**Praise for the novels of *New York Times*
bestselling author**

RACHEL VINCENT

"Compelling and edgy, dark and evocative, *Stray* is
a must read! I loved it from beginning to end."
—*New York Times* bestselling author Gena Showalter

"I liked the character and loved the action. I look
forward to reading the next book in the series."
—*New York Times* bestselling author
Charlaine Harris

"Her first-person perspective, dialogue, descriptions,
and even her sound effects are phenomenal
(I heard the noises, I swear it!).... I think Vincent
has a hit on her hands."
—*Romance Reader at Heart*

"The second installment of Vincent's urban fantasy
series (after *Stray*) features a well-thought-out vision
of werecat social structure as well as a heroine who
insists on carving her own path, even if it means
breaking some of her society's most sacred taboos."
—*Library Journal* on *Rogue*

"Vincent's smart, sexy sequel to *Stray* continues
in the same vein, but this story has more emotional
resonance. Faythe's as sassy as ever,
and her first-person observations add greatly
to the reader's experience."
—*Romantic Times BOOKreviews* on *Rogue*

RACHEL VINCENT
PRIDE

MIRA®

MIRA

Recycling programs
for this product may
not exist in your area.

ISBN-13: 978-0-7783-2908-4

PRIDE

For questions and comments about the quality of this book please contact us
at Customer_eCare@Harlequin.ca.

www.MIRABooks.com

Printed in U.S.A.

To my critique partner, Rinda Elliott,
whose advice and opinions I could not make do
without. Your generosity knows no bounds,
and your talent is without end. Your time's
coming, and I can't wait!

ACKNOWLEDGMENTS

Thanks first of all to #1,
who keeps me up and running.
I wouldn't be here without you.

Thanks to Jocelynn Drake,
Vicki Pettersson and Kim Harrison for being there
with me for both the cheers and the tears.

Thanks to Elizabeth Mazer,
for all her work behind the scenes, and for holding
the whole thing together. To D. P. Lyle, MD, whose
medical expertise kept my corpses realistic.
Any medical mistakes in this book are mine, not his.

Thanks to my agent, Miriam Kriss,
for support and encouragement
that goes way beyond her job description.
You give me confidence, without which it would be
so much harder to face that blank screen.

And a huge thank-you to my editor,
Mary-Theresa Hussey, for showing me the path
and letting me wander from it as necessary. Your
guidance has been invaluable. You make me shine.

One

"**M**iss Sanders, tell us why you killed your boyfriend."

Fresh irritation swelled in my chest like heartburn, bringing with it the first twinges of a migraine behind my right eye. I turned away from the fall-color panorama visible through windows spanning the south wall of the dining room to stare down the long mahogany table at a much less pleasant sight: Calvin Malone, Alpha of the Appalachian territory. As I watched, the left corner of his mouth began to twitch above his thin, trim beard, a sure sign that he was having fun. The pompous bastard loved pushing my buttons. He'd just found the one labeled Use with Caution, then poked it anyway.

"*Ex*-boyfriend." I spoke through gritted teeth, my hands clenched on my black cotton slacks. "And it was self-defense. Which you'd know if you'd listened the *last* time I answered that *exact same question*."

Michael cleared his throat from the chair on my right. Dark brows rose over the rim of his glasses, urging me to be good. Since he was acting as my adviser, the werecat version of a defense attorney, rather than as my oldest brother, I took his advice without argument. Possibly for the first time ever.

Sighing, I forced my attention back to the tribunal—three

Alphas chosen by the highly regarded "short straw" method to sit in judgment of me. Officially, the hearing was to determine my guilt or innocence on two capital charges. However, the grudge Malone held against me was old long before each of my crimes took place. *Allegedly.*

But that wasn't right, either. Unlike the human justice system, in the werecat world, the accused was considered guilty until proven innocent. And the burden of proof was on the defendant—me.

I was charged with infecting Andrew Wallace, my human ex-boyfriend, which I'd already confessed to doing—*accidently.* I also stood accused of murdering him to cover up my crime, which I'd vehemently denied. I'd killed Andrew in self-defense, and while I felt guiltier about that than any of my judges could possibly understand, I'd had no choice. It was either kill or be killed, and my stubborn sense of self-preservation insisted on the former.

If the tribunal found me guilty, in addition to a lengthy stay in the cage, I'd be facing some kind of corporal punishment. Possibly the loss of my claws, which was motivation enough to keep me on my best behavior.

"But you do admit to biting him?" Malone prompted, his mouth twitching again as he tapped a thin stack of papers lying on the table in front of him.

"Yes," I said through clenched jaws, gripping the lacquered arms of my chair to anchor myself to the seat. "I did bite him, but the infection was an accident. I didn't know my teeth had Shifted."

"So you still claim to have experienced this…" Malone paused, glancing at his notes for effect. "'Partial Shift?'"

His patronizing smile made my stomach churn, but in light of the circumstances, I was trying very, very hard to be good. "Yes."

Malone huffed in disbelief, glancing around the room to

make sure everyone else shared his skepticism. On his right, Paul Blackwell placed one wrinkled hand on the table. He scowled, scraggly gray eyebrows drawing low over small, dark eyes. "Why is it, then, that you can't show us this 'partial Shift'?"

Because I'm not quite ready to give in to murderous rage. Fortunately I was getting pretty good at not saying the first thing that popped into my head. Mostly. "I can't do it on command. Not yet anyway. I have to be in a certain mood— excited, in one sense or another—to make it happen."

"Well, isn't that *convenient?*" Malone said with a conspiratorial glance at Blackwell.

"Quite the opposite, actually," I snapped, and Michael kicked my shin under the table.

Malone's fist clenched around his notes and his mouth opened. But before he could speak, the Alpha on his left cleared his throat conspicuously, drawing all eyes his way.

"Calvin, I assume you have a legitimate question for Faythe?" By some miracle, my uncle Rick Wade—my cousin Abby's father—had been selected for the tribunal, and in my father's honor, he'd made his allegiance to my family well-known. If not for him, I'd have already been convicted and sentenced.

"Of course." Malone shot an annoyed glance at my uncle, then adopted a professional pose. But when he faced me, I saw that same gleam of animosity in his eyes. "So you were in an…*excited* state when you bit Mr. Wallace?"

A mischievous grin lurked behind my solemn courtroom face, and it took all my self-control to stifle it. As well as a hard, self-inflicted pinch on my arm, through the white blouse my father had chosen to make me look innocent. And to cover the new belly-button ring he didn't think projected the right image during my hearing.

"You might say that. We were at school, on our lunch break. Neither of us had a class for a couple of hours, so we wound up at his apartment."

"In bed?" Paul Blackwell leaned forward from Malone's right side, gripping the curve of his cane hard enough to make his withered fingers creak.

Blackwell was the senior member of the tribunal, as well as the Territorial Council, and had been clinging tenaciously to his position as Alpha of the southwest territory for years, in spite of urgings from his family and several other Alphas to turn the reins over to his son-in-law. He was mulish, outspoken, and hopelessly old-fashioned, stubbornly adhering to outdated ideas about premarital sex and a woman's place in the world. In fact, he seemed as scandalized by my "indecent" relationship with Andrew as by the thought that I'd infected and murdered him.

But according to my father, Blackwell was both honest and honorable. He would vote based on his conscience, rather than on any political alliance or previously held grudge. So I'd just have to make sure his conscience knew I was innocent. Mostly. And that I respected myself enough not to apologize for something I hadn't deliberately done.

I met his eyes boldly, to show I wasn't ashamed. "Yes. In bed. We were having sex, and I just…nibbled his ear a little too hard."

"And your sworn testimony is that you never actually Shifted during this…occasion?" Malone asked, as if to confirm facts he'd already heard half a dozen times.

I nodded, then turned my head from side to side to ease the stiffness that had settled into my neck from sitting in the same position for hours at a time. "Only my teeth Shifted, like I told you last time. And the time before that. And the time before that—"

"Faythe…" Michael warned, and wood creaked behind him as our father moved in his seat.

In spite of his position as head of the council, my father hadn't been allowed to serve on the tribunal overseeing my trial because of his relationship to the accused—me. But he'd insisted on being present the entire time, though he wasn't permitted to actually speak during the proceedings. He sat directly behind Michael in a straight-backed chair against the wall, as he had for the last three hours, one ankle crossed over his opposite knee, hands resting on the chair arms. By all appearances he was relaxed and confident, but I knew by the firm line of his mouth that he was every bit as irritated as I was. And a lot more nervous, which made me wonder if there was something he wasn't telling me.

Frowning, I crossed my arms over my chest and leaned back in my chair, awaiting the next question. Which would no doubt be something I'd already answered.

Malone looked up from the slanted scrawl on his legal pad. "Did Mr. Wallace notice that your teeth had Shifted?"

"No. I didn't either."

Malone's head jerked up and his eyes found mine, his brows high in surprise. Evidently I'd said something new. "If you didn't know your teeth had Shifted at the time, how can you possibly be sure that's what happened?"

Shit. I sat back in my chair, going for calm confidence. "Because that's the only logical conclusion. I infected Andrew somehow—" we knew that for a fact based on his scent "—and I never intentionally Shifted in front of him. So it stands to reason that I did it by accident. And the day I bit him was the last time I saw him until the day he died. It must have happened then."

Blackwell appeared unconvinced, and Malone looked downright dubious. "Since you brought it up, let's talk about the day Mr. Wallace died," he said, shuffling though his papers again.

My head throbbed as I massaged my temples. Whatever amusement I'd felt over the proceedings drained from me, replaced by dread and a horrible, hollow ache. "I've already told you everything."

"Tell us again." Malone didn't look up from his pages.

We'd been over every single aspect of their accusations and Andrew's death in the past thirty-six hours, only taking short breaks for food and rest. There was nothing to be gained from repeating any of it, except possibly to wear me down, which had to be their goal. They were trying to trip me up. Catch me in a lie. But that wasn't going to happen; I was telling the truth, whether they believed it or not.

My eyes closed, and the memory rolled over me, rendered no less horrible by the number of times they'd made me relive it. I flinched as Andrew's face came into focus in my head. I couldn't help it. Watching him die was one of the most difficult things I'd ever endured, and knowing I'd been the cause, however unwillingly, was the biggest regret of my life.

"What do you want to know?" I couldn't keep weariness from my voice, but I made myself meet their eyes, knowing they'd see guilt rather than grief if I didn't.

Malone scanned his notes. "Where did you get the spike?"

The railroad spike. That horrid, seven-inch iron spear, which had gone right through Andrew's neck, spilling his life along with his blood. "They were all over the floor…" I trailed into blessed silence when I couldn't purge the image from my mind.

"Why did you stab him with it?"

My hands clenched into fists again, this time on top of the table, where everyone could see them. "I was trying to knock him off me. He was going to crush my head!"

Malone leaned back in his chair, narrowing his eyes at me. "Or maybe he was threatening to tell everyone what you did. That you infected him. I imagine that would seem reason enough to kill him."

I took a deep, calming breath. "Look, I didn't mean to kill him, and I certainly wasn't trying to cover anything up. There were five other people with us minutes earlier, and even if I hadn't already told them I'd infected Andrew—and I'm sure any one of them will swear I *had*—they could smell my scent in his blood. It wasn't a cover-up. It was self-defense."

Malone's eyes narrowed, his mouth already opening to argue, but Uncle Rick beat him to the punch. "We've heard all of this before," he said, and I glanced at him in gratitude. "Let's move on."

"Fine." Malone scowled, leafing through his papers until he found whatever he was looking for. His eyes settled on me again, and I didn't like the eager look in them. "Is it true that you've turned down *multiple* proposals of marriage over the past six years?"

What? My face blazed in anger. "What the f—" I paused for a quick rephrase, because cursing at a panel of Alphas was a very, *very* bad idea. "What does that have to do with anything? Andrew never asked me to marry him."

"Answer the question please, Miss Sanders," Blackwell ordered, clearly irritated by my near slip.

Michael didn't look any happier than I was about this new line of questioning, but he nodded for me to answer.

"Yes."

"How many proposals have you turned down, total?" Malone continued.

I closed my eyes, pretending to think, though I was actually trying to get a grip on my temper before my mouth dug a hole too big for the rest of me to crawl out of. "That's hard to quantify," I said finally, opening my eyes to meet Malone's gleeful stare.

"Why is that?" he asked.

"Because I received multiple proposals from the same person." Marc, of course.

"I see." Malone nodded, as if he understood. And he probably did. Rumor had it he'd been after his wife for years and years before she finally agreed to marry him. My private theory was that he wore away at her defenses. But I knew better than to say that to his face.

"How many toms proposed to you, then? Surely *that* can't be hard to quantify." Malone said as my uncle scratched something I couldn't read on the notebook in front of him.

I sighed. "Four."

"And you weren't tempted by any of these proposals?"

Sudden understanding clicked into place in my head, but instead of calming me, it made me angrier. One of the marriage offers had come several years earlier from a young man two years my junior, whom I'd barely known. Brett Malone. Calvin Malone's firstborn son. The petty son of a bitch was mad because I'd opted not to give birth to his descendants. That wasn't the reason for the hearing, of course. But it was surely the source of his malicious, twitching smile.

"Of course I was tempted." It took most of my remaining self-control not to roll my eyes over such a petty grudge. "But I had reasons for turning them down."

"What were those reas—"

"Calvin, I think you've gotten your answer." Uncle Rick cut Malone off in midword, having obviously come to the same conclusion I had.

Malone frowned. "Fine." He consulted his notes again. "I understand that you are no longer involved in a relationship of any kind. Is this also true?"

Fuming, I glanced at Michael, but he only nodded, telling me to answer.

"Yes."

"And is it also true that you have no plans to marry, or to ever have children?"

Fury singed through my veins, lighting tiny fires throughout my body. No longer satisfied by my brother's passive nodding, I whirled on Michael again, my long black hair swinging out behind me. "Why are they asking me this crap?

It's none of their business, nor is it even *vaguely* related to what happened to Andrew. Shouldn't you…*object,* or something?"

"This isn't a court of law, Faythe," Michael reminded me for at least the hundredth time. "They can ask you anything they want. The best way to help yourself right now is to answer their questions." *With as little information as possible.*

I'd heard that line often enough to know what he wasn't saying, and to know that the unspoken part applied as much then as it ever had.

Unsatisfied by his answer, I dismissed Michael entirely, focusing on my father instead. "Daddy?" I begged him with my eyes to step in. To somehow liberate me from the indignity of discussing my sex life—or lack thereof—in front of a trio of old men, two of whom I barely knew. But there was nothing he could do, and we all knew it. He shook his head, the opposite of Michael's typical response, but it meant the same thing: answer the question.

Beyond angry, I tried to relax, sinking into my chair as if there were nowhere else I'd rather be. "Yes. I am no longer in a romantic relationship, and at the present, I have no plans to marry. Or have children. And for the record, I object to this entire line of questioning on the basis of relevance."

Michael coughed to disguise a laugh, and Malone frowned, already opening his mouth to ask another question. Fortunately, Uncle Rick stepped in again, eyeing me intently, as if to tell me something other than what he was about to say aloud. "But are you prepared to swear right now that you will never, under any circumstances, marry and start a family?"

"No, of course not." I shrugged. "I can't say for sure what I want for dinner tonight, so how can you possibly expect me to know whether or not I'm going to want kids five years from now?"

My father chuckled quietly, and Uncle Rick smiled. I must have done something right.

Malone scowled again. "Is it true that even in your relationship with Marc Ramos, you took active measures to prevent pregnancy?"

My hand clenched around the arm of the chair, and distantly I heard wood creak. My teeth ground together audibly. "You have *no* right to ask me these da—"

"Gentlemen, I think we're ready for a break." Michael stood, pulling me up with him. "Thirty minutes?"

"Of course," Uncle Rick said, just as Malone said, "Ten."

Michael didn't hesitate, already hauling me away from the table. "Let's meet in the middle and call it twenty." Malone nodded reluctantly, and my brother shoved the door open, tugging me into a short carpeted hallway.

My father followed us into the living room of the rented lodge, where he stopped to stare out the broad picture window at a breathtaking view of the Rocky Mountains, so different from the Lazy S, my family's East Texas ranch. My father peered out at steep, tree-covered slopes and snow-topped peaks, lit by the afternoon sun. He'd been doing that a lot lately—staring at nothing in particular, as if he had something important to say but couldn't quite figure out how to say it. Which wasn't like him at all.

"What's going on?" I demanded, jerking free from my brother's grasp to settle onto the arm of a worn couch.

Before Michael could answer, a door opened on the far side of the room, revealing a young tomcat in jeans and an open button-down shirt, munching from an orange bag of Doritos. Behind him, I glimpsed two unmade beds and a pressboard dresser like those found in hotels all over the world. Though his name wouldn't come to me, I recognized the tom as one of Blackwell's enforcers—one of his grandsons, in fact. Blackwell and the toms accompanying him were staying in the main lodge, where my hearing was being held.

To the immediate east of the main lodge, out of sight from

the front window, sat three smaller cabins, the first occupied by Malone and his men, the second by my uncle and the enforcers he'd brought. My father and I shared the last cabin with Michael, Jace and Marc.

Michael's wife, Holly—an honest-to-goodness runway model—thought he was off on a father-son camping trip with our dad. Since there were no children to miss either of them, she was spending the week in Acapulco with her sister.

Our group had reserved the whole Oak Trails cabin complex for an entire week, though no one expected the hearing to take that long. It would have been a lovely place to vacation, complete with private hunting and fishing sites and beautiful nature trails, but that wasn't why the council had chosen it. Oak Trails was the only location both neutral and isolated enough to suit all the Alphas, and we'd had to wait more than two months to reserve the entire complex. Giving all the employees time off had raised a few eyebrows, but they'd been delighted to have a free vacation.

Michael frowned at the young tomcat for breaking through our semblance of privacy. "In there," he commanded me, gesturing toward an empty bedroom opening off the other side of the living room. "We need to talk."

We needed more than that. We needed fresh air. I'd been in the Rockies fewer than forty-eight hours, and I got angry every time I passed a window, because I longed to be out in the open on four paws, exploring unfamiliar ground, and trees, and streams. But instead I was stuck inside, repeating myself over and over to a tribunal who didn't seem very interested in my answers to the questions they kept repeating. Although the whole marriage-and-children angle was a new development…

"What's going on?" I repeated, sinking onto the plaid comforter as my father followed us into the room, closing the door at his back. "Why are they asking me personal questions? My social life has nothing to do with Andrew's death."

Michael flicked the wall switch and light flooded the room, illuminating more motel-quality furnishings. One whiff told me the room belonged to one of the Pierce boys—Parker's brother, who was another of Blackwell's enforcers.

Michael sat on the bed next to me and my father took the desk chair, meeting my brother's eyes instead of mine. That couldn't be good.

"Are they going where I think they're going with this?" Michael asked our father, and again my temper flared. I hated being in the dark, especially on things that concerned me.

Our Alpha sighed. "Yes, I think they are."

Michael's eyes closed, and he cradled his head in his hands. "I didn't think they'd really do it."

"Do what?" I demanded.

My brother looked up, but not at me. "You have to tell her, Dad."

My father nodded solemnly. Angrily. Then he met my eyes, and I saw in his the strength I'd always admired, and the brutal honesty I'd never been quite so fond of. "You aren't on trial anymore, Faythe."

"What?" I glanced at Michael, hoping to find something I understood in his expression. And I did. I found pain, and regret, and more anger than I'd ever seen on his face. "What does that mean?" My hands clenched around the comforter, and I couldn't seem to uncurl them.

"They think you're guilty, and they're now debating your sentence."

"What? No." My head shook in denial of the truth even as it sank in. "Uncle Rick wouldn't do that."

Michael took my hand in his, drawing my attention along with it. "They don't need him to find you guilty. They need a simple majority. Two out of three." His focus shifted back and forth between my eyes, searching them for understanding.

"This can't be happening." I pulled my hand from his grip

and rose from the bed, pacing the width of the room before I realized what I was doing. "This isn't real. I didn't mean to kill him. I infected him, but that was an accident. It was all an *accident*."

"I know." Michael followed me with his eyes, trying to comfort me with the right words and a gentle tone. But I didn't want comfort. I wanted answers.

"What does this mean? The cage?" I stopped pacing to look at Michael. "How long can they keep me locked up?" No one answered, so I asked again. "*Daddy?* How long?" Two weeks in the cage had nearly driven me crazy. My father had threatened to put me away for a year once, but I couldn't imagine surviving that long without sunlight. Without trees, and grass, and hunting, and physical contact with…well, with *anything*.

But before he'd answered my first question, another, more startling one occurred to me. "Where?" They wouldn't leave me at home; I knew that with a sudden devastating certainty. "Where will they put me?" I was *not* spending the next year of my life in Malone's cellar.

My father closed his eyes and inhaled deeply as another knuckle cracked. "They aren't planning to lock you up."

"What then? Declawed? I'm going to be *declawed?*" My pitch rose on the last word, and I heard panic in my voice. Michael glanced at my father, and fear danced up my spine. "No. I can't be declawed." My nails bit into my palms, as if to remind me they were still there. "I can't work as an enforcer without my claws. I can't fucking *defend* myself without them."

Maybe that was the whole point. If I couldn't take care of myself, I'd have to let someone else do it. I'd have to stay home and get married and have babies.

"Faythe, they're going for the death penalty." My father spoke so softly that at first I thought I'd misunderstood him. "They think you murdered Andrew, and they want to execute you for it."

"No." I couldn't think clearly enough to say anything else. It wasn't possible. "Tabbies don't get the death penalty. We're too valuable. You've said it all my life." And that's when I finally understood. "That's why they're asking me about children…"

Michael nodded. "To them, you're only as valuable as the service you provide the werecat community. If you aren't willing to perpetuate the species, you're no more valuable than any enforcer would be. And an enforcer can be replaced far easier than a dam."

A sudden wave of nausea made my stomach clench. I leaned against the dresser, then let myself slide to the floor. My spine scraped three drawer handles on the way down. I couldn't seem to draw a deep breath.

"Faythe?" Michael knelt at my side, but I barely heard him. *I'm going to die.*

The hard wood was cold against my legs, even through my slacks, and I shivered uncontrollably. For what I did to Andrew, I was going to die. And the real bitch was that I probably deserved it.

I hadn't meant to infect him, much less to kill him, but that made no difference in the long run. None of it would have happened if I hadn't insisted on doing things my own way, on going to school instead of getting married. Dating humans, instead of tomcats. If not for me, Andrew would still be alive, probably dating some grad student who never did anything more violent than crush spiders.

But it was too late to take it back now. The only way to save my life was to prove my own worth—by agreeing to have some random tom's baby.

Manx had known the truth all along. No wonder she was so happy, in spite of her constant heartburn and swollen feet. Her unborn child had saved her life, and she damn well knew it.

A warm hand touched my shoulder, then smoothed my hair down my back. "We won't let this happen, Faythe. I swear on my life that we will not let this happen. We'll find a way around it."

I lifted my head to find my father kneeling next to me. My father the Alpha—head of the Territorial Council for as long as I could remember—was on his knees on a dusty, rented cabin floor, still wearing his usual suit and tie. I smiled at him. It was either that or cry, and I was determined not to cry in front of him again.

"I know you will. Just tell me what to do, and I'll do it." For once, I'd do exactly what he wanted. No questions asked.

He opened his mouth, but before he could speak, the bedroom door flew open behind him, and Jace burst into the room. "Greg! There's a bruin out front, and he's demanding to see whoever's in charge."

Two

"A bruin? Are you sure?" my father asked.

Jace snorted. "Um, yeah. He's huge, and he smells like a bear. He's arguing with Calvin, and it looks like it's about to get ugly."

My father turned from Jace back to me. "I meant what I said, Faythe. This isn't over."

I nodded. I recognized the dismissal, but knew it wasn't personal. As the head of the council, he *had* to go deal with the new crisis, even if we hadn't yet resolved the previous one. "Go."

My father was off the floor in an instant, rising with the speed and grace of a tom half his age. In spite of the circumstances, I was happy to see him move like that because each new line that appeared around his eyes and each gray hair that grew at his temple reminded me that he was just as susceptible as the rest of us to the devastation of time, the wear and tear of constant use. One day he would retire, and that would break my heart. But one day further down, he would die, and that would crush my soul.

If I'm still around to see it...

Michael followed our father from the room, and Jace started to go after them, then stopped when he noticed me sitting on the floor. "Faythe? What's wrong?"

"I killed Andrew, haven't you heard?"

"What are you talking about?" In several long steps, he was in front of me, pulling me off the floor. "It was self-defense. The panel will see that eventually. They have to." He wrapped his arms around me, and I let my head fall on his shoulder, breathing in his scent, which brought with it memories of warmth, and safety, and comfort.

I shook my head, and my cheek rubbed against his cotton T. "They think I did it on purpose. All of it. They're going after the death penalty."

"What?" Jace held me at arm's length, searching my face for an explanation. He frowned in confusion. "Calvin told you that?"

"No, my father. And Michael."

He shook his head. "That makes no sense. You're a tabby," he said, echoing my own thoughts.

"They don't seem to have noticed that yet."

Jace smiled, and his eyes roamed south of my chin. "I don't see how they could keep from—"

In the main room, the front door creaked open, and heavy footsteps clomped on the hardwood floor. Voices spoke over one another, in every pitch and timbre, until finally one broke through them all "—don't care *what* you're in the middle of." The voice was deep enough to rumble, and loud enough to shake the walls around us.

"The bruin," Jace whispered, and I nodded, still listening.

"I wanna speak to someone in charge, and if you point that finger at me again, I'm gonna break it off and shove it someplace uncomfortable."

Jace grinned and tossed his head toward the sound of the voice. I nodded again and followed him into the main room, mingling with the various enforcers standing against the walls, most with their hands clenched into fists at their sides. They were agitated, on high alert from having our rented territory invaded by a stranger. A very *large* stranger of another *species*.

The bruin wasn't hard to spot. In fact, he would have been impossible to hide.

The largest tomcat in the room was my cousin Lucas Wade, who'd accompanied my uncle Rick to the hearing. In human form, Lucas was six and a half feet tall and more than three hundred pounds of solid muscle. He had to enter most rooms sideways. Running into him was like hitting the side of a house.

The bruin was more than a foot taller than Lucas, and I couldn't begin to imagine how much he weighed. His hair was light reddish-brown, which I hadn't expected, and plentiful, which I had. It hung to his shoulders in thick, tangled waves, blending seamlessly with a beard of the same length and color. His cheeks were ruddy from the cold, and above them shone eyes that were proportionately small, dark brown and surprisingly expressive. And what I saw in them at the moment was anger. Unfiltered, unmistakable anger.

"You can't just walk in here and demand an audience," Calvin Malone insisted from the center of the room where he, like everyone else, was dwarfed by the angry bear. "This is neither the proper place, nor the proper way to address our council. I'm going to have to ask you to—"

"Calvin." My father's voice cut through Malone's with the confidence of long-held authority. Malone faded into silence, but he didn't move. My father was unfazed. "I'm sure we can spare the time to meet with a member of our brother species. In fact, I think that's the least we owe our guest. That, and perhaps a cup of coffee?"

On his left, Uncle Rick nodded, as did Paul Blackwell, who watched from the kitchen doorway. Malone scowled, then conceded the point with a brisk nod. "Of course."

My father's gaze settled on me and Jace. "Jace, bring some coffee for…" He paused, addressing the bruin again. "I'm sorry, I didn't catch your name."

"Elias Keller," the giant rumbled.

"Some coffee for Mr. Keller?" my father continued, and Jace nodded, already headed toward the kitchen. "Mr. Keller, will you have a seat?"

Keller nodded, apparently surprised by the offer of hospitality. But there was barely enough space to breathe, much less sit, in the crowded room. My father looked almost amused by the extra security. "Gentlemen, could you give us a little room?"

The tomcats hesitated, glancing around at one another. Then, almost as one they migrated toward the exits, some headed for the front door, others for the hallway. When the room had cleared, except for the four Alphas, my father considered me for a moment, then tossed his head toward the kitchen. I went willingly, because if I sat quietly and chose my seat carefully, I'd be able to see and hear everything that happened in the main room. A minor bright spot in what was shaping up to be one of the worst days of my life.

Jace stood in front of the coffeepot, pouring creamer into a plain white mug. "You think he takes it with hazelnut creamer?" I leaned with one hip against the counter next to him.

"I'm guessing black." He stirred, then tapped the spoon against the rim of the mug before dropping it into the sink. "This one's for you." Winking, he handed me the cup of doctored coffee, then carried a second mug—black—into the living room. He was back a minute later, pouring a third mug for himself.

I sat at the small round table, my chair positioned as far to the right as possible. From there, I could see the bruin, who took up most of the ugly beige sofa all on his own. I could also see my father, in the armchair nearest the couch, and Malone, opposite him in a matching chair.

"…can we do for you, Mr. Keller?" My father asked, his hands templed beneath his chin, fingertips brushing a slight shadow of stubble.

Across from him, Malone faced mostly away from me, so

that I saw only a slice of his profile. But that was enough for me to recognize the scowl dominating his expression. He was clearly irritated with my father for taking charge, which sent a petty surge of glee through me. Did Malone think chairing the tribunal sitting in judgment of me gave him enough power to displace Greg Sanders as the head of the entire Territorial Council? If so, he was sorely mistaken, and at that moment I wanted nothing more out of life than to be present when my father made that fact clear.

And maybe a full pardon. That would be nice, too.

Jace slid into the seat on my right, setting his own mug on the table in front of him. I mouthed, "Thanks," and held up my cup before sipping from it, my attention already focused on the Alphas and the bruin.

"What can you do for me?" Keller ran one broad, thick-fingered hand along his scraggly beard, tugging it as he stared down at my father. "Keep your cats off my mountain."

Bruins, like the bears they Shifted into, lived almost exclusively in the northern rocky districts—mostly Alberta, British Columbia and Alaska. Very few lived in the continental U.S., and those who did stuck to isolated regions of the Northwest—including the werecat free zone in Montana, where we'd come for my hearing.

"*Our* cats?" My father glanced at his fellow Alphas, but none seemed to have any idea what our ursine guest was talking about.

"Well, they certainly aren't *my* cats," Keller scoffed. He lifted his mug—which looked like a toy cup in his tennis racket-size hand—and drained the contents in one long swallow. Then he set the empty cup on the coffee table and eyed my father steadily.

"What are these cats doing, exactly?" Calvin Malone asked.

"They're carrying on like a pack of rabid dogs, not five miles from my place." Keller shifted in his seat, and the couch groaned with his movement. "Hunting and fighting in the daytime. Making all kinds of racket. It's a bad time for such ruckus, what with humans crawling all over the mountain looking for those missing hikers. Damn fools. Those cats of yours are either gonna *make* trouble, or *be* trouble, and I want no part of it either way."

Missing hikers?

On my left, the kitchen door creaked open, and I turned to see Marc step inside. His gaze found me instantly, the gold specks glittering in his brown eyes. He looked away first, as had become his habit since we'd broken up ten weeks earlier. Ten weeks and four days, to be exact. And approximately ten hours.

But who was counting?

A familiar ache settled into my chest, and I tried to drown it with coffee.

"Are you sure they're Shifters, and not natural cats? Cougars, maybe?" Uncle Rick asked from the living room. I tried to concentrate on what was being said, but I couldn't seem to drag my gaze from Marc.

"What's going on?" he whispered to Jace, avoiding my eyes as he sniffed in the direction of the living room. "And what's that smell?"

"Of course I'm sure," Keller rumbled from the other room, and Marc froze at the sound of the strange voice.

"Is that what I think it is?" Marc murmured, crossing the kitchen to stand behind us, where he could see into the living room. "A *bruin?*"

Jace nodded, a grin practically splitting his face in half. Bruins were rarer than thunderbirds. Rarer even than tabby cats, at least in the U.S. My father said they'd be gone for good someday. Maybe during my lifetime. I'd never expected to see one in person.

"They're bigger than cougars, and jet-black, every one,"

Keller continued. "Smarter 'n cougars, too. But they lack the common sense to be frightened when they ought."

Definitely tomcats, then, I thought. *And probably teenagers.*

"I expect you boys to round 'em up, and soon," the bruin said, glancing from one Alpha to another. "I've already buried one—figured you'd wanna know why he didn't come back— and I don't mind diggin' more holes, if need be. Seems only fair to warn you first, though."

My father frowned, and I knew exactly what he was thinking. What they all must have been thinking. We weren't missing any cats. Though he didn't seem to know it, Keller was talking about strays. Reckless, likely suicidal strays. He had to be.

"We'll take care of the problem." My father tapped his index fingers together beneath his chin. Then, as if he'd read my mind, "Can you describe the scent of these werecats? They were male, I assume?"

Keller nodded. "No doubt about that. Not with 'em pissin' on every tree and rock for ten square miles."

My father cleared his throat to disguise a smile, but Jace wasn't so fortunate. He choked on a gulp of coffee, spewing it across the table and down the front of his shirt. I bit my lip to keep from laughing, and Marc grabbed a pile of paper napkins from the counter behind him, dropping them over the mess on the table.

"Could you tell anything else from their scents?" Uncle Rick asked, while my father glared at us from the living room. I shrugged at him in apology, while Jace tossed the soggy napkins across the room into the trash can. "Were they Pride or stray?"

Keller stroked his beard again. "Can't say as I know the difference."

My father nodded, as if he'd expected that very reply. "A stray is a werecat who was born human, then infected by being scratched or bitten by one of us in cat form."

I squirmed in my seat, uncomfortably aware that nearly every eye in the living room had just focused on me. Always in the past when the topic of strays came up, Marc became the unwilling center of attention. But that was no longer the case. I was now infamous for having created a stray. In fact, I was the only Pride cat in living history to admit to such a thing. No one else was that crazy. Or stupid.

But things were different for bruins, as Elias Keller had just reminded us. His species wanted nothing to do with the human population. Or with each other, for the most part. Unlike werecats, bruins lived alone, typically in rough cabins in isolated mountainous regions virtually untouched by civilization. They were the "mountain men" of legend, reclusive giants in huge flannel shirts, fur hats and colossal boots, stomping through the forest with an ax over one shoulder and a dead deer over the other. They were likely the source of the Paul Bunyan stories. Hell, in one form or another, they were probably also Bigfoot, almost never seen, because there were very few of them to *be* seen.

Bruins weren't rare only because they bred slowly, though that was certainly part of it. The rest of the problem was that like thunderbirds, they could only be born, not made. Being mauled by a bruin would not turn a human into a "werebear." It would kill him or her. Period. Which was why the concept of a stray was completely lost on Keller.

"And there's a difference between the smell of a stray and a…Pride cat?"

Malone nodded. "We're all Pride cats. This cat you… *buried?* Did it smell like us?"

Keller sniffed the air dramatically, and his entire beard twitched with the motion. It might have been funny, if he didn't look so very serious. "Yes. You're all cats. *They* were all cats. You all smell like cats to me."

"He needs to smell a stray," Paul Blackwell said, and dread

settled into my stomach. I knew what was coming. I just didn't know who'd be dumb enough to do it.

But I *should* have known.

"Where's Marc Ramos?" Malone demanded, glancing around at his fellow Alphas, as if he expected Marc to suddenly appear in their midst. "*He's* a stray. Someone bring Marc in here."

I dared a peek at Marc and found him standing behind Jace, fists clenched around the back of the chair, face scarlet. He growled, very low and deep, and I ached to put a sympathetic hand over his.

"Marc?" Malone called again from the living room. He twisted in his chair, glancing down the hall first, then toward the kitchen, where he found us all frozen in place—Marc in anger, me in dread, and Jace in what could only be humiliation. I hadn't noticed his reaction earlier, because Marc was clearly about to blow his top. But when I looked at Jace, I saw that his jaws were clenched, muscles bulging in his cheeks, and that he stared at Malone in nothing short of rage. Pure, murderous rage.

"Ramos, front-n-center!" Malone shouted, apparently oblivious to the fact that he was insulting my father's top enforcer—the tomcat who got paid to bust heads in defense of our territory.

Marc growled louder, and the chair back creaked beneath his hands. He watched my father instead of Malone, waiting for either a nod or a shake of his Alpha's head to tell him what to do. But instead, my father shrugged. He was leaving the decision up to Marc, and I loved him for it. For not demanding that Marc present himself to be sniffed like a bitch in heat.

However, before Marc could make up his mind, Keller spoke again, slicing through the tension with a single, insightful statement. "I can smell you from here, son. No need to put yourself out on my account."

Marc nodded. He didn't smile—he was much too angry for that—but I could see respect for Keller in his eyes.

"So." Malone dismissed Marc as casually as he'd called for him. "Did these werecats smell like us, or like *him?*"

I never actually heard Keller's answer because the wood splintering under Marc's hands drowned it out. An instant later, Marc held the detached back of Jace's chair—a solid strip of oak attached to four thin spindles—in one hand. Jace jumped from his seat just as Marc hurled the wood through the window over the kitchen sink. Glass shattered, spraying the ground outside. Heads swiveled our way, eyes wide, mouths gaping. Then, before anyone seemed to realize what had happened, Marc was gone, and the screen door slammed shut.

Malone practically shook with fury, now standing in the middle of the living-room floor. "Jace, bring him back. Now!"

Jace's hands curled into fists at his sides, and anger smoldered in his eyes. He ignored Malone and watched his own Alpha for a signal.

"Let him go." My father didn't shout. He didn't need to.

Jace's hands uncurled, and he sank back into his broken chair, ears flaming as he stared at the table.

Calvin Malone turned to face my father, and again I saw him in profile. "Do you let that kind of disrespect go unpunished among your men?"

"You mind your Pride, and I'll mind mine." His carefully blank face was the only hint at how very angry my father was. At Malone, not Marc or Jace.

Malone's mouth twitched. He was furious, but making an obvious attempt to rein his temper in, at least until the bruin was gone. "We'll discuss this later."

My father nodded curtly. "We certainly will."

"Well, I'll get out of your fur." Keller rose from the couch, and its springs screeched in relief. He stepped toward the door, and had to duck beneath the fan overhead.

"Mr. Keller, wait," Uncle Rick called, and the bruin paused several feet from the door. "Where did you last see these strays?" *So they* were *strays…* "And how many are there? We'll send some men out on patrol, and they'll need to know where to start."

Keller's face relaxed. "There's a good-size pond not six miles north of here. I scented at least two of them there this morning, and several more before that. That good enough to get you started?"

"Yes, thank you. We appreciate the warning." My father escorted Keller to the door, step by creaking step. The bruin had to bend to fit through, and when my father turned to the rest of us, his face was all business. "Can you spare two men apiece?" he asked, glancing around the room from Alpha to Alpha.

"Of course," Blackwell said, "More, if you need them."

My father nodded, acknowledging the commitment.

"You're not serious about this, Greg?" Malone demanded, looking around the room for support from his fellow Alphas. My father, the head of the Territorial Council, walked past him without responding, and it was all I could do not to laugh out loud. He'd been using that tactic on me for years, but I'd never expected to see him ignore a fellow Alpha's question, as if it wasn't worthy of reply. Though, for the record, I agreed with him completely.

Malone shouted after him. "We all took time away from our jobs—our *lives*—to come here on *werecat business,* not to take tea with Yogi Bear!"

My dad strolled through the living room and into the kitchen, where we all watched him pour the last of the coffee into a clean mug, as if his authority wasn't being questioned in front of Alpha and enforcer alike.

Malone followed him, stopping on the worn linoleum. "This is free territory. Of *course* there are strays here. *We* put them here!"

Daddy poured a packet of sugar into his coffee and stirred, looking no more annoyed than he might be by a fly buzzing near his ear. Malone seethed. "You can*not* seriously be asking us to set aside your daughter's *criminal* behavior in favor of chasing a few stray cats up the side of a mountain."

That did it. My father brought the mug slowly to his lips. He sipped from it, eyeing Malone with all the patience in the world, and I understood in that moment why my father was the head of the council, and Calvin Malone never would be: Malone had no patience. No sense of timing. He wanted instant gratification, even on little things like getting a rise out of my father.

"No," Daddy said. "I'm not *asking* you to do anything." With that, he turned his back on Malone, showing the entire room that he had nothing to fear from his fellow Alpha. For toms like Malone, fear was synonymous with respect, and my father had just insulted him on a *massive* scale.

I think I was starting to rub off on him.

My father set his mug on the counter and turned to face the room. "We'll send everyone we can spare. Jace, will you round them up, please?"

Jace was out of his chair and through the back door in less than a second.

As the first of the enforcers straggled in, I rose to refill my mug and found the pot empty. I had a fresh pot going when Marc followed the last tom in, at which point my father finished his coffee and cleared his throat for our attention. "In case anyone's eavesdropping efforts failed—" quiet chuckling echoed across the living room "—we have agreed to investigate a matter brought to our attention by Elias Keller, the bruin we all just met. Mr. Keller says a group of strays has been making trouble near his home. You should be able to pick up their scents at a pond about six miles north of here."

Excited murmurs rose throughout the room as anticipation

of the chase swelled. I shared the guys' eagerness, but knew without being told that I would not be participating. The council would never let me run free—even on an important assignment—while the hearing was in progress, and once it was over, the point would likely be moot. I might never run anywhere again.

That thought sent a jolt of fear through me, and the coffeepot shook in my grip, clattering against my empty mug. Marc lifted it from my hand, filling first my cup, then one for himself. I met his eyes—and he didn't look away.

"I want you in pairs," my father called out from the living room, drawing my attention back to the hunt I would take no part in. "One man from each team on two feet, the other on four paws. Stay ten yards apart, and head north to start. Check in with your Alpha by cell phone every hour. Got it?"

Several toms nodded, but Brett Malone—he of the unaccepted proposal—spoke up with a question, drawing a scowl from his father. "What should we do with the strays, if we find them?"

"Bring them back. Alive. Unconscious, if necessary."

Brett frowned. "Should we use tranquilizers?"

My father's brow rose in mild surprise, no doubt only a fraction of what he was truly feeling. Then his mouth turned down in what I knew from experience to be *extreme* displeasure. "We have *tranquilizers?*" He glanced at his brother-in-law for confirmation, and Uncle Rick nodded.

"Yes," Malone chimed in, a slimy smile taking over his face as he glanced pointedly at me. "We have *plenty* of tranquilizers." His implication was clear. They hadn't come expecting trouble from strays, but they'd obviously expected some from *me*.

Fortunately, my father knew how to roll with the punches. "Then yes. If any of the strays are in cat form, tranquilize them and bring them back. We'll have more than a few questions for them to answer." He looked at Marc, who nodded in acknowledgment of his role in the process. Marc was the enforcer's enforcer. He was my father's big gun, the one in charge of *convincing* unruly cats to do what they should. He was also our executioner, when the situation called for one.

Which meant that if Calvin Malone got his way, Marc's would be the last face I ever saw.

But my dad would never let that happen. Hell, *I* would never let that happen. And neither would Marc.

"Any more questions?" my father asked. When no one spoke up, he waved one thick hand toward the front door. "Good. Stay in sight of your partner at all times. Use your head, as well as your nose." One corner of his mouth quirked up in an amused smile. "And see Brett for a tranquilizer before you go."

Brett was already on the job. He'd just come in from the hallway with a big cardboard box, from which he pulled a handful of preloaded hypodermic needles, capped in red plastic. "You'll have to get close to use these, of course," he said, handing the first two needles to Jace, and the next two to Blackwell's young grandson. "But they'll work pretty fast."

Frowning, I settled back into my chair at the table, thinking of where I'd like to shove Malone's hypodermics.

In the living room, my father leaned against the wall next to his brother-in-law and both Alphas eyed the absurdly large box of sedatives. "Expecting trouble, were you?"

Uncle Rick chuckled. "Malone's a frugal bastard, and they're cheaper in bulk."

"I bet." But Daddy smiled. He was amused by all the needles, and so was I. The fact that they were prepared to sedate me—for the rest of my natural life, apparently—meant that they took me seriously. Were maybe even afraid of me, just a little bit.

Fear wasn't quite as good as respect—but I'd take it.

My father cleared his throat, and everyone stopped what

they were doing to look at him. "I'd like to speak to the council members in the dining room, please."

Malone frowned and jerked his head in my general direction. "What about her?"

"She'll have to come along."

Oh, goodie! Insider information... I sipped from my mug to hide my smile.

"No," Malone said, and I twisted to look at him so fast a jolt of pain shot through my neck. He shook his head firmly.

Blackwell stood. "She can*not* sit in on council meetings, Greg. Not before we have a verdict. She hasn't earned enough trust."

My father nodded in concession, and a pang of disappointment leached through me. *More sitting around, bored. I should have packed more books.*

"Someone will have to watch her," Blackwell continued, and I stiffened. The tribunal had put me under round-the-clock guard until the hearing was over, like I was some psychopath who might run off to infect and murder more humans if they lost sight of me for more than a five-minute bathroom break.

"Fine," my father said, because he clearly had no choice. But there were only two toms left to watch me: Brett Malone and a Nordic-looking Canadian transplant named Colin Dean, who'd been hired by Paul Blackwell a few months earlier. I'd never said a word to him, and wasn't eager to, based on the sheer number of times I'd caught him staring at my chest.

I turned from Colin to look at my father, pleading with him with my eyes to give me an out. "I can help. Let me help."

"No." He didn't even hesitate.

"I'll hunt with Brett and Colin, and I won't Shift." Being trailed through the forest by strange men was much better than being cooped up in a small cabin with them. "You can call me anytime you want."

"No," my father repeated, and Malone smirked, the arrogant bastard.

"You're wasting your resources." I pushed back my chair and followed my father down the hall. "You could have three more noses out there looking!"

"That's enough, Faythe." Three feet from the dining room, he spun in midstep, frowning at me in warning. "Don't make this worse. Go wait at the cabin. I'll be there when we're done here."

At home, I probably would have argued further, but I wasn't going to embarrass my father in front of his fellow Alphas. Not while he was trying so hard to maintain his authority. The last thing he needed was me making more trouble.

"Fine." Brett and Colin waited by the front door while I gathered what I'd brought to the main lodge—a novel, a bottle of water and a bag of Chex Mix. Before I left, I drained my mug, and as I set it in the sink, snatches of conversation floated to me from the dining room.

"You let him run wild, Greg, and it has to stop."

Marc. Malone was complaining about Marc.

With nothing left to do in the lodge, I headed for the front porch, and the last thing I heard before the door swung shut behind me was my father's reply. "He runs no wilder than your mouth, Calvin, and no one's tried to muzzle you yet. But I promise you this, if you don't get control of your tongue right now, I'll make sure it never gets you in trouble again."

A smile bloomed on my face as I bounded down the front steps. I couldn't remember ever being so proud to call myself my father's daughter.

Three

My father had rented cabin number four, a quarter-mile walk from the main lodge. On the way, as I stomped through dry brown grass, sandwiched by Tweedledee and Tweedledum, I nursed serious resentment toward both the Alphas, who'd made me stay behind, and my fellow enforcers, who'd gone on without me. I hadn't done anything more exciting than brush my own teeth for more than two months, since I'd been suspended from active duty as an enforcer in September. And now I was missing an opportunity that might never come again: the chance to take a run through bruin territory. To sniff out scents foreign to East Texas. To the entire southern and eastern sections of the country, for that matter.

From the woods to the north came the sounds of tomcats making their way through the forest—twigs breaking, leaves swishing, and entirely too much gallivanting to be productive. The racket—probably barely audible to the human ear—had to come from the enforcers walking on two feet, because when a cat stalks on four paws, he makes no sound. Not if he knows what he's doing, anyway.

I knew what I was doing. But I was *not* doing what I wanted.

Stifling a frustrated sigh, I wedged my novel into the crook of my left arm and opened the squirt cap on my water with my teeth. "Why don't we blow off this whole 'house arrest' thing in favor of a rousing game of touch football." I gulped from the bottle, then wiped my mouth on my sleeve. "You guys look like you could use the exercise."

I was kidding, of course. Brett was slim but well toned, and Colin looked like a towheaded Rambo. Or that Russian boxer from *Rocky IV*. He scowled down at me from at least six inches over my head. "If you're looking to get tackled, I'm sure we can work something out."

My temper flared, but then Brett made a strangling sound, and I glanced at him, expecting to see him choking back a laugh. To my surprise, he looked nervous rather than amused, his focus shifting back and forth between me and Colin, as if he expected me to explode any second, raining blood and guts all over them both.

I turned back to the Nordic giant. "You even *try* to tackle me and I'll hang your favorite parts from my rearview mirror in place of my fuzzy black dice." Okay, I didn't actually have a car—or a pair of fuzzy dice—but Colin didn't need to know that.

He laughed, and a snarl rumbled its way from my throat.

"You think I'm kidding? Try me." When he didn't answer, I jogged up the steps of cabin four and shoved the door open. I dropped my armload on the coffee table, then plopped onto the couch, where I stared out the front window at the beautiful fall afternoon wasting away without my participation.

Brett dropped onto the armchair to my right, and Colin headed straight to the kitchen to forage.

For several minutes, Brett and I sat in silence, listening to cabinets slam and pots clang in the kitchen. Twice his lips parted, as if he might say something. But each time, a single glance at my expression—a carefully crafted scowl—changed his mind.

Finally, around the time sizzling sounds floated in from the kitchen, along with the aroma of melted butter, Brett worked up the courage to speak. "You wanna play cards?"

"No." Instead, I stared out at the line of trees two hundred feet from the cabin's front door.

Ten minutes later, Colin lowered himself onto the cushion next to me, holding a paper plate piled high with western scrambled eggs. Brett sat straighter, his nose twitching. "Got enough to share?"

Colin shook his head, and several strands of straight, white-blond hair fell over his pale blue eyes. "You're on your own," he said, barely sparing his fellow tom a glance. Then he favored me with a satisfied smile, set his plate on the wood-plank coffee table, and slid one arm across the back of the couch behind my head. He held a forkful of eggs inches from my lips. "*You,* I'll share with."

Clearly my reputation had yet to spread to Canada.

"If you want to keep those fingers, I suggest you pull them back. By about five feet."

Colin laughed, under the mistaken impression that I was joking. I snatched the fork from his hand and hurled it end over end across the room. Chunks of egg and vegetable dropped to the ratty carpet. Stainless-steel tines sank into the fake oak paneling. The handle was still vibrating from the impact, Colin's wide-eyed gaze glued to it, when I twisted his entire arm with a grip on his first two fingers.

"Ow, shit!" he shouted, leaning toward me to ease the pressure on his shoulder.

"You come within two feet of me again, and I'll break the damn things off. Understood?"

Fury rushed in to cover the pain on his face, and for a moment it looked as if he'd make trouble. I twisted harder.

"Fuck! Yes, I got it! Let go!"

I released his hand, and Colin launched his bulky frame off the couch with a werecat's peculiar grace and flexibility. On my right, Brett laughed. He'd seen the show once before, years earlier.

"You could have warned me," Colin grumbled. He snatched his fork from the wall, then sank into the only other chair in the room and reclaimed his meal.

Brett huffed, and shot me a blatant look of approval, which I hadn't expected. "She's on trial for *murder*. I figured that was explanation enough."

Colin focused on his eggs, steadily whittling away the yellow mountain, glaring at me like a spoiled child the whole time. Brett stared out the window in silence, because the television didn't get cable and we hadn't brought any movies. I ignored them both and picked up my novel.

When he finished his meal, Colin stood to take his empty dish into the kitchen. I glanced up to see him balance the paper plate on top of the full trash bin, rather than emptying it. I started to berate him for being lazy, but stopped when I realized he'd just given me the perfect excuse to go outside. Not for long, granted, but it would be worth playing nice for even a few minutes of fresh air and privacy.

"That needs to go out, before it starts stinking up the cabin," I said, careful not to voice my offer too soon.

"It can wait." He pulled open the fridge and snagged one of Marc's Cokes from the top shelf. Normally I would have warned him not to do that, but I was trying not to piss him off at the moment. Plus, I kind of wanted to be there when Marc found out.

"No it can*not* wait. That's disgusting. You filled it up, you take it out."

Colin glared at me over the top of Marc's Coke. "I'm not taking out your trash. If you want it out, take it yourself."

And just like that, Tweedledum had told me to do what I wanted to do in the first place. *Idiot.*

"Lazy tom…" I muttered, stomping past him as if in aggravation. I was three feet from the back door, garbage bag in hand, when he caught on.

"Stop. Nice try, but the council doesn't want you out alone. Brett, you take it."

Damn it.

Brett started to complain, but Colin was bigger and stronger, which meant he called the shots, in the absence of a higher-ranking enforcer or an Alpha. Grumbling beneath his breath, Brett plodded into the kitchen and took the bag from me. He headed into the backyard, and I returned to the couch and my novel, fuming silently.

A minute later, something heavy thumped at the rear of the cabin. Probably the trash bag hitting the bottom of the metal can. But then I heard another thump, and a wave of alarm surged through me. I looked up from my book and froze, listening. There were no more thumps, but I picked up a muted whispering sound, too soft for a human to have heard.

I jumped up from the couch and bolted into the kitchen to peer through the window over the sink. At first I saw nothing, but by the time Colin joined me, leaning much closer to me than necessary, the source of the sound had come into view. Sort of.

It was a tail, solid black and twitching in nervous excitement. I smiled. One of the guys had returned from the hunt and was obviously trying to cheer me up with a game of stalk-and-pounce. It wasn't Marc or Jace; I knew that even at a glance. Maybe my cousin Lucas?

But as the hindquarters wriggled farther into sight, I realized they didn't belong to anyone I knew.

"Who's that?" Colin asked, and as I took in the confused look on his face, my apprehension deepened. My pulse pounded. An instant later, the cat came into full view, and I gasped, startled into inaction for a moment longer than I should have been. He was no one I knew. But he was *dragging* someone I knew: Brett, unconscious and bleeding from his stomach, the starched collar of his shirt clamped between the cat's sharp front teeth.

"Shit!"

The cat started at the sound of my voice. He dropped Brett's collar and met my stare through the window. His fur stood on end. He hissed, baring two-inch canines, white whiskers standing out against the black fur on his face.

"Who the *fuck* is that?" Colin demanded, louder that time.

I glanced around the kitchen, searching frantically for something to use as a weapon. "It's one of the strays, genius. Who else could it be?" My focus settled on a block of knives near the stove, and I pulled the butcher knife free, hefting it in one hand to test its weight. *Not bad.*

"What are you doing?" Colin stared at me like I'd lost my mind.

"Hurry, before he gets to the woods." I was halfway to the door when my gaze caught an ice pick lying on the counter by the refrigerator. I grabbed the pick and dropped the knife in its place, sparing time for another glance out the window. The cat and his prey were now a third of the way to the tree line.

Colin hesitated, then his head bobbed in reluctant concession. "Just give me a minute." He bent to take off his shoes. Then he unbuttoned his pants.

"What the hell are you doing? You don't have time to Shift." Werecats have very powerful jaws and legs. I'd once seen a tom haul an entire deer into the branches of a tree to protect it from scavengers. Once he got into the forest, the stray could drag Brett anywhere he wanted and we'd never catch him.

"We can't go out there like this. He'll shred us. Unless you can use that partial Shift trick to come up with a quick set of claws…" The bastard actually smirked at me, like we had all afternoon to trade insults.

"That's not how it w—" I stopped, sucking in a deep breath. There was no time to argue, much less to defend my partial Shift claims. "Get your ass out there and help me, or I swear I'll tell the entire council that you're a spineless, dickless fur-ball whose dam should have eaten him at birth."

Colin's smirk faded into cocky sneer. "Like anyone listens to *you.*"

Disgusted, I turned my back on him and caught sight of the meat mallet stuck upright in the dish drainer. It was bulky, with a sharply textured, two-sided aluminum head, a one-and-a-half-pound monster, which I could attest to, having taken out my frustration on a couple of sirloins the night before. Dropping the ice pick into the sink, I snatched the mallet and ran for the back door. My left fist closed over the doorknob as Colin grabbed my right arm, halting my progress and nearly pulling my shoulder out of its socket.

I whirled on him, fury and fear battling for control of my expression. The left hook flew out of habit; I'd been practicing with my southpaw during my recent period of unemployment. The practice paid off.

My fist hit Colin's chin. His head snapped to the side with a grunt of pain and surprise. He stumbled backward several steps, then tripped over his own foot. Colin's skull hit the countertop, then his back hit the linoleum. His eyes fluttered, then closed. He was out cold.

Shit! I needed his help. *Good going, Faythe!*

Flustered and out of time, I waited a second to make sure he was breathing, then shoved my way through the back door before I had a chance to consider my odds and chicken out. I raced across the grass toward the cat, now less than twenty feet from the tree line. A shriek of fury split my skull as I ran, and it took me a moment to realize it was coming from me.

When I reached Brett's feet, the stray dropped his prey and bared his canines at me. His fur stood on end, gleaming in the midafternoon sun. His tail swished back and forth in equal parts fear and aggression. He was going to attack.

So was I.

I planted one foot on the ground and knelt as I swung the mallet. The stray hunched, preparing to pounce. My scream became a cry of triumph even before the hammer made contact. And it *did* make contact.

The mallet slammed into the left side of his skull.

A sickening thud-crunch raised goose bumps all over my skin. Blood and fur flew from the point of contact. The impact traveled up the handle to vibrate in my arm. The cat fell over sideways. Then there was silence. And stillness. Nothing moved, other than the rise and fall of my chest on the bottom edge of my vision as I sucked in air and spit it back out, over and over again.

Sound came back slowly, and the first thing I heard was my own rasping breath. The cat didn't breathe. I knew he was dead without checking for a pulse. I'd caved in his skull. Ripped flesh and fur from bone. Whoever the bastard was, he'd never bother Elias Keller again. Or anyone else.

After several seconds of shock, my senses came back enough that I knew I should check on Brett. At first I couldn't bring myself to touch him. Blood had soaked through his shirt, drenching his torso and crotch so badly that I couldn't find the wound. I saw no movement from him at all. No breathing. No pulse jiggling in his throat.

Then, suddenly, he seemed to be moving everywhere all at once. *Shaking.*

No, wait. He wasn't shaking. *I* was shaking. I was shivering all over.

I dropped to the ground on my knees, and my left hand landed on Brett's chest. And that's when I realized he was moving after all. Breathing shallowly, but steadily. Thank goodness.

My fingers uncurled, and the mallet fell onto the grass. I explored his stomach with both hands, and found several deep gashes across his abdomen. They were bad, and he'd bled a lot, but he was still alive. And so was I.

My eyes closed, and I sat still next to Brett, my hands covered in his blood. And that's how my father and the other Alphas found us, minutes later.

Four

"Here. This will warm you up." Something soft and heavy slid between my back and the spine of the kitchen chair, and Jace leaned over me from behind to drape the material over my shoulders.

"I'm not cold." Yet I clutched the blanket anyway, because it was chenille, and it felt good, while I felt like shit.

Jace stepped around my seat and pulled an empty chair closer, and when he sat, his knees brushed mine. "You're shivering."

"No I'm n-n…" But I was. My hair was still damp from my shower. That was it.

"It's okay." His cobalt eyes met my yellow-green ones. "You saved his life."

I shook my head, thinking of the Alphas gathered in the dining room to discuss my latest mishap. "They won't believe that."

"Screw 'em." Jace scowled, and I knew what he really meant was, "Screw *Calvin*." "They'll figure it out. And if they don't, Colin will tell them what happened when he wakes up."

"Sure." *Assuming he* does *wake up*. He'd hit the counter-top pretty hard.

The Alphas had put Colin and Brett in one of the downstairs bedrooms of the main lodge so they could be cared for more easily. Neither tom had opened his eyes in the hour since, which was starting to seriously worry everyone.

And frankly, the outcome wasn't looking good for me either—apparently being found with two unconscious guards and one dead stray did *not* cast a favorable light upon my innocence.

The kitchen screen door squealed open behind me. "What happened?" Marc demanded as it thumped shut.

My eyes closed, and my pulse jumped. I inhaled deeply to get a whiff of his scent, which made my blood rush even faster.

"Short version?" Jace headed for the coffeepot as Marc crossed the room toward me. "Brett got mauled by a stray. Colin wouldn't help, so Faythe knocked him out and killed the stray. With a meat mallet."

"You okay?" Marc knelt at my side, brow furrowed in concern.

"Fine." I sat straighter and shrugged off the blanket to hide how shaken I really was. "He never laid a claw on me."

"I didn't mean physically."

I blinked up at Marc, aching to touch him. To deserve his comfort. "I'm fine. I did what had to be done."

"Spoken like a true enforcer," he said, and I smiled. That was a very big compliment, coming from Marc.

Ceramic clinked against Formica, and Jace handed me a fresh mug of coffee as Marc slid into the chair on my left.

"Thanks." I'd already had enough caffeine to kick-start Frankenstein's monster, but I took the mug anyway, grateful that anyone was willing to speak to me—much less fix me coffee—in spite of the blood on my hands. *Literally.* I eyed the reddish crust dried beneath my right thumbnail. Apparently I'd missed a spot in the shower.

"How are Brett and Colin?" Marc asked.

Jace pulled out the chair on my right and sat. "They're as comfortable as we can make them until the doc gets here."

Dr. Carver. He was already on his way to testify about the condition of Andrew's body when we'd brought it home for disposal, but he'd find his bedside manner more in demand than his testimony.

I stared into my mug, treasuring the warmth of my coffee even more than the scent. "What'd they do with the body?"

"It's out back under a tarp," Jace said. "We'll bury him in the woods when they're done examining him."

"They find anything?"

Jace shrugged. "He's newly infected. Less than a week, most likely, since his original scratches haven't healed yet. They think he was still feverish, and that's why he came so close to the complex. He was probably looking for food, and found Brett instead. Hell, he might've thought Brett *was* food."

Still feverish. I sipped from my mug, thinking. Newly infected strays suffered from disorientation, high fever and intense hunger for several days after being scratched or bitten. Many strays did not survive the transitional illness—called scratch fever—and of those who did, many more died during or soon after their first Shift.

The stray in question had obviously survived both. But he hadn't survived me. And as justified as I felt in killing the strange cat to save Brett, I couldn't suppress a pang of sympathy for the stray, who was likely out of his mind with pain and hunger when he'd attacked.

"What can they tell about his infector?"

Marc leaned with one shoulder against the living-room doorway. "Only that it's no one we know." Which meant that the trace of his infector's base scent, which ran through the stray's blood, belonged to a stranger. Likely another stray. In theory, we could trace a stray's lineage from his base scent back to his infector's scent, and back even further if that cat were also a stray. But that ability would do us no good without a suspect with whom to compare scents.

"So whoever infected him is local." Because no stray could have traveled far from wherever he was attacked while still in the grip of scratch fever. "But that could be anyone." Since we were in a free zone, whatever local werecat population there was would be made up of strays and wildcats, who were not known for cooperating with Pride authority.

But before I could take that thought somewhere productive, the makeshift-infirmary door opened into the living room and the Alphas filed out, Malone going off at the mouth as usual. "…and I want *her* locked up, until we can figure out what really happened."

"Why don't you ask her?" I snapped, both brows raised at the Appalachian Alpha. All heads turned my way, and my father shook his sharply, warning me to let *him* handle Malone. But it was too late for that.

Especially once Malone answered, glaring at me from across two rooms. "You'll be interviewed soon. Don't worry about *that*."

"The only thing I'm worried about is hell freezing over before I get a chance to speak freely in my own defense," I snapped, fury scalding my cheeks.

"Faythe, that's enough!" My father was mad. Very, very mad. But beneath the rage turning his face a scary shade of crimson lurked an even more frightening fear. He was afraid for me. Afraid my own mouth would seal my fate. And he was probably right to worry.

I averted my eyes, submitting to my Alpha without actually apologizing—a face-saving technique I'd picked up from Marc.

"I think she deserves to be heard." Marc's voice was quiet, not quite a whisper, but perfectly audible.

Malone scowled. "The tribunal will question her when we reconvene."

"This isn't part of the hearing." Marc pushed back his

chair and stood, facing off against Malone. "She saved your son's life, and the least you owe her is your gratitude. In lieu of that, she deserves the chance to tell us what happened."

My heart thumped against my rib cage, and my skin tingled with excitement. Marc was saying everything I wanted to say to Malone, and I felt as if I should contribute something to his argument. A show of solidarity. But other than a thick, foggy amazement, my mind was a complete blank.

Normally, I would take my cue from my father, but he seemed uninclined to interrupt, probably curious to see how far Marc would take his stance. Our Alpha was training him—training us *both*—to take over for him someday, and he considered experience an invaluable instructor.

I had my doubts, but I wasn't going to argue with any tactic that gave me the chance to be heard.

Malone didn't even glance at me, though that tick was back at the corner of his mouth. "I'm sure Faythe doesn't mind waiting for the appropriate forum."

"She can speak for herself," I snapped, forcing him to acknowledge me.

"That's what he's afraid of," Jace whispered behind his mug.

"What was that?" Malone demanded.

Bold anger shined in Jace's eyes. "Marc's right. This has nothing to do with the hearing, so you have no authority in the matter. She doesn't need your permission to speak."

For a moment, there was shocked silence as everyone processed Jace's reply. Even my father looked astounded, both brows rising over wide eyes.

Then rage flooded Malone's face, and his jaw bulged beneath a thin, trim beard. "No one pulled your string, boy!" he shouted, anger thickening his Appalachian accent. "You keep sticking your muzzle in where it doesn't belong and someone's going to break it off."

Suddenly my father seemed much taller than his six-foot

frame, much bulkier than his solid-but-trim build. "You threaten another one of my men, Calvin, and you and I are going to have a serious problem."

Malone spoke through clenched teeth. "He's *my* son."

"*Step*son," Jace spat, as if even the legal connection to Malone left a bitter taste in his mouth. "Marrying my mother did *not* make you my father."

Even *my* father flinched over that one. But he didn't back down. "He's *my* enforcer, and as such, you *will* respect him." He turned toward those of us in the kitchen and continued before Malone could respond. "And you will respect him as an Alpha. Mutual respect. Understand?"

Marc and I nodded silently.

"Yes, sir." Jace looked simultaneously nauseated over his own gall and relieved by my father's interruption.

Malone nodded curtly, still obviously fuming.

My father's shoulders relaxed and tension drained from his face as easily as if he'd pulled a plug. But anger still churned beneath the surface of his new calm, and those close to him knew it. "Now, Faythe, tell us what happened. Quickly."

I spoke fast, eager to get the words out before I lost my chance. "There isn't much to it. Brett took the trash out—" no need to mention my ploy for fresh air and solitude "—and a minute later we saw the stray dragging him across the backyard. Colin wouldn't go out without Shifting first, but I didn't think we had enough time for that. He tried to stop me from going to help, so I hit him. He fell backward and smacked his head on the counter—out cold." I shrugged, scanning the half-dozen faces watching me. "Then I went out and took care of the stray. End of story."

Blackwell narrowed his eyes at me. "You weren't trying to escape?"

"Escape what?" I shrugged, still holding my mug. "If our

justice system is as fair as everyone claims it is, I have nothing to fear from the tribunal, because I did nothing wrong. I look *forward* to a chance to defend myself. Besides…" Another shrug. "I sat there covered in blood and gray matter for several minutes before you guys got there. If I were going to run, I'd be halfway to Canada by now."

My father's proud smile faded into a deep scowl. I probably should have left off that last part.

My uncle's mouth twitched in a good-humored grin. Blackwell looked skeptical. And though Malone frowned and shook his head, I was suddenly sure he believed me— and just as sure that he didn't give a damn. He wanted me locked up anyway.

"Do we know how many strays we're dealing with here?" my father asked, and just like that, I was dismissed in favor of more important business. I could have kissed him.

"At the pond, we smelled, what? Four? Five?" Marc glanced at Jace for confirmation, and Jace nodded. The other enforcers had been sent back to search, and Michael had stayed to watch me and care for the injured. "But we didn't find any fresh trails. The newest was at least a day old, except for the one from the stray Faythe killed."

"Any connection between the scents?" Uncle Rick asked. "Same infector?"

Jace shrugged. "Can't say without a fresher scent."

Marc nodded in agreement. "One thing's for sure, though. Humans have been stomping *all over* that mountain. If they don't find those missing hikers soon, the strays *will,* and…" Marc trailed off, and we seemed to come to the same conclusion together.

"Son of a bi—" I censored myself just in time. "The hikers are dead. The strays *already* found them and killed them. Otherwise, the timing's too much of a coincidence."

Marc nodded grimly, and my father sighed, but Blackwell

looked less than convinced. "You don't know that. They could just be lost."

"Maybe, but Marc's right. If the strays haven't found them yet, they will soon," my father said. "The human search party only complicates things. Call your men and have those in cat form Shift back for now, to blend in with the human search parties."

The other Alphas pulled out phones and began dialing as my dad continued. "We need information about the hikers—what trail they were on and how long they've been missing. Michael?"

"Yes?" My brother stepped into the room from the make-shift infirmary.

"Can you get Internet access out here?"

"There's a patchy broadband signal from the tower on the mountain. I can give it a shot."

"Good. Bring us what you find," my father ordered, and Michael jogged out the door, headed for our cabin and the laptop he never traveled without. "Someone turn on the news."

The lodge didn't get cable reception, but there was a radio on top of the ancient yellow refrigerator. Jace plugged it in and rolled the dial until he found a strong local station.

After that, things got quiet for a while. Blackwell and Malone retreated to the dining room with a bottle of scotch for a private anti-Faythe party. My father and Uncle Rick settled around the kitchen table with a platter of cheese and cold cuts, the radio playing in the background. Jace plopped down on the floor in one of the bedrooms to play a shoot 'em up game on someone's PS3.

I made myself a sandwich and sat in the living room, from which I could see the kitchen, the front window, and the dark, quiet bedroom where both Colin and Brett lay unmoving.

Several minutes later, Marc settled on the other end of the couch, twisting to face me with one leg bent on the cushion in front of him. "So, how you holding up?"

I stared at the gold flecks in his deep brown eyes, thinking of how they sparkled in the moonlight, even in cat form. "I'm fine. What's the worst they can do? Kill me?"

He frowned. "That's not funny."

"Michael told you?"

"Jace."

Oh. So that's why he looked so…irritated.

Leaning forward, he plucked a bread crumb from the dingy upholstery and dropped it on my plate. "Why did you tell him, but not me?"

Because he doesn't look at me like I'm what's wrong with his life. Because he takes what I can give him without pouting over what I can't. "Because he found me on the verge of tears and gave me a hug. Any man who catches me crying gets a free peek at my thoughts. House rule."

"I'll have to remember that."

I took my time chewing, hoping some of the wistfulness would drain from his face before I had to answer. No such luck. "If you want to know what I'm thinking, ask me."

"What are you thinking?"

I sighed, dropping my sandwich onto the plate. "I'm thinking this needs more tomato."

Marc frowned. "I wasn't kidding."

If he'd been any one of my other fellow enforcers, I'd have stretched out and put my feet in his lap, begging for a massage. The others would take such a gesture as I meant it—a sign of trust and friendship. A werecat won't touch someone he or she doesn't trust. Not without bared claws, anyway.

But touching Marc was never a good idea. Not since we'd broken up. Touching him reminded me of what we'd had. What we'd been. What was gone.

"What do you want me to say? 'Hey, Marc, it turns out you were right. If I'd married you instead of going to school, they'd think I was worth what it costs to feed me. But since

I'm only as valuable as my uterus—which is currently unoc-cupied—this time next week, I'll probably have gone the way of the dodo bird.'"

His frown deepened. "This is because you're single?"

"No, this is because I infected Andrew and opted to defend myself when he tried to kill me. But when they find me guilty, being single will mean the difference between losing my claws and losing my life. Peachy, huh?"

Marc shook his head slowly, his hand clenching around the back of the couch. "They won't do it. Your father won't let them."

"What about you?" I shouldn't have said it. I had no right to ask that of him.

But he answered anyway, staring at me with eyes full of hurt. "I won't, either. Did you really have to ask?"

"No. I'm sorry."

We sat in awkward silence for the next ten minutes, me chewing and him…watching. I'd just swallowed the last bite of my sandwich when a silver sedan pulled into the gravel driveway. Danny Carver sat behind the wheel, his short, neat brown beard adding a bit of softness to sharp cheekbones and an angular nose.

"Daddy, Dr. Carver's here. I'm going to walk him in." Without waiting for a reply, I jogged out the front door and down the steps, eager for any excuse to breathe fresh air, even if only for a minute. "Hey, Doc."

Danny Carver pushed open his car door and stood, stretch-ing short, thick arms and legs after the long drive from the airport. "Faythe, you're in fine spirits for someone facing a disciplinary board." He opened the rear door and pulled out a small, hard-shell suitcase.

"Eh, what can I say?" I crossed both arms beneath my breasts, shrugging as if I weren't in the middle of the most stressful week of my life. "I'm seething on the inside."

Dr. Carver laughed. "Attagirl. What's the worst they can do? Execute you?" He winked in jest.

Marc was right. It wasn't funny.

"What, they didn't tell you, either?" I arched one brow and took the suitcase from him. "Malone's shooting for capital punishment. Apparently I don't contribute enough to the werecat community to justify the expense of my upkeep."

"What?" Carver frowned, walking alongside me toward the lodge. "It won't come to that. There's no way he'll get a majority vote of guilty."

I wanted to believe him. I really did. Uncle Rick was definitely on my side, and Malone definitely was *not*. Blackwell was the swing vote. My life depended on convincing the stubborn old crow that I had value as something other than a walking incubator.

Inside, I set Carver's bag by the door, and Uncle Rick stepped forward with a glass of sweet tea for the doctor, who didn't drink coffee. "Good to see you, Danny."

Dr. Carver returned the greeting, and several more, as everyone was reacquainted with the south-central Pride's resident physician.

By profession, Dr. Carver was chief medical examiner for the state of Oklahoma, which led to all the usual jokes about him "carving" up dead bodies. As always, the doc laughed the remarks off, then he looked around for Malone. "My flight leaves tomorrow afternoon, gentlemen. So, shall we get started?"

Malone cleared his throat and glanced at me, anger flickering across his expression before his gaze settled again on the doctor. "First, I wonder if you'd take a look at my boy. And Paul's new enforcer, too."

"Oh?" Carver's brow rose in interest. "You've had some excitement?"

"Brett met with a stray in cat form," Malone held out one

arm to indicate the open front bedroom. "And Colin met with Faythe's fist."

I flinched as Dr. Carver's head swiveled in my direction. "He was trying to stop me from going after Brett."

Carver's mouth curved into a grin, and my own smile answered his. "Okay, let's see what we have."

The doc started with Brett, pulling back first the blankets, then the huge bandages covering the young tom's stomach wounds. Air hissed as I inhaled through clenched teeth. Somehow, the wounds looked worse clean and bare than they had hidden by blood.

Brett had four deep, curved gouges across his stomach, tapering to an end below his navel, just above the waistband of his ruined jeans. Someone had cut his shirt off, but left his pants, so the entire room reeked of the blood saturating them.

After carefully examining Brett's injury, Dr. Carver asked Jace to fetch his medical supplies from the backseat of the rented car. While Jace was gone, the doctor knelt to examine the purple swelling on the right side of Colin's jaw. Then he gently turned Colin's head to get a look at the massively swollen lump on the back, where he'd hit the counter. Colin moaned, and settled back into silence.

Dr. Carver glanced up at me. "What happened?"

"I hit him with a left hook, and he fell back and hit the counter." I crossed my arms over my chest in an unconscious defensive posture.

The doctor turned for a second look at Colin as Jace slipped into the room carrying a large vinyl first-aid kit. "Well, he definitely has a concussion, but it looks like Colin could wake up anytime. When he does, he'll have a hell of a headache. Give him an ice pack and some Tylenol." Carver smiled at me, and his eye twitched, like he wanted to wink.

I barely resisted a smile.

Tylenol wouldn't do a thing for a werecat's pain. We metabolize it too fast. But the good doctor wasn't going to give Colin anything stronger because the Nordic asshole didn't deserve it.

"That's it?" Blackwell frowned.

Carver's smile broadened. "Time is the best medicine for a wound like this. And if you ask me, you should all be thanking Faythe." His eyes settled on Malone, who only scowled.

"Why is that?"

"Because Colin's going to wake up wishing he were dead. But if he'd stopped her from killing that stray, your son would never wake up at all. Now, let's clear the room so I can sew this poor kid up."

As we filed out of the bedroom, Michael stepped through the front door, carrying a yellow legal pad covered in notes. "Well?" My father asked as I snagged a leftover piece of ham from the plate I'd left on the coffee table.

Michael sighed and glanced at his tablet. "The hikers are Bob and Amanda Tindale—newlyweds on some kind of back-to-nature honeymoon. They reserved a campsite about eight miles from here for an entire week. They should have come down two days ago, and when they didn't show up, her parents called the forest rangers. The searchers have been walking an organized grid for two straight days, from dawn to dusk. No sign of them so far."

Uncle Rick scratched his chin in thought. "Anyone here think there's any chance they weren't killed by the strays?"

Heads shook all over the room, and Michael held up his notebook. "Not one in a thousand. She's an inexperienced hiker. He goes out for a week every fall, as some kind of confidence boost—because he lost his left leg in an accident five years ago."

Five

An hour later, I sat in the dining room again, staring out the window. But this time, the setting sun cast a deep reddish light on fall leaves and brown grass. And this time Dr. Carver had the seat of honor. I sat against the wall, between my father and brother. I was allowed to listen to the good doctor's testimony, but *not* allowed to open my mouth since I wasn't on the stand. I didn't even get to cross-examine him, which I only found out when I overheard my father and Michael arguing over who had to tell me.

To help keep my temper in check, Michael had given me a stress ball painted to look like the earth. I'd excised most of South America when Malone asked Dr. Carver if he knew of any medical reason I seemed "disinclined to breed."

"How long after Mr. Wallace's death were you able to examine him?" Malone's narrowed eyes and cold tone said he didn't like Danny Carver any more than he liked me. But that was too damn bad, because the doc was an expert witness if I'd ever seen one. Dr. Carver was a *coroner*. He spent more time with dead bodies than a dog spends licking itself, and if his expert opinion was that Andrew's death was an accident, the tribunal would have to accept that.

Right?

Dr. Carver didn't hesitate. "Less than six hours."

"And could you tell the cause of death?"

Harsh, barking laughter burst from my throat before I could stop it, and several disapproving eyes turned my way. They'd called in an expert for *that?* I could tell them the cause of Andrew's death. I *had* told them.

"Yes, in fact the cause of death was rather obvious. Blood loss, from a massive puncture wound on his neck." Dr. Carver's expression was appropriately somber, but I thought I saw a spark of humor in his eyes. He'd testified in actual courts of law, and I got the distinct impression our little play-trial didn't compare.

"How would you say he came by his wound?"

I rolled my eyes at Malone's phrasing, but Dr. Carver looked like he wanted to smile. "I would say someone shoved a railroad spike into his neck. In fact, it was still lodged there when I examined him."

"So someone killed him." Malone glanced expectantly at the other tribunal members. "And by her own admission, Ms. Sanders was the only person present when Mr. Wallace died."

"I've already *told* you I did it," I shouted, jumping from my chair. "But it was self—" My father jerked me back into my seat by one arm, just as Michael slapped a hand over my mouth.

Malone tried to look angry, but his satisfied smirk ruined the image. "Miss Sanders, if you lose control of your mouth one more time, we will have you removed from the room."

"Like it matters," I mumbled, staring at the battered stress ball clenched in my fist. *I can hear just as well from the living room.*

Michael pinched my arm hard enough to leave a welt, and I glared at him. I would have pinched him back if I hadn't seen concern behind the irritation etched across his face.

"I don't think you understood what I was saying," Dr. Carver said, shifting attention away from me. "Because I wasn't finished." His pointed look at Malone made me smile. "Yes, Faythe killed Andrew Wallace. She's never denied it. But she says she had no choice, and I have no reason to doubt that."

Uncle Rick leaned forward in quiet eagerness. "So you could tell it was self-defense based on the body?" I have no doubt he meant to help my case. Unfortunately, his question forced Dr. Carver to backtrack.

"Well, not for sure, no." He moved uncomfortably in his chair. "But neither could I say for certain that it *wasn't*. But beyond that, her story checks out, medically speaking."

Uncle Rick nodded encouragingly. "Meaning…?"

"I also examined Faythe that night, and her injuries are consistent with her explanation of what happened. Cuts on the backs of her arms, from being pinned to the floor on top of broken glass. Severely bruised cheeks, from several blows to the face. Bruised ribs from blows to the torso. She was obviously the one on the ground—that much is clear from her injuries. And that implies that Mr. Wallace was the aggressor. Faythe says she was acting in self-defense, and I believe her."

I exhaled in relief. I wasn't out of the proverbial woods yet, but it felt so damn good to know someone else was willing to stand up for me. Someone who had no personal stake in my future.

"Dr. Carver, we have no doubt that Ms. Sanders was injured in the exchange. But we can't ignore the possibility that Mr. Wallace was the one acting in self-defense, injuring Ms. Sanders in an attempt to preserve his own life. An effort which ultimately failed. So, implications aside, can you say for certain, based on the state of his remains and Ms. Sanders's injuries, that this was not the case?" Malone's voice was as persuasive as he could get.

"I most certainly *can* say that." Dr. Carver's tone was firm, and anticipation pulled my spine straight in my chair. "I just can't prove it."

The frustration in his voice was mirrored in my posture as I slouched lower in my seat.

Malone rolled his eyes. "Dr. Carver, we are interested in actual evidence here."

"Only because you don't have it," the doctor snapped.

The room went completely, eerily silent as all eyes settled on Danny Carver, in his chair at the end of the table, face pink with irritation, gaze focused intently on Malone.

"If you had proof it was an accident, you'd want expert testimony to tell you that proof was wrong. But there *is* no irrefutable evidence in this case, and when that happens, you have to make your decision based on the testimony and opinions of others. And my testimony—my gut instinct—is that Faythe had no choice but to defend herself against Andrew Wallace. As she's said repeatedly."

"So she has." Malone's disbelief sent a fresh surge of irritation through me. My fist clenched around the stress ball again, and I glanced down to see that I'd carved a new tectonic-plate boundary down the middle of Central Europe. Thank goodness I wasn't into voodoo.

"Speaking of Ms. Sanders's testimony…" Blackwell began. "Are you aware of her claims that the infection was an accident, caused by a—" he glanced at his notes "—'partial Shift.'"

The doctor nodded curtly.

"And have you ever seen this…phenomenon?"

"Unfortunately…no."

"What a coincidence," Malone spat. "Neither has anyone else."

I shot up from my chair in indignation, my latest warning forgotten. "That's—" Michael's hand clamped over my mouth again, and he shoved me back into my seat, much harder than necessary.

—*not true!* My protest ended in my head, as my teeth sank into my brother's finger. He snatched his hand from my mouth, shaking it. And too late it occurred to me that biting was probably a bad idea, considering I was on trial, in part, for that very offense.

Still, Malone's crack was an outright *lie*. Several people had seen the partial Shift. Of course, one of them—Eric, the psycho kidnapper—was now dead, so his testimony would be pretty damn hard to scrounge up. And none of my other potential vouchers—Marc, Michael, my father, and my cousin Abby—were considered reliable witnesses because they all loved me and would presumably lie to save me.

The tribunal had voted in favor of excluding their testimony by a margin of two to one, and no matter how fiercely Uncle Rick had argued, he was unable to gain even one vote. *Stubborn bastards.*

But he wasn't done trying to help me. "Dr. Carver, do you think such a Shift is possible, medically speaking?"

Dr. Carver sighed. "No. Medically speaking, *no* Shift is possible. Our very existence should be a physical impossibility. But we *do* exist. And so does the partial Shift. I see no reason for it not to. It takes intense concentration to Shift intentionally, so it stands to reason that intense concentration focused on a particular part of the body would cause only that part to Shift."

His gaze swung left to include only Malone and Blackwell. "What makes no sense to me is that men like you—creatures whose very existence humanity has denied for centuries— refuse to believe something that requires only a small portion of the transformation you put your entire body through on a near-daily basis. The only reason you don't believe in the possibility of the partial Shift is because you don't *want* to believe."

Yeah! I wanted to stand and clap, or cheer, or…sing the national anthem. In a matter of minutes, Dr. Carver had driven home the very point I'd been trying to make for the last five months. And he'd made it look easy, and *honorable,* as if he were saying something that *needed* to be said, for the moral well-being of all involved.

To my utter surprise, though Malone still scowled, Paul Blackwell looked half-convinced. He placed one thin, wrinkled hand on the table. "Dr. Carver, I have to admit this partial Shift gibberish is starting to sound less and less like nonsense. But we still need proof Ms. Sanders can actually accomplish such a thing, even if it *is* possible."

Okay, it could have been worse. Blackwell was the swing vote, and he was definitely coming around. But he wanted proof—which I still didn't have.

In a real court of law, where the burden of proof was on the prosecution, I would have been good to go. There was plenty of doubt about my guilt. But here, I had to prove myself *innocent* beyond all doubt, which seemed less and less likely with each hour that passed.

The doctor nodded. "Of course. But let me point out that Faythe's explanation for why she can't prove it yet makes sense. Medically speaking." Carver was taking no chances on his testimony being thrown out because it didn't pertain to his area of expertise. "We all know most werecats experience their first Shift at puberty. But you may not know, or recall, that many of these first Shifts are actually brought on by bouts of strong emotion. Anger, fear, excitement…even lust."

Calvin Malone squirmed in his chair. Rumor had it his first Shift was triggered at age fourteen by *heavy involvement* with his human girlfriend. He'd reportedly barely made it into the empty field behind her house, shedding his clothes along the way like a madman.

So if anyone understood about emotion bringing on a Shift, it should have been Calvin Malone. But his stiff posture and angry eyes said Malone was *not* pleased by the trip down memory lane. Nor was he willing to acknowledge it, even indirectly—especially not to help me.

"Dr. Carver, what happens to preteenagers at the mercy of their hormones is not relevant to this hearing," he snapped. "Ms. Sanders is twenty-three years old. She had her first Shift at least a *decade* ago, and should long ago have learned to rule her emotions, rather than being ruled *by* them. The fact that she has *yet* to reach that level of control does *not* speak in her favor here. It is simply one more example of her inability to restrain her impulses, which no doubt led to both Mr. Wallace's infection and his death. If you have another point, I suggest you make it before you bury the defendant any further in the pit you're digging for her."

That son of a bitch!

Every pleasant, tingly feeling left over from Dr. Carver's speech drained from me, leaving behind a cold, clammy feeling of exposure. And…*shame.* Had my lack of control really caused all my problems?

Before I could decide whether I should be ashamed or royally pissed, footsteps pounded down the hall, and all heads turned toward the door as it flew open. On the other side stood Jace, his face grim, full lips drawn into a taut line.

My father rose in one easy, graceful motion. "What's wrong?"

"They found a body."

"*Who* found a body?" Dr. Carver asked, rising just as Michael said, "Is it one of the hikers? The man or the woman?"

Every man in the room stood in the next two seconds, and I followed suit, not about to be left behind.

Jace shook his head sharply. "Neither. According to the radio, the victim's an off-duty cop—one of the human volunteers. His own search group found him."

"Wonderful." My father exhaled in frustration. "I'm assuming this cop didn't fall on his own gun?"

"They haven't released the details yet, but I seriously doubt it," Jace said, and around the room, heads nodded in agreement. "Should I bring the radio in here?"

"No, thank you, Jace. We could all use a break." Without waiting for permission to suspend the hearing, my father marched past the long dining-room table and out the door, Michael and Dr. Carver on his heels. I jogged to catch up with them before Malone could detain me without my familial-support system.

In the kitchen, Marc stood next to the ancient radio, and when we filed into the room, he turned the volume up. "They're supposed to give an update on the search in about ten minutes."

In the interim, the Alphas waited in the living room, and the rest of us gathered around the kitchen table, where we demolished two cartons of cookies and a bag of chips before the radio announcer fulfilled his promise of more information.

The dead volunteer, who was indeed an off-duty policeman, had wandered away from his group and been mauled by some kind of large animal—possibly a cougar. Searchers had withdrawn from the woods for the evening and would resume in the morning, with each group led by an armed forest ranger on the lookout for the offending cat.

"Well, I'd say that changes things a bit." Uncle Rick turned down the volume on the radio.

My father nodded. "Since the humans' search is over for the night, our men can Shift into cat form. But no one goes out furry after dawn. Spread the word."

The other three Alphas dug out their cell phones and began calling their men. Including Blackwell, who'd been forced into the twenty-first century when he'd lost an enforcer because he was unable to pass along crucial information in time.

When the calls were made, my father sent Jace into the sickroom to check on the injured toms. He came back an instant later, smiling at me in anticipation. "Colin's waking up."

Malone rose immediately, but Dr. Carver beat him to the door—then blocked the Alpha from entering. "Let me examine him, then you can all ask him your questions." Doc stepped back and closed the door before Malone could reply.

I bit into another cookie to keep from smiling when Malone turned his furious gaze on the rest of the room.

A few minutes later, Dr. Carver emerged from the bedroom. "He's fine. Dizzy, and a bit cranky, but he should be able to tell you what happened."

The Alphas filed into the bedroom. I started to follow, but my father shook his head and pointed to the couch. Scowling, I sat, trying to bolster my mood with thoughts of the apologies I'd soon bask in. Colin would tell them what happened. He was no doubt pissed about the big bump on his head, but he'd have to admit to trying to stop me, and I'd be cleared of suspicion in at least one crime. Which was a damn good start.

"…bitch is crazy. Homicidal. She nearly took my head off." Colin's voice floated to me from the bedroom.

"Now, that's hardly fair." I glanced around for support from my fellow enforcers. "It was just a little left hook."

Marc frowned and shushed me. Jace turned off the radio.

My irritation mounted as I realized no one was yelling at Colin for cussing in front of four different Alphas. Which was just plain wrong. *I'd* probably be brought up on more charges.

I crossed the room silently, and Michael scooted to make room for me in front of the closed door.

"Do you remember *why* she hit you?" Paul Blackwell asked, and I tensed, bracing myself for vindication. Absolution. Complete exoneration.

What I got was total bullshit.

"Yeah." Springs creaked as Colin shifted on the bed. "I was trying to stop her from going out. Just doing my job."

Yeah, right, you worthless lump of fur. Tell them why *I was going out.*

"Where was she going?" Malone asked. "Was she trying to get away?"

Objection, Your Honor? Leading the witness? I glanced at Michael, but he only frowned and shook his head, telling me to keep my mouth shut. Clenched jaws kept my complaint locked up tight. Clenched fists kept my temper in check. Barely.

"Yeah." Colin grasped eagerly at the straw Malone had just given him. "That's exactly what she was doing. She was trying to escape."

Fury blazed its way through my veins, scorching me from the inside out. The rotten bastard was outright *lying* to a room full of Alphas! On those not-so-rare occasions when I needed to avoid telling the whole truth, I simply evaded the question, but Colin was pinning his lie to his chest like a fucking medal of honor. And he seemed completely unaware that such a badge was not of courage, but of cowardice and shame. Or maybe he didn't care. Either way, enforcers should not possess such traits. Ever.

I opened my mouth to protest, but again Michael shook his head, this time adding a severe frown to his silent warning.

"What about the stray?" Uncle Rick asked, and when Colin made no reply, he continued. "Wasn't Faythe trying to save Brett Malone from a stray in cat form?"

Colin hesitated for a moment. Then he cackled with laughter so sudden and forced that everyone surely knew it was fake. That he was overcompensating. But no one questioned Colin's sincerity. Not aloud, anyway.

But the bedroom door opened, and I jumped back to avoid Dr. Carver when he stomped out, a disgusted look plastered on his normally jolly face. When no one closed the door behind him, Michael and I stepped silently into the room, where all four Alphas stood around the twin bed on which the towheaded tom lay propped against several pillows.

"*Faythe?* Save Brett? Is that what she said?" Colin glanced from face to face in overplayed incredulity, daring a grin when he caught sight of me watching. "No. *I* was trying to save Brett. *She* was trying to get away while I was distracted."

"Are you sure that's what happened?" my father asked, and the disbelief thick in his voice did little to smother the flames of anger shooting up and down my spine. *My* Alpha wasn't the one I needed to convince.

"Of course I'm sure. I was about to go out after Brett when Faythe took off for the front door. I had to choose between the two of them. Her stupid stunt could have gotten him killed."

My fingernails bit into my palm. My teeth ground together. My nostrils flared as my body demanded more oxygen to feed the fire of indignation burning deep in my chest. If Colin didn't spit the truth out soon, I was either going to spontaneously combust or lose my temper. I could *not* stand there and watch that lying coward of a pussycat ground my name and reputation beneath his filthy paws.

I should have hit him harder.

"If she was trying to get away…" Uncle Rick asked, eyes narrowed at Colin, "why would she kill the stray? Why not just run?"

"You think a *girl* on two feet could outrun a tom on four?" Calvin Malone demanded, glaring across the room at my uncle. "She had to kill the stray to keep him from killing her. She wasn't trying to save Brett. She was trying to save *herself.*" He practically spat the last word, and a fresh flare of anger shot up my spine and over my neck, where little flame-tongues licked at my chin. Pain lanced through my jaw, and I gasped.

Michael turned toward me with that same warning on his

face, but it drained from his features with one look at the pain on mine. "You okay?" he whispered.

I nodded, even as dread and rage churned in my stomach. Stress sent bolts of pain through my forehead, and tension made my face ache, probably from clenching my teeth.

Or maybe not. That pain was familiar, and more than welcome...

Suddenly Marc's scent enveloped me, and he took my hand. I should have been surprised by that, but I could barely think through the throbbing in my mouth. He squeezed my hand as my jaw popped, and I turned to find him watching me intently. Watching my *jaw* intently. He knew what was about to happen. What *would* happen, if I could exploit my anger without losing my temper.

A harsh smile hovered behind his expression, and he glanced at Colin. He had an idea; I could see it. "Actually." He spoke loud and clear, drawing glances our way. "Faythe can outrun any one of us. If she'd wanted to escape, she would have."

I started to squeeze his hand in thanks, but winced instead as my jaw...*rippled*. Then Colin opened his big fat lying mouth again, sucking up all the attention before anyone could look at me too closely.

"She *was* trying to run. I was getting ready to Shift—so I could go fight the stray—and she took off for the front door. She was taking advantage of me trying to save Brett, and she could have gotten us both killed. She ought to be locked up for her own good. For the good of us all."

My arms went stiff at my sides. My jaw cracked again, but I barely noticed. Colin's lie would add another charge to the list against me, and Malone would have more ammunition than he needed to cleave my head clean off my shoulders. My good deed had become Colin's get-out-of-jail-free card, and he was using it against me. The bastard.

Suddenly my tongue seemed to take up too much room in

my mouth. It broadened and flattened, itching unbearably. My teeth rolled along my gums. I groaned as my jaw stretched, the bones lengthening. All eyes turned my way. And while everyone else stared at me, I stared at Colin, who had become the focus of all my rage and frustration.

Then, as suddenly as my face had begun to change, his did too. His pale blond hair and bright blue eyes lost some of their real-world color. The green and yellow hues in the room deepened as everything else melted into muted shades of gray.

And that's when I realized Colin wasn't really changing.

Cat vision and cat teeth. I'd partially Shifted in front of the entire tribunal.

I should have been delighted, having just proved I could partially Shift. And even better, that the process was unintentional. Unfortunately, I wasn't thinking clearly enough to experience relief or pride. I felt only instinctive fear and aggression. My inner cat—now peeking out through my human face—was threatened by this tomcat and his homicidal lies.

While everyone stared at me in shock, I watched Colin, unable to look away from the focus of my rage.

Marc whispered in my still-human ear, so softly I could barely hear him. "You want to pay him back?"

I nodded.

"Pounce." Marc's lip brushed my earlobe, combining with his scent to add a new layer of emotion to those already fueling my partial Shift. "Pretend you want to rip his lying head off."

Pretend? No problem. I *did* want to rip his head off. My rage was overwhelming. The human in me wanted justice, but the cat wanted blood. I'd spent most of my life curtailing such urges, and now Marc wanted me to indulge one instead?

I raised an eyebrow at him, not entirely sure what he had in mind, but absolutely certain it wasn't a good idea. The last thing I needed was more trouble.

Trust me, he mouthed silently. And I did. Even after all

we'd been through together—*because* of what we'd been through—I trusted him with my life. So I took a deep, noiseless breath, then I let my anger unfurl like a whip snapping loose of its coil.

I leapt between my father and uncle, and the floor lurched past beneath me. Startled gasps surrounded me. My feet hit the carpet, and I jumped again. I landed on my knees on Colin's bed, straddling his shins. The mattress squealed beneath my weight. My fingers curled in the ancient afghan.

I was dimly aware of movement and frantic whispers around the room. But I left the shocked Alphas to Marc. I only had eyes for the terrified tom beneath me.

Colin stared at me in horror. His jugular vein jiggled madly in his throat. The stench of fear trickled into my nostrils, and I realized my nose had Shifted too. Or maybe the scent sensors in my brain had changed.

"Get her under control, or I'll do it myself!" Malone shouted. But I neither heard nor felt movement in the room around me.

"Calvin, look at her face," my uncle ordered softly, and I caught a twitch of movement in the mirror on the edge of my vision—someone moving to better see my reflection.

Fine, let them see. Turning my head, I bared my canines and hissed into the glass without actually looking at my face. I was oddly pleased by the resulting gasps. My smaller stature would afford them no advantage this time; if I caught an arm between my jaws, my cat teeth would cleave straight through to the bone in a single bite. No one seemed willing to risk that. Yet.

The blankets moved beneath me, and my attention snapped back to the bed. Colin edged away from me slowly, cautiously, his legs sliding between my knees. He scooted until his spine hit the headboard. A growl of warning rumbled from my throat, and he jumped. Sweat trickled down his bare chest.

Bloodlust surged through my veins. Chill bumps burst to

life on my arms as some distant, still-human part of me understood what was happening—what my cat-self wanted—and was horrified. But before I could impose logic on my feline brain, Colin glanced to his right, clearly considering an escape, and the sudden movement triggered my pouncing instinct.

A roar ripped free of my throat. I lunged the last few feet. Something heavy landed on the bed behind me. Strong hands grabbed my upper arms, holding me inches from my goal. Marc's scent washed over me. "Good," he murmured in my ear. "Let it loose. I've got you."

Not at all sure we were still playing, I struggled and lunged again, pulling him with me. My pointed, feline teeth snapped closed an inch from Colin's nose.

"Take her down!" Malone shouted, anger and panic saturating his voice.

"Don't move," my father ordered with his usual quiet confidence.

Marc ignored them both.

Colin whimpered like a little bitch, and my not-so-inner cat soaked it up. His eyes flicked from mine up to Marc's. "Call her off!" he sniveled, this time careful not to move.

Marc's grip tightened on my arms, and I struggled instinctively. Cats hate being restrained. "I can't," he said. "She's strong when she's pissed off, and I can't hold her for long. If you want to calm her down, give her what she wants. Tell the truth. And do it fast. If I lose my grip, she'll go straight for your throat. She's done it before."

Ohhhh. Suddenly I understood Marc's plan—a bit late, considering it was well under way. He was fucking brilliant! And surely if my brain weren't foggy with cat-thoughts, I'd have gotten it earlier.

Colin glanced at me and I let loose the growl I'd been holding back, confident now that even if I lost control of myself, Marc wouldn't.

Colin opened his mouth, hesitated, then finally spat, "That *is* the truth." His gaze shifted to someone at the foot of the bed. "The bitch is crazy! See?"

"Jace, get me a syringe," Malone ordered.

Jace must have refused silently, because I couldn't hear him. But I heard Malone loud and clear. "Fine, I'll get it myself." Harsh footsteps stomped out of the room.

Another slow, soft growl trickled from my throat, and a bead of sweat rolled down the side of Colin's face, over the purple lump on his chin.

"Can you get her off the bed?" Paul Blackwell asked hesitantly. It sounded as if he'd backed toward the door. Colin wasn't the only one buying our act.

"I'll try," Marc said.

The bed shifted beneath me, and Marc let his hand slip on my arm. Taking my cue, I sprung at the injured tom again, probably more surprised than he was when my teeth raked his nose.

Marc jerked me back again, but it was too late. Blood ran from a jagged cut on the end of Colin's nose to drip down his chin.

Shit! That wasn't supposed to happen.

The scent of blood exacerbated my bloodlust, and this time when I growled, it wasn't on purpose. My fists clenched around the afghan on either side of Colin's knees. My toes curled in the rough cotton yarn, stabilizing my body for another lunge.

Colin's eyes widened, then his focus shifted to something over my shoulder as footsteps shuffled on the carpet. One whiff of the air told me Malone was back. A tiny pop, and I knew he'd uncapped the syringe. The sharp chemical scent of the sedative stung my nose. "Hold her still."

"What is that?" Dr. Carver asked from my right. I hadn't heard him come back in.

"It's just a tranquilizer," Malone said. More firm footfalls, and I bucked wildly. I had prior experience with syringes, and the memories were *not* pleasant. Marc's grip on my arms tightened, and he pulled back, putting pressure on my shoulders.

"Stop, Calvin," my father ordered, and I stilled to listen, still pinning Colin with my glare. "You wanted a demonstration, and now you're getting one. She's fine, aren't you, Faythe?"

Marc answered for me. "She'll be fine once she calms down. And she'll calm down as soon as Dean tells the truth."

Malone's footsteps stomped closer.

"One more step and I'll let her go," Marc warned, and I expected to hear my father object, but he didn't. "Dean's the only one who can end this. Do it, Dean. Tell the truth. You owe her that."

Colin whined, and I opened my mouth, showing my willingness to follow through on Marc's threat. "Fine! You're right!" He faced away from me on the pillow. "She was going after the stray, and I wanted to Shift first. He could have shredded us like he did Brett. I just wanted a fair fight."

"Yet a tabby half your size was willing to face him with nothing but a meat mallet and a prayer. You're useless, Dean, and you're not worth her mercy," Marc spat, releasing my arms.

Gratitude swept through me, chased by a familiar pang of loss I was coming to associate with Marc.

Justice is a powerful concept, and it was not lost on me, in spite of the more feral righteousness the cat in me demanded. Triumph penetrated my rage and soothed my bloodlust like balm on a burn. I swung one leg over Colin's stomach and stood. He exhaled in relief, but watched me warily, as if I might yet decide to rip his throat out.

Dismissing Colin, I turned toward the rest of the room and smiled to the best of my ability. I crossed my arms beneath my breasts in a show of confidence, as if I'd never doubted the outcome.

"Well played," Marc said, grinning at me proudly.

Malone's face flushed beneath his obvious horror at my appearance. He knew he'd been conned, and he was pissed. But he was too much of a coward to complain while I still had the physical advantage.

"Wow," Dr. Carver said, and my head swiveled in his direction. A sharp gasp came from behind him, and Paul Blackwell stared at me in undisguised revulsion. Evidently most of the room's occupants hadn't gotten a good look at my in-between face in the mirror.

Their reactions were what I expected. They were horrified. Repulsed. Every last one of them, except Marc, my father and the doctor. Even Jace looked…*uncomfortable,* at best. Later, they might realize what a wonderful thing the partial Shift was. That if we mastered it, we would gain the use of our werecat's enhanced sight and hearing—and one hell of a set of canines—without losing the use of our fingers, and those handy semi-opposable thumbs. But for now, all they could think about was my deformed face.

I had to look. I'd had no intention of doing it, but when the moment came, when I stared at each of them in turn, meeting stare after disgusted stare, I had to know what they saw.

Smoothing my shirt into place, I turned slowly toward the dresser, only dimly aware of the people around me as my face came into focus in the mirror. I'd only really seen the in-between face once before, but I'd felt the features with my hands often enough to know that what I saw in the mirror was unlike anything I'd Shifted into before.

Before, my jaw had always Shifted to one degree or another, and my eyes had taken on slitlike pupils and irises, if not their actual cat shape. This time, in addition to that, my jaw had elongated into a hairless muzzle, complete with an entire set of cat teeth. My nose was feline too—black, and flat, with the familiar thin split between the nostrils.

I plodded toward the mirror in a daze, and my fingers found

my nose. It was damp and warm, as it should have been—on a cat. But that wasn't the worst part. Or the best. Or...whatever.

Though my forehead was smooth, and still completely human, sticking out of my normal, human eyebrows were several stiff white hairs on each side. Whiskers. I had brow whiskers. And cat eyes, in human sockets.

My face held the single-most bizarre combination of features I'd ever seen. And by "bizarre," I mean ugly as shit. But on the bright side, if the whole enforcer thing didn't work out, I'd have a long career waiting for me in the circus.

While the tribunal met in the dining room—I knew they were arguing because they'd turned on loud classical music to cover up their voices—I sat on the side of a bed in the empty first-floor bedroom, while Dr. Carver peered at my face with undisguised eagerness. "So, you can't do this at will?"

"'Aw eh," I mumbled, forced to work around jaws more suited to chomping than enunciating.

For an interpretation, Dr. Carver looked to Marc, who stood peering through a gap in the blinds at the darkness outside. "What'd she say?"

"'Not yet,'" Marc translated without turning. "She can't do it on command yet, but she thinks she could, with some practice. She thinks we could do it, too."

Dr. Carver nodded, shining his penlight in my eyes. "I don't doubt that."

Growling softly, I winced and closed my eyes against the light.

"Try to keep them open for me, hon. This won't take long."

I opened my eyes and kept them wide as his light traveled back and forth between my pupils. Tears formed to defend my eyes from the invasion, and when I could finally blink, they rolled down my cheeks. When the light went off, I closed my eyes and pressed the heels of my hands against them.

"Here." Something soft brushed my cheek, and I looked up to find Marc offering me a tissue. Smiling in thanks, I blotted my eyes, then wiped my cheeks, watching the doctor on the other bed as he scribbled in a notebook.

"Your eyes themselves appear to have Shifted completely," he said, finally looking up from the paper, though his pen was still poised over it. "And you have brow whiskers, though the bone structure above your nose is still completely human. What about your vision? How do you see things?"

"'ike a aaa."

"What?"

"Like a cat." Marc settled onto the bed next to me, close enough that our knees touched.

"Mmm-hmm. That's what I thought. Let's take a look at your mouth."

I rolled my eyes and opened my mouth. The tribunal had asked for a report on the examination, so I submitted, though it irked me to be inspected like a fucking show dog. It would irk me much more to be convicted, then executed.

After noting the shape of my nose, the fact that my sense of smell was enhanced, and the number and form of each of my teeth, Dr. Carver let me Shift back. He wanted to watch, though, which was a bit unnerving. I've Shifted in front of my fellow werecats literally hundreds of times, but only once could I remember actually being watched, and that memory wasn't exactly pleasant. I'd killed the guy who'd ogled— Eric—shortly thereafter.

Dr. Carver was another case entirely, of course. He made notes, and commented on the relative ease of Shifting back to fully human form, in contrast to the difficulty I had doing the reverse. When the change was complete, he examined my human face, made several short notes on his yellow pad, thanked me for my cooperation, then headed for the door, clearly eager to report his findings to the tribunal.

And suddenly I was alone with Marc for the first time in weeks.

At first, neither of us spoke. Strains of classical flute and violin floated in from the dining room, and some radio announcer was giving a weather report in the kitchen, where Michael, Jace, and my father sat around the table, demolishing a huge platter of homemade nachos while they waited for the next update on the dead cop.

Marc was looking out the window again. There was nothing out there; he was just avoiding me.

Sighing, I got up and closed the door quietly, then leaned against it with my arms crossed over my chest. In all the years I'd known him—since he was infected at fourteen—he'd never once made an empty threat. He'd learned from my father that if you don't follow through on your threats, people will stop believing you. The same goes for promises, as I'd learned the hard way.

Yet for me, he'd bluffed Colin and a whole roomful of Alphas. And now he wouldn't even look at me.

From the kitchen, the weather report—calling for light snow overnight—gave way to another bouncy disco tune from the seventies.

I inhaled deeply, then exhaled slowly. "Thank you."

Marc turned from the window, and the blinds snapped back into place. "For what?"

I frowned. He knew damn well what I meant. "For bluffing Colin. I've never seen you make an empty threat before."

He sat on the edge of the far bed. "You still haven't. *I* wasn't threatening him. *You* were."

Riiiight. "You're walking a pretty thin line there, Marc."

"Yeah. I am." He frowned in reproach. "I wish you'd walk it with me, just long enough to get the tribunal off your back."

No wonder they wouldn't let Marc testify. He really *would* do anything to save my life.

I flopped onto the empty bed on my back and stared at the ceiling. "What do you want me to do?"

He leaned forward, both elbows resting on his knees. "If you play the game their way—just tell them what they want to hear—life might go a little more smoothly. Or at least last longer."

I huffed in skepticism, but hadn't yet thought of an intelligent reply, when someone knocked softly on the door. "Faythe?" Jace called hesitantly.

"Yeah, come on in." I turned onto my side and propped myself on one elbow as the door opened.

Jace glanced from me to Marc, then back to me, and his creased forehead relaxed. He was probably relieved to find us both clothed. Marc and I had rarely been alone together since we broke up, but in the past, privacy had always been enough of an excuse to make up.

But things were different now. This time *he'd* dumped *me*.

Jace smiled like he had a secret. "The tribunal's ready to see you."

Based on his expression, I was guessing the news was good. They wouldn't have told him anything official, but the kitchen was much closer to the dining room than the bedrooms were, so he'd probably overheard enough to warrant the giddy grin.

Thank goodness.

Five minutes later, I sat at the end of the dining-room table, yet again. Michael had gone back to our cabin to search for information on the hikers and the dead cop, so the chair on my right was empty. Dr. Carver and my father sat against the right-hand wall. The doc looked eager. My father looked deliberately uninterested, as if the future of our Pride didn't depend on whatever the tribunal was about to say.

At the other end of the long table, my uncle and Paul Blackwell flanked Malone, who stood and scowled down at me. I gave him a saccharine smile, gaining as much confidence from his displeasure as I had from Jace's grin.

No counting chickens, Faythe, my mother's voice said from some distant memory. *Nothing's hatched just yet.*

And as usual, she was right.

"As I'm sure you know by now, Ms. Sanders, this tribunal needs a simple majority vote to render a verdict. In light of your recent exhibition and Dr. Carver's expert opinion on the matter, we've discussed the demonstration of your partial Shift and have taken a vote. Since each member is confident enough in his vote to swear that it will not change after further discussion or evidence, we are now ready to announce our decision."

My breath caught in my throat, in spite of my confidence a moment earlier. I uncrossed my arms and laid my palms on the cool surface of the table, but they were damp with nervous sweat and left wet smears across the wood.

Uncle Rick smiled reassuringly at me, and I tried to smile back. But though I was in a roomful of people, I'd never felt more alone. Sure, the tribunal's verdict was important to the entire south-central Pride. Might even decide its future. But ultimately, I was the one who would live or die based on the next words spoken.

"On the charge of infection of a human, our vote was unanimous. As one, we find you guilty."

My heart thumped painfully in my chest, and with each beat I could almost feel my sternum pushed out of line with my ribs. But I wasn't really surprised. After all, I'd *admitted* to infecting Andrew. The real revelation had yet to come.

"Some of us are ready to hand down a sentence right now. But because others—" Malone glanced at my uncle, on his far right "—evidently believe the infection was an accident, we have decided to forgo sentencing until we are ready to render a verdict on the second allegation."

"Wait, you're not ready on the murder charge?" I sat straight in surprise. *Then what was the point of all this?*

Malone's scowl deepened. Apparently he was the only one

who got to talk. "One member has yet to reach a decision about his vote."

I fully expected to see him frown at Paul Blackwell. But he didn't. He glared at my uncle Rick.

At first I thought it was a ploy—that Malone was just trying to upset me. But my uncle stared straight at me, not even bothering to deny the accusation. I arched my brows at him in question, and he nodded. He'd held up the vote.

Disappointment and confusion swept through me like a chill wind, raising goose bumps on my arms and legs. Uncle Rick knew me better than anyone else on the tribunal. How could he doubt my innocence?

"Later," he mouthed, assuring me less than subtly that there was a method to his madness. I had no choice but to trust him.

Uncle Rick leaned back in his chair, crossing thick forearms over a still-firm chest. "Tell her the rest of it, Calvin." Though he spoke to Malone, he never looked away from me.

My eyes narrowed as my gaze returned to Malone. What else could the bastard possibly have to say? They were canceling my birthday? Shaving my head? 'Cause there wasn't anything else left to take from me, short of my life. And they were still working on that one.

Malone inhaled deeply, and dread settled into his expression, which sent a flash of hope through me. "It appears you were telling the truth about…what you did for my son." Reluctance was written in the wrinkles around his eyes and the downward cast of his mouth. He couldn't bring himself to actually say that I'd saved Brett's life.

The councilman gulped thickly, like he was trying to literally swallow his pride. "You risked your life to help Brett, and for that I must thank you."

Not *I want to thank you,* but *I* must *thank you.* As if he had no choice. And knowing my uncle as well as I did, I doubted he *had* given Malone a choice. That must have been the part of the meeting Jace had overheard. The part that had put that secretive smile on his face.

"Don't misunderstand me," Malone backpedaled. "That won't sway any of my decisions on this tribunal. But if there's any way I can take myself out of your debt, I wish you would tell me."

From the pained look in his eyes, I gathered that he meant that last statement literally. He didn't want to thank me. He wanted to absolve his debt to me.

Not the most heartfelt offer, but I'd take it.

I watched Malone for several seconds, considering my options. And when the first flash of irritation crossed his face, I spoke. "Actually, there is something you can do for me."

"Yes?" Suspicion oozed from his voice like puss from an infected sore.

"I've been twiddling my thumbs behind a desk for more than two months now. I'd like to help with the search. I'm finished testifying, right?" My uncle nodded, so I continued. "I'm not doing anyone any good hanging around here all day when I could be out helping. Besides, you guys must be tired of having me in your fur all the time."

On my right, Dr. Carver snickered like a teenager.

Paul Blackwell frowned, rubbing one wrinkled hand over his bare, pointy chin. "You want to go back to work?"

"Yes." I nodded eagerly. "Here, of course. I'm not asking you to send me home. I just want a little fresh air. And I want to help with the search."

"No." Malone didn't even *consider* my request, though *he* was the stingy asshole who owed me.

"Oh, come on, Calvin," Uncle Rick snapped. I'd rarely heard him take such an openly hostile tone, and I'd *never* heard him take it with a fellow Alpha. "She's not asking for a full pardon. Just a chance to do what she's best at."

Gratitude flooded me, and I tingled with warmth. Did he

really think enforcing was what I did best? Chasing down trespassers and patrolling our territory, rather than renting out my
uterus for the greater good of the species?

I shot my uncle a smile of thanks, which he returned with
a nod of acknowledgment—an Alpha-move if I'd ever seen
one. "Besides," he continued, "is your son's life worth so
little that you can't grant the cat who saved it a few hours
liberty in the woods? Doing work for us? That's practically
community service, and she's offering it in exchange for your
debt. I think it's pretty damn generous of her."

Malone fumed. I expected to see flames burst from his ears
at any moment. But on his left, Paul Blackwell was nodding,
probably eager to make up for the embarrassment Colin the
Cowardly Lion had heaped upon his pride. And his Pride.

"It's too much freedom," Malone insisted. "What's to keep
her from running?"

My love for my friends and family? My obligation to my
father and Alpha? My need for vindication? My honor? Take
your pick. But Malone wouldn't believe any of that.

"What if she goes in human form?" Dr. Carver suggested,
and I wasn't sure whether to thank him or curse him. I didn't
want to go in human form. I hadn't fully Shifted in more
than a week, and tripping over twigs and vines on two feet
wasn't going to soothe the need crawling beneath my skin.
The urge to Shift was so strong in me now—perhaps
strengthened by the partial Shift—that I felt distinctly
snappy and irritable. It was like having an itch in the middle
of my back, just out of reach. I could scratch all around it,
but until I hit the right spot, it wasn't going to go away. I
needed to Shift.

But that wasn't going to happen anytime soon, because
Malone was nodding slowly in favor of the doc's suggestion.

"Yes. She can go in human form, but only for tonight. Supervised, of course. She's not to leave her partner's sight."

Uncle Rick nodded. "Done."

My father cleared his throat, drawing attention to the right side of the room, where he still sat next to Dr. Carver, who appeared amused by our informal negotiation. "There's no one left here to partner her but Marc and Jace."

Malone scowled. We all knew he neither liked nor trusted Marc. And he could barely stand the sound of his stepson's name. "Send them both."

My father nodded. "The three of them can replace two of the teams out now. We're going to need someone rested enough to go back out tomorrow." He paused, turning toward the closed hallway door. "Marc!"

The door opened instantly, and I grinned. Marc had been listening from the hall, and I had no doubt Jace was with him. "Yes?"

"You and Jace are going to rejoin the search. With Faythe." He stood, smoothing down the front of his suit jacket. "Go see if Michael's found out where the cop died. If he has, start there. I want Jace on four paws, and you and Faythe on two feet. If anyone's at the scene, send Jace into the trees to get close enough to pick up the killer's scent. Don't get yourselves spotted, and don't make any trouble. Understand?"

Marc nodded, and behind him Jace's mop of brown waves bobbed in unison.

"Grab something quick to eat before you go, and take a tranquilizer with you. If Faythe makes a run for it, shoot her up and drag her back." My father's eyes sparkled in mirth at Malone's expense, and I laughed out loud.

"No problem," Marc said around a big smile of his own. If he thought he'd get away with knocking me out, he'd have tried it a long time ago. But he knew better. He met my eyes briefly, then headed off down the hall, calling over his shoulder to tell Jace to make us a snack.

My father was already halfway to the door, Dr. Carver on his heels. Malone stayed in his seat, staring at the table as the other Alphas pushed their chairs back.

"Councilman Malone?" I said, and he looked up, meeting my eyes in annoyance. "Thank you."

He nodded once, curtly, then shoved his chair back and marched out of the room.

My father paused in front of the door and gave me a nod. It was nothing big, and certainly nothing as obvious as a smile. Yet it warmed my insides as much as the thought of the fresh air I was about to breathe. My father had just acknowledged my gesture—and the effort it had taken—with a sign of respect and approval.

And though I didn't want anyone else's opinion of me to hold value over my own, my father's did.

It always had.

Six

Shortly after seven, I set off toward the woods with Marc on my right, Jace on my left, a canteen of water clipped to my belt and a ham sandwich in each hand. Moonlight lit the yard around us, with no sign yet of the clouds in the forecast. My smile was so big it had taken over my face. I hadn't felt so good in weeks, even with the tribunal withholding the verdict on my murder charge.

Uncle Rick had explained the delay. He'd refused to cast his vote because Paul Blackwell still thought I was guilty, and two votes were enough to convict me. His delay had bought us more time to change Blackwell's mind.

My hiking boots crunched on dead grass, and the rich brown leather of my coat sleeves *swooshed* as they rubbed against my sides. I inhaled deeply and my smile broadened as crisp fall air brought with it the scents of pine needles, several species of forest animal, and wood smoke from some camper's grill in the distance.

No, I hadn't been completely confined to the cabin. I'd walked to and from the main lodge several times since our group arrived in the mountains. But somehow the great outdoors smelled so much sweeter when I wasn't dreading my return to captivity.

At the tree line, as I munched on the first of my sand-wiches, Jace handed Marc the nature-trail map my brother had marked with the location where the cop's body was found. Marc stuffed the map into the inside pocket of his own leather jacket, then reached out for the hypodermic needle Jace handed him. Next came my uncle's handheld GPS, which Marc kept out, to guide us on our hike.

Then Jace stripped, handing his clothes to Marc to be stuffed into his backpack. Naked now, he dropped to his hands and knees on a bed of dead leaves and began his Shift.

I tried not to be jealous. I really did. Part of me felt fortu-nate to be outside at all, even confined by my human form. But there was still that stubborn part of me that refused to be sat-isfied with receiving only a portion of what should have right-fully been mine. I hadn't intentionally done anything wrong, and "permission" for one evening hike in human form wasn't going to make up for weeks of desk duty and stolen freedom.

"This is really a compliment, you know," Marc said, his gaze sliding from Jace's writhing form to my face.

"How do you figure?"

"They know they can't keep up with you on four paws. Their refusal to let you Shift is an admission of their own inferior abilities. See?" He smiled. "A compliment."

"A backhanded compliment, maybe." I tore another bite from my sandwich before I could indulge in any more verbal abuse against Malone.

"Well, this one's for real." Marc tugged up the hem of his jeans and dug at something from inside one sturdy hiking boot. "In light of your recent interest in nontraditional weapons, your dad thinks you may be ready for a real one."

Something thin and hard hit my palm, still warm from Marc's body heat. When I held it up, moonlight revealed a simple, sturdy folding knife.

"It's just in case. Since they're not letting you Shift. That button opens it—" he pointed out a small raised circle on one side "—and you can close it one-handed by folding it against your leg. But *please* don't cut yourself."

I huffed in response and pressed the button. A two-and-a-half-inch stainless-steel blade popped out, and I gripped the knife for business, testing it out.

I liked the feel of the knife. It wasn't as good as having claws at my disposal, but at least I wasn't defenseless and completely dependent on Jace and Marc to protect me in the big bad woods. "Thanks. Where'd you get this?"

"Your dad borrowed it from Lucas. But if you don't have to use it, let's not mention it to anyone else, okay? Malone and Blackwell would not be pleased to find out you're walking around armed."

"Spoilsport." I grinned and folded the knife closed, then slid it into my back right pocket. The bulge felt good. Comforting, though enforcers don't usually carry weapons, other than what they're naturally gifted with.

A hoarse grunt drew my attention to the ground, where Jace was in the last stages of his Shift. He looked like a huge shaved cat with a deformed head. No, it wasn't pretty, but werecats grew accustomed to such sights early in life—long before puberty brought on a cat's own first Shift.

The potential horror inherent in the in-between stages of a Shift was balanced by its temporary duration. By the knowledge that the very body currently suffering serious pain and monstrous mutation would soon be a beautiful, sleek, graceful animal capable of feats of speed and balance a human could never even imagine, much less experience.

But apparently—based on my fellow werecats' reaction to the partial Shift—the knowledge that my partially Shifted face was the goal of my transformation, not just a necessary transition, made my fellow cats uncomfortable, all except for

Marc. And Dr. Carver, who no doubt thought of me as a living science experiment.

As I chewed the last bite of my sandwich, dense black fur sprouted in a thick wave across Jace's back. He opened his mouth and his canines elongated, growing to match the other sharp, curved teeth in his newly feline jaw.

A moment later it was over. Marc and I stood in front of a one-hundred-eighty-pound stalking, hunting machine. I'd seen the transformation a thousand times—hell, I'd done it nearly as often—but it never failed to amaze me.

Jace padded over to us and sniffed Marc's feet. Marc chewed his sandwich with no regard for the cat. His tolerance was all Jace needed as a sign of approval.

Then Jace twisted around with a smooth, slinky grace, rubbing the entire right side of his body against Marc's leg as he glided toward me. His head nudged the empty hand at my side, and I held my palm out for him to rub against. It was a familiar greeting, and a show of trust and affection. Not too much affection, because Jace knew better than to linger too close to me while Marc was around. Even though we'd broken up, and even though Marc was in human form, he wouldn't hesitate to show Jace his place—which was nowhere near me, according to Marc.

I put up with Marc's conduct because I didn't want anyone else in my life—or in my bed—and I wanted him to know it. But we both knew that if Marc's protective—or possessive—behavior got out of hand, I'd put an end to it. So far, that knowledge had been enough to keep him in line.

Jace purred, rubbing his head against my palm. I smiled and scratched between his ears. Then, with no warning but the tensing of muscles between his shoulder blades, he leapt out from under my hand and soared between two trees. He bounded up a steep bluff, around a clump of thorny bushes and out of sight.

Marc and I glanced at each other. I raised one eyebrow. He nodded, and we were off, legs flying, arms pumping, Marc still clutching the uneaten half of his sandwich in one hand. My canteen bumped my thigh and I laughed as I ran. It was probably a waste of air in my inefficient human lungs, but I didn't care. Running wasn't about work. It was about *running*, whether on two feet or four. Whether in fur or denim. Exercise was exercise, and I hadn't been getting anywhere near enough of it lately.

Cold air stung my throat as I sucked in huge mouthfuls. My muscles gloried in the freedom of movement without restraint. My legs itched for speed I couldn't give them in human form. But I could damn sure try.

A sudden burst of energy pushed me ahead of Marc, and I grinned at his grunt of frustration. Shaggy evergreens and skeletal deciduous trees raced past as I ran, blurs of green and brown on the edge of my vision. Ample moonlight filtered through the bare branches above, alternately illuminating my path and cloaking it in deep shadow. I was hot on Jace's tail when that first surge of euphoria hit me. Adrenaline flooded my bloodstream. Dead grass crunched beneath my boots. Naked branches slapped my jacketed arms and my bare neck and face, and still I ran, paying no heed to the cuts and scrapes I'd probably regret later.

Even in human form, to smell the forest was to know it. Scents swirled all around me, so strong and varied I could almost see them in the very air, churning in the dark as my motion disturbed them. Rabbits, squirrels, possums, deer, moose—or was that elk? And wolf. I was surprised there were any of those left, with so many cats running around.

Next came charcoal and pungent cedar ash, from an old, dead campfire. Were those even legal here? Leaf mold, tree moss, crushed pine needles, and…*barbecue sauce?* Someone had neglected to clean up a campsite.

Jace darted left around a red fir and across a distinct hiking trail. I rushed after him, and Marc's footsteps fell at my heels.

Jace's tail disappeared over another small hill, and I dug

in with the toes of my boots, climbing the incline after him, grabbing exposed roots and dangling vines for support. The only advantage my two-legged form carried in the forest was the convenience of human speech. Everything else was harder—more work for less result. Especially jumping. Jace had soared right over the hill, barely pausing halfway up for a powerful shove against the earth with his hind legs. But I actually had to *climb,* pulling with my arms and pushing with my feet. I slid, and would have lost my footing entirely if not for Marc's hand on my rear, heaving me up.

At the top of the hill, I took two running steps after Jace, then hesitated as a familiar scent rose above the tangle of forest smells surrounding me. *Bear. A bear's been through here recently.*

No, not just a bear; a bruin. *Keller.*

Marc had cut ahead of me when I'd slowed, but he stopped when he noticed me lagging behind. "What is it?"

"Nothing. I picked up Keller's scent."

"Yeah, he came through here on his way to the lodge. His cabin's about six miles northwest of here."

I nodded, and slowed to an actual stop beside him to rest. My human lungs were winded by what would barely have been a workout for a cat. "How close are we to where they found the cop?"

Marc pulled the GPS unit from his jacket pocket and pushed a couple of buttons. Then he turned to his left, and glanced at the screen again. "We're going the wrong way. It's about two miles northeast of here."

"Better call Jace back then."

Marc shoved the GPS back into his pocket and slid two fingers partway into his mouth, leaving a gap between them. He inhaled deeply, then blew over his fingers, producing a very shrill, very loud whistle, which I couldn't replicate to save my life.

Seconds later, Jace burst from between two bushes and

plopped down on the ground at our feet, licking dirt from one paw as if there was nothing more important to be dealt with at the moment than personal hygiene. Which was pretty damn typical of a cat, honestly.

"Wrong way, dumbass," Marc said genially.

Jace paused in mid-lick, rolling his eyes up to meet Marc's. He blinked once—in dismissal, I'm sure—then returned to his grooming, apparently unconcerned with either the name-calling or his own flawed sense of direction. Also typical of a cat.

"Okay, Fabio, that's enough primping. Let's go." Reaching down, I grabbed a handful of fur and skin from the back of Jace's neck and pulled. He growled lightly—a mock warning—and rose with my hand. I rewarded him with a stroke down the entire length of his back, which he extended by trailing his tail through my palm too. Greedy tomcat.

Chuckling, I scratched his head, then headed off in the direction Marc had pointed out. He followed, still chewing on the scrap of meat and bread that had survived our race through the woods. Half an hour later, I was cursing my human legs. Hiking through the forest on two feet was serious work, and the constant incline—we were literally climbing the side of a mountain—didn't help.

Around the halfway point, we stopped to drain our canteens. Marc refilled them with two bottles of water from the pockets of his baggy pants, while Jace lapped from a stream he'd found. Twenty minutes later, we were half a mile from the sight of the murder, according to Uncle Rick's GPS. But we never made it that last half mile.

I'd just shoved aside the millionth branch to slap me in the face when sudden stillness in front of me dragged my focus from my own scrapes and bruises to Jace. He stood frozen, ears twisted to the sides, tail twitching nervously.

He smelled something, and my automatic reaction was to

sniff along with him, though the chances of my human nose picking up whatever he smelled were slim to none.

So I was shocked when it actually did.

A stray.

I stiffened, and Marc's hand settled silently on my shoulder, letting me know he'd noticed it too, and warning me not to speak. And as if it mattered. Our sudden silence and stillness would tell the stray—wherever he was—that we'd noticed him.

The very fact that I could smell him in human form meant two things. First, the scent was fresh. Second, the stray was close. He had to be, or his scent wouldn't be so strong. And it *was* strong. The stray must have been exactly where we now stood only moments earlier. We'd practically tripped over him.

Jace's tail twitched faster, and he stared into the branches of a tree to our left. He'd spotted something. I followed his gaze, peering into the heavily laden pine branches, but could make out nothing more than needles and shadows.

Then, suddenly, Jace snorted through his nose and dismissed the distraction, like he might dismiss a mouse too small to bother chasing. He started walking again, continuing on our current heading as if he hadn't noticed anything.

I stared after him, then glanced at Marc, who grabbed my upper arm and hauled me after Jace, warning me not to speak with a single glance. That was a talent I'd always envied. The only thing I could do with a single glance was piss people off. Which was not a very valuable skill to have when one is on trial for her life.

When we'd walked for several more minutes, Marc sticking close to my side without actually touching me, I realized the stray was following us. I could no longer smell him, and I only heard him because I knew what to listen for. But he was definitely there, and the guys definitely knew it.

They'd also definitely altered our course, so that we were no longer leading the stray to the murder scene.

"What are we doing?" I breathed so softly I barely heard my own voice. But Marc heard me.

"Drawing him out," he murmured as softly as I'd spoken. Memories of us whispering to each other on much more pleasant nights almost made me miss his next words. "We're going to have to let Jace take him."

"He won't go near Jace," I whispered. "The claws are too much of a threat. One of us will have to draw him out."

"I'll do it." His response was automatic, and it was exactly what I'd known he'd say.

"He won't be interested in you. I'm better bait."

"No."

I'd known he'd say that, too. It was a direct quote from my father.

"Fine. Lose him." I resisted the urge to shrug and let the stray know we were whispering. "Malone's just waiting to see all three of us humiliated, and this will make him pretty damn happy."

"You can be a real bitch sometimes," Marc said without pausing even a second in his smooth, relaxed gait. But there was real irritation in his tone.

"So I've heard." I smiled in the dark, knowing I'd won. "We gonna do this or not?"

"Fine. You get to play your favorite role. I'll kiss you, and you slug me. Make it good, then run off."

He was going to kiss me? "He'll never buy that," I said, stepping over a fallen pine branch. But in truth, my hesitation came from the potential kiss—our first since we broke up. Kissing Marc was not a good idea. It would just make me want more of what I could no longer have.

"Of course he will. He'll buy it because he wants to. And so what if he doesn't? No stray's going to give up his shot at a tabby. You'll run off, he'll follow you, we'll follow him, me on the ground, Jace in the trees."

Jace fake-sneezed to let us know he understood his part.

Before I could argue further, Marc grabbed my arm and swung me around. He kissed me so hard and fast I didn't have time to think. Which was bad, because I forgot I was supposed to be resisting. Instead, I *settled,* sinking into him like I might my favorite armchair.

Some unacknowledged tension in me eased, and I felt myself relax, both mind and body. Even with Jace listening and the stray no doubt watching from the brush, Marc's scent and touch—as familiar to me as the planes of my own face—triggered responses I'd thought never to feel again. At least, not until I'd convinced him to give me another chance.

I tasted Marc, and recollection merged with reality, leaving me hopelessly confused, and craving something that was no longer an option. For several moments I kissed him back, and he let me, our role-playing forgotten amid the assault of memory and craving.

Then, when I'd nearly forgotten not only where I was, but *who* I was, his left hand snuck beneath my jacket and up my shirt. He pinched the flesh over my ribs, twisting brutally.

I gasped and shoved him away, furious until I remembered that I'd missed my cue. "Son of a bitch! That—" *fucking hurt!* "—was *completely* out of line!" My right hand curled into a fist, and when I let it fly, Marc didn't duck. He took the blow as planned, on his left jaw. His head snapped back, and before he could "recover," I took off through the brush.

Before I'd gone twenty feet, I stumbled over an exposed root, and had to grab a branch to stay upright. *Stupid human feet.* I glared at a clump of brush I could have bounded right over on four legs, but had to go around on two, my arms pumping furiously at my sides. I kept one eye on the ground, desperately wishing for my sharper cat's vision as I searched the shadows in vain for obstacles before I tripped over them.

I had to concentrate so hard on staying upright and in motion that at first I thought of nothing but outrunning the stray. I paid little attention to where I'd been or where I was headed—or where Marc and Jace had gone—because I was accustomed to running in cat form, with a sensitive nose and ears to guide me.

After a couple of minutes of running, I realized I was alone. I stopped in a small clearing to listen. My own heart-beat drowned out the ambient chirps, croaks, and slithers of any woodland creatures not scared off by my mad dash through their forest home, but above even that I heard the distant sounds of a human crashing through the woods in my direction. *Marc.*

He and Jace had probably hung back at first, to let the stray think he had a chance, but they were no longer playing around. They—though I couldn't hear Jace, in cat form—were racing toward me now. However, even as I listened, the sounds veered to the west. If they didn't correct their course, they'd miss me. But if I alerted them too soon, they might arrive before the stray, and ruin our chance to catch him.

On the other hand, if the stray arrived too early, I'd be well and truly *fucked*.

From the south, dry leaves crunched and a twig snapped. It was Marc, not quite as stealthy on two feet as he was on four. Or maybe he was letting me know he was near. I strained against the near silence, listening so hard my own pulse roared in my ears, but I heard nothing from either Jace or the stray. Neither could I smell them, which was starting to make me nervous in spite of the breezeless night and my less capable human nose.

I turned a slow circle in the clearing, eyes open for any sign of sleek, glossy fur amid the shadows and thick brush. Before I'd completed an entire rotation, a sudden awareness sent chills up my spine, and neither it nor the goose bumps sprout-ing on my flesh were due to the mid-November cold.

I was being watched. Some subconscious cat part of me

had picked up a subtle scent or sound and raised a red flag for my conscious human half.

My heart hammered hard enough to bruise me from the inside out, and I could barely hear over it. I turned slowly, and at first saw nothing but more trees and bushes. But then there was a small flash of light in the dark. No, not *a* flash. *Two* flashes of white light in the deep night shadows. Moonlight reflecting off cat eyes.

I slid my right hand slowly into my back pocket and pulled out the folding knife, my finger on the button and ready to press. But I kept it behind my back, out of sight. A surge of adrenaline raced through me, and my free hand curled into a fist. Those were *not* Jace's eyes. They were a pale, earthy greenish-brown, with no hint of blue. My pulse rang in my ears.

The stray had found me first.

Seven

The cat blinked, and I shuffled backward. Dead leaves crunched underfoot, and I winced at the sound, as if it might give away my position. But I'd already been found by one tom, and needed to be found by two more. *Maybe I should start shouting...*

No.

Foliage rustled as he stepped out of the bushes, tail swishing slowly, head high, ears pricked and on alert. I studied him, memorizing his form for possible identification later— one of the first things I'd learned as an enforcer. I inhaled, learning his scent, too, which told me without a doubt that he was male. And that he had *not* infected the stray I'd killed with the meat mallet. But just because he hadn't scratched *that* stray didn't mean he hadn't infected another. Or done something worse.

He carried no stench of disease or infection, and he walked without a limp, both of which indicated good health. He looked young—I was guessing early thirties—and was smaller than Marc. Unfortunately, for werecats, size wasn't the only determining factor for danger; I was proof enough of that.

But the bottom line was that he was a stray tom, and I was a tabby. He was drawn to me by curiosity, and by an instinct he hadn't been born with and probably didn't yet understand. To walk away unscathed, I'd have to satisfy his interest and keep him calm until Marc and Jace arrived.

"Good kitty, kitty," I murmured, unwilling to release the blade on my knife until or unless he looked openly hostile. Wielding my weapon too soon would almost surely provoke that hostility.

Marc, where the hell are you?

The stray took another step toward me, his ears folded back, tail held low and stiff. He was still more curious than aggressive, which was no big surprise. I was typically the first tabby most strays had ever seen, and they generally had no idea there was anything to fear from me until it was too late. Of course, I was usually in cat form too, and I was *never* unaccompanied…

Okay, there has to be some kind of protocol for this. Still eyeing the cat, I searched my memory, running through everything I'd learned since becoming an enforcer. What did the guys do when they were stuck in human form, barely armed, facing a stray with full use of his claws and canines?

The answer did nothing to reassure me: They fought, or they died.

Fighting was a last resort, and dying wasn't an option. *So, what are you good at?*

Talking. According to Marc, I could talk the color off a crayon. Of course, that usually got me *into* trouble, rather than out of it. But it was worth a shot.

I got as far as, "Hi," then I was stuck. I couldn't decide between, "What's your sign?" and "Please don't eat me."

The cat ignored my greeting, and his nose twitched as he took in my scent. He hadn't seen my weapon, and if he'd smelled the metal, he didn't seem bothered by it. He edged closer and I backed up, but after one step my foot landed unevenly on a mound of dirt, and my right hand—still clutching the knife at my back—scraped a tree trunk. There was nowhere else to go, unless I was willing to run from the cat. But that would be suicide. Even if he didn't *plan* to attack, if I ran, he'd chase me out of instinct.

"Do you live around here?" I asked after a moment's hesitation.

To my surprise, the stray cocked his head to one side, as if in question. Or confusion.

"Here." I raised my left arm to take in the immediate surroundings, and the cat jerked. *No sudden moves, Faythe. He's already jumpy.* "Do you live in these woods? On this mountain?"

That time he bobbed his head once, then tossed his muzzle toward the north.

"You live that way?" I asked, and he nodded again. Suspicion sent a vine of doubt twisting through me. Keller hadn't mentioned any werecats *living* near his territory—only loud, obnoxious invaders.

I glanced toward the north, as if I might be able to see his home through all the trees and brush—not to mention the mountainside—and thus verify his claim. And when I turned to face him again, the stray stood less than five feet away, still watching me. He'd distracted me, then snuck up on me, and I'd fallen for it, thrown off by his apparent cooperation.

"Clever kitty." Unlike the last stray, *this* one was neither sick nor confused, so I saw no reason not to gut him if he pounced.

The cat's nose twitched again, and his whiskers arced forward. He froze, and his ears swiveled one hundred and eighty degrees, listening to something outside the range of my regrettably human ears.

Marc and Jace? *Please let it be them.*

Eyes still on me, the stray began to swish his tail slowly. His ears returned to their normal position. I had his full attention now, and could practically see eagerness in his very feline expression.

He was preparing to make a move. Either Marc and Jace were too far away to worry about, or they were close enough to rush him into action. I was betting on the former, since I could neither hear nor smell them.

I swallowed thickly and inched another step to the right, my spine still pressed against the tree, the knuckles of my right fist scraping against bark. "What do you…?" *Damn it, yes-or-no questions, Faythe.* "Do you want something from me?"

The stray bobbed his head again, and a soft, low-pitched bleating sound rumbled up to me. He was purring, now less than a foot away. His gaze was glued to my face, his mouth open, teeth exposed.

Unfortunately, I was pretty sure I knew what he wanted, and "companionship" didn't quite cover it. That was the problem with being one of very few tabby cats in existence. The supply doesn't meet the demand, so those demanding often got a little…*eager.*

The cat closed the distance between us. My heart thudded in my throat. He nudged my left hand with his head, and I tried not to flinch. I consider uninvited physical contact grounds to bite off some part of the offender's body.

My dull human teeth would only piss him off. But even with it behind my back, my knife was inches from his throat. I could end our little standoff with the press of a button and one quick slash.

But he hadn't actually hurt me, or even really threatened me, so killing him seemed a little…rash.

Dread settled into my stomach like sour milk at the realization that unless I was willing to kill him, I had no real recourse, other than cooperation. I spread my free hand, hoping to pacify him—though the very *thought* of playing along struck discordant notes of fury and disgust in me. He rubbed one cheek against my palm, much as Jace had done minutes earlier. He was replacing Jace's scent with his own, effectively claiming me.

My skin crawled with revulsion. Casual physical contact among littermates or Pride members was both accepted and expected. But between strangers, it was an insult. A threat. A social faux pas about the size of the Grand Canyon.

I told myself the stray probably didn't know that; he hadn't grown up in our society. But I had, and I couldn't help feeling disrespected. The best I could do was cringe quietly, knowing any resistance I gave could get one of us hurt, if not killed. And since survival trumped pride any day of the week, I was more than willing to play along. Just not happily.

I was just getting a handle on my own revulsion, when a feline snarl ripped through the forest from a distance, shredding our pretense of friendly petting as well as the eerie hush around us.

The stray froze beneath my hand. My fingers went still and my eyes closed in silent prayer. The snarl hadn't come from Jace, but I had no doubt it involved both him and Marc, and that it was the reason they had yet to arrive.

Leaves crunched at my feet, and suddenly my hand was empty. Something tugged on my jacket sleeve and I opened my eyes to find my left cuff pinched between the cat's front teeth.

"Hey, let go!" I demanded, summoning anger to replace the fear curdling the contents of my stomach. Fear cripples you, but anger helps you fight, and I now knew without a doubt that I would soon be fighting. "You do *not* want to know what happened to the last cat who pissed me off."

Okay, technically all I'd done was scratch the end of his nose with my partially Shifted teeth, but the cat *before* that… *He'd* gotten his brains splattered all over both me and several square feet of dry brown grass.

In response to my blatant but evidently unbelievable threat, the stray rolled his eyes—an oddly human gesture for a cat— and tugged urgently on my sleeve.

What he wanted was clear. It was also not going to happen.

"Uh-uh!" I shook my head. "No way in *hell* am I going to wander off through the woods with the first tom who rubs up against me."

The stray growled fiercely, and my pulse thundered in my ears. My nose picked up a sudden surge of the stray's scent in the air. He was pissed, and likely scared, and his body was releasing extra pheromones to warn everyone near him. Which would be me. Only me. All by myself.

However, even if he *was* trying to help me, I couldn't leave Marc and Jace behind, especially when one or both of them might be injured.

He pulled my sleeve again, hard this time. "You can't just *grab* strange girls and start dragging—"

But apparently I was wrong, because he planted his rear feet firmly in the ground and gave my jacket a mighty yank. I had to brace a hand on his shoulder, curling my fingers in thick, unfamiliar fur to remain standing. The next tug moved us several feet, me hunched over and tripping in the meager moonlight, him stepping quickly and confidently, even moving backward.

"Stop it!" I shouted on purpose this time, hoping Marc and Jace were close enough to hear me. But my words gave the stray no pause. The time had come for more offensive measures. *Damn it*.

I drew the knife from behind my back, slamming one finger down on the button. The blade popped out with a satisfying metallic thunk. "You're not giving me many options here," I warned as his eyes lit on the blade, gleaming in a stray beam of moonlight.

He growled again, and for a moment, neither of us moved. Then he braced his front paws on the ground and jerked me to his right by my arm. I stumbled, off balance, and only remembered to swing the knife up at the last second. But that was a second too late.

His left paw arced toward me and slapped at my hand. Even with his claws retracted, the powerful shot knocked the knife from my fist and left my whole arm numb and tingling.

The knife flew off to my right and clattered against a tree trunk, then disappeared, buried within a pile of leaves. Now I was alone with an unknown stray, in the dark, in unfamiliar woods—and completely unarmed. If I remained stuck in human form much longer, I was clearly going to need some serious training with a blade.

Until then, all I had was anger and instinct, now singeing every nerve ending in my body. I was one big live wire, buzzing with fear and indignation. But my indecision was gone. "Let me go!" My arm flew along with my last word, and my fist slammed into the side of his skull before the cry had faded from my mouth.

Stunned for a moment, the stray swayed on his feet—all four of them. He blinked, then his mouth opened, and I was free.

I raced down the dark hillside in the direction I'd come from. Hopefully. At my back, the stray roared in fury, and thundered after me. "Marc!" I yelled as the running pant closed in on me from behind. "Jace!"

"Faythe!"

My head whipped around in search of Marc's voice. He was at least okay enough to yell, and he wasn't too far away now. I veered toward him, confident he would never have revealed his location if the cat who'd snarled was still a threat.

From behind me came a harsh crunch-sliding sound and the pant of labored breathing as the stray made a sharp turn to follow me. His next huff was too close for comfort—too close for *survival*—so I shot forward to gain a little distance, then skidded to a halt, spinning on a bed of leaves before I'd even stopped sliding. I grabbed a bare branch overhead with both hands. The stray lunged for me. Grunting, I swung myself forward. Bark cut into my palms. My legs arced into a beam of moonlight, knees bent.

I didn't make it into the tree—a world-class gymnast I am *not*—but my legs swung high enough that the stray passed right under me. By the time he skidded to a halt, I was racing in the opposite direction, away from both friends and foe.

I couldn't outrun the cat, much less outclimb him, and I could only avoid him until he tired of the chase. Or until I grew too exhausted to continue—which would be any moment. Already my lungs burned, and my side felt like it was being ripped open with each deep breath.

Out of options now, I slowed to first a jog, then a walk, one hand pressed to my left side. Then I stopped entirely. Behind me, the cat's steps slowed too, which I took as further proof he was trying to catch me, not kill me. Unfortunately, that knowledge wasn't very reassuring. If he got close enough, he could knock me out with the swipe of one sheathed claw, then drag me anywhere he wanted.

I turned to face the stray, leaning against the nearest tree trunk, and immediately held my palm out in the universal signal for "stop."

The stray threw his head back and roared, and his fury echoed throughout the trees. It was pretty impressive. But it didn't change my mind. I was *not* going with him.

He started forward, determination written in each firm step, and I backed away slowly. I was trapped again, and too exhausted to run. But I was my father's daughter, and I would *not* go down without a fight.

My right hand curled into a fist, and I took my "ready" stance, showing the stray my intent. Then a deep growl rumbled over me, humming in my very bones. It was aggressive and angry—a very fine threat. With a very *familiar* feel…

Jace.

The stray's head flew up, his focus fixed on the branches

above me. I followed his gaze—briefly—and there was Jace, hunched on a thick limb to my right, canines bared, fur gleaming in a broad beam of silver moonlight.

The stray's tail twitched once, drawing my eye. Then he pounced.

I screamed as his huge front paws slammed into my chest. The forest pitched wildly. My back hit the ground. My head thumped against an exposed root. Massive weight drove the air from my body, cutting off my cry of terror.

The stray glared down at me, teeth inches from my neck, breath hot against my chin. Panicked, I shoved at thick, fur-covered ribs, my mouth open and gasping for air my lungs had no room to accept, thanks to the hundred-and-seventy-plus-pound cat on my chest.

Jace growled above us, wordlessly warning the stray to release me or suffer the consequences. But he couldn't pounce on the cat without squishing me, too.

That's when I realized I was a hostage. The stray was threatening to kill me if Jace didn't back off. And if one of them didn't make a decision soon, the point would be moot, because I was suffocating.

Terror clawed at my chest, scorching my throat. My arms flapped helplessly, beating ineffectively against the stray's sides.

"What good is a dead captive? She can't breathe!"

My vision was already going gray when Marc's voice cut through the buzzing in my ears. It was the sound of mercy. The sound of salvation.

It was likely the last sound I'd ever hear.

But then the stray removed one paw from my chest, settling some of his weight on the ground between me and Marc, and suddenly I could breathe again. Not well, but good enough.

I swallowed air in huge mouthfuls, spitting it out as fast as I pulled it in, and only a concerted effort on my part stopped me from hyperventilating. When I could see clearly again, I turned my head, pressing my cheek into soft, cold, fragrant dirt as I peered around the stray's leg. Marc stood fifteen feet away. He had a gash on his forehead, blood smeared across the left side of his face, and a bloody rip in the corresponding sleeve of his coat. But he was alive and upright, and everything else would come in time.

"Let her go," Marc ordered, in near-flawless imitation of my father's obey-or-die voice.

The stray growled and dropped his muzzle to my neck. Stiff fur brushed my skin, and I whimpered before I could stop myself.

Marc jerked into motion, snatching a long, thick branch from the ground near his feet. He swung his club up and took two steps forward.

Four shards of pain pricked my chest, above my left breast, and I screamed, more shocked than really hurt. Startled by Marc's sudden movement, the stray had unsheathed his claws, which pierced my leather jacket, shirt, then my flesh.

The cat resheathed his claws immediately, reinforcing my theory that he didn't want to kill me—unless he had to. And when my eyes found Marc again, I saw something flicker in the dark behind him, in the hand he held behind his thigh. A flashlight? How was that supposed to help me? Was he planning to blind the damn stray?

Marc's hand moved again, and the light flashed brighter this time. Only it wasn't really a light. It was more like a glint—moonlight flashing off something...metal? Had he found my knife? No, it was too thin. More like a...

Syringe. He had the tranquilizer.

Wonderful. Unfortunately, Marc would never get close enough to use it without startling the stray into killing me. But evidently he didn't plan to.

Marc glanced up at Jace, and gave him a tiny nod—a signal for something.

Jace roared—an impressive display of anger and dominance, I must admit—and the stray hissed, his head whipping toward the sound instinctively. While the cat was distracted, Marc tossed the syringe toward me. It thumped onto the ground near my hip.

The stray turned toward the sound, hissing, and one heavy paw landed on my stomach.

"Do it!" Marc whispered urgently to me, and my hand flew to my side, fingers scrambling in a mound of moss for the syringe—almost literally looking for a needle in a haystack.

My sudden movement startled the cat—or maybe angered him—and four pinpoints of agony sank into my stomach, deeper than they'd gone into my breast. I screamed, and my hand clenched around a clump of moss. The scent of my blood saturated the air. Each breath I dragged in pulled at my torn stomach, sending new waves of pain through me. Yet some distant part of me wondered if he'd accidently ripped out my belly-button ring.

The stray growled at me and retracted his claws, and overhead Jace hissed in fury, drawing the cat's attention.

I dropped the handful of moss and let my hand skim the ground once more, this time moving slowly, to keep from startling the tom again. My fingers brushed the cold plastic plunger. My hand curled around the syringe, and I exhaled in relief.

I swung my arm up. Claws sank into my flesh again. Hot blood poured over my stomach and down my sides. One last scream ripped free from my throat. I shoved the syringe into the cat's neck, wincing as it met gristly resistance. I pushed harder and the needle slid in.

The cat roared in pain and surprise. I shoved the plunger home. Something heavy thumped to the ground on my left, then soared toward us. My scream ended in a terrified yelp as the stray flew off me. His claws ripped loose from my flesh and I screamed again. My hands clutched at my stomach, slipping in my own blood.

Marc was at my side in an instant, pressing something to my stomach. It was his shirt. His jacket lay forgotten on the ground, his chest bare in spite of the cold. "Don't move." He stroked my hair with his free hand. "You're bleeding."

I laughed, but that hurt my stomach, so I stopped. "Ya think?"

He smiled, and pressed harder on my abdomen. "Shh," he said, and I nodded, compliant now that I hurt too badly to argue.

Marc pulled out his cell phone and autodialed my father with one hand. Distantly I heard him read coordinates from the GPS unit, and tell our Alpha that we'd caught a stray. And that I was hurt. After that, I heard panic on the other end of the line and quit listening.

I turned my head to find Jace standing over the strange cat, who lay unmoving on the ground, the syringe still protruding from its neck. Jace had knocked the stray off me, accidentally ripping its claws from my stomach, but probably saving my life. "Thank you," I whispered.

At the sound of my voice, Jace padded to me silently and rubbed his cheek on my shoulder. He lay down at my side, purring, and I put one bloody hand on his paw then closed my eyes.

Marc's phone clicked shut, and he took my free hand in his, still putting pressure on my abdomen. "You're gonna be fine," he said. "Your dad's sending help." Then, so low I could barely hear him, "I should never have let you go."

Eight

I'm not sure how long it took for help to arrive, but it felt like forever.

While we waited, Jace kept his body between me and the unconscious stray, just in case, and Marc applied pressure to my wounds. He didn't actually look at them, and even in my pain-filled fog, I understood that he was too scared to. He could apply common-sense first aid to slow the bleeding, but looking at the damage might tell him more than he wanted to know. More than I wanted to know, too.

We heard our backup long before we saw them, and knew from the racket that most of those sent were in human form. Since speed was the issue, they wasted no time on stealth, instead crashing though the woods like a bear on fire, pounding feet, breaking branches, and crunching leaves. Jace roared to help them find us; there was little else he could do to help me in cat form.

To my complete surprise, and more than a little relief, my father was the first man to burst through the brush. He still wore the suit he'd donned that morning, including shiny dress shoes that should never have seen action in the woods. They were now ruined by mud and scratches from exposed roots.

He stopped as soon as he spotted me, one thick hand holding back a branch he'd shoved aside. Alarm flickered across his face, then was gone, but I was surprised to have seen it at all. My brothers had been wounded dozens of times, and my father had always taken charge with calm professionalism. Yet for me, he'd shown fear.

Did my stomach look that bad?

No! It was only a few puncture wounds, and surely he couldn't see the details without more light. My father was just upset because I was his baby—his only daughter—whom he'd never seen sliced open. Would this scare him into removing me from the field? Putting me on permanent desk duty?

Hell, no. I wouldn't let that happen.

I grinned through the pain at my father, assuring him I was okay, and he smiled back in relief and knelt next to Marc in the crowded clearing, taking my right hand in his. He stroked my hair back from my damp cheeks, much as Marc had done, but didn't say a word. I didn't know what to say, either. When he found out it was my idea to play bait, his concern would likely be eclipsed by anger, and even in the grip of abdominal agony, I knew the ensuing argument would not be pleasant.

Behind my father, two dark, furred forms stepped into the clearing—extra security, in case we ran into more trouble on the way back. The first I recognized as Paul Blackwell's grandson, and the second was…

Uncle Rick! I couldn't remember the last time I'd seen him in cat form, but he'd come along as a public show of support for me, as much for Malone's sake as for mine. But that didn't matter. An Alpha doesn't play security guard for just anyone. I was honored, in spite of the fire enveloping my stomach.

My cousin Lucas followed his father out of the brush, towering over everyone, including Dr. Carver, who carried his first-aid bag in both hands. His eyes widened as he took in first the unconscious stray, then me.

All business now, he dropped to the ground at my side, pushing my father over without so much as an "Excuse me." Daddy moved without argument, and I was pleased to see that an M.D. trumped Alpha status in an emergency. *Good to know.*

Dr. Carver set his bag down, then carefully peeled Marc's ruined shirt away from my stomach and dropped it into a plastic bag Lucas held ready. Then he took the bottom of my T-shirt in both hands and lifted it gently. I sucked in air through clenched teeth as the material tugged at my open wounds. When the injury was exposed, the doc ripped my shirt open from hem to collar. It tore easily, if not neatly— even in human form werecats are very strong—and suddenly my entire torso was exposed, bloody wounds, scarlet-stained bra, and all.

Marc winced, and Jace whined over the state of my stomach. But no one even blinked at the partial nudity. We saw each other naked all the time, because Shifting with clothes on would have been ridiculous, not to mention expensive after a while.

Marc's face reflected my own fear and horror, and I didn't need any more of that, so I tilted my head to look at my father instead. His jaw was clenched tight, like mine, and I couldn't help wondering what his was holding back. He smiled when he noticed me watching him. "You're going to be fine." He nodded, as if to convince himself. "It doesn't look that bad."

I flinched as Dr. Carver began mopping up the blood gently, and breathed a sigh of relief when he held my still-there navel ring to clean around it. But I never took my eyes off my father. "Where'd you get *your* medical degree?"

Daddy laughed hoarsely as Dr. Carver sat back on his haunches, drawing my attention. "Actually, he's right. You've got four puncture wounds in the chest—I'm guessing claws?"

I nodded, and he continued. "I'm sure they hurt, but they're shallow and don't appear to have done any real damage."

So far, so good.

"The wounds in your abdomen are a bit more serious, but at a glance they don't seem to have ruptured any organs. Of course, I'll want to keep an eye on you to make sure. And the tears coming from the puncture wounds sliced through the skin pretty good, but I don't think they've gone past the muscle. I'd say you're damn lucky. I don't think there will be any permanent damage."

The forest itself seemed to sigh, and it took me a moment to realize I was actually hearing the men around me exhale in unison.

"Don't get me wrong." Dr. Carver frowned down at me. "It's going to hurt for a while. You'll need to be still for at least twenty-four hours, then Shift as soon as possible after that to speed up the healing. It won't be fun, but that's better than lying around here for the next month, wincing every time you laugh."

"I can handle it, Doc."

His frown eased. "I'm sure you can." His gaze rose to meet my father's. "Let's get her out of here so I can sew her up."

Lucas offered to carry me, and Jace wanted to Shift back and help, but Marc wouldn't let either of them near me. He carried me cradled in his arms all the way back through the forest to the lodge, then another quarter mile to our cabin. I winced with every step, finally burying my head in his neck for the comfort of his smell. Marc nuzzled the top of my head with his chin, which did more to ease my pain than anything Dr. Carver could give me.

Lucas walked behind us, the unconscious stray tossed over his shoulder like a sack of feed. Dr. Carver said he'd be out for hours, based on the dose I'd given him of…whatever Malone had loaded in those syringes, which was evidently much stronger than what I'd been shot up with in the past. And the very thought of how long I would have been unconscious on such a dose, considering how much smaller I was than the stray, was enough to make me sick to my poor, abused stomach.

When we got to our cabin, Marc placed me gently on the shiny green-blanketed bed in the room I'd claimed. He found a pair of scissors in the kitchen and cut the rest of my shirt off, then propped my head up with an extra pillow from his own room—I could tell because it smelled like him. He was doing his best to make me comfortable, and even though fire lanced my stomach with each breath, I was much too happy to have him touching me to ruin it by complaining, even about the pain.

My father sat in a chair in one corner of the room, refusing to let anything impede his view of me while he called the tribunal at the main lodge to give them an update. Dr. Carver rushed to and from my room, getting everything set to sew me up. He removed the shade from the lamp to give him as much light as possible. Then he arranged an assortment of medical supplies—scissors, flosslike thread, and a couple of other scary-looking instruments—on a clean white towel on the nightstand.

I flinched as he set an empty syringe on the towel, followed by a small, rubber-topped glass bottle. "What's that for?"

Dr. Carver smiled gently when he saw the fear in my face. I'm not big on needles. They always seem to precede me being taken somewhere I don't want to go. "That's for our new guest. I'm going to force his Shift with a mix of adrenaline, and some other drugs."

"Oh." That made sense. We couldn't let the stray wake up in cat form, because he'd be dangerous, hard to control, and impossible to handcuff. And because we had no cage in which to confine him. On two legs, he could be properly bound, thus unable to slice and dice anyone else.

"The rest of those are for me, though. Right?"

"Um…yes." Dr. Carver zipped his nylon bag and sat on the

empty bed facing me. "Is this your most serious injury in the line of duty?"

I tried to shrug, but even that slight movement hurt my stomach. "It's the first to nearly disembowel me."

Carver laughed. "Well, if that's what he was going for, he did a very poor job of it. Your guts would never fit through these tiny holes. You're gonna be fine. Sore for a while, and possibly scarred, but completely fine."

"Thanks," I said, and the doctor nodded brightly, then picked up the needle and the small glass bottle on his way into the living room to deal with the stray. And oddly enough, that comforted me more than his verbal assurances. My injuries couldn't be too bad if he was willing to deal with the other guy first.

But then again, I wasn't a threat to anyone. The stray was.

On his way out the door, Dr. Carver passed Marc, who carried a kitchen chair to my bedside then dropped into it and cradled my hand in both of his. With Marc there to keep me company, my father left to call my mother with an update from the semiprivacy of his own room.

"The doc's right, you know." Marc squeezed my fingers.

"How do you know?"

He leaned back to give me an unimpeded view of his gorgeous, sculpted chest, marred only by the four long claw-mark scars that had brought him into our world, and into my life. Those old scars had an oddly fresh look now, smeared as they were by my blood. "If I survived this, you'll survive that."

I blushed and glanced away, ashamed of whining over a relatively minor injury. Hell, Jace had been *shot* three months earlier and had recovered just fine.

"You're right. I'm a wimp."

"Nah. You looked pretty bad before the doc got you cleaned up. I saw all that blood, and at first I thought the bastard nearly ripped you in half."

"I don't think he meant to hurt me."

Marc's gaze flicked to my stomach, then back to my face. "What he *meant* to do doesn't matter."

"Don't you think it should?" But I wasn't thinking about the stray. I was thinking about myself, and the fact that I hadn't meant to infect Andrew. And the possibility that Marc was right—whether or not I meant to wouldn't matter in the end.

But instead of answering, he dropped his gaze to my bare stomach, and a grin tugged at one side of his mouth as I heard his pulse jump. "You know, you're lucky he didn't rip that thing right out." He nodded at my navel ring, and I flushed to realize he was really looking at it for the first time.

Ethan had taken me to get it done less than a month earlier, and had spent the entire time flirting with the multipierced girl behind the glass counter, in spite of the fact that he had a long-term girlfriend, for the first time ever. Well, if three months could be considered long-term…

My brother had pronounced my new—and *only*—piercing "awesome." But I hadn't done it for him. I'd done it on a whim, when the display in the shop window reminded me that Marc had once said he found belly-button rings sexy.

I'd worn skimpy tops for a week, trying to get a response out of him, but he'd never even looked at my pierced navel. At least not that I'd seen. Evidently putting a single hole through my stomach wasn't enough to get his attention.

Though *four* of them did the job nicely…

"Do you like it?" I asked, fully aware that my bloody gashes marred the view.

"Um, yeah. I do." His voice went hoarse with yearning, and I smiled.

My eyes roamed Marc's chest, taking liberties because I hadn't been invited to look in quite a while. He was beautiful; I'd always thought so. Even when we were both children. Even now that he was covered in my blood.

No, wait, that's not all mine. Marc had already been bloody when he and Jace found me in the woods, and now that his shirt was off, I saw why. His left biceps was scored by four brand-new claw marks, and I could tell by the scent of the wound that they hadn't come from Jace. They'd run into another stray. No wonder it took them a while to find me.

But before I could ask him what happened, several thumps and a soft grunt drew my attention to the living room, where Lucas and Jace—who had Shifted back and re-dressed—were carrying a limp, naked male form. *The stray.*

Dr. Carver's magic needle had worked—further evidence that if given enough time, science could overcome nature entirely. Maybe someday it would be able to reverse werecat infection, giving strays back their human existence. But so far, the only hope available to strays was learning how best to play cards with the hands they'd been dealt. Marc coped very well. Andrew had not.

The last thing I saw from the living room before Dr. Carver stepped into my room and pulled the door shut was Lucas duct taping the stray's wrists together while Jace worked on his ankles. Then Dr. Carver sat in the chair Marc vacated, and I exhaled slowly, mentally preparing myself for the stitches to come.

Marc held my hand while Dr. Carver gave me a local anesthetic to numb the site of the sutures. When I realized the local anesthetic involved a needle, I nearly crushed his fingers. After that, when the actual stitches began, he switched to stroking my hair, and sent Jace for the stress ball Michael had given me. By the time the doctor had me patched back together, that stupid squishy ball lay in tiny clumps of foam all over my comforter.

But that wasn't what got me through the stitches, every one of which I felt as little painless-but-weird tugs in my flesh. Neither was it my father, who returned to pace at the end of my bed. What got me through was Marc, holding my attention with one old enforcer tale after another. Some were funny. Some were dumb. But all of them were better than listening to my father's anxious pacing, or Dr. Carver mumbling to himself as he counted my stitches.

Once again, Marc had come through for me when I needed him, though I'd failed him time and again.

When my stomach was finally stitched up, and my father had both inspected and approved of his work, Dr. Carver covered my belly with several large pieces of gauze, which he held in place with thick white medical tape.

Marc pulled the blanket from the unoccupied bed and draped it over me. Then he slid one firm, warm hand behind my neck to help me hold my head up long enough to wash down the pills Dr. Carver brought me, with the accompanying glass of water.

"These will make you sleep for several hours," Dr. Carver said as I gulped more water to rinse away the bitter aftertaste. *Smart man.* If he'd told me that before giving me the pills, I probably would have refused them. "You won't need anything for pain while you're out, but I have something good for you when you wake up."

I was sure I would need it. The local was already wearing off, and just holding my head up made my stomach feel like flaming knives were being driven through it. I'd had no idea I used those particular muscles so often, but I made a mental note never to take them for granted again.

"I don't want to leave you alone," Dr. Carver said, looking at my father, even though he seemed to be speaking to me. "At least until we rule out internal bleeding. Let me know immediately if you feel dizzy or nauseated, or if there's blood in your urine. And someone will need to watch you for swelling, tenderness, or bruising."

My father nodded, but Marc was the first to speak. "I'll stay with her."

Daddy frowned, and looked as if he might argue for a

moment. But then his face went carefully blank, and he simply nodded. "Fine. I'll send someone to relieve you if the stray wakes up before she does." Because Marc was in charge of inter-rogations. He was really good at *convincing* people to talk.

Apparently satisfied, Dr. Carver nodded at Marc, already moving toward the door. "I'll be back to take care of your arm in a few minutes."

My eyes were already getting heavy, probably as much from exhaustion and shock as from the pills, which couldn't have kicked in so quickly. Either way, the very thought of being sucked into sleep against my will was starting to panic me. I hate being left out of things, and if the stray woke before I did, I wouldn't even get to hear what he had to say, much less ask him my own questions. *No fair.*

"Wait, I want to talk to him," I insisted as my father bent over me, studying my eyes, as if to determine my awareness. "I want to ask him—"

"Believe it or not, we can handle it without you." But his gentle smile softened the blow to my ego. "You get some sleep and let us worry about the stray."

"I'm not *worried…*" I started to protest, but he was already looking at Marc, his expression now hard and angry. Whatever *that* was about, I didn't want to miss it, either.

"Step outside with me for a moment," our Alpha ordered. Then, before Marc could answer, my father turned to me again, and his eyes had gone soft, which irritated me because it meant he was treating me like a daughter instead of like an enforcer. Smiling, he planted a soft kiss on my forehead, which I couldn't remember him doing since the morning of my tenth birthday. "Good night, kitten. We'll be here when you wake up."

"I'm not a kitten!" I snapped, but no one was listening. My father ushered Marc into the living room and shut the door behind them, as if that would block out their conversation. But

I could still hear them arguing about me, and surprise registered even through the thick sleeping-pill fog rapidly enveloping my brain. I couldn't recall Marc ever arguing with his Alpha before. But then I understood: My father wasn't acting like an Alpha. He was acting like a father, and Marc was calling him on it.

"…could you leave her unsupervised? She could have been killed!"

"Yes, she could have." Marc's voice was calm, with an undercurrent of quiet confidence, which sent a silent thrill through me. He sounded like an Alpha. "Any one of us could be killed on any given day of the year, Greg. We're enforcers. Risk comes with the job."

"And that's why you work in pairs. To watch each other's backs."

"In a perfect world, yes," Marc admitted. "But our world is far from perfect, and sometimes things come up. Opportunities present themselves, and that's what happened here. Faythe saw an opportunity, and she took it. The whole thing was her idea. She said she'd make better bait than either one of us, and she was right. He would never have shown himself with me and Jace hanging around."

"No rogue is worth her life."

"I agree. But if you really expect her to take over for you, you have to let her learn *how*. And you have to let her know you trust her. Especially now, when no one else seems to. This was her idea, and it was a good one. She's stubborn as hell, and if we hadn't played along, she would have taken off on her own, anyway. We both know that. I did what I thought was best at the time, and so did she. But no one feels worse about her getting hurt than I do."

"I know."

I swallowed thickly, discomforted by my father's acknowledgment of Marc's feelings for me, in spite of the pain and frustration my presence put him through on a daily basis. Privacy was nonexistent in our world, and most of us saw no reason to pretend *not* to know something everyone else knew anyway. The only person I pretended with was Jace, and that was only because he seemed to prefer it that way.

"This is about more than that, though, Greg."

"Hmm?" my father said, and I smiled to realize he was avoiding something. Could there actually be something the great Greg Sanders wasn't comfortable admitting to himself?

"The tribunal is probably going to convict her on both charges. We all know that. What they need now is a reason to let her live. An excuse that will let her walk away without making them look like weak fools. They need to know she's useful to them—to all of us—as something other than a dam. Saving Brett and bringing in the stray will show them that. Yes, she was hurt in the process, but she's going to be fine. The ends justified the means, Greg, and she believes that just as much as I do. If you don't believe me, go ask her yourself."

Silence spoke for my father. Marc was right, and he damn well knew it. But he couldn't truly ease a father's fears. "Fine. As soon as the tribunal hands down a verdict, she's back on the clock, and back at work for real. But until then, she takes it easy. Especially now that she's hurt. Keep an eye on her."

"Of course."

The Alpha's distinctive smooth-but-heavy footsteps moved away from the door, and I called out to him in spite of the pain in my stomach, just to let him know I'd been listening. "'Night, Daddy!"

His steps paused, and he chuckled softly. "Good night, kitten."

"I'm not a kitten!" I shouted as Marc pulled the door open. "I'm fully grown!"

"You two are going to butt heads on that one for the rest of your life," he said, smiling. "You'll always be his little girl."

"And he'll always be an overprotective, know-it-all pain in my ass," I snapped.

Marc nodded, still smiling as he sat on the side of my bed. "Like father like daughter."

I couldn't quite pull off a frown. He could call me whatever he wanted, because that meant he was talking to me. "So why are you being so nice to me all of a sudden. Because I'm hurt?"

"Maybe."

"You mean, all I had to do was spill a little blood?"

"Or maybe a little kindness."

Ouch. That was hardly fair; I was rarely mean to him. But I didn't say it out loud, because that was one of the things we could never agree on. He thought it was cruel of me to refuse to marry him, and I thought it was cruel of him to make me choose between marrying him and losing him completely.

Marc's world was defined by bold streaks of black and white, and mine was consumed by shades of gray. He saw good and bad, but all too often I saw only the lesser of two evils. Oddly enough, however, we seemed to have reversed our usual positions on this whole me-standing-trial thing.

"I'm sorry," he said, stroking my hair again.

"Don't be. I deserved it."

Before he could disagree—and he *would* have disagreed— the bedroom door opened again.

"Okay, Marc, let's get a look at that arm." Dr. Carver sat on the chair between the beds and waved him over, gesturing for him to sit on the empty bed. Marc did as directed, and Dr. Carver carefully extended the injured arm toward the lamp to inspect it.

"Well, the scratches are clean, and they aren't very deep. Looks like you got lucky, too."

The only reason Marc still had his arm, not to mention full

use of it, was because he was a damn good enforcer. His reflexes were the fastest I'd ever seen, and he was always on alert. Marc made his own luck in life.

All *I* ever seemed to make was mistakes.

As my eyelids grew heavy, I watched Dr. Carver sew Marc up, making one small, hypnotically even stitch after another. He actually wound up with more than I did, because his scratches were longer than mine, if not as deep.

"I want you to Shift in the morning," Dr. Carver said to Marc as my eyes started to close. "It'll shorten your healing time considerably, and it sounds like they're going to need you in top shape around here."

I opened my eyes one last time to see Marc nod, and to realize he was still watching me over the doctor's shoulder. The last thing I saw before succumbing to drug-induced slumber was his mouth quirking up at me in an achingly familiar half smile.

Nine

When I woke, Marc was gone. My room was dark, and the red alarm-clock numbers on the nightstand said it was 3:13, but I was too disoriented from the sleeping pills to know whether that meant a.m. or p.m. I twisted to my right, intending to glance at the window, but I didn't make it that far, because pain sliced through my stomach at the first movement.

"Oh, shit," I moaned, and laughter floated to me out of the dark.

"Did you think that would feel *good?*"

Jace.

I fell back onto the pillow, relieved that I wasn't alone and that Marc had been replaced by Jace, rather than by…well, anyone else. "I didn't think at all, actually. I forgot how much moving hurt."

"It'll get better soon." And he should know. In the last six months alone, in addition to the usual scrapes and bruises accrued in the line of duty, Jace'd had the living shit beat out of him by Marc and been shot by Manx. He'd spent so much time in my mother's sickroom that she'd offered to let him redecorate it.

"I certainly hope so. Could you turn on the light?"

"Sure." Chair springs creaked and footsteps shuffled across the floor. A muffled click echoed through the dark room, and light flared to life from the lamp near my bed to illuminate Jace, one hand still on the switch.

"Thanks." Squinting, I slid one hand beneath my head, trying to prop it up without moving my stomach.

"No problem. You want some water?"

"I would, actually. My mouth's pretty dry." And my tongue tasted bitter too.

"That's from the sleeping pills." Jace handed me a plastic cup of water from the nightstand, drawing my attention back to the clock.

"That's a.m.?" I asked, having finally decided there wasn't enough natural light in the room for it to be afternoon. And surely I hadn't slept that long…

"Yeah. You've been out for nearly five hours. Doc says you can have whatever you want to eat."

I smiled as he sank into the chair by my bed, holding the cup near my face, straw bent toward my mouth. "Pizza. I want pizza."

He chuckled. "Except that."

Of course. The Alphas would never let a pizza driver on the premises.

I sipped from the straw, and my throat felt better immediately. When I'd had enough, Jace replaced the cup. "Want me to help you sit up? The doc left some pain pills for you, but you'll probably choke on them if you try it lying down."

"Yeah, thanks."

Jace bent over the bed and hooked his hands under my arms, supporting my weight as I slowly pushed myself into a sitting position, leaning on a pillow propped against the headboard. My abdomen screamed in protest, and my skin seemed to pull tight around the stitches. I couldn't squelch the fear that if I moved too suddenly the threads would rip through my flesh and I'd have to be sewn up again.

Fortunately that didn't happen. The worst of it was finding a comfortable position once I was upright. I squeezed my eyes shut and clenched the blanket in both fists as the first wave of pain washed over me.

"Here, take these. They'll help." Jace poured three round white pills from a bottle beside the nightstand, and my eyes widened in surprise over the size of the bottle. He smiled. "You'll be thankful for that soon. You're supposed to take these for the first twenty-four hours, then try Shifting to speed things along."

I stared at the pills on my open palm. "Three of them?"

He shrugged. "I took four every four hours after Manx shot me. They wear off fast. Anyway, your dad told the doc to make sure you feel good. I think he's afraid to put the hearing off any more than necessary."

He wasn't the only one. I was more than ready to have it over with, even if I had to hear the verdict flat on my back. I washed the pills down with another gulp of the water he held for me.

"Where's Marc?" I asked, suddenly concerned by the silence from the rest of the cabin. A frown flitted across Jace's face, and I immediately felt guilty. Like everyone else, he knew Marc and I had broken up, and he probably knew why. Secrets were hard to keep in a werecat household, because everyone could hear through the walls.

But Jace had to know I wanted Marc back, so I tried not to talk about one in front of the other. And to move on quickly when I forgot. "They're not questioning the stray without me, are they?"

"Not yet. He woke up about an hour ago, but the Alphas are still talking to Marc. They called him in after me, to question him about what happened out there." His sweeping gesture took in my entire body, and a second pang of guilt followed hot on the heels of the first.

"They're not blaming you guys for this, are they?"

Jace glanced away and gave me a noncommittal shrug. "Calvin would love to, but your dad's running interference." Since the rogues in the forest technically had nothing to do with my hearing, my father would lead the inquiry. Thank goodness.

"I'll set them straight," I promised, frowning in anger. "It was my idea, and neither of you could have stopped me if you'd tried."

Jace smiled as his hand settled over mine. "That's exactly what your dad said."

I grinned, pleased to hear that my father was coming around. That he was thinking of me as an enforcer again, instead of as a child to be protected. Now if I could only make the tribunal see things my way...

"What happened to you guys out there anyway?" I asked, remembering the screech of an unfamiliar cat and the fresh claw marks on Marc's arm.

Jace leaned against my headboard and rubbed his forehead, then met my eyes with regret shining in his. "Damn, Faythe, I am so sorry about that. We heard someone thrashing through the forest. It was so loud and obvious, we thought it had to be you baiting the stray." He shrugged. "Obviously it wasn't, but by the time we figured out it was another of the strays, he'd circled behind us.

"Marc must have heard him pounce, because he dodged just in time, but the bastard still got in one good swipe before I could get there. He ran off when I arrived, but by then we'd lost you. If you hadn't shouted, we might not have found you in time." He shook his head again, and his face held so much shame and guilt I could hardly stand to look into it. "I'm so sorry."

I waved off his apology. "Hey, I'm a big girl. I got myself into this mess." Fortunately, it all worked out in the end. *Except for these damn stitches.*

I reached for the water on the nightstand, and the blanket whispered against my legs as I moved. Jace tried to get the cup for me when I winced in pain, but I shook my head. Being babied wouldn't get me out of bed any faster. Determined to get up and going, I drained the cup in several long gulps.

"Want some more?" Jace asked.

I set the cup down and sat straighter in the bed, ignoring the tugging sensation in my stomach. "Think you could snag me a Coke instead?"

"Absolutely." Jace carried my cup through the living room and into the kitchen. He left the bedroom door open, and I was surprised to realize that the stray was visible through the gap.

He lay nude on the floor in front of the couch, on his stomach, with his head turned away from me. Thick coils of duct tape secured his wrists behind his back, and matching strips bound his legs at the ankles and again just below the knees.

A booted foot sat in front of the armchair next to my bedroom door, its owner no doubt guarding the stray while everyone else was busy with me or answering questions for the Alphas.

I couldn't see the prisoner's face, but a quick sniff of the air verified his identity. He had nondescript straight brown hair, tousled from his run in the woods. Or maybe from trying to wrestle free from his bonds. He was thin but obviously strong, lean muscles standing out from slim arms and legs. I considered calling out so he'd turn his head, because I was curious to know if his eyes were that same greenish-brown color in human form. And I was even more curious to hear what he had to say for himself.

But before I could act on my curiosity, the cabin's front door opened. I couldn't see the door from my bed, but another sniff told me who had entered: Marc, my father and Michael. *The gang's all here.*

"He's awake," Marc said, and the stray's head jerked up at the sound. He struggled against his bindings, thrashing on the floor and kicking his legs as best he could with them bound together. From the muffled sound of his cries, I was guessing the stray's mouth was taped shut, probably over a gag of some sort.

"Pick him up." My father's distinctive footsteps headed away from my room. "Faythe's awake, too?" The new echo of his voice said he was in the kitchen now, where soda fizzed as Jace filled my cup.

Jace must have nodded, because I didn't hear his answer, but a moment later, my father stepped into my room, cup in hand. "How do you feel?" he asked as Jace followed him in.

Like crap. "Fine. Much better." I smiled and accepted the soda he held out.

"Good. After I take care of our guest, I'll give you an update," my father said. I nodded, and he returned to the living room while Jace sat in the chair by my bed.

Framed by my doorway now, Marc and my cousin Lucas— the owner of the boot I'd seen—lifted the thrashing stray, each gripping one of his arms. They set him on his knees in the middle of the bare floor, and I could see his profile, a long, crooked nose and a single thick brown eyebrow.

Marc bent close to the detainee and gripped his chin in one hand, and the stray tried to shrink backward. Marc tended to have that effect on people. "I'm gonna take this off your mouth, but that does *not* mean you get to talk. Got it?"

The stray hesitated, and Marc's expression hardened, his gold-flecked eyes darkening, beautiful lips thinning in anger. It was the face he saved for trespassers. The one that said he'd broken plenty of skulls before, and wouldn't hesitate to do so again at the slightest provocation. That face was how he got his job done so quickly and so thoroughly. Along with those fists.

Sometimes it was hard for me to reconcile the angry fists clenched at his sides with the gentle hands that touched me. That *used* to touch me, anyway.

"Got it?" Marc repeated, and the stray nodded hesitantly. Marc scratched at one corner of the tape to loosen it, then ripped it off in one quick motion. The stray screamed around whatever was in his mouth, and I got the distinct impression that in this case, ripping the Band-Aid off quickly wasn't so much a mercy as a brutal warning.

The stray's jaw worked, muscles flexing behind the furious red skin of his cheek as he tried to spit out his gag. Marc and Lucas watched with cold detachment born of years of training. Half a minute later, the stray finally spit a damp white cloth onto the floor at his knees, and I noticed with a jolt of alarm that it was spotted with blood.

Straining forward in spite of the pain in my stomach, I studied what I could see of the stray's face and decided he had a fat lip, no doubt the source of the blood. Someone had roughed him up pretty good, hopefully in response to some resistance he'd offered after waking.

My father stepped into sight beside Marc. "I miss my basement already," he mumbled. "Take him outside."

"No!" I shouted, and all heads turned my way. I threw back the comforter, mildly surprised to find my legs bare. Pressing one hand to my stomach, I shifted my left leg onto the floor in spite of the pain ripping through my middle with each movement.

"What are you doing?" Jace demanded. "Get back in the bed." He cradled my calf gently in both hands—as if the damn thing might break—and firmly guided it back onto the mattress.

"Let go, Jace." My voice came out calm and commanding, and I must not have been the only one impressed by that fact, because he paused in midmotion. Evidently I was actually *learning* something in my training…

"What's wrong?" Marc asked, and I looked up to find him taking up most of the doorway. My father shot me a questioning look over his shoulder.

I scowled at them both. "I helped catch this stray and I'm damn well going to be there when you question him. If you're taking him outside, I'm coming with you. And quit glaring at me—you'd all do the same thing in my place, and you know it."

Marc sighed and glanced at Jace. "Did she take the pills?"

He nodded. "About five minutes ago."

Marc frowned and shook his head at me. "You're causing yourself more pain than necessary. Besides, you shouldn't walk before you've had a chance to heal."

I shrugged. "So I'll Shift."

"No." His eyes were kind, but his tone was not. "Doc says you need at least twenty-four hours to heal naturally. *Then* you can try Shifting to speed it up."

"*You* didn't wait that long." I stared pointedly at the new claw marks on his arm, which were little more than scabbed stripes now.

"Mine were only scratches, and I couldn't afford to wait. You can."

"Whatever. If you take him outside, I'm going, too." I pivoted slowly, grimacing when I swung both legs carefully over the side of the bed. Jace sighed and rolled his eyes, shrugging helplessly at Marc.

"Get your *stubborn* ass *back* in that bed before I tie you to it!" Marc growled, and irritation shot up my spine, hot, fast, and invigorating.

"If you think you can do it, come give it a try!" To prove my butt was firmly in place behind my mouth, I gripped the nightstand hard enough to make the wood creak and stood carefully, gritting my teeth against both the pain and that creepy *tugging* sensation in my stomach.

An angry growl rumbled from Marc's throat, and he marched toward me. But he only made it two steps before my father spoke from the living room. "We'll stay inside. Jace, bring her in here. If she wants to be a part of this and is willing to work through the pain, so be it."

Smirking at Marc, I wrapped one arm around Jace's shoulder

as he bent for me. But then Marc cleared his throat and nodded pointedly at my bare knees. "Forgetting something?"

Shit. Pants. Jeans would be too rough on my stomach, but I was *not* going to face the asshole who'd nearly disemboweled me without the dignity of being fully clothed. Even if *he* wasn't.

Jace smiled in sympathy. "I'll help you get dres—"

"Out," Marc snarled. "I've got it covered."

Jace closed the door as he left and Marc was already rooting through the suitcase on my dresser for something suitable. "How 'bout *this?*" He held up a new pair of low-slung red satin pajama pants, clearly trying to picture me in them.

I grinned. "That's fine. Find the shirt and help me change." I'd planned to wear the real pj's around the cabin to tempt him. But I hadn't counted on injury dictating the timing.

A minute later, I stood in nothing but the scarlet pajama halter top and my underwear. My heart lurched when Marc knelt in front of me. My breath lodged in my throat when his hands slid slowly up my thighs and over my hips, pulling the waistband of my pants into place. His fingers scorched my skin, yet left chill bumps in their wake, and I nearly moaned aloud when he sat back, dropping those gifted hands into his lap.

I gripped the headboard, hoping he'd think the throbbing in my stomach was what threatened my balance. But it wasn't. As usual, my problem was Marc, and the taste he'd just given me of what we used to share. But a taste wasn't enough, not then, and not ever. I wanted the whole damn meal.

Frantic for some semblance of self-control, I stared into the mirror, silently ordering myself to forget about Marc and focus on the job at hand. And when that didn't work, I flexed my stomach, counting on the fresh wave of pain to ground me.

It worked, and I sucked in an agonized breath. *Son of a bitch!*

Marc stood and I had to look up to meet his suddenly grave expression. "You don't have to do this," he said, rubbing my arms, as if to warm them. "It won't be pretty."

"I know." I'd never seen an actual interrogation, but I knew the basics of what it would entail, and I knew that watching Marc beat information out of a bound and helpless man—even one who'd nearly disemboweled me—would likely horrify me.

I also knew it was necessary. We needed information. The stray probably had it, and almost certainly wouldn't want to part with it. The lives of the human men and women scouring the mountain were worth more than the comfort of one man who might know something that could save them.

No *real* enforcer would be squeamish about doing what had to be done. And red satin pj's notwithstanding, *I* was a *real* enforcer.

Marc saw the decision in my eyes and nodded solemnly. Without another word of protest, he scooped me into a careful cradle-hold, and I smiled through the pain as he edged us out the door into the living room.

He carried me past the stray, who still knelt—naked—on the floor, then lowered me into the chair Michael had taken from the breakfast table. I sat nearer the kitchen than the couch, well out of the action, should something go wrong. But I was out of bed and officially part of the proceedings, so I was pretty pleased, all things considered.

Now if only those damn pills would kick in...

Michael and Jace took up posts on either side of my chair, while Lucas sank onto the couch behind the kneeling stray, one hand on the prisoner's bound wrists, to hold him in place. Marc assumed the position of honor in front of our unwilling guest. He towered over the stray, who hung his head, refusing to look at any of us.

"Let me explain how this works." Marc's voice was colder and more detached than I'd ever heard it. "We ask the questions. You get one chance to answer on your own. If you don't take that chance, I convince you to cooperate. This can be as easy as you want to make it. Of course, the opposite is also true. Ready to give it a shot?"

The detainee made no response.

On the edge of the room, my father stood with one arm folded over his chest, the opposite hand stroking the graying stubble on his chin. "Let's keep this one neat, please." He paused to survey the arrangement of old, worn furniture and the dingy walls. "I don't want to have to repaint the place before we go, like in Abilene."

"Yeah, sorry about that." Marc nodded grimly, and the stray's Adam's apple bobbed as he swallowed.

Repaint? I didn't even want to *know* what they'd had to cover up in Abilene. *Maybe I'm not as ready for this as I thought...*

Ten

Marc stood in front of the stray kneeling naked on the floor. "What's your name?" he asked. The stray didn't move. Didn't even acknowledge the question. "Your name, or your nose." Marc's fingers popped as they curled into a fist at his right side, and my mouth went dry.

The stray scowled up at Marc, defiance stark in his bearing, in spite of his nudity and humbled pose. "You have no right to—"

Marc glanced at my father, who nodded, and my throat constricted around the heart-size lump lodged in it.

"Wrong answer." Marc's fist flew. Bone crunched. Bright red droplets sprayed his jeans and the floor. The stray gurgled, coughing and choking on his own blood as it poured down his face and over his chest.

My eyes closed and I swallowed back revulsion. *It's part of his job,* I told myself, uncomforted by the truth much as I was by the necessity. And by the knowledge that in the line of duty, I'd punched several strays in search of a name. But I'd never made one kneel naked and bound on the ground before me, and that part of the procedure bothered me more than I wanted to admit. It reminded me of a time when *I'd* been bound and at the mercy of a man standing over me.

Jace's hand landed on my shoulder, and I opened my eyes to look at him. His face was carefully blank, a skill I envied.

"Your name," Marc repeated, and I turned my attention back to the spectacle in progress, which didn't appear to be upsetting anyone else.

"Zeke." The stray spit blood on the floor at Marc's feet, eyeing him in defiance, which I had to kind of admire. "Radley. Zeke Radley."

"And what are you doing here, Mr. Radley?"

The stray cleared his throat and spat more blood on the floor, tossing a strand of brown hair from his forehead. "I was chasing a downed alien spacecraft." No one seemed very amused by Radley's ill-timed attempt at humor, least of all Marc, whose arms bulged in anger. But the stray was unperturbed. "I thought this was free territory. Was I wrong?"

"Where did you hear that?"

Radley shrugged, which looked painful with his hands taped behind his back. "Some cat told me. Did I cross some kind of boundary? If so, you guys do a piss-poor job of marking your territory. No pun intended."

On my left Jace growled, and Lucas smacked the back of Radley's head with one huge hand. "You're in no position to smart off."

Radley ignored Lucas in favor of Marc, who looked amazingly calm and in control. "You didn't answer the question," the prisoner said. "Is this your land or not?"

"No." My father clasped his hands behind his back, standing straight and tall in his suit and tie, even at three in the morning. "This is not our land. But this is my *daughter*—" he gestured toward me with one outstretched hand "—who now has twenty stitches in her stomach, thanks to you."

My left hand settled lightly onto my abdomen. *Twenty? Really?*

Radley rolled his eyes. He actually rolled his eyes at my father, Alpha of the south-central territory and head of the Territorial Council. Sure, I did that all the time, but I'd also peed on his lap when I was two. No one else got away with such disrespect toward an Alpha, which meant Radley either didn't know who my father was, or didn't care. Either could have been true, because most strays didn't understand the werecat social hierarchy, and those who did had little reason to respect our Alphas.

Still, I wasn't the only one surprised into silence.

"That was an accident!" Radley snapped, shuffling on the floor to find a more comfortable position for his bruised knees. He glanced from my father to me, then back to my father. "I was just trying to get out of there alive, and I knew they wouldn't hurt me while I had *her*."

"Why did you 'have her' in the first place?" Marc demanded, his voice low and dangerous.

"She set me up. You *all* set me up. You dangled bait in front of my face, and now you want to know why I took it!"

I tried not to squirm. He was right; we *had* set him up. Was it possible Radley knew nothing about the missing hikers and the slaughtered cop? Could he have simply been in the wrong place at the wrong time? That was almost too much of a coincidence to believe.

"You didn't have to chase her." Jace squeezed my shoulder protectively. "Why did you?"

Radley huffed impatiently, which seemed odd coming from a man in his position. "Look, you assholes may have dinner with a tabby every night of your life, but for a tom like me, running into a puss like that is a once-in-a-lifetime opportunity." His gaze raked over me boldly, as if we weren't surrounded by five other tomcats, including my father. And Marc.

Well, at least he's honest. I had to give him that.

Jace seemed much less inclined to give him a break. "So you followed her because you've never seen another tabby?"

The stray blinked, and indecision flashed across his face so fast I wasn't sure I'd seen it in the first place.

Whatever he'd started to say was gone, but Radley's confidence was back, bolstered by another dose of anger and resentment. "I followed her because she looked upset. She ran off by herself. It's not safe for a girl to be on her own in the woods at night."

"I'm not a *girl*," I snapped, but my ferocity floundered as Radley's nostrils flared, obviously taking in my scent. Marc tensed, and I rushed on before he could interrupt. "In fact, I've probably been alone in the woods more times than you've pissed in private."

"Lovely, Faythe," Michael murmured on my right as Jace nearly choked trying to hold back laughter.

"And completely beside the point." My father frowned sternly, then faced the prisoner, dismissing me entirely.

Marc cleared his throat, drawing Radley's attention away from me and pulling the interrogation back on track. "So you followed her to *protect* her? What were you going to do— serve her cocoa, then walk her home?"

I laughed aloud, drawing more disapproving glances from my father and Michael, and another stifled chuckle from Jace.

"I don't know." Radley sniffed at a drop of blood trailing from his nose. "I didn't have a plan. I just saw her run off, and when neither of you went after her, I figured *someone* should."

"It was an act—you said it yourself," Marc growled through gritted teeth, and I knew it irked him to let Radley think I'd run to get away from him.

The stray shrugged, as if he couldn't care less. "Whatever. I didn't think she should be alone in the woods."

Jace inhaled softly, and his hand tightened briefly on my shoulder. "Why were you following us?"

"Because I'm not as dumb as I look." Radley lowered his weight, so that he sat on his feet. "If you saw three strange cats walking through your territory, wouldn't you follow them?" He bent to one side, extending his arms behind his back so we could all see the tape binding them. "I'm guessing you wouldn't stop there."

"This isn't your territory," Michael pointed out calmly, ever the voice of reason.

"It's as much mine as it is yours."

Even more so, I thought, but had the good sense to keep my mouth shut for once.

Marc nodded. "Fair enough. So you followed her—for her own protection, of course…" The sarcasm in his voice could have sliced through glass. "Why was she running from you when we found her?"

Radley shrugged. "How should I know? I must have scared her. I didn't mean to though." He peered around Marc's arm to address me directly. "I didn't mean to scare you."

"The hell you didn't!" I leaned forward in my chair, and the medication-dulled pain in my belly roared into focus with the sudden movement. *Damn it!* I pressed one hand to my stomach, breathing deeply until the sharp throbbing ebbed. When I looked up, everyone in the room was watching me, including my father, which reminded me that no one had heard my side of the story yet. "He wasn't going to let me leave. He was trying to take me somewhere."

Radley shook his head, this time rolling his eyes at me. "There was someone else out there. Another cat," he said. His eyes were wide and earnest, but I couldn't shake the feeling that he was trying a little too hard to convince us. Still, there *had* been another cat…

Marc glanced at Jace, and I knew they were thinking the same thing I was.

"I was trying to stop her from running off again," Radley

continued. "For all I knew, she'd run right into that other cat, and I doubt he's as friendly as I am. Not that being friendly's helped *me* much today."

If he was telling the truth, we were seriously mistreating Zeke Radley. But though I couldn't find an inconsistency in his story, neither could I swear it wasn't a lie. I couldn't read Radley, and that knowledge gnawed at me from the inside, mirroring the now mercifully dull pain in my stomach.

Though I could interpret neither my father's expression nor my brother's, Marc wasn't buying Radley's innocence in the least. "Maybe you should have Saint Zeke tattooed on your rump…" he muttered, turning away from the bound tom in disgust and frustration.

Facing me now, Marc closed his eyes and inhaled deeply. When he opened them a second later, his face was carefully blank, his hands open at his sides instead of curled into fists. He turned slowly, ready for another round of questions. "Where do you live, Radley?"

"Nearby, for the moment."

"On this mountain?" Marc swung one hand toward the window to indicate the swath of forest barely visible in the dark. Radley sighed and nodded, so Marc continued. "A cabin? A house? What?"

"Anyplace that will keep me warm for a few hours. I don't have the deed, if you know what I mean."

We knew what he meant. He was a drifter.

While most strays used the stability of an established human lifestyle to balance out the volatility of life as a stray, some new werecats never readjusted to a normal human existence after being infected. Drifters roamed from place to place, hunting when they were hungry, sniffing out water when they were thirsty, sleeping wherever they found warmth, and only venturing into human society when they were too lonely to think straight. However, attempts at socialization rarely lasted long for a drifter, because he would soon come to realize all over again that he had little in common with the human world, and thus no real place in it. And back to the woods he would go.

But Radley didn't strike me as a typical drifter. His hair was trimmed and his teeth were in good shape, both of which are hard to accomplish in an existence with no scissors or toothbrushes.

"Where are you from?" Marc asked.

"My birthplace." Radley smirked.

"Specifically…?" Marc rolled his shoulders, making it clear that he was ready for more *persuasion,* should it prove necessary.

Radley licked blood from his lips in a slow, deliberate motion. Then he closed his mouth and met Marc's eyes boldly.

Marc shrugged. "I wouldn't want to lose *my* canines. But that's your call." He uncrossed his arms, elbows bent, fists clenched. He dropped one hip and leaned in for a kick, no doubt aimed at the stray's jaw.

My father went completely still. Jace's hand tightened on my shoulder in anticipation. My breath caught in my throat. My brother Ethan told me once that Marc could throw a kick with enough precision to knock out a single tooth. But I had no desire to see it happen.

"All right!" Radley shouted, wincing back from the blow before Marc could release it. "Vancouver! I'm from Vancouver, but I moved closer to the mountains several years ago."

Most strays eventually wound up living near large forested regions of land, where they could roam in cat form without too much risk of being spotted.

Marc nodded and relaxed his stance. "Better." He glanced over his shoulder at my father, brows raised in question. Daddy nodded for him to continue, his satisfaction with the progress evidenced only in the relaxed line of his forehead.

Marc turned back to the job at hand. "Canada, huh? You wandered a good way from home, Radley. What the hell are you doing here? Other than searching for aliens among us."

"I needed a change of scenery."

"Why?" Lucas jerked back on the stray's wrists, so that he almost lost his balance. "Things get too hot for you up there?"

Radley opened his mouth to answer, but Marc cut him off. "Think carefully before you speak. It'll only take one phone call to verify whatever you tell us." With the Canadian Territorial Council, of course. If he'd ever caused trouble in his homeland, they'd have a record of it.

"I don't know what you're talking about." Radley glanced from face to face in apparent confusion. "I just needed a change. How many times can you sniff the same trees and hills before dropping dead of boredom?"

Either he was telling the truth, or he was a *really good* liar. And it irked me that I couldn't tell which it was.

"So, what, you wanted to sniff *different* trees and hills?" Marc sighed and shook his head. "Never mind. How long have you been here?"

Radley shrugged. "In the U.S.? Or on this mountain?"

"Both."

"I crossed the border a few weeks ago. Why? What's all this about, anyway? You guys set me up, knock me out, drag me up here, and I wake up with my hands and feet taped together in human form. How the hell did I even *get* hands, anyway? I have no memory of Shifting. And what the hell do you people want?" Radley sat on his heels and stared up at Marc defiantly. "I'm not answering any more of your questions until you've answered a few of mine."

"If you like your face intact, you'll do whatever you're told," Lucas said.

My father studied Radley with his eyes narrowed in thought. "We forced your Shift," he said finally. "The process was overseen by my personal physician. You were perfectly safe, I assure you."

I frowned at my father, confounded by his sudden—and much more thorough than necessary—explanation. But he was still watching the stray, his face now deliberately blank.

Radley's eyes grew wide, his expression eager. "How? How did you force my Shift? Some kind of drug?"

"Yes." Daddy nodded once, adopting a stronger-than-usual appearance of authority. "But that's all you need to know about it."

Radley frowned. "Why?" He ignored Marc now in favor of the Alpha, whom he'd finally identified as the one in charge. "What do you want with me?"

"You're being held by our Territorial Council, headed by me, on the charge of attempted murder. Of my daughter."

Surprise tingled up my spine. That was news to me, and based on Lucas's expression, he hadn't known, either. Evidently that's what the Alphas were talking to Marc and Jace about for so long.

Yet in spite of my obvious surprise, the stray showed no fear. He showed nothing but confusion, balanced by a hint of righteous anger. He clearly had no idea how serious his predicament had just become.

My father continued, without even glancing my way. "Officially, you're facing a probable death sentence, Mr. Radley. *Un*officially, however, we want information from you. If we get it, and if you can convince us that what you did to my daughter was an accident, the charge will be amended to assault, which carries a much lighter sentence."

Radley's brow furrowed, and his shoulders tensed. "Sentence? Wait, you're serious?"

"Perfectly," Michael said from my right.

Radley glanced from him to our father, then briefly at me. "What the hell does that mean? You guys are like…what? Werecat law enforcement?"

Jace chuckled. "We can't be the first Pride cats you've ever run across."

"No. I know what a Pride is. Elitist pricks won't let anyone else play their reindeer games." Though a flicker of doubt crossed his face as he glanced at Marc, who was clearly a stray and yet a Pride cat. "What I don't understand is where you get off bringing me up on some kind of bullshit charge. You're not the police. The police don't even know you fuckers exist."

"Watch your mouth," Marc said, the warning rumbling from his chest like a growl. "Or I'll watch it for you."

Radley barely glanced at him, having obviously decided there were bigger things to worry about than Marc. But what he didn't realize was that if the council sentenced him to death, that death would come in the form of a certain six-foot-two, tall-dark-and-scary enforcer who had absolutely no incentive so far to administer a merciful demise.

Michael stepped up to our father's side. "Werecat business doesn't fall under any police department's jurisdiction, Radley. State and local law enforcement aren't even in the same *galaxy* as the Territorial Council, and right now you're in our world. Until we decide to either let you go or put you in the ground, you live, breathe and speak on our collective whim. At the moment, you exist only to please the Territorial Council, and if you cease to please them, you'll cease to be. Period. You get it now?"

Aaaand here comes the panic…

Okay, Radley didn't exactly panic. But he did look like he was about to spew his guts all over the floor, which was already splattered with his blood.

I could totally sympathize.

"What do you want?" he demanded, bolstering his floundering courage with a heavy dose of anger. "You bastards are crazy, and I just want to get—"

Marc exploded into motion, moving almost too fast to see. His fist slammed into the stray's cheek. Radley's words ended in a surprised *oof* of pain, and his head rocked to one side. For a moment, his eyes fluttered as if he might lose consciousness, and only Lucas's grip on his shoulders kept him upright.

My father made a harsh, disapproving sound in the back of his throat, and Marc stepped back, accepting his wordless rebuke with his hands still clenched into tension-white fists. He'd forgotten the cardinal rule of interrogation: an unconscious cat can't answer questions.

Daddy did *not* look pleased. But then, neither did Marc. He lost his temper fairly regularly in his personal life, but I'd never heard of him losing it at work before. Something else had to be wrong with him. Something unrelated to Radley. Or at least unrelated to Radley's foul language.

For several seconds no one breathed, waiting to see whether or not Radley would pass out. But then he blinked to clear his vision, and his eyes focused slowly on Marc, whose penitent expression was now gone.

"I told you to watch your mouth. Consider that your last warning."

Radley cleared his throat and spat more blood on the floor. This time when he looked up, his eyes were filled with a cold, detached fury. "What do you want?"

Marc crossed his arms over his chest, hiding his fists. He stood several feet back from Radley, removing himself from the temptation to strike out again. "What do you know about the two human hikers who went missing on the mountain several days ago?"

"Nothing." That was it. No further explanation or questions. Radley was going to give us exactly what we asked for, and no more. Marc's temper had just erased any progress my father had made toward convincing our informant to cooperate by choice.

"What about the human cop mauled yesterday afternoon? Know anything about that?"

"No." Radley glared at Michael now, pointedly ignoring Marc completely. So, at my father's silent signal, Michael took over, stepping forward as Marc slunk back to lean against the wall by the door, the fury in his expression rivaling Radley's.

Michael slid his hands into the pockets of his slacks, still sharply creased even in the middle of the night. "Have you seen any other strays on the mountain in the last week?"

"Yes."

"How many?"

Radley thought for a moment, ducking his head to wipe blood from his face onto his bare shoulder. "Three. Maybe four?" he said finally, shuffling backward to lean with his left arm against the front of the couch. "I didn't know I was supposed to be counting."

Michael pushed his glasses higher on the bridge of his nose, peering down at Radley through lenses he didn't even need. He wore them because he thought they made him look more like a lawyer. He was right, especially in that moment. "Do you know their names and current whereabouts?"

"No."

"Do you have any knowledge of their activities on the mountain?"

"No."

Sighing dramatically, Michael dropped into a limber squat in front of Zeke Radley, looking into the stray's eyes from an equal height. His tone became friendly, confidential, as if they were the only two people in the room. "Mr. Radley, I want to help you. I believe you didn't mean to hurt my sister. I think you were just in the wrong place at the wrong time, but I have to be honest with you—that was a *very* wrong place to be at that particular wrong time. We're looking for murderers, Mr. Radley, and we came across you instead. Can you see how that looks? You being all alone on the mountain, less than a mile from where a police officer was slaughtered only hours earlier?"

Radley frowned and nodded reluctantly.

"If you want us to help you, you have to help us first. Help *yourself*. Someone on that mountain is murdering humans, and I think you've seen something. Or know something. You may not have seen it happen, but you've seen the other cats. Right? Smelled them, maybe?"

Radley nodded hesitantly, and my heart thumped in surprise and suspense. Michael was doing it. His good-cop routine was breaking through where Marc's bad cop had gone horribly wrong. This was no ordinary drifter, accustomed to being threatened and coerced into cooperation. Radley was smart, and he was proud. He could not be pushed past the point defined by his self-respect.

There was more to this stray than we were seeing. I would have bet my life on it.

"Can you help us?" Michael paused before adding the final touch—that last nugget of respect he knew Radley couldn't resist. "Please?"

Radley stared at the blood-splattered hardwood, as if mentally trying to talk himself out of whatever he was about to do. When he looked up, he met only Michael's eyes, as if that would block the rest of us from hearing him. We hadn't respected him—hadn't earned his cooperation. Michael had.

"Look, I mind my business and try to stay out of trouble." He shrugged. "But I might have seen these cats you're talking about."

Michael nodded, playing his part while the rest of us watched in tense silence. "Where?"

Radley sighed, resigned. "There's this cabin on the other

side of that hill." He tossed his head toward the window, and the mountain I could barely see past the inky predawn darkness. "Ten, maybe twelve miles to the northwest. There were several cats staying there a couple of days ago. They may be gone now. I don't know. But that's the last place I saw them."

"Who are they?"

"I told you, I don't know." Of course, he'd also told us he didn't know where they were, but no one seemed inclined to mention that and risk him bottling up. "They're just cats. All toms, of course. And all strays from what I can tell."

Which made me wonder how Radley had become a stray. I didn't recognize the scent of his infector.

"Can you show us this cabin?" Michael asked, rocking slowly back and forth on his feet.

Radley shook his head vehemently. "No. Hell no. In one breath you tell me these jokers are killing people, and in the next you want me to *take* you there? No." Blood-matted brown hair slapped his brow as his head whipped back and forth.

"You seem to be under the mistaken impression you have a choice in the matter," Lucas growled, jerking him back sharply. One curt shake of my father's head, and Lucas shoved him forward in frustration.

Without his hands free, Radley fell forward and would have tipped over if not for the hand Michael steadied him with. "Please." My brother held the stray's gaze. "You could save us hours of stomping through the woods."

Radley hesitated, and I could practically taste temptation in the scent pouring from his body. "Can you get them to drop this bogus charge?"

Michael closed his eyes, as if the stray were asking for the impossible, and I bit my lip to keep from smiling. This was where they'd been heading all along with the whole attempted-murder bit. If Radley had wanted me dead, he could easily have killed me. We all knew that.

Not that I believed his wholesome and gallant act either, though…

Exhaling audibly, Michael glanced over his shoulder at our Alpha, who'd retreated to the edge of the room, next to Marc. My father nodded, arms crossed over his chest.

"I'll see what I can do." Michael stood as he faced the stray who'd just agreed to help us in exchange for his life, which probably hadn't been in much danger anyway.

He should have bargained for his freedom, I thought, barely stifling the smug smile stealing over my face. *That's what he's really in danger of losing.* Then a sudden chill washed over me as I realized that the stray who'd practically ripped open my stomach in front of two witnesses was facing a lighter sentence than I was.

Michael gathered his legal pad and pen from the end table and was already scribbling furiously when he glanced at our father. "Think we can do anything to make Mr. Radley more comfortable?" And with that, my brother's status as good cop was firmly established.

"Of course." The Alpha stepped into the dim light from the dusty bulb overhead and made a slicing gesture to Lucas with one hand. Lucas nodded and pulled a pocketknife— nowhere near as nice as the one I'd lost for him—from his back pocket. As my cousin worked his blade between Radley's wrists and the first band of duct tape, my father turned his attention to Jace. "You and Lucas see that Mr. Radley gets a shower and something to wear. I'll put together a team to find the cabin, and you can all leave after our guest has had something to eat."

What? The bastard nearly cut me in half, and my father was practically rolling out the red carpet for him.

Jace nodded and offered Radley a hand up as Lucas jerked the last wad of tape from the stray's bare ankles, accompanied by his hiss of pain. Then they each took one of his arms and escorted him down the hall toward the bathroom, his toes barely brushing the floor with each step.

As soon as the door clicked shut behind them, I twisted to face my father, encouraged by how dull the bolt of pain in my stomach now felt. "You're giving him a shower? And a meal?" I demanded. "Why don't you just lay me out on the floor and let him finish the job?"

"Faythe, stop—"

"Shut up, Michael," I snapped, one hand gripping the back of my chair in preparation to stand. "When there's nothing but twenty stitches standing between *your* guts and the mother-fucking floor, *then* you get to talk. Until then—"

I stood, anger pushing me past growing pain and the fear of ripped stitches. And suddenly the whole damn room went black. *Those must be some pills,* I thought, just before my legs buckled beneath me.

Eleven

"—many did she take?" My father's voice sounded oddly hollow, as if he were speaking into one of those tin-can telephones Ethan and I played with as kids. And everything was dark, but with a weird sort of backlit glow—light shining through my closed eyelids.

"Jace said he gave her three."

Marc. I opened my eyes to find him staring down at me, dark curls shining in the dim glare overhead. "Here she comes," he said, concern audible in his voice and visible in the worry lines etched across his forehead. "Feel any better?"

"I'm fine. What happened?" My fingers brushed velour at my side, and I realized I was on the couch. Lying down. "Well, crap. I fainted?"

Marc chuckled, worry melting from his face to reveal relief and more than a little sympathy—definitely not my favorite of his expressions. He lowered himself onto the edge of the couch next to me, careful not to jar me. "Nah, you just passed out. You stood up too fast, and you probably took one too many of those little white pills."

"But Jace said—"

Marc frowned, cutting me off. "Jace weighs a lot more than you do. He's also an idiot."

"It's not his fault." I took the hand Marc offered and pulled myself upright slowly, ignoring the dull protest from the stitches in my stomach. As I leaned against the back of the couch, the rest of the room came into sharp focus. My father sat on the coffee table in front of me, slumped in his wrinkled suit jacket, his elbows propped on his knees.

Michael stood in the kitchen doorway behind him, watching me with a steaming mug in one hand. Coffee, based on the scent. Other than the three of them, the living room was empty, but the splatter of running water came from down the hall. Radley was still in the shower. I couldn't have been out for more than a few minutes.

"How's your stomach?" My father asked, peering into my eyes.

"Still hurts, but it's only unbearable when I move."

"Well, I have to give you credit for creativity, at least." Michael ran one hand over his face, as if trying to rub the feeling back into his features. "I can't remember anyone ever passing out to avoid being scolded before."

"What?" Then I remembered what I'd been doing when my legs fell out from under me: complaining about my father's decision to offer hospitality to the cat who'd left his mark on my stomach. Permanently. "Oh, yeah. I probably got carried away. But seriously, Daddy, if *I'd* carved up some poor cat's stomach, you guys would have me bound and gagged. But you're feeding and clothing *him*. How exactly is that fair?"

"He *was* bound and gagged," Michael reminded me, betraying no trace of a smile. I couldn't remember ever seeing him look more exhausted. He'd been working long hours with the tribunal on my behalf, and now thanks to Radley and the strays, he'd gotten less than three hours' sleep in the last twenty-four.

"*Was.*" I stressed. "He *was* bound and gagged. *Now* he's

probably in there using the last of my shampoo. He better not come out smelling like lavender."

Marc's hand landed gently on my knee, and a jolt traveled up from the point of contact. "I don't like him either, but your dad's right. We don't have any real reason to hold him. Or any *place* to hold him."

"What happened to the attempted-murder charge? Was that just a ploy?"

"Not *just* a ploy…" Michael mumbled.

The coffee table creaked when my father stood, then lowered himself into the armchair on my right. "We reported the incident to the entire council via a conference call, while you and Radley were both still out. I suggested the charge because all we knew at the time was that he'd chased you and punctured your stomach."

"Isn't that enough to hold him on?"

"Of course it is." He frowned, eyeing me sternly. "If you can honestly tell me you believe he meant to kill you. Can you? Because Marc says you were alone with him for several minutes before they found you, and that he could have killed you anytime he wanted to."

I glanced at Marc, surprised he would speak up in Radley's defense. He shrugged. "The truth is the truth, whether I like it or not."

Impressed all over again with his professionalism, I nodded. I was a big fan of the truth. Usually. "Oh, fine. He wasn't trying to kill me. But he wasn't trying to save me from anything *else* bumping around out there, either. He never intended to let me go. I have no doubt about that."

All three men nodded in agreement, and my father picked up a mug from the end table. "I don't doubt that. But the fact is that he's worth more to us out there—" he gestured toward the window and the great outdoors "—than he is tied up in here, where we'll trip over him every time one of us crosses the room."

"Not to mention the fact that we don't need him overhearing our every word." Michael swept a limp strand of brown hair from his forehead. "I don't think he's *that* innocent."

Overhearing us. Of course. That's why my dad had put the prisoner in the shower: so the running water would block out our discussion. *Damn, I have a lot to learn...*

I nodded. "So what's the plan?"

"Radley's going to lead a large team to that cabin, on the off chance they're still there. If they are, we bring them in. If not, Radley goes about his business with his eyes and ears open for any trouble. He's been here longer than we have and no doubt knows the woods much better."

"And if he doesn't want to play along?"

"He doesn't have that option." The hard line of Marc's jaw said he wasn't as happy with the plan as he wanted me to think. He'd go along because Zeke Radley held our best chance of catching the strays. And because our Alpha was calling the shots. But Marc didn't trust the stranger any more than I did.

From the end of the hall, the sound of running water dribbled to a halt and metal rings rattled as the shower curtain was pulled back. Radley was out of the tub, and our privacy had expired.

A quarter of an hour later, a clean, dressed Zeke Radley sat at the kitchen table, ignoring us all as he scarfed down his second microwavable chicken potpie. Michael and Jace sat on either side of him, silently chewing canned clam chowder, and the combined scents of their odd, predawn breakfast were not appetizing, even from the living room where I sat on the couch, trying to move as little as possible.

Radley wore a tattered but fresh pair of jeans and a solid black T, both donated by Marc, just to piss our "guest" off, even though Jace was closer to the stray's size.

In guy logic—an oxymoron if I'd ever heard one—since Marc had technically done Radley a favor by clothing him, the stray was now in debt to him, even though he'd only accepted the clothes because refusing them would have been a blatant insult to the lender. And the best part was that now Radley had to walk around smelling like Marc, which was practically an admission of Marc's dominance. And the source of our *guest's* steady scowl.

Someone knocked on the front door as Radley spooned the last drops of gravy from the paper pie plate, and Lucas stood to admit the last two members of the team my father and the tribunal had assembled. First through the door was Nate, Paul Blackwell's grandson, whom I'd expected. But I had *not* expected Danny Carver, who came in right behind him.

"Hey, Doc." I leaned forward to see around Marc, who sat very close to me. "You here to see me, or to play in the woods with the other boys?"

His ubiquitous smile widened when his eyes met mine. "Both." He shrugged. "I haven't gotten my paws dirty in a while. Thought it might be fun."

"That, and we're running short on uninjured, available enforcers," Marc murmured into my ear. Logically, I knew he was just trying to keep Radley from overhearing anything about our manpower shortage. Still, my pulse jumped and my face flushed when his lips brushed my ear.

Dr. Carver edged between the couch and the coffee table and held one hand out to me. I took it, and he helped me gently to my feet. "How you feeling?"

"Like I'm already tired of answering that question."

He nodded, laughing softly. "Sounds about right. Let's take a look."

I let the doctor lead me back to my bedroom, where I lowered myself gingerly onto the bed and pulled the hem of my shirt up to my sternum. He carefully peeled back the tape holding my bandages in place and inspected the stitches, talking the whole time.

"I just treated similar wounds on Brett Malone, and I have to say, you're a much easier patient to deal with. You haven't hissed at me once." He grinned. "Of course, you only have twenty stitches. He has closer to one hundred."

Smiling, I closed my eyes as the doctor spread clean squares of gauze over my stomach. "Is he okay?"

Dr. Carver nodded, taping the new bandages in place. "He's gonna be fine. Not as soon as *you* will, naturally. Your gashes are closing up nicely." Standing, he tossed the used gauze into the trash can by the door. "But I want you to go to sleep."

I nodded, but he ignored my assurances as if he knew I didn't really mean them. "I'm serious, Faythe." He frowned down at me, showing the strict-doctor side of him I rarely saw. "If you don't get some rest and let your body do its job, you won't be ready to Shift tomorrow, and you'll have to spend another day sitting on the couch."

"I got it, Doc." Surely my wide-eyed, innocent look was more convincing than a mere nod. "Stay in bed, sleep all night." Fortunately, the night was nearly over.

"Exactly. And this is to make sure you do as you're told for once." From his pocket, Dr. Carver pulled a brown plastic prescription bottle, from which he poured two more of those stupid sleeping pills. "Don't worry," he said in response to the panic that must have been written all over my face. "These don't work very well on us, as you may have noticed. You'll only be out for a few hours, and you're not going to miss anything."

"Oh, fine." I swallowed the pills with a gulp from the water he handed me. Then I had to stick my tongue out and wiggle it up and down to convince Dr. Carver that I'd actually ingested the damn things.

Ten minutes later, the guys filed out the front door, Zeke Radley sandwiched between Marc and Lucas. Marc and Jace both said good-night before leaving, but neither of them even hesitated to go on without me. They'd made the usual promises to come back safely, and to tell me the whole story when they returned. Then they'd left me alone with my father and brother, both of whom refused to speak to me for fear of keeping me awake.

I don't remember falling asleep, but I definitely remember waking up. When my eyes opened, the first thing I noticed was how bright my bedroom was, even though the lamp was unlit. The alarm clock read 8:04.

Damn. It's morning. I'd slept through the whole rest of the night—nearly three hours.

But the annoyingly bright sunlight wasn't what woke me. Voices had interrupted my sleep. Angry voices, one of them my father's.

"—let him go? Why would you *do* that?" Malone demanded. From the sound of it, he and my father were arguing in the living room, right outside my door. And they clearly had no idea I was awake.

"It was *my* call, and I made the decision I thought best. I stand by that decision. The cabin was empty—probably had been for a couple of days—and Radley stands a much better chance of finding them than we do. He knows the forest, and they have to be familiar with his scent by now, so they won't think twice about him wandering around, whereas one whiff of any of our toms would send them running. We need Radley's help, and we're not going to get that with him wasting away in front of the television."

"He's a *criminal,* Greg. I know your perspective on criminal behavior has changed a bit lately, but Radley's a stray. You have no reason to protect him. He nearly killed your daughter, for crying out loud. You should have his rear paw hanging from your key chain like a rabbit's foot. Instead, it's prancing around the woods with his other three, without a care in the world."

"You'd see my daughter executed tomorrow if you could, Calvin." My father's voice was dangerous, and so low I could barely hear it. "Should I take your paw, too?"

A thrill raced up my spine and down my limbs at Malone's silence. I would have given almost anything to see his expression at that moment. It was fear. It *had* to be. Surely he was about to mess in his pants after being threatened by my father, even indirectly. Anyone else would be.

"That's not the same, and you know it," Malone finally said. "I'm *not* out to get her, no matter what you think."

Yeah, right, you sorry bastard. I had to shove my knuckles into my mouth to keep from shouting it out loud.

"It's my job to make sure Faythe's hearing is fair, not just to her, but to the entire werecat community. She infected her boyfriend, then killed him to cover up her crime. She's *dangerous,* whether you can see that or not, and it's not fair to the rest of us to leave her free to do it again."

"She killed him in self-defense, and you *damn well* know it." The floorboards groaned, and I pictured my father stepping closer to Malone, invading his personal space. "Having my daughter executed won't get you a seat at the head of the council. You must know that."

"*My* position within the council has *nothing* to do with this. This is about *your* priorities, and the fact that they no longer represent the interest of the majority."

"That's out of line. I released Radley in hopes that he can help us. No, I'm not certain he will. But neither am I certain we can find the strays on our own before they do any more damage. Trusting Radley was worth a shot, so I took it. If it was up to you, you'd probably have had him executed."

"Damn right. That'd be one less str—"

The bathroom door creaked open from down the hall, then silence fell, as sharp and sudden as the blade of a guillotine. I wanted to get out of bed and creep closer to the door, but I was afraid the rustle of my blankets would cover whatever happened next.

"One less what?" Marc demanded, his voice as cold and hard as steel.

Oh, shit.

"This is none of your business." Malone wisely refused to complete his aborted thought, but I couldn't let him get away with that. If he was going to hate Marc, he was damn well going to be honest with himself—and with the rest of us—about why.

"One less what?" I shouted, pushing myself into a sitting position with my back against the headboard. The pain in my stomach was sharp at first, but had already faded into a dull throb before my father threw the bedroom door open.

He didn't say a word. He simply warned me with his eyes to stay out of it.

Over the shoulder of my father's navy terry-cloth robe, I saw Malone, already fully dressed. And beyond him stood Marc, wearing only the shorts he typically slept in, his hair wet from the shower he'd just taken.

"One less what?" I repeated, narrowing my focus on Malone, wondering if he could possibly know what a complete ass he was. Surely not. Surely no one could possibly maintain such a repulsive personality without a blanket of ignorance insulating him from reality.

"One less…*criminal* running loose." Malone's face flushed in either fury or humiliation, but I didn't know him well enough to decide which it was. "I was going to say *criminal.*"

"We all know what you were going to say," I spat, tossing the covers back to expose my lower half—still clothed in the red pajama pants, thank goodness. "It doesn't take a genius to fill in the blanks. Though apparently it takes a pedigree to get in your good graces."

"Faythe…" my father warned, but his expression, rather than matching his carefully stern tone, was completely blank.

Did that mean he didn't really want me to shut up? Or just that I hadn't yet reached "critical" on his internal political-disaster dial?

Malone turned back to my father, ignoring both me and Marc. "I assume you'll let us know if Radley contacts you."

"Certainly. And I assume *you'll* let *us* know when you've agreed upon a verdict on the murder charge?"

"Of course." Malone's glance landed on me briefly before he stomped across the living room and out the front door.

"Get some sleep," my father said to Marc, then he turned to me. "And *you* don't overdo it today. Danny will be back this evening to see if you're ready to Shift."

With that, my father retired to his own rented bedroom, where he probably spent more time staring at the ceiling than actually sleeping.

The rest of the day dragged by slowly while Jace, Marc, and my father tried to catch up on sleep. Jace and Marc had been sharing one of the two upstairs rooms, but since I was awake, I let Marc borrow the spare bed in mine, for a little privacy. That left only Michael to keep me company/watch to make sure I didn't escape, which was obviously a *huge* risk, considering I'd nearly been disemboweled twelve short hours earlier.

My brother spent the entire day on the couch next to me, his laptop balanced on both knees, clacking away at the keyboard as if there weren't a real world all around him, ready and willing to keep him busy.

Fortunately, he didn't want to talk, so I had plenty of time to catch up on my reading. As luck would have it, during one of Michael's two short bathroom breaks, the cabin's landline rang for the first time all day, and there was no one else around to answer it. I dropped my novel on my lap and carefully stretched toward the end table, hoping to reach the phone before it woke anyone up.

"Hello?" I gritted my teeth as the pain in my stomach faded.

Naturally, it was my mother, since there was no one around for me to pass the phone to. "Faythe, dear, how are you feeling?"

"Like a pincushion. How 'bout you?"

To my surprise, she actually laughed. "Well, you *sound* good. And I'm fine. We're all doing very well, in fact. Manx finally decided on colors for the baby's first picture outfit. We're going with stripes in cornflower, periwinkle, sapphire and midnight."

"Lovely." I couldn't help rolling my eyes. "And…monochromatic."

"I know." My mother chuckled again. "She's still insisting on all blue."

Dr. Carver had confirmed the unborn infant's gender a couple of months earlier with an after-hours ultrasound at his office. Far from being disappointed with another boy, Manx was thrilled. She was determined that regardless of her own fate, this baby would live, and that the world would welcome him in spite of his gender. Unlike his brothers. And to prove her point, she and my mother were knitting the poor thing an entire closetful of hats, sweaters, mittens and blankets in every shade of blue imaginable.

My mom talked my ear off for the next five minutes, telling me she'd finally met Angela, Ethan's girlfriend, and how often Manx's baby was kicking now. Owen had sold the last of the season's hay, and Vic and Parker were doing regular patrols. The only one she didn't mention was Ryan, perhaps because nothing had changed with him, in his basement prison cell. But more likely, she was still trying to pretend her favorite-son-turned-traitor had never returned. And I could hardly blame her for that.

When Michael emerged from the bathroom, I tossed him the phone, mouthed the word *Mom,* and went back to my book.

"Hello?" he said into the mouthpiece, already heading into the kitchen to scrounge up some lunch.

I didn't even pretend to read as I eavesdropped. My mother hadn't asked me about the hearing, though I knew damn well that was why she'd called, probably hoping I'd be the one to bring it up. But that wasn't my style. If she wanted to know something from me, she'd have to ask.

Unfortunately, that wasn't *her* style. My mother was more the hint-dropping type, at least with me.

My mother and I had never been the best of friends. She was grace, and tact, and poise, while I was bruised, and blunt, and loud. But despite our differences, I'd recently discovered that *she* was the source of my steel backbone, and quite possibly the root of my own stubbornness—discoveries that both surprised and pleased me.

Still, she was more comfortable discussing serious things with Michael, and, sure enough, as he dug through the freezer, Michael fended question after question, leaving me to puzzle out her side of the conversation on my own, because the rumbling of the ancient refrigerator blocked most of it out.

"Guilty." He held up a box of frozen lasagna and a pepperoni pizza, asking me silently to choose. I pointed to the pizza, and he shoved the lasagna back into the freezer. "Not yet. Uncle Rick's buying us more time." Another pause as he closed the microwave door on the pizza and pressed some buttons. "Yeah, she did. It was really…interesting. Didn't look much like the last time."

She was asking about the partial Shift—not my favorite topic at the moment. Fortunately, when the microwave dinged, Michael begged off the line, promising to have our father call her back later.

While we were eating, Jace padded downstairs, clad only in a pair of blue plaid pajama bottoms cinched around his narrow waist. He mumbled a groggy hello on his way into the kitchen, where he nuked five frozen burritos and started a fresh pot of coffee, his eyes still half-closed. Minutes later, the scent of coffee brought Marc out of his coma, looking irritatingly fresh and alert.

I'd slept ten out of the last twenty-four hours and still felt like crap thanks to painkillers and the constant throbbing in my stomach. Marc had only had four, and looked like he could climb Mount Everest without breaking a sweat. The claw marks on his arm were little more than puffy red scars now that he'd Shifted into and out of cat form twice.

When he and Jace had Shifted, they headed off into the woods for a four-hour session to relieve one of the teams out looking for the human hikers. Marc and Jace returned around five-thirty, exhausted and disheartened at having made no progress.

The human hikers had been missing for three days. Brett Malone had been mauled twenty-six hours earlier, and we'd found no sign of the strays we suspected were responsible for both. And to top all that off, I felt completely useless, because my stomach still hurt like hell.

As I watched Marc pop open a can of Coke after his shift in the woods, my gaze fell on his newly healed wounds and I knew what I had to do.

It was time for me to Shift—the sooner I healed, the sooner I could get my butt off the couch and into gear. My eyes slid briefly to the closed bedroom door next to mine, behind which my father had finally fallen asleep.

I should probably ask him first. But I didn't, because he'd tell me to wait until the twenty-four-hour mark. Instead, I dug my cell phone from my pocket. While the guys watched, Michael frowning in disapproval, though he couldn't have known what I was doing, I speed-dialed Dr. Carver's cell, which we all kept programmed for medical emergencies. He'd talked the guys through more than a few tourniquets over the years. And a couple of broken bones, as well.

"Hello?" Dr. Carver answered on the second ring. "Faythe? What's up?"

"I'm going to try Shifting."

Silence settled over the line for a moment, and in the background Brett asked if it was supposed to hurt when he inhaled. "Give me ten minutes to get done here." The doc's voice held no doubt or judgment of any kind. I heard only acceptance of my decision and a willingness to help, which was a really nice change.

My father was awake by the time Carver arrived—I strongly suspect Michael woke him—which meant there were four extra sets of eyes staring at my stomach when Dr. Carver examined my lacerations beneath the fluorescent fixture in the kitchen, the brightest source of light in the cabin.

"Excellent needlework, if I do say so myself." The doc leaned forward in one of the dining chairs to peer closer at my stitches. "Well…" He sat up, making contact with my eyes this time, instead of my abs. "It's not going to feel good, that's for certain. Are you sure you're ready to try? It won't hurt to wait one more day…"

"I can*not* sit on that couch doing nothing for the next twenty-four hours. All I want to know is whether or not Shifting will actually accelerate the healing. Is there any chance it could tear the skin more?" The very thought of which was enough to make me sick to my stomach.

Dr. Carver blinked, then glanced at my father before answering me. "It would have done more damage than good if you'd Shifted last night. But a few hours can make a big difference. You've already started to heal, and with any luck, the stitches will hold." He shrugged. "If you're feeling up to it, I say give it a try. Assuming that's okay with the powers that be, of course." And with that, his gaze slid back to the Alpha.

My father frowned as he studied the earnest hope surely plain on my face. I knew what he was thinking: Malone would never go for it. The tribunal didn't want me to Shift because they knew that if I decided to run, they probably couldn't catch me. I was the smallest—therefore the lightest—cat in our cabin complex, and I'd spent my entire life outrunning my four brothers just to emerge from childhood intact. That, plus my recent enforcer training labeled me a huge flight risk in their eyes, and no matter how often or sincerely I promised them I wouldn't go, they didn't believe me. The real bitch of it was that considering my history, I couldn't really blame them.

But now that I was injured, things had changed. I couldn't outrun an *armadillo* with four holes in my stomach, not to mention the ones in my chest. Surely even Malone would understand that.

Finally my father exhaled slowly, and the mischief sparkling in his eyes lent youth to his features. "Danny, are you saying Faythe *needs* to Shift to facilitate healing her lacerations?"

Wide-eyed, Dr. Carver nodded eagerly, clearly catching on. "The sooner she Shifts, the quicker she'll heal, thus the faster she'll be ready to continue with the hearing."

"We don't really have a choice, then." A hint of a grin peeked through my father's typically stern expression. "Faythe, you're going to have to Shift for your own good, and you may as well get it over with now, so the tribunal doesn't accuse us of trying to delay your hearing."

Jace scratched his nose to hide a smile, but I didn't bother. I'd only been allowed to Shift once every two weeks—currently considered the bare minimum for a werecat to maintain good physical and mental health—and even then I'd been heavily supervised. I was nearing the end of my two-week cycle of abstention, and the thought that I might have to leave the mountains without experiencing them on four paws was making me almost as crazy as the accusation that brought me there in the first place.

"I'd like to observe your Shift," Dr. Carver said. "In case anything goes wrong."

"Fine." As badly as I hated having my Shift ogled, I was

not going to give up my chance to frolic in the woods over something so trivial.

My father nodded, and it was official. "After you Shift, you have half an hour to exercise. Make sure everything still works."

"I'm injured, not eighty," I complained, but he ignored my interruption.

"The strays are still out there, Faythe, and the fact that they've abandoned their hideout means they probably know we're looking for them. Stay close to our cabin and away from the main lodge. And stay within sight of your escorts at all time. Escorts?" My father's eyes roamed the room, and no one was surprised to see Marc and Jace each raise one hand silently. "Fine." His gaze returned to me. "After your half hour, come back here and let Danny watch over your Shift back. And Faythe?"

"Yes, Daddy?" I stared up at him with my innocent face fixed firmly in place. He wasn't falling for it. He never had.

"Don't do anything stupid or dangerous. Understand? You are *not* fully healed, and you won't be after a single Shift. Doing too much too fast will only hurt you worse. No tree climbing, no long-distance leaping, and no hunting. Just a little light exercise. Got it?"

"Yes, Daddy."

Of course, like "be good," "mind your own business," and "play nice with the boys," "light exercise" was open to interpretation. Right?

Twelve

Stretchy red boyshorts slid down my legs to land inside my pajama pants, already pooled on the ground around my feet. Tempering my eagerness with a slow breath of caution, I stretched my arms over my head, pulling my pajama top along for the ride. It landed with my other clothes, and I shivered as the frigid breeze brushed my goose-pimply skin. It wasn't every evening I stood naked in the mountains.

On either side of me, Marc and Jace were well into their respective transformations, writhing on all fours among dead leaves and cold dirt.

Teeth chattering, I glanced over my shoulder at our cabin, easily visible through gaps in the bare branches. We'd stopped a few feet into the woods so that if anything went wrong, the doc wouldn't have to go far for help. In fact, he'd only have to shout, because my father's silhouette was clearly outlined in the front window, holding a mug-shaped shadow.

"Ready?" Dr. Carver asked, and I turned to face both him and the Shift that was starting to make me nervous, in spite of my earlier bravado and enthusiasm. I nodded, and he smiled supportively. "Now remember, if it hurts too badly, you can always reverse the Shift and wait another day. Or even a few hours. And if you feel any unusual ripping or popping sensations in your stomach, stop Shifting immediately and let me take a look."

I nodded again, too nervous to speak. After more than a decade of Shifting on a mostly regular basis, I knew what was normal for my body and what wasn't. "If anything goes wrong, you'll be the first to know."

"Good." He made a sweeping gesture at the ground. "Have at it."

Marc had fully Shifted by then, and he sat on his haunches next to the doctor, where they could both watch me carefully. Jace was entering the final stages of his own transformation, so I lowered myself carefully onto my knees next to him, distracting myself from the painful tugging sensation in my gut by breathing deeply to take in the recognizable yet different scents of an unfamiliar forest.

As I put weight onto first one hand, then the other, I mentally cataloged the scents of pine needles, which we had in East Texas, bear dander, which we *didn't* have in East Texas, and some kind of sweet, winter-blooming vine I *wish* we had in our private slice of nature.

Something crackled through a pile of leaves on my right, and my nose twitched, easily identifying a mouse fleeing from my scent even as I discovered his. *If I had paws, you'd make a good snack, little mouse.* As if the thought triggered my Shift, the first surge of pain rippled across my back and down my limbs, convulsing my major muscle systems in a graceless dance of agony.

I gave myself over to the pain, letting the Shift choose its own path through my body, as I'd learned to do more than a decade earlier. If I tried to force it in one direction or another, I'd pay the price with more and prolonged pain.

For several minutes, as my body ripped apart and restructured itself, the sharp bolts of pain in my bones and joints overshadowed the throbbing in my stomach. My spine bowed. My hips and shoulders popped in and out of their sockets. My elbows and knees made hollow cracking sounds, accompanied by vicious spears of agony.

Dry grass pricked the palms of my hands and the soles of my feet as they swelled into paw pads. My nails thickened into hard, sharp claws. I let my mouth go slack when the Shift reached my head, distorting my face in a stream of excruciating bulges and new hollows. A moan escaped my disfigured throat as my jawbone rippled with the transformation of my human teeth into long, sharply curved points. My tongue tingled when several hundred tiny barbs sprouted from it, arcing toward my throat.

My skin began to itch as fur rippled across my back, surging to cover my extremities before flowing rapidly over my face. And last of all, just when I was starting to think Shifting with an injury wasn't so bad, the irregular line of fur surged down my sides toward my stomach.

My body had saved the worst part for last, when it was too late for me to turn back.

I screamed as my torn flesh stretched, burning unbearably as new hair follicles opened and sprouted fur. My stomach throbbed, muscles bunching and expanding to support my re-structured physiology.

Then, finally, it was over.

I lay panting on the ground as if I'd just run several miles. The sharp pulse of pain in my stomach had dulled to a mild ache, a reminder of what I'd been through, as well as a promise that things would get better. Soon.

As always after a Shift, my new body felt awkward—stiff, like I'd just woken up and needed a good stretch to settle everything into place. To ease the bad-weather ache in my joints, I stretched my front paws toward Jace, who now sat on his haunches beside Marc, both of them watching me for any sign of a problem. I sank my claws into the winter-cool earth and stretched my belly carefully, hindquarters in the air, tail waving slowly toward the mostly bare branches overhead.

I felt a sharp twinge in my stomach, and the tug of the stitches, which seemed to have survived my Shift pretty well, so I eased out of my new-body stretch and into a sitting position, very pleased to note that the pang faded immediately.

A hand landed gently on my head, scratching behind both my ears at once, and I arched into the touch as Dr. Carver's scent washed over me. "Turn over and let me take a look at your stomach, please," he said, scratching his way down my neck to that hard-to-reach spot between my shoulder blades.

Happy to oblige, I lowered myself to the ground and rolled onto my right side, my tail swishing among the fallen leaves, a purr rumbling softly from my throat as Marc rubbed his cheek against mine, and Jace did the same with my exposed left flank. Dr. Carver knelt beside me, shining a flashlight on my underbelly. He combed his fingers carefully through my thick black fur, and I huffed, the cat version of soft laughter. I hadn't realized I was ticklish in cat form, probably because no one had ever touched my stomach so softly before. It was nice, in a cozy, reassuring way.

So different from the touch that had necessitated the stitches.

"Well, the stitches survived, which is good. These new, thicker sutures make it so much easier to Shift while injured…" His voice trailed into silence as he peered closer at his handiwork, parting my fur with a single cold finger. "The skin has mostly mended everywhere but this one deep cut, and hopefully that one will seal itself when you Shift back. But the muscle beneath will take longer." Dr. Carver rocked back on his heels, then stood, which I took as my signal to roll onto my feet.

"Remember what your father said. No climbing, no tackling—" he glanced at Marc and Jace on that one "—and no long-distance pouncing. Give yourself a chance to heal." We all nodded obediently, which Carver surely knew to disregard completely, as he glanced at his watch. "You have thirty minutes. Make it count."

He could pretty much put money on that one.

As Dr. Carver picked his way through the thin strip of trees and into the yard, I headed in the opposite direction, tempering my ingrained need for speed with fresh memories of pain and ripping flesh. If I overdid it now, it could be weeks before I saw the woods again through cat eyes.

Marc and Jace walked alongside me at first, giving me very little space, as if they might lose me forever if I wandered more than three feet away. But the truth was that there was very little trouble to be found so close to the cabin complex, where our combined Pride-cat scents surely worked as stray repellent. Especially considering that the last stranger who'd wandered near had gotten his brains bashed in with my meat mallet. The scent of his blood—now soaked into our front yard—was pretty good advertising for an ass kicking.

After several minutes, I began to test my limitations, and the guys stepped back to give me more room. Jace played alongside me, swiping at pinecones for me to bat away and sniffing out field mice for me to pounce on—carefully, of course. But Marc stayed on my far side, keeping me between himself and the cabin to stop me from wandering too far as I grew more bold and more confident in my healing body.

Unfortunately, as my father clearly knew, half an hour wasn't enough time to do anything too adventurous. It was just long enough to realize what I'd been missing over the last two weeks—namely, fresh game. Well, the thrill of the hunt was what I really craved, but since such strenuous exercise was off-limits, I'd settle for a little fresh meat.

And when I caught the scent of a rabbit as I nosed through a pile of dead foliage in search of a pinecone Jace had swatted,

I made up my mind. I was *not* leaving the woods without a bite to eat. Period.

My nose twitched in the undergrowth, taking in as much of the prey-smell as possible. I wasn't trying to pinpoint its location; cats don't track by scent. I was just whetting my appetite. And hoping to scare the little morsel into making some noise, because cats *do* hunt with our incredibly well-tuned sense of hearing. And our eyesight.

My pause in the game did not go unnoticed. Jace whined at me in question, and I purred in response, telling the guys there was something I wanted in the bushes. I rested my muzzle on my forepaws and stuck my rump in the air, wiggling it back and forth to signal that I wanted to pounce.

I wasn't really going to pounce, of course. But just in case, Marc swatted my flank, then nosed me out of the way, which was feline-ese for "Scoot over and I'll catch your dinner." It was downright gallant of him, considering.

Marc bounded into the undergrowth, and the rabbit shot out the other side, bouncing off toward the west. Marc went after it, and both predator and prey disappeared around a dense clump of brush.

Jace stayed with me, and we experienced the hunt vicariously though a series of deep feline grunts, high-pitched squeals of terror and shaking foliage. Two minutes later, Marc slunk back into sight, a rust-colored rabbit pinched between his jaws. The damn thing was still twitching, trying in vain to get away. It was a miracle it hadn't had a heart attack.

I purred loudly in thanks, and Jace edged closer to get a good whiff of my dinner. He rubbed his cheek against my shoulder, begging politely for a taste, but I shrugged him off. There was nothing wrong with his stomach. He could go hunt his own dinner.

Marc dropped the rabbit at my feet, and the poor thing tried to hop away. It didn't get very far, in part because its left rear leg was broken. But also because I lunged for it, hoping to capture at least the *feel* of catching my own meal, even if I'd had to forgo the actual hunt.

Marc growled at my sudden movement, but I ignored him as my teeth sank into the fuzzy rabbit, his rapid heartbeat emptying its lifeblood into my mouth to dribble over my chin and onto the ground. I shook my prey until it was dead, then pinned it to the ground with one paw while I ripped its stomach open with my teeth.

Such a small creature was little more than a snack to a cat my size, but the meal was just as much symbolic as practical. The Territorial Council had figuratively clipped my wings, robbing me not only of my job as an enforcer, but of my inherent right to run with my fellow werecats. To taste speed and freedom a human could never understand or enjoy. And to my relief and surprise, half an hour in the woods and a fresh snack were enough to restore part of what I'd lost. Namely, my pride.

By the time I finished eating, which Marc watched with the satisfaction of a true provider, and Jace watched with more than a little envy, it was time to go back. Probably past time, in fact, but even so, I spared a couple of minutes to clean my fur. Fresh meat is messy, and even injured, a girl has her standards, right?

When Marc thought I was clean enough, he swatted my rump and nudged me in the direction of the cabin. I went willingly, my mood bolstered by the taste of freedom. And rabbit.

At the cabin, my father scolded us for being late, but there was no real anger in his tone. He'd probably been listening to us from the front porch the entire time.

I Shifted back in my bedroom, with Dr. Carver observing, and to my relief, my second transformation was easier and less painful than the first. And faster. We were both pleased to discover that the lacerations in my stomach were now fresh pink puckered scars, and though they still ached when I twisted from side to side, that weird flesh-ripping sensation was gone, along with most of the pain.

As I made my way down the hall toward the bathroom, tying my robe around my waist, Dr. Carver called after me from the living room, where the guys were sprawled across the furniture watching a DVD they'd borrowed from Lucas and passing around two bags of Doritos in lieu of a real dinner. "Brett's been asking to talk to you. If you want, I'll take you over after your shower."

"We'll all go." My father stepped into the hall from the kitchen. "We need to report to the tribunal anyway. And get something more substantial to eat than corn chips."

While I showered, Daddy sent Jace ahead to tell everyone we were coming, and to put four frozen lasagnas in the oven. Dr. Carver went with him because after what happened to Brett, no one was allowed out alone until the strays were found and dealt with. We'd always *worked* in pairs, and now that we were officially on alert, we'd do everything in groups of two or more.

Twenty minutes later, freshly showered and dressed in jeans and a snug, long-sleeved green T-shirt, I knocked on Brett's bedroom door. Behind me, the aromas of cheese, garlic and tomato sauce were just starting to flood the spacious living room from the kitchen, where Nate Blackwell and Jace were chopping vegetables for a huge salad.

"Yeah?" Brett called from inside his room, and I pushed the door open, stomping down a thread of anxiety winding its way up my spine. Dr. Carver had said Brett wanted to thank me, not threaten me. Even if he *was* Malone's son, Brett shared a mother with Jace, so he couldn't be *all* bad. Right?

"Faythe." Brett lay on the right-hand bed, blankets pulled up to his chest. Blue eyes almost as bright as Jace's met mine. His voice held pain and relief, and I could empathize with both.

"Hey." Tucking a strand of shower-damp hair behind my

ear, I settled into the chair by his bed, which still smelled like Danny Carver. "Doc said you wanted to talk to me."

"Yeah. I just wanted to—" He broke off and one hand went to the blankets over his stomach as his face twisted in pain, and I was reminded how much worse his injuries were than mine. How much blood he'd lost, much of it covering me as I'd tried to stop his bleeding without further injuring him.

Composed again, Brett turned his head on the pillow to face me more directly, springs creaking beneath him. "I wanted to thank you. Jace told me what happened. What *really* happened."

He'd spoken to Jace? Curious, I fiddled with the watch on my left wrist. "What did he say?"

"That I owe you my life."

I glanced at my hands in my lap, surprised to feel my cheeks flush. "Anyone else would have done the same thing."

Brett shook his head. "Colin would have let me die. Blackwell let him go. He called home for a replacement, and they're taking Colin to the airport in the morning. Shipping him straight back to Canada."

I didn't bother to hide the satisfied smile blossoming across my face. Vindication felt every bit as good as I'd hoped it would. Petty, but true.

"I want to make it up to you."

I shook my head. "I'm an enforcer, too—we look out for each other. That's the way things work."

"No." His voice was firm, his lips drawn into a thin line. "You went out there with no claws and no backup. That's not the way things work, and you didn't have to do it. I owe you. Let me owe you."

Before I could think up a new argument, much less voice it, a loud banging from the front room cut through the cooking noises and background chatter coming from the rest of the lodge. "Hey, Pride cats!" Elias Keller's voice was typically loud but muffled, and I realized the banging was his fist on the front door.

Around us, the lodge went silent.

"Open up!" Keller called, pounding again, this time hard enough to shake the walls. "I found something of yours and thought you might want it back."

Several sets of footsteps clomped toward the front door, and I recognized my father's distinctive tread among them, as well as the squeak of Malone's shiny new loafers. I glanced at Brett to find his eyes wide and curious, as my own no doubt were. Then the squeal of hinges drew my gaze to the living room, where Marc, Jace, Nate, and Michael stood clustered in the kitchen threshold, staring at the front door, which I couldn't see. Jace held a serrated bread knife, Nate a carrot peeler.

"There y'are!" Keller bellowed as heavy boot soles clomped on the hardwood. "Got somethin' for ya."

"Holy shit!" Jace whispered, and I was on my feet in an instant, desperate to know what had stunned an entire roomful of werecats. What could make Jace cuss in front of at least four different Alphas? Better yet, what could keep them all from noticing?

I rushed to the bedroom door, but hesitated there when Marc shook his head at me and showed me his open palm— a clear signal to stop.

My gaze followed Marc's to the center of the living room, where Keller towered over the Alphas gathered around him, staring at the limp black bundle tossed over his shoulder. *What the hell?* As I watched, the bundle seemed to swell, then shrink. Then it swelled and shrank again. Then again. It was breathing. The bundle was *alive.*

And suddenly I understood. Keller had brought us a cat. One of the strays? Radley, maybe?

One sniff in the bruin's direction put that theory to rest. The cat was definitely *not* Zeke Radley.

"I found her rootin' through my trash and thought you might want her back." Keller heaved the bundle from his shoulder and dropped it nonchalantly onto the empty coffee table, where the long black tail dangled to the floor. "She smells a bit diff'rent with fur. But seein' as how you don't have many girl cats—right?—I'd think you'd wanna keep a better eye on this'un."

Keller had brought us an unconscious cat. *A tabby.* And he thought it was me.

Thirteen

Surprise still tingling in the tips of my fingers, I stepped into the living room and felt all eyes turn my way. Including Keller's. A frown took over his broad forehead as confusion filled his face. He looked from me to the near-still form on the coffee table. Then back to me.

Keller blinked, then his eyes sought out my father's. "No wonder she smells different. If that one's yours—" the bruin nodded in my direction "—who's this?" He bent to stroke the fur atop the unconscious cat's head, as if to comfort her.

"That's a wonderful question, Mr. Keller."

Keller made a surprised noise in the back of his throat and sank onto the couch in front of the strange tabby. "You don't know her?"

Paul Blackwell answered, gaze zipping between the tabby and the bruin. "No. If one of our tabbies was missing, we'd know it."

My father nodded in agreement, but he had to ask, just in case. "Anyone recognize her?" He glanced around at the growing crowd of toms, who had begun to creep forward as one, for a better look. "Let's give her space to breathe, shall we?"

The guys backed up, and I rolled my eyes as they sniffed the air dramatically. Still, their curiosity was understandable. It wasn't every day we met a new tabby. In fact, that had only happened once in my lifetime—with Manx, who'd promptly discharged her nine millimeter into Jace's shoulder.

But this tabby was unarmed. And obviously unconscious. And completely unfamiliar.

There were only ten U.S. Prides, each of which had at most one dam and one tabby—all of whom I knew personally. But I didn't know this tabby. Whoever she was, she wasn't ours.

When none of the toms or other Alphas recognized her, my father's frown deepened. "Danny, what can you tell us about her?"

Dr. Carver stepped forward, a forgotten bowl of Froot Loops in one hand. He set the bowl on the nearest end table and wiped his hands on his pants, then knelt next to the tabby.

The doc started his examination by running his hands over the unconscious cat, pausing several times to part her fur and look closer. "Well, she's young," he said, fingers working their way from her right flank to her shoulder. "Midteens, I'm guessing, though I can't be sure without seeing her in human form."

I'd had the same thought, based on her size; she was small, even for a tabby.

"What on earth is a teenage tabby doing alone in the woods?" Calvin Malone demanded, taking up a position at my father's side, probably to place himself within the sphere of authority. "And in free territory, at that? Not to mention *bruin* territory. Where is her family? *Who* is her family?"

He'd said what we were surely all thinking. Tabby cats don't grow on trees. Most dams wind up giving birth to several toms before finally conceiving the tabby necessary to continue her family line. No Pride in the world would let its tabby—the very key to its future—run around unsupervised in the free zone.

Trust me; I've tried.

"That, I don't know," the doc said in response to Malone's likely rhetorical question. He peered up at Keller. "Where did you say you found her?"

"Out behind my place, sniffin' through the trash."

"And how did she get this?" Dr. Carver parted the fur on the back of the tabby's head to reveal a large purple lump, actually throbbing with her heartbeat.

Keller flushed beneath the thick fuzz on his weathered cheeks. "She got all riled up when I tried to get hold of her. See?" He held up his right arm, which was bleeding through several long rips in his flannel shirt. "I had to whack her on the back of the head with a piece of firewood just to get a good grip on her."

I wasn't sure whether to scowl or laugh at his approach to taming the shrew. Nor was I quite sure what to think of Keller's willingness to whack the shit out of a tabby he mistook for me.

"I think she was lookin' for food. I wish she'd just knocked on the door. I'd gladly 'ave given her some fresh deer meat."

Dr. Carver smiled, wordlessly reassuring the bruin that he'd done no harm. "I think she'll be fine. I don't think it's fractured. She should wake up soon, but we'll need to keep an eye on her until then." He glanced up at my father, then over at Paul Blackwell. "Where do you want to put her?"

Daddy shrugged at Blackwell. "It's your lodge."

Blackwell nodded. "Colin, clean out your room. You're sleeping on the couch tonight." He glanced at my father. "He's leaving tomorrow anyway."

"Paul—" Colin started from the kitchen doorway, where he was standing with an ice pack pressed to his jaw over the lump I'd given him.

Blackwell frowned, and I was kind of impressed by how stern the old man looked, in spite of the frailness of age.

"Now." Like the rest of us, he knew that if Colin had chick-ened out while defending his boss, the southwest territory would be looking for a new Alpha.

Colin stomped up the stairs to pack his bags, looking for all the world like a spoiled preschooler. A very *large* pre-schooler. I'd have gladly given up a week of my freedom to see the look on his face when his sire found out why Black-well was sending him home.

"Greg, could you send someone for my medical kit, please?" Dr. Carver said, circling the coffee table to examine the tabby's underbelly. "I left it in your cabin."

"Of course." My father scanned the faces still staring rapt at the tabby. "Jace?"

Jace handed the bread knife to Nate and headed out the front door without a word, trailed by Michael, since they weren't supposed to go out alone. Shortly after they left, a buzzer went off in the kitchen, and Nate scurried to take the lasagnas out of the oven before they burned.

After that, Keller excused himself, and as the other Alphas shooed their men from the crowded room, I made my way slowly toward the tabby, expecting someone to stop me any minute. When no one did, I sank to my knees next to Dr. Carver and reached out hesitantly to touch her fur. My curi-osity was trumped only by my sympathy for the prone tabby, who was in pretty bad shape, above and beyond the fresh lump on her head.

Dr. Carver smiled as I stroked her side gently. "What do you think? Any guess as to her age?"

"Young." I frowned as my fingers skimmed ribs far too delicate and pronounced. "*Too* young." In cat form, she was about the same size as my cousin Abby, which worried me more than I wanted to admit. Abby was seventeen and a half, but very petite; at a glance, she could pass for twelve.

Surely the tabby wasn't *that* young. What the hell was she doing alone in the Rockies?

I inched closer to the table, one hand hovering over my still-tender abdomen, and my jeans whispered across the worn carpet. "She's so thin," I said, carefully working a cocklebur free from the fur over her left flank. "Why is she so thin?"

Glass clinked against glass in the kitchen as someone pulled bottles from the refrigerator. Dinner was almost done, but for once I wasn't thinking about my stomach. I was thinking about the tabby, who clearly needed food worse than I did.

Dr. Carver's eyes found mine again. "She's malnourished. Half-starved. And this kind of damage doesn't happen quickly. Either whoever's supposed to be watching out for her is guilty of long-term neglect, or she's been on her own for quite a while."

My fingers skimmed a patch of fur matted around a clump of something soft and sour smelling. "How long?"

"A few weeks at least. See here?" The doc ran his hand backward across her fur, revealing a patch of dry, scaly skin. "She's peeling. And look how bloated her stomach is."

Her belly *was* a little poochy, in contrast to her otherwise bony appearance. A devastating pang of sympathy rang through me, bringing tears to my eyes. But an instant later my pity was replaced by blazing anger. Whoever this tabby was, she hadn't simply winked into existence. Some tom had sired her, and some dam had given birth to her.

Someone, somewhere was responsible for this poor girl, and someone was going to pay for the sorry state she was in.

I would see to that personally if I had to.

"What happened here?" My mood sank even further as I lifted her left front paw to show him an open wound oozing a thin, clear fluid.

"She cut it on something, probably glass from someone's trash can, if that's how she's been feeding herself. It's infected, and since she's malnourished, it won't heal. Not until we can get some nutrients into her, anyway." The doc stroked her side, petting her like he might a scared kitten. "Something tells me she won't want much to do with us once she wakes up, so I'm going to do what I can for her now. Want to help?"

I nodded, mute, my head spinning as I tried to figure out what had happened to her. How the hell had a cat so small and young survived on her own long enough to become so malnourished?

Jace and Michael returned with the medical kit just as Nate yelled for everyone to grab a plate. While the toms formed a line behind the Alphas for dinner, I stayed on the floor with Dr. Carver, taking the supplies he handed me as he dug them one at a time from his bag.

Several minutes later, as I shone a flashlight at the tabby's paw so the doc could see better, Marc sank onto the couch at my back and held a full plate of food toward me. "Here." He nudged my shoulder with the plate rim. "I brought you some dinner. You should eat."

"Thanks." I glanced at him long enough to see the concern in his eyes, and to know it was for me, not for the tabby. "You go ahead. I'll eat when we're done here."

"The food'll be gone by then."

"Then I'll grab something else. I want to help." I couldn't have said *why* I wanted to assist the doctor, but the urge was there, nonetheless. I couldn't get up to stuff my face while this poor young tabby lay unconscious on the table, thin to the point of emaciation, with knots in her fur and unhealed wounds on her feet. It wouldn't be right.

Still… "I'd love a Coke, though, if you don't mind."

"Sure." Marc set the plate of food on the middle couch cushion, to save his place, then marched into the kitchen like a man on a mission. I smiled as I watched him, amused by how happy he was with a task to perform, until my father crossed my field of vision. He carried his dinner to an armchair against the far wall, where he sat and balanced his plate on his lap.

As an Alpha, my father could have demanded a seat at the kitchen table, where he could easily have kept an eye on me while eating in comfort. Yet he came into the living room, not to monitor me, but to *watch* me. To observe me and study my motives. And he looked pleased, which drew an odd blush of pride from me.

Though I'd never given his disapproval of my wardrobe, my big mouth, and my craving for independence much thought, his opinion of me as a person—as a possible *successor*—well, that meant the world.

The approval in his eyes was worth listening to my stomach growl for a few more minutes.

Marc returned with my soda and sat on the couch behind me. In the kitchen, Jace sat around the table with Lucas, Michael, and my uncle Rick, all of them watching as I helped Dr. Carver clean the tabby's paw and treat it with some kind of goopy cream and a gauze wrap. Everyone else had filed into the dining room, where there was space at the long table for fourteen.

When Dr. Carver and I had done what we could for the tabby, he carried her upstairs to the bedroom Colin had vacated for her at the end of the hall, and I followed, carrying his supplies. When he had her settled on the bed, he thanked me for my help and sent me downstairs to grab some dinner.

I was loath to leave because I wanted to be there when the tabby opened her eyes. But I went because I didn't want my growling stomach to be what woke her up.

However, I was only halfway through the hunk of lasagna Marc had set aside for me when a thump shook the ceiling over my head, followed by a roar and a vicious, frightened growl. Dr. Carver screamed, and every cat still in the lodge jumped to his feet, until my father called a halt and nodded for Marc to follow him and my uncle upstairs.

While they were gone, the rest of us listening in absolute silence, Blackwell and Malone emerged from the dining room demanding answers. Before anyone could tell them we had no idea what had happened, a door closed on the second floor and Dr. Carver appeared on the stairs, a bloodstained towel wrapped around one arm.

"What happened?" I asked when he settled into the kitchen chair next to me. The Alphas gathered around the table and I felt all eyes on us.

"She woken up, and I must have startled her, because she took a swipe at me. Cut my arm wide open." Dr. Carver lifted the towel gingerly to expose three bloody claw marks bisecting the top of his forearm.

"Wow." I inhaled sharply. "You're going to need stitches."

"If only there were a doctor in the house…" Carver laughed, his tone heavily ironic. He had a pretty good attitude for a man bleeding so heavily.

I shrugged. "Marc's done his fair share of emergency stitching…" Lots of the guys had, actually, but other than my mother's and Carver's own, Marc's stitches were the neatest I'd ever seen.

"Marc?" my father called, and Marc stepped forward with the doctor's supply bag already in hand. I kicked a chair out for him and he sat, already pulling out disinfectant and a wicked-looking curved suture needle.

"I had to tranquilize her," Dr. Carver explained, as if to distract himself as Marc poured peroxide over the cuts. Evidently doctors don't make very good patients. "But it should wear off in a few hours. Let's hope she's in a better mood then, because I'm going to have to treat her sooner rather than later."

"I don't think you should go in there alone, if she's dangerous," Uncle Rick said.

"Surely she's not *dangerous*." I scowled. "She's probably just scared, and Dr. Carver *said* he startled her."

"I see no reason to take that chance," Malone said.

My father nodded, turning to the doctor. "I agree. When she wakes up, we'll send several toms in with you, in case she needs to be restrained or tranquilized again."

Dr. Carver frowned. "I'm afraid that won't make her very easy to care for. Or very willing to cooperate."

"That's better than having anyone else injured." Uncle Rick leaned against the kitchen door frame. "We need all the able-bodied toms we can get right now, so no one goes into the tabby's room alone. Understood?"

We all nodded, but Dr. Carver looked just as frustrated as I felt. And something told me the tabby wouldn't take the news any better.

Fourteen

"Faythe!" A cold hand touched my arm as a whispered breath brushed my ear. "Faythe, wake up."

My eyes opened, then closed when they met only darkness. The sun wasn't up yet, and neither was I. Instead of answering, I snuggled closer to the warm body pressed against my chest, stomach, and legs, too tired to care who I'd curled up next to, since I was still fully clothed.

"Faythe, come on!" the voice whispered again, begging that time.

I sucked in a deep breath to give the rest-stealer a piece of my mind, but froze instead when the scent of the body in front of me penetrated my exhausted, medicated brain.

Jace? I'd slept in *Jace's* bed? Or had he slept in mine?

Either way, this was very, very bad. My father was going to have *kittens* when he found out, which wouldn't be long, considering someone had just discovered us together. If I was going to screw everything up by sleeping with Jace, I should at *least* have some really hot memories to balance out my father's fury. Not to mention Marc's...

Wait. If I'd spent the night with Jace, why was I still

dressed? And why couldn't I remember what we'd done? More important, would I get away with blaming this on the pain pills?

"Faythe…"

"I'm up," I mumbled, rubbing sleep from my eyes. I rolled onto my back carefully, then went still again as a warm, heavy arm draped across my ribs. From my *other* side.

Who the hell is that?

One whiff gave me the answer. *Marc*. I was in bed with Marc *and* Jace? *I should sure as* hell *have some memory of that!*

Wait… Whose bed were we in? And more important, what the *hell* was I thinking?

Moving slowly this time, I completed my rollover and my cousin Lucas's red curls came into focus, backlit with light from the living room. As soon as I saw him, the requisite memories slid into place, along with a pang of mild disappointment.

Nothing bad had happened with Marc and Jace—nothing good either, for that matter—and we were in Nate's bed. Nate and his roommate were on the nightshift in the woods, still searching for the strays and the missing humans.

The young tabby had still been unconscious when my father was ready to retire for the evening, so I'd asked to stay in the lodge. I wanted to be there when she woke up because she would no doubt be frightened by the strange surroundings and the gaggle of unknown toms ready to hold her down and sedate her.

My father let me stay at the lodge because Marc and Jace said they'd stay with me, and Nate and his roommate offered us their room. And because Dr. Carver had removed my stitches an hour earlier, proclaiming my recovery to be right on schedule. But since the guys wouldn't sleep in the same bed, and neither were willing to let the other sleep in *my* bed, we wound up snuggled together on the two twin mattresses, pushed together to form one big bed. Another potential catastrophe averted by a werecat's affinity for lying around in big piles.

Naturally, I got stuck on the crack in the middle.

"What's wrong?" I whispered, blinking sleep from my eyes as I removed Marc's arm carefully to keep from waking him.

"Dr. Carver's asking for you. The tabby woke up again."

Sleep fog drained from my body, leaving me alert and cold. I was up in an instant, using my werecat's balance and stealth to crawl from the bed without disturbing either of the toms sandwiching me. Or reopening my own half-healed wounds.

Standing, I straightened my shirt and tugged my jeans into place, staring in regret at the bed I'd just left. It wasn't every day I got to sleep between two such yummy morsels of masculinity, and part of me wanted to crawl right back between them. But the rest of me was too curious about the strange young tabby to give up the chance to see her while everyone else was sleeping.

I trailed Lucas into the living room, then detoured into the bathroom before following him upstairs, where Dr. Carver waited in the hall outside her bedroom. "When did she wake up?"

The doc rubbed the bandage on his arm absently. "I heard her moving around about half an hour ago, but I just listened for a while, because she was pacing." A pacing werecat is either nervous or upset—or both—and *not* to be approached. "When she settled down, I opened the door a crack. She was curled up in one corner, and she started hissing at me. I told her who I am, and that I wasn't going to hurt her. But when I tried to open the door farther, she started hissing and growling."

"I take it she hasn't Shifted yet?"

"No. I asked her to, but I can't even tell if she understands me. She just stares at me and swishes her tail." He paused, and tucked his injured arm behind his back, as if out of sight really meant out of mind. "Anyway, I thought the scent of another tabby might help calm her down…"

My pulse spiked in excitement. "You want me to go in with

you guys?" I'd never expected to get more than another peek at her until the Alphas had pronounced her safe to approach.

"No."

I twisted to find Marc on the top step, Lucas towering over him from behind, though he was one tread lower.

Marc marched toward us, censure heavy in each step. "Faythe's still recovering from a serious injury, and she is *not* going to get another one on my watch."

Irritated, I propped both hands on my hips. "I can speak for myself."

He nodded. "So long as you say something sensible."

Before I could start yelling, Dr. Carver cleared his throat to get our attention. "Marc…" His fingers picked uneasily at the edge of his bandage. "We need to know who the tabby is, and I don't think she'll talk to any of the toms. But more important, she needs food and medical treatment, and I doubt she'll take either until she feels safe. I can't even get her to Shift. Faythe is probably the only one of us she'll trust, at least at first."

"Then go get Greg's permission." Marc stopped three feet from the doctor, clearly prepared to stand his ground. "He'll see your point, and probably go in there with you both."

Carver sighed, and suddenly looked very tired. "I'm afraid she won't cooperate—even with Faythe—with the rest of us standing around ready to knock her out the first time she twitches. She needs to feel safe, not threatened."

My blood raced, my skin tingling in excitement. He wanted me to go in alone!

"Absolutely *not*." Marc's eyes went hard. "He'd never let Faythe confront a feral cat alone while she's still injured from her last adventure."

The doc closed his eyes briefly, then opened them to meet Marc's. "Exactly."

"And if *I* let her, he'll have my head." Since Marc was the senior ranking enforcer present, in theory, if he gave me an order, I'd have to follow it. Of course, in practice that didn't always work out very well—for *him*. "And there's no telling what the rest of the council would do. I value *both* of our lives too much to risk finding out."

"What about *her* life?" Dr. Carver tossed his head toward the closed bedroom door. "That tabby's emaciated and dangerously dehydrated. She has a concussion and an infected laceration on one paw. She needs food, water and medical attention. Immediately. If you wake Greg up, he'll say no out of an understandable but overprotective need to keep his daughter safe. But the tabby's the one who will suffer."

"So you're willing to risk Faythe's life to help some cat you don't even know?"

I gaped at Marc, surprised by how callous he sounded. "She's not just *some cat*. She's practically a child. A sick, scared child who probably has no idea where she is or how she got here." Not to mention the fact that she was a tabby. Some Alpha's *daughter*. And whoever her father was, he would *not* be pleased to know we let her suffer, especially out of cowardice.

When Marc appeared unmoved by my argument, Dr. Carver stepped in again, the dim light from the hall fixture shining on his short brown beard. "Faythe won't be in any real danger, Marc. We'll be right here with tranquilizers, and if anything goes wrong, we can sedate the tabby and get Faythe out immediately."

"Why don't you just shoot her up now and force her Shift?" Marc asked.

"Because I need her responsive to properly treat her. I don't have the supplies for an IV with me, so she'll need to take liquids and medication orally. If I *have* to knock her out again, I will, but I'm leaving that as a last resort."

Finally, I saw conflict in Marc's eyes. It wasn't that he didn't care about the tabby, but that he cared too much about me to let me risk injury—even to help a scared young woman. But I couldn't leave her alone and suffering, even long enough for the Alphas to argue their way to a decision. My mind kept returning to the memory of my cousin Abby, alone and scared in a basement prison, and I just couldn't do it.

I turned my back on Marc to face the doc. "What do you need me to do? Get her to Shift?"

Dr. Carver nodded. "For starters. Then talk her into letting me treat her. And her name would come in handy too."

"Got it."

Marc scowled, an impressive imitation of my father. "Faythe…"

I whirled on him, irritation sparking in my veins. "I'm going in there to help her. You can either stay here and watch my back—and you know there's no one I trust more—or you can go tattle and get us all in trouble."

"The shit will hit the fan anyway, once the Alphas wake up. You're just delaying the inevitable."

"Precisely. By the time they find out, the tabby will be eating breakfast—in human form—and ready to spill her guts. And I'll be safe and sound. That has to count for something."

Marc sighed, and I knew I'd won. He'd just told my father that I needed to take on more responsibility, and he wasn't about to go tattle on me now for doing that very thing. "I'll be right here listening, and if she takes so much as a *step* in your direction, I'm pulling you out of there, so stay clear of the door. Got it?"

I nodded. "Fine."

"And you're going to take something to defend yourself with. Where's that damn meat mallet?" He glanced pointedly at Lucas, who took off immediately for the stairs.

"Stop it, Lucas." I glared at Marc. "She's never going to trust anyone who comes in wielding a weapon."

Marc rubbed his forehead, as if staving off a headache. "At least take one of those damn tranquilizers."

"Done." I could live with that. "Where…?"

Dr. Carver pulled a red-capped syringe from the pocket of his khakis and set it in my outstretched palm. "Loaded and ready to go," he said as I slipped the slim needle into the hip pocket of my jeans. "Be careful not to break it."

"No problem."

I reached for the doorknob, and the first threads of doubt wound through me, in spite of my bravado for Marc's sake. Even the smallest, least experienced tabby cat in the world could do serious damage to an unarmed human if provoked. Dr. Carver's arm was proof of that. Sucking in a deep breath, I wrapped my hand around the knob. "Here goes nothing."

I turned the knob, pushed open the door, and stepped into the room, pleased to note that Dr. Carver had left the light on. No furry black blur leapt out of nowhere to maul me, so I exhaled in relief and closed the door. *So far, so good.*

For a moment, I stood still and silent, taking in the two twin beds, each beneath a small window, and identical plywood nightstands. Between the beds was a bare strip of wall and an oval braided rug. Against opposite walls sat cheap matching dressers, one for each theoretical occupant. Other than that, the room looked empty. The tabby was either under one of the beds or in the closet.

As the sound of my own rushing pulse faded from my ears, it was replaced by a low-pitched rumbling sound. The tabby was growling at me.

Suddenly I wished I'd knocked before opening the door. I didn't like it when people walked into my bedroom unannounced, so why should she?

"Um…hi," I said, still scanning the apparently empty room. "Where are you? Under the bed?" I took a step forward, and reached to lift the blanket draping the nearest bed, but before I could, the growling grew louder and its source moved. She wasn't under the bed; she was between it and the right-hand wall.

One more step forward, and I could see her. She lay curled up in the corner, every muscle tense, her head high and alert. Her ears swiveled in my direction, to best catch the sounds of my approach. With each breath, her chest rose and fell, ribs standing out in the glare from the light overhead.

I squatted slowly, to put myself on her level, and big greenish eyes followed my movement. "My name is Faythe, and I'd really like to help you. Can I get you anything? Something to eat?" She *had* to be hungry.

Though her eyes never left my face, the tabby stopped growling, and I took that as a sign she understood me. *Love, my ass. The international language is* food.

Encouraged by the fact that she hadn't yet tried to kill me, I took another step forward—then froze in place when her growl rumbled back to life.

Okaaaayy, we'll take it very slooowly.

"You know, this would be much easier if you would Shift. That way you could actually *tell* me what you want to eat. Or your name. Or exactly how far you'd like me to shove this olive branch up my ass."

The tabby snorted. She was laughing! "Aaaah, you *do* understand me." I smiled, and pride bubbled up inside me. *I bet Dr. Carver didn't get her to laugh. Or even listen.* "So what do you say about Shifting? If you're worried about your clothes, I'm sure I have something you can wear for now."

The tabby's eyes narrowed, an oddly human gesture, but perfectly understandable, especially once she cocked her head to one side. "You don't understand me?" I paused, as another possibility occurred to me. "Or you don't like what I'm saying… Is it the clothes? You don't want to wear my clothes?"

That made sense. Werecats have very sensitive noses, even in human form, and she'd be surrounded by my scent if she wore my clothes, even if they came right out of the dryer. I wouldn't want to walk around smelling like anyone else. *Except maybe Marc…*

"I can send someone out for new clothes, if you want. And you can wear a sheet or a towel in the meantime. Would that work?"

She tilted her head again, and I frowned. Maybe she really didn't understand me…

"I need a sign that you know what I'm saying. How 'bout a head nod? Nod your head if you understand me." Of course, if she didn't want to do that either, I'd never know whether we were having a communication problem, or she was just stubborn.

The tabby nodded hesitantly.

"Good. Wonderful." *Now we're getting somewhere.* "Okay, are my clothes the problem? You don't want to wear my clothes? Nod for yes, shake your head for no."

This time she just stared at me, not moving her head in either direction. *Hmm.* Maybe my questions weren't very clear. She'd responded to the mention of food earlier…

"Are you hungry?" I asked, and the tabby nodded in slow, exaggerated motions. *Awesome.* "Can I send someone to the kitchen for food?"

Instead of nodding, she glanced at the door. In cat form, she could probably hear them breathing, whereas I only heard feet shuffle on carpet as they listened to our one-sided conversation.

"So, no food? Or no *guys?* You want me to get it myself?" I backed toward the door, and the tabby swung her head back and forth vehemently, rising to sit on her haunches. "No? You want me to stay?"

Her head bobbed again, and a smile stole over my face. She liked me. Or she at least preferred me to a group of strange men. Either way, it was a good start.

"How 'bout lasagna? I think there's some left from supper."

The tabby shook her head, so I tried again. "Chicken? We had fried chicken last night."

She nodded again, and the tips of my fingers tingled in excitement. Accepting food from me meant she was starting to trust me. Either that, or she was starving, and the clear view of every one of her ribs told me which answer was more likely. "Okay, I'll be right back. I'm just going to give your order to the waiter. Okay?"

After a moment's hesitation, she nodded reluctantly, and I slipped into the hall before she could change her mind.

"What happened?" Carver asked the minute the door closed behind me. He and Lucas stood across from the door, eyeing me eagerly. Marc stood to the left, syringe in one fist, ready to burst in, should I need him. But I was pretty sure I wouldn't now.

"She's hungry." I stuck my hands in my pockets and glanced up at Lucas. "Could you stick some of that leftover chicken in the microwave?"

"Sure. Potatoes too?"

"Nah. I think she wants meat." He nodded and took off down the hall, and I turned to Marc and the doctor, who was practically humming with excited energy. "She's still in the corner, but she's trying to communicate."

"She ready to Shift yet?" Marc asked, clearly less than pleased with my progress.

"We haven't gotten that far." I ran my finger down a groove in the rough wall paneling. "But she's answering yes or no questions."

"She's not violent?"

"Of course not!" I scowled at Marc until he nodded pointedly toward Dr. Carver's arm, and I had to concede his point. *Damn it.* "She hasn't lifted a paw against me. She's just scared and hungry, but I'm sure I can get her to open up." I was also sure she was listening to every word we said.

"Well, hurry up then," Marc snapped, crossing his arms over his chest. "It'd be nice to have something concrete to show your father when he's trying to decide whether or not to skin us alive for this."

He was right, so I slipped back into the bedroom, pleased to see the tabby still sitting on her haunches, watching the door for my return. "Your chicken's coming." I headed for the nearest bed, and her eyes followed my progress. When she voiced no objection to my approach, I settled onto the mattress and tucked my feet beneath me. We were now separated only by several feet of empty floor space.

"Are you cold?" I asked, remembering how frigid the floor-boards were against my bare feet.

She nodded, and curled her tail around her body.

I started to tug the blanket from the bed beneath me, but stopped when the tabby started growling. Again. "Sorry." *You must not be too cold.*

"You know, I like to talk as much as the next girl, but con-versation really is a two-player game. I'd love it if you could Shift back and talk to me. Maybe tell me your name? You do have a name?"

She nodded again.

"Good. I'd love to hear it. So, you feel like Shifting back?" I leaned forward in anticipation of an answer.

The tabby's head tilted to one side again, and my finger-nails bit into my palms in frustration. What didn't she under-stand? These were not hard questions!

"Okay, let's see if we can figure out where we're going wrong. 'Kay?" She nodded, so I continued, twisting one corner of the blanket between my fingers. "You have a name. Do you want to tell me your name?"

Another nod.

Good. She was still trying to cooperate. "You're gonna *have* to Shift to tell me your name, because I'm really no good at charades. And honestly, I'd much rather hear your voice. So…do you want to Shift?"

Again she cocked her head to one side, this time following the familiar gesture with a whine of frustration. I knew exactly how she felt.

Hmm. She looks confused when I mention Shifting. Maybe her Pride called it something different. That was pretty unlikely, if she was born in North America. But then, if she were a North American cat, I'd probably already *know* who she was.

"Do you know what I mean by 'Shift'? Do you know what I'm asking you to do?" We were close to a breakthrough; I could feel it.

She shook her head firmly from side to side, sitting straighter, as if eager for my explanation.

I didn't even know I was holding my breath until it burst from my throat. Now *we're getting somewhere*. The problem lay with the terminology. "I'm talking about your transformation. Changing yourself from cat form to human form. We call it Shifting. I want you to Shift into your human form so we can talk like people, without all this nodding and whining. Does that help?"

The tabby shook her head again, and my own fell into my palms with the dull slap of flesh against flesh. "I don't know how else to say it. I need you to Shift. Just…turn yourself back into a human." My hands flailed in the air, in search of a gesture to get my meaning across. "You know…hands, semi-opposable thumbs, articulate tongue, the whole thing. Now. Please."

Instead of answering, the tabby lowered her head to the floor and curled into a ball. She wasn't even looking at me anymore. I'd been dismissed. Damn it.

What's the big deal? I demanded silently, barely able to hold the words inside. *It's just Shifting.* Even if she was only fourteen—though that was *waaaaaay* too young to be out on her own—she'd probably already done it dozens of times.

Though she'd likely never Shifted in a strange place, with some strange woman watching her. I, of all people, should have been able to sympathize with those circumstances. Especially if she had some kind of stage fright, like Abby'd had in Miguel's basement…

Of course. She's too upset or scared to Shift. Just like Abby.

"Are you scared? Is that the problem?" Without waiting for her response, I rose from the mattress and sank onto my knees fewer than five feet from the tabby.

Her ears perked up when the bedsprings creaked, but she didn't look up. She was ignoring me like a damn toddler.

"Hey. I'm trying to help you. I have a cousin about your age." At least, I *hoped* she was as old as Abby. "Several months ago, she and I found ourselves in a very scary situation. We…" I hesitated, unsure how much to tell her. I didn't want to frighten her further. But then I realized she was watching me, actively listening again, so I continued. "We thought we were going to die. We needed to Shift into cat form to protect ourselves, but Abby was too scared to Shift, and just thinking about that made it worse." I paused, meeting the tabby's eyes with what I hoped was frank concern on my part. "Is that what's happening here? Are you scared?"

Sitting up now, the tabby nodded, but before I could get my hopes up, she shook her head in the negative, just as firmly.

Yes *and* no? Or did that mean she wasn't sure? Wait, I'd just asked two questions at once. The poor thing was trying to answer them both. "I'm sorry. One question at a time. Are you scared?"

A single, short nod. So far, so good.

"Is that why you can't Shift?"

She shook her head.

Damn it. I was running out of yes-or-no questions.

"Okay, you're scared, but that's not why you're not Shifting." I ticked that morsel of knowledge off on my index finger, then moved on to my middle finger. "And you know what Shifting is, so…"

Movement caught the corner of my eye and I looked up to see the tabby shaking her head back and forth so hard I thought she'd fall over.

"Wait, you don't know what Shifting is? Didn't we just cover this? Shifting is what we call the transformation from one form to another. Maybe your Pride calls it something else." Shit. Was her Pride even called a Pride? Was it possible we were speaking two completely different languages?

Encouraged by the curiosity obvious in her eyes, I edged forward cautiously. "Do you have a Pride?" She shook her head again, so I forged on. "Okay, they probably call it something different. But you live with a group of other werecats, right? Your dad's the boss—the Alpha—and your mom's the dam? And you probably have several big brothers? I only have four, but most tabbies have five or six…" My voice faded into silence. She'd been shaking her head steadily through my last few questions.

A weird, antsy feeling sizzled in my stomach, surging upward like acid reflux as I watched the tabby stare at me steadily. She didn't live with a Pride? How was that possible? Surely I was misunderstanding…*something*.

"You…" I wasn't even sure how to approach the swarm of questions swirling in my head. There were too many to grasp. "Your father's not an Alpha?" She shook her head again, once, and I exhaled slowly. That was rare, but by no means unheard of. Jace's father wasn't an Alpha; he was dead. And I'd once heard about an Alpha who was deposed for failure to act in the best interest of his Pride, which was basically what Malone was accusing my father of. Though that charge was completely unfounded.

Okay, so her father wasn't an Alpha. "Your mother's a dam, though, right?" There was really no way around that one—once a tabby had children, she was a dam by definition. Yet the tabby shook her head, again, and I steeled myself to ask what was possibly the most difficult question I'd ever had to pose to anyone. "Did your mother die?"

The tabby blinked at me slowly and lowered her chin to rest on one paw. After a moment, she lifted her head and nodded, then set it back down.

Damn. She was an orphan. The only other orphaned tabby I'd ever met was Manx—who was fully grown—and thinking about Manx made me wonder if *this* tabby's mother had died in whatever incident removed her father from their Pride. Still, orphan or not, she was born into a Pride *some*where, and no Pride would give up its tabby, even if they'd lost—or over-thrown—her parents.

She's a runaway. I should have realized it earlier. I'd done enough running myself to recognize the signs, and she had obviously been on her own for quite some time. But the immediate question, at least as I saw it, was whether we had any right to turn her over to a Pride she clearly wanted no part of.

"Honey…" *Damn, I wish I knew her name!* "I'm not going to let anyone hurt you. We won't send you anywhere you don't want to go. I swear on my own life. You're safe here. Do you understand?"

She lifted her head long enough to nod one more time.

"Good. Do you want—" A knock on the door preceded the aroma of fried chicken, and my mouth watered instantly. The tabby wasn't the only hungry girl in the room. "That's your food," I said, already headed for the door.

As I let Lucas in, I kept one hand on the doorknob, prepared to shut it quickly if the tabby freaked out at the sight of another tom. But she made no sound as the door creaked open and didn't even growl when Lucas stepped past me into the room, a huge plateful of chicken pieces in one hand. Evidently hunger superseded any residual fear and misgivings.

"She still hasn't Shifted?" A frown marred Lucas's curiosity as he brushed a red ringlet from his forehead. He'd probably been hoping for the first glimpse of our guest in human form.

I followed his gaze to the tabby, who sat watching us alertly, her eyes on the food in his hands. "Yeah, there seems to be a bit of confusion on that point. I don't think she understands what I want her to do."

He handed me the plate. "Like, she doesn't know how to Shift? How is that possible?"

"It's not. She can't possibly—" I froze, the plate hot in my hand. "Son of a bitch!"

The problem wasn't that she didn't know what I wanted her to do, but that she didn't know *how* to do what I wanted.

Somehow, as impossible as the concept seemed to me, the tabby didn't know how to Shift.

Fifteen

Eager to explore my new theory, I ushered Lucas from the room much more quickly than he wanted to go, without updating Marc or the doc. I closed the door on them all and turned back to the tabby, the platter of chicken cradled in both hands. "Do you mind if I join you?"

She made no response, which I took as consent. Honestly, though, by that point, I would have taken anything short of an outright attack as consent.

I made my way to the tabby slowly, giving her time to warn me if she got cold paws. But her eyes didn't leave the plate until I set it on the bare floor between us.

The tabby glanced from the chicken to me, asking permission to eat. In a hunt, the highest-ranking werecat eats first, like the male in a pride of lions. But something told me that wasn't what she had in mind. She was using plain old human manners, taught by someone who cared about not only her physical well-being but her upbringing.

How had she gone from that to this? From loving parents who taught her manners, to eating leftover fried chicken in cat form on the floor of a rented lodge with a perfect stranger?

I nodded toward the food as I sat cross-legged on the floor, across the plate from her. For several minutes, we ate in silence. In the time it took me to eat a single breast, she polished off a breast and two drumsticks, skin and all, licking the last of the flesh from the second leg bone with one end of it pinned to the floor by her front paw.

She definitely *ate* like a werecat, even if she seemed to know nothing about us.

Three wings and a thigh later, when the tabby started to slow, I drew my knees to my chest and wrapped my arms around them. "I have some more questions, if you're up to it." I rocked back and forth slowly as she licked her right front paw, then used it to clean her muzzle. "Is that okay?"

She nodded, and a small bud of satisfaction blossomed in my chest—pride in myself for earning her trust, and a little edge of confidence. Or maybe that was heartburn from the chicken...

Inhaling slowly, I crossed my mental fingers, hoping I'd truly hit upon the problem with our method of communication. "Do you know how to Shift?" The tabby's head swiveled back and forth firmly, and I exhaled. "Do you know what Shifting *is?*"

This time the tabby nodded, but very slowly. Hesitantly. Just as I'd expected. She let her paw fall to the floor, abandoning her grooming efforts altogether. I had her full attention now that the food was gone.

"Did you know what Shifting was before tonight? Before I came in here to talk to you?"

She shook her head, and I dared a small smile. I was starting to get a clearer picture, though I couldn't for my life understand how she could have Shifted into werecat form without knowing what Shifting *was*. Maybe she'd been alone and starving so long she'd contracted some sort of Shifter amnesia. Weirder things have happened, right?

Okay, maybe not.

"Do you remember Shifting into your current form?" I

asked. She cocked her head again, punctuating her confusion with a soft whine. Hmm. "Do you remember being a human? A girl, like me?"

The tabby nodded, slowly at first, then more enthusiastically, as if she'd just discovered the very memories I spoke of.

I sat straighter as an exciting possibility pinged through me, making my skin tingle and my heart beat faster.

"Good. Now…do you remember being scratched or bitten by a big black cat?" She shook her head, but I pushed on because even if she *had* been infected by another werecat, she probably wouldn't remember the actual attack, or much of what happened next, including scratch fever and her initial Shift.

Her memory loss, while frustrating, was pretty common for newly infected strays and did not, in itself, rule out the possibility that she was one.

But tabbies are *girls,* and though the existence of a female stray hadn't technically been ruled out, it had never been proven either.

In all of werecat history, the only mention I'd ever heard of a female stray came from Manx, who claimed to have seen one in South America, where they'd both been imprisoned by Miguel and his band of tabby-nappers. But the Territorial Council was no more willing to believe Manx's unsubstantiated claim of a scratch fevered tabby than they were willing to believe mine about the partial Shift.

But they were wrong about the partial Shift. Maybe they were wrong about female strays too…

"I'd like to try something, if you're feeling up to it." *And even if you're not…* "When my cousin Abby and I were… locked up that time, and needed to Shift for our own safety? Do you remember me mentioning that?"

She nodded.

"Well, she was nervous and had trouble Shifting, so I tried

to help her." No need to mention the fact that my help didn't actually *work*. "I can try to help you the same way, if you want."

The tabby hesitated, and I could practically track her thoughts as her gaze flitted from me, to the plate of mostly eaten food, to the soft, warm bed, back to my very human-shaped clothes. The temptation was there. Now to sweeten the pot…

"How long has it been since you walked upright?" I asked, knowing she couldn't answer with a wag of her head. "Don't you want to talk? Take a shower, and wash your hair? Maybe play some video games? Do you like PlayStation?"

She nodded, less hesitantly this time, and I wondered if she was a Rock Band player, or more the God of War kind of gal.

"If you Shift back, we can get you some clothes, and you can eat your next meal at an actual table. Where you can sit on a *chair,* and still reach the floor with your feet. How 'bout some shoes? Whatever you want, we can get it. You say the word and I'll send Lucas into town." Her eyes were glued to my face, and I could see longing in her still-feline features. "You interested?"

This time she nodded her head firmly. Eagerly. *Good girl.*

"Great. Let's get started." I set the empty plate on the nearest bed and stood, facing the cat, who still sat on her haunches. "Now, I know you don't remember Shifting into cat form this last time, but do you remember Shifting *at all?*" Might as well cover all the bases, just in case.

The tabby shook her head. I'd expected that. She truly had no idea what she was supposed to do, or what it was going to feel like. Poor girl. "Well, I have to warn you that this is gonna hurt. But I promise it's worth it. The pain is temporary, and it's nothing compared to regaining the use of your fingers and your voice box. You still up for this?"

She nodded, and while she definitely looked scared, she also looked eager. She was ready to Shift. Probably even overdue.

"Okay, the first thing I need you to do is stand up." I

dropped onto my hands and knees to demonstrate, reminding myself *not* to go through the transformation myself, as I'd done when I tried to help Abby. If I wound up as a cat while she Shifted into a human…well, she probably wouldn't like being defenseless and at my mercy.

The tabby stood two feet away facing me, and I realized with a jolt of alarm that she could now kill me easily with the swipe of one paw. If she wanted to.

She won't do it. I had little doubt about that, because if she killed me, I couldn't teach her how to Shift, and her eagerness to reassume human form was obvious. So I shoved my own fear to the back of my mind so I could concentrate on hers.

"Good. Now, the rest of this is mental. Whether you realize it or not, your body knows how to do this, and *all* you have to do is relax and let it take over." After all, she hadn't been *born* in cat form, so she'd clearly Shifted at *some* point in the recent past, whether she remembered it or not. The details were buried in her brain somewhere. They had to be.

"But just in case, we're going to give your body a little nudge in the right direction. I usually start with my feet." I wiggled the bare toes of my left foot for effect. "Or back paws, in your case. Concentrate on only that one part of your body. Feel your toes. Move them if you want. Sheathe and unsheathe your claws."

Her eyes closed, and I knew without looking that she was doing as I'd suggested.

"Good. Now, instead of your cat paws, picture your human feet. Remember what they look like. If you have any scars on your foot, think about them. Where are they? What are they shaped like? How did you get them?"

Her eyes were scrunched shut in concentration now, and I couldn't help smiling at her honest effort.

"Your toes…" I continued. "Are they long and thin, or shorter and thicker? Is your big toe the longest, or your middle toe? Picture the fine, thin hairs on your big t—"

The tabby sucked air in sharply, and it came back out as a hiss of pain. With the next breath, she mewled, deep in her throat.

Her Shift had started.

I sat on my feet, my fingernails scraping the hardwood in excitement. "It's happening, isn't it? Do your feet hurt?" For a moment, there was no answer but more mewling, with her eyes still shut tight. "Wait, now, look at me." No change.

"*Look* at me." I demanded, firmer that time. I was emulating my father now, and doing a damn fine job of it, in my own estimation.

Whether surprised into compliance by the change in my tone or desperate for more instructions, the tabby opened her eyes, staring straight into mine in pain and in growing fear.

"Do your feet hurt?" I repeated, and this time she nodded. "Good. I know this part sucks, but it's supposed to feel like that. Really. That means this is working."

She shook her head, and I sighed silently. "No, don't try to stop it. You want to be human again, don't you?"

She nodded and closed her eyes again, this time in concentration. She was trying so hard to deal with the pain, and the poor thing now had my respect, as well as my sympathy.

"You're doing great. Seriously. The next step is to push it forward, instead of pulling it back. Picture your legs, like you did your feet." Her eyes were still closed, so I leaned to the side to check her progress. There was no visible change in her yet, but I could hear the muted popping as her bones began to rearrange themselves.

To keep the pain to a minimum, she needed to Shift evenly—put each part of her body through the same stage at the same time. In short, her top half needed to catch up.

"Okay, you're still doing very well. Now let's work on your hands. Do you have long, pretty fingernails, or short stubby ones like mine?" Not that it mattered. If she'd been in cat form for a matter of weeks, rather than hours, her nails were going to be long, and likely ragged in human form. But for the sake of the imagery exercise, picturing them the way she liked them would work just as well.

Movement near the floor caught my eyes; the toes on her front paws were wiggling. She was really trying. I had a soft spot for people who did what I wanted without questions or complaints. I got that from my father, too.

Another tiny joint popped, and the tabby's right front leg buckled beneath her. Before she could shift weight onto the other leg, she overbalanced, toppling to the ground on one side.

Oops. Forgot to warn her about that part.

"Are you okay?" I stamped down the urge to pet her, to somehow comfort her—I knew better than to touch a cat in mid-Shift. As long as her cat jaws were still in place, she could take off my hand with one good bite. Even if she didn't mean to.

When she didn't answer, shaking all over now that the changes were visible, I tried again. "Hey! Nod your head if you're all right!"

She nodded, an unstable up-and-down motion in the grip of the full-body tremors that ushered in her human skeletal structure.

As I watched, her tail seemed to shrink into her spine—easily the most amazing part of the process—and the fur across her back began to recede in a broad arc, as if the follicles were sucking each hair back into her skin. I'd done it at least a thousand times, but it was still amazing to watch. Riveting. Though the tabby probably wasn't enjoying it quite so much.

Fortunately, by then she was past the point of needing my guidance. And past the point of no return, at least for such a young werecat. A more experienced cat could probably have reversed the Shift at such a late stage, if he was willing to put up with the extra pain and extended duration. But the tabby was over the hill and on the way down, with nothing to stop her progress now but completion of the transformation.

A few minutes later, her bare paws twisted and stretched into hands, and her claws thinned into fingernails, long and dirt-caked, as I'd expected. Then she went still, lying on the floor on her stomach, one leg out straight, the other bent at the knee. A long, matted mane of thick brown hair covered her head, shoulders, and much of her back. When it was clean and healthy, she would probably have one of the most beautiful heads of hair I'd ever seen. A true mane.

For several moments, she didn't move, other than the rising and falling of her chest as she panted beneath that blanket of hair, winded from the most strenuous and unique exercise she'd ever endured. I thought back to my first few Shifts, trying to remember if I'd been so exhausted, or looked so incredibly frail. I didn't think so. But then, I'd known what to expect. And I'd never in my life been as weak as she had to be, nor half as thin.

Between matted strands of hair, I saw bony shoulders stretching into a pair of arms so fragile-looking and thin that her elbows had actual corners. Her waist was impossibly tiny, and her hips so narrow I would have assumed she was prepubescent, if it wasn't impossible for a werecat to Shift before puberty sent hormones raging through a body, triggering much more than just breasts and menses.

But that was impossible. She was probably just petite, like Abby.

Or so I thought, until she lifted her head, pushing tangled strands of hair aside with one arm while she supported her slight weight with the other. Huge hazel eyes stared up at me, a little browner than they'd been in cat form, and much larger than they should have appeared because of how thin her face was. Her cheeks had more hollow than bone, and her chin looked sharp enough to draw blood.

Still, she had the makings of true beauty, and I had no doubt that once she'd put on a few pounds—like, twenty or so—she was going to break tom-hearts all over the world. And, if she was half as fierce as the gleam in her eyes suggested, she might break a few heads, too.

I liked her already.

Sixteen

I smiled at the now-human tabby and rose onto my knees, extending one hand to help her up. But as soon as I moved, she scuttled away from me on all fours, hair trailing the floor, eyes wide and frightened.

As she moved, I caught fleeting glimpses of the front of her body, and the enforcer part of my brain kicked in, looking for wounds or scars that could have come from an initial infection. She was almost certainly *not* a stray, but I didn't want to overlook any evidence in what could turn out to be a landmark case.

Unfortunately, she had no such marks. Other than odd scrapes and several deep bruises, the most serious injury I saw was the medicated gash on her hand, exposed because the bandage had fallen off during her Shift.

When her back hit the corner, the tabby hugged bare legs to her chest and stared at me over a pair of dirty, bony knees. Her focus roamed from my face to my tee, then to my faded jeans, as if seeing them for the first time. She'd seen them before, of course, but not with the full range of colors the human eye dealt with.

Then she twitched, as if with sudden understanding, and her gaze flicked back to mine. Her cheeks flushed, and she looked away, hugging her legs tighter.

She was…*embarrassed*.

My Pride—*all* Prides, as far as I knew—paid little attention to nudity associated with Shifting. And even some nudity *not* associated with Shifting. But there *were* some exceptions. My mother, for instance. As with humans, levels of comfort and acceptance varied widely, most of us falling somewhere in the middle of the spectrum, with the odd few on either end.

So it was possible that the tabby's entire Pride was more conservative regarding gratuitous nudity than we were. But this wasn't unwarranted bare skin. She'd just *Shifted*. There was no way to do that with clothes on. At least, not without ruining them.

"It's okay." I edged closer on my knees. "You did it! I knew you could." I didn't play cheerleader for just anyone, but I was hoping the pride and enthusiasm in my voice would be contagious.

The tabby said nothing. She only stared at me with those huge eyes, her chin resting on her knees. She looked shocked. Terrified. And not just of what she'd done. She looked horrified to find herself naked in front of a stranger. That was *not* the typical werecat response. Not even after a first Shift, though that couldn't possibly have been her first. She'd had to get *into* cat form somehow.

I knee-walked a step closer, and my leg came down on something sharp. "Ow, shit!" I looked down to find a cocklebur stuck in the denim over my knee. *What the hell?* I plucked it out and dropped it on the wood floor, where it landed next to another just like it. Glancing around, I found several more, and only then did I understand. They'd fallen from the tabby when the fur tangled around them receded into her skin.

Huh. Look at that.

Wary now, I scooted around the litter of cockleburs. As I drew closer, the tabby squeezed her legs tighter to her torso, her fingers going white under the strain. Her gaze skipped to my left, and I followed it with my own.

The bed. She was looking at the bed. *She wants the blanket.*

Of *course* she wanted the blanket. She was naked, and probably cold. I stood slowly to keep from frightening the tabby with sudden movements. As I pulled the top blanket from the mattress—fortunately *not* the one Colin had slept on—I deliberately turned my back to her, hoping she recognized—at least subconsciously—the demonstration of my trust. A werecat almost never turns his back on someone he doesn't trust. To do so can get you killed.

I held the blanket high as I turned, showing her I meant no harm. She let me approach, but her eyes didn't leave mine until I draped the blanket over her and left it for her to arrange it as she saw fit. The bulk of the quilted material pooled on the floor around her, and she huddled beneath one small section, looking impossibly small. Impossibly young.

"Are you warm enough?" I sat cross-legged on the floor, several feet in front of her. The tops of my feet itched, and I rubbed them, surprised to find the imprint of the wood grain still there from when I'd sat on them.

The tabby nodded, even as her teeth started chattering. I wasn't cold in the slightest. But then, I was neither underweight nor naked. "Just a minute. I'll send one of the guys to get something of mine for you to wear. We'll get you something new as soon as you decide what you want. Okay?"

She nodded again, and I smiled, trying to set her at ease as I crossed the room and opened the door just wide enough to slip through the crack, to keep from frightening her with the sight of several strange men. The guys were lined up against the opposite wall, Dr. Carver clutching his clean, bandaged arm to his chest.

Jace had joined them, and he looked irritated, probably because he'd woken up alone in an empty bed. I knew exactly how he felt. Usually *I* was the one left out of the action.

I closed the door behind myself as I stepped into the hall, and the eagerness in Jace's eyes died with the click of the latch sliding into place, but Lucas looked annoyingly smug. He was tall enough to see easily over my head and had clearly gotten a glimpse of the tabby. Suddenly I was glad I'd covered her. Seeing her naked would mean nothing special to Lucas—his curiosity was completely innocent—but it would probably mortify her.

"She Shifted!" Lucas's excitement was practically palpable, but Marc rolled his eyes. They already knew that, having heard every word we'd said for the last forty-five minutes or so.

"Yes." I glanced from face to face, and my words came out rushed with my own excitement. "I need someone to go get clothes for her from my suitcase." My gaze stopped on Marc first, because he knew where most of my stuff was and what I wouldn't mind lending out. But the steel-edged glint in his eyes told me his answer. I should have known better. He wouldn't go, not because he was worried about my safety—he trusted all the toms present—but because he wouldn't risk running into my father and having to explain what we were doing.

We'd be in enough trouble once they found out on their own.

But Jace would go. He'd go because Marc would make him. And because I would ask nicely. "Please?" I pinned him with my eyes.

"What? You leave me out of all the fun and now you want me to fetch clothes for you like some kind of fucking gofer?"

"Please," I repeated. "I'd do it myself, but I don't want to leave her alone."

"Whatever." Jace huffed, his eyes never leaving mine. "What do you want?"

I smiled my thanks at him. "Um…my black pajama bottoms, I guess. The ones with the drawstring. And a black T-shirt. And that soft, cream-colored sweater. She's in there shivering."

"Socks?"

"Yeah. Get the fuzzy ones." Something told me she'd like those. "My shoes won't fit her, so once I get her sizes someone will have to go shopping." Until then, she'd have to go without underwear, because I was *not* sharing mine. There was a limit to my generosity, after all. Fortunately, she didn't have enough up top to need a bra for comfort.

"Anything else?"

"Nope. Hurry, please." Jace took off down the hall at a jog, bare feet silent on the hardwood, and when he reached the top step I remembered the last crucial detail. "Jace!" I hissed, hoping not to wake the rest of the lodge.

He stopped, one hand already on the banister. "Yeah?"

"*Please* don't wake up my father. Or Michael." Nothing in the world could make my father's firstborn keep a secret from him.

"No worries," Jace said with that irresistible grin, his blue eyes sparkling like the sea at midday. Then he bounded down the steps, and out the front door a moment later.

"Get her name," Marc said, his voice the very essence of authority. "You need at least that by the time everyone wakes up, if you don't want to get us all in serious trouble."

"I know." *Boy,* did I know.

My hand was already on the doorknob when Dr. Carver spoke up for the first time. "You really believe she didn't know how to *Shift?*"

I met the skepticism in his eyes with certainty in my own.

"Yes. I don't know why yet, or how it's even possible, but I believe she has no memory of ever having Shifted. Her reactions are too genuine. She was legitimately scared to Shift." Which I knew because I'd heard her heart beat harder and smelled fear in her sweat as she'd prepared for the transformation.

My eyes were drawn to Marc's when I felt him watching me. He knew what I was thinking: that Elias Keller might well have stumbled upon the first female stray in recorded history. At least, the first *verifiable* female stray in history.

But neither of us said that. My reputation wasn't solid enough for me to start spouting the werecat equivalent of conspiracy theories and alien-abduction stories. I'd need concrete proof before making such claims.

"Go on," Marc said, telling me with his eyes to keep quiet.

I stepped back into the tabby's room and closed the door, and the first thing to catch my eye was not the small girl still huddled beneath a blanket in her corner. It was the window over the closest twin bed. Or rather, the first rays of sunlight peeking through said window.

Oh, shit. I glanced at my watch, dismayed when the time confirmed my suspicion. Our privacy was about to expire. Marc probably wouldn't let any of the tribunal members into the room, but he wouldn't even *try* to stop my father.

In a blink, my focus shifted from the window to the girl curled up in the corner. My opening line was already on my lips when I saw her mouth stretch open in a yawn much too big for such a small face. She was about to fall asleep. Again. She'd been out cold for hours, but I knew better than most that being unconscious isn't the least bit recuperative. You need actual sleep to feel alert and rested.

"You want to lie down?" I sank onto my knees in front of her.

She shook her head adamantly, and the harsh motion seemed to wake her up a bit. But it was only a matter of time before sleep would claim her. I didn't think anyone would wake her intentionally once she passed out, but I had to find out her name before then.

"I sent one of the guys to get some clothes for you. When he gets back, you can get dressed and curl up in the bed." She shook her head again, and I conceded. "*Or,* you can stay awake. But before he gets here, we need to talk. You can talk, right?"

She nodded solemnly, and one thin hand went to her throat, as if checking to make sure it was still there. "I thi—" Her voice broke into a hoarse croak after only two syllables. "I think s—" But again her effort ended in a dry strangling sound.

"You need something to drink?" I asked, and she nodded, her hand still pressed to the base of her dirt-streaked neck. Lucas hadn't brought a glass of anything along with the plate of chicken, and I wasn't sure we had time to send him to the kitchen again now. But surely one of the first things a doctor would offer a newly awakened patient was something to drink…

I scanned the room, but saw nothing to drink from. No paper cup, no coffee mug, and certainly no nice tall glass of ice water.

The tabby cleared her throat for my attention. "There," she croaked, pointing toward the foot of the nearest bed. I followed her finger to find the edge of something white and round sticking out from under one corner of the bed. I lifted the sheet to reveal a white plastic cereal bowl, about one-third of the way full of water.

A bowl. Of course. The tabby had still been in cat form when he'd visited.

When I pulled the bowl out, my hand landed in a small, cold puddle on the floor, and I understood where the rest of the water had gone.

"Here you go." I held the dish out, and she snatched it from me with both thin hands, exposing the stark lines of her collarbones, a nearly flat chest, and more ribs than I cared to count when the blanket slid from her shoulders.

The tabby drained the bowl in a blink, then held it out to

me, her eyes flashing bright in satisfaction. "Thank you," she said as I took the bowl from her.

"You have a lovely voice," I said, and I meant it. Her voice was clear and young, as was her complexion, in spite of having spent at least the past few weeks without access to soap and showering facilities. Her voice, skin and manners gave the only hint that her life had once been something else. Something pure and good, and completely unrelated to the wilderness nightmare that had become her reality at some point.

The tabby didn't return my smile. She blinked, and that gleam in her eyes was gone. She wrapped the blanket around her torso, tucking it beneath her arms like a towel, likely a habit left over from her life before…whatever had brought her here.

From downstairs came the sound of water running. Someone was taking a morning shower. I had to get her talking *posthaste*.

Struggling to maintain a smile that now felt painted on my face, I set the bowl on the floor and faced the tabby. "Feel any better now?"

She shook her head. "Not much."

"I'm sure you're exhausted. But if you can answer a couple of questions for me, I'll go away and let you sleep for a while." *Just as soon as the doc has examined you…*

That time she didn't deny her exhaustion—a definite step in the right direction. "What kind of questions?"

I smiled encouragingly. At least, I *hoped* it was encouraging. "Your name, for starters."

"Kaci Dillon," she said, and my heart tried to burst straight through my sternum.

Success! I'd now gotten the tabby to eat, Shift, talk and tell me her name, when she wouldn't even tolerate the doctor's presence. No matter what happened next, the Alphas couldn't deny that I'd gotten the job done. That I had value as something other than an incubator.

But the tabby wasn't done. "Kaci-with-a-*K*-and-an-*I*." She said it as if the whole phrase was one word, and her speech had the distinctive cadence of long-term habit, as if she'd said that same thing nearly every day of her life. I could sympathize. No one ever spelled my name right the first time either.

"Nice to meet you, Kaci. I'm Faythe-with-a-*Y*-and-an-*E*." My smile widened, and I was delighted to see a tiny echo of it on her face. She was happy to have made me happy. Or else she was laughing at me silently.

Hoping fervently that it was the former, I said, "You look pretty young." *Hopefully much younger than you actually are.* I inhaled slowly, then asked the question before I could chicken out. I needed to know, whether I *wanted* to or not. "How old are you, Kaci?"

"I'm not that young." She twisted her face into a look of displeasure; it was a bit like watching a pixie frown. A very thin, dirty pixie. "I'm just a late bloomer. At least, that's what my mo—" She stopped in midword and looked away, but it didn't take a genius to figure out how the sentence ended in her head. "Anyway, I'm not as young as I look."

Thank goodness. But her reassurance wasn't enough to unclench my hands in my lap. "So? How old are you?" *Please, please, please say seventeen. Sixteen, even.*

"Thirteen. And a half."

Shit. Ohhhh, shit. Thirteen and a half was too young for… *anything.* There was no way any enforcer worth his own canines would let a tabby that young out of his sight. Especially with her parents dead.

"Thirteen and a half?" I heard the flat, shocked quality of my own voice and winced at it, even as Kaci frowned. How the *hell* had a thirteen-year-old survived on her own long enough to become so thin and malnourished? It just wasn't possible, even if she *had* been stuck in cat form the whole time, which was how the story seemed to be shaping up.

"Where are you from, Kaci?" I tried to hide the horror in my voice, without much luck. But before she could answer, a loud, persistent knock came from the other side of the door.

Knowing none of the toms I'd left in the hall would interrupt us, I sniffed in that direction and felt the blood drain from my face, even as the voice bellowed from the hallway.

"Katherine Faythe Sanders, get your *tail* out here *now!*"

Damn!

"I'll be right back," I whispered to Kaci. Swallowing thickly, I started to stand, but then sank back onto the floor when I noticed that Kaci's eyes had gone huge. "Don't worry," I mumbled, shoving sleep-tousled hair back from my face. "It's just my dad."

Seventeen

"What were you *thinking,* disobeying a direct order?" my father demanded, and I had to stand on my own foot to keep from scuffing my bare, freezing toes in the dirt. I hadn't even had a chance to put shoes on before he marched down the stairs and out the back door, his very posture an unspoken command for me to follow. All the way to the woodpile stretched between two trees behind the main lodge.

"I was thinking about what Marc said earlier. Right now the council has no use for me—no reason to keep me alive. The best way I can help myself is to prove them wrong. To prove myself useful. *Indispensable.* So when Dr. Carver said she might calm down for another woman..."

My father's scowl deepened.

Shit. I shouldn't have mentioned Dr. Carver's part in the whole thing. Now he would get his ass chewed, too.

"It's not his fault, Daddy. He didn't make me do it. No one did." But that wouldn't matter. If I went down, the doc would go down with me. And we probably wouldn't be alone.

I stared into the skeletal branches overhead, trying to remember what I was originally getting at. *Oh, yeah...* "But my point is that I finally had something to offer. Something no one else could do."

Early-morning sunlight highlighted the gray patches at his temples as he shook his head, mouth already open to interrupt. I rushed on before he could. "No one else could have gotten her to Shift, Daddy, much less talk. She was too afraid of the guys to relax enough to even *listen*. She split Dr. Carver's arm wide open!"

"Which is *exactly* why we said no one was to go in there alone! We're all here trying to keep your head attached to your shoulders, yet for some reason, you feel the need to flaunt your disobedience in front of the very tribunal demanding your life! Not to mention how badly hurt you could have been. You had *twenty* stitches removed from your stomach not *ten hours* ago. We can*not* afford to have you injured again."

"I'm fine." I spread my arms, showing him how perfectly intact I was.

"You could have been mauled."

"Yes. I could also be struck by lightning on my way back to the cabin. Or I could be hit by a falling tree. Or run over on the crosswalk. Life isn't safe, Daddy. Not for your little girl, and *certainly* not for one of your enforcers. I saw an opportunity to prove my own worth and help that poor child, and I took it. I stand by my decision." Though I was so nervous about it my hands were starting to sweat in spite of the cold…

"And furthermore…" I rushed on, ignoring both my own nerves and whatever he'd been about to say. "I think you should be *proud* of me, instead of mad. I think I did exactly what *you* would have done in my place."

My father's face turned purple faster than I could backtrack. "What *I* would have done is irrelevant." He stepped into my personal space and I backed up instinctively, groaning inwardly when my spine hit the tree trunk. "I am your sire and your Alpha. I do whatever has to be done, in large part because whelps like *you* can't remember to follow orders!"

"Okay, yes. You're right." Like he needed me to tell him

that. I exhaled slowly, gathering my wits as I grounded myself with the feel of the bark beneath my fingers. "But what you would have done is *not* irrelevant. It's imperative. You're training me to take over for you one day, right? To be as good a leader to the Pride as you are now."

I probably shouldn't have played the successor card, especially coupled with a heavy helping of sycophancy. But if the ends justified the means… "How can I do that better than by emulating you?"

His scowl deepened. "You're not going to get out of this with flattery, so don't even bother."

Damn. "Fair enough." I sighed and made myself meet his angry stare. "But can you honestly tell me you would have let that poor girl—that *child*—suffer alone out of fear for your own safety, when you could help her and everyone else by simply showing a little courage and compassion?"

For a moment, my father only looked at me, and I held my breath in anticipation of his reaction, mortified to realize I was scolding my-Father-the-Alpha. *Oh, shit.*

Then, to my absolute amazement, my father crossed his arms over his chest and nodded, by all appearances conceding my point. "Well said." His face showed no hint of a smile, meaning that while he might—by some miracle—be proud of me, he was far from happy. "I hope you can say it again just like that, because no matter how good your intentions were, they don't excuse you disobeying a direct order. The tribunal is going to want a word with you."

"Yeah, I figured." I closed my eyes for a moment, thinking. When I opened them again, I found my father watching me, still in that same closed-off posture. "I'll do whatever I have to do. Apologize, take another suspension, or even a night in the cage." Since we both knew there *was* no cage here. "All I ask is that you protect Kaci."

His brows rose in surprise, and his expression softened ever so slightly. "She told you her name?"

"That's what I was trying to tell you. I was in there *working,* not goofing off with my girlfriend. We didn't paint a single toenail!" Not that I'd ever done that in my entire life.

He actually smiled at that one briefly before recomposing his business face. "What did she say?"

"Just her name and age. She was about to say more when you…*arrived.*" My father scowled again, and I rushed to fill the pause. "Her name is Kaci Dillon, and she's thirteen and a half years old."

"Thirteen…?" His words faded into horrified silence and he reached for the woodpile, as if to steady himself. "That isn't possible."

"That's what I thought." I glanced at the lodge, where several gaps had appeared in the blinds covering the windows—toms watching us from relative safety. Evidently everyone was awake now, which made me *really* glad my father had posted Marc and Jace at the tabby's door with orders not to let anyone in—or out—until further notice from him. Including the other Alphas.

It was a risky move, and they wouldn't be able to hold the door themselves if the entire tribunal decided they wanted in. But that wasn't likely to happen, thanks to Uncle Rick, and even if it did, we'd hear the ruckus from outside and come running to straighten things out. So for the moment, I was confident that the tabby was safe.

"Who is she?" my father asked, now pacing the length of the woodpile, crunching dead leaves beneath his feet. The question was rhetorical, fortunately, because I certainly didn't have the answer. "I've never heard of the Dillons, or their Pride. How could I never have heard of them?"

No, we didn't know every Pride in the world personally, but my father knew every Pride in North America, by name and reputation at least, and several of those in Middle and

South America, as well as Europe. And Kaci spoke English. *American* English, as far as I could tell, with no accent I could discern in what few words she'd said so far. It made no sense.

"It gets even weirder than that. She didn't know how to Shift. I had to talk her through it step by step." I rocked on my heels, my hands clasped nervously at my back. "You know, there's a possibility no one else seems willing to say out loud…"

"No." He stopped near the far end of the woodpile, to glare at me over one shoulder. "She was probably too nervous to Shift on her own, which makes sense considering how young she is. She is *not* a stray, Faythe."

"Why? Because we've never seen a female one? There's a first time for everything, Daddy."

His eyes glazed over and the pacing recommenced, and just like that, I was dismissed, along with my theory-threatening, comfort-zone-shattering, too-new-to-be-considered yet perfectly-possible idea.

Irritation clenched my jaws, so I spoke through them. "Why is it that when Manx claims to have *met* a female stray, everyone smiles and says anything's possible, but when I merely *mention* that very possibility, the same people roll their eyes and laugh in my face?"

My Alpha reached the end of the woodpile and turned. "They're humoring her. They expect more of you. You're well educated, well trained, and even well respected in certain circles."

I was? *Cool.* A tingle of pride shivered its way through me, though I knew the downside was coming…

"Spouting nonsense like that makes you sound like those idiots who turn up in the woods with their cameras every year hoping to spot Bigfoot."

"You know, they're not completely off base." I plucked a lone brown leaf dangling from the branch over my head and broke off the first lobe. "Someday one of them might get lucky and capture a shot of Elias Keller."

He growled softly in reproach. "You're missing the point. She's *not* a stray, and I'm basing that on nothing more than the fact that she doesn't *smell* like a stray. If she did we'd all have noticed immediately."

"She doesn't smell like a *male* stray, but maybe she *does* smell like a *female* stray and we don't know because we've never smelled one."

He huffed in exasperation. "We've smelled female cats, and we've smelled strays. It's not too hard to imagine what a combination would smell like. She's *not* a stray, which means she had to come from somewhere. From some Pride. We need more information from her." Having obviously come to a decision, he stopped pacing to face me. "You'll have to ask her some more questions."

Ya think? I rolled my eyes. He'd interrupted us and practically dragged me from the room by my hair, only to tell me to go back and do more of what I'd been doing in the first place. Lovely.

"Don't start, Faythe. This is different. Now you'll be going in with permission and an approved agenda, not disobeying a direct order in the middle of the night."

Technically, it was five-thirty in the morning…

I ripped the last of the leaf in half and let the pieces flutter to the ground. "You think Malone will go for it?"

He hesitated, obviously thinking unpleasant thoughts. "After he's had his say and you've taken whatever's coming to you, I don't see that he'll have much of a choice. *He* won't be able to get her to talk." Without another word, my father headed for the lodge, his steps firm and heavy.

As I followed, trying to catch up without actually running, one last whispered sentenced floated back to me on the chilly, early-morning breeze. "By damn, they can't call her useless *now*."

I smiled in spite of myself, and in spite of the tribunal, every member of which no doubt sat waiting for me inside.

Twenty minutes later, I sat on the living-room couch trying not to nod off on Dr. Carver's shoulder. Lucas was perched in the armchair on our right, much too stiff and nervous to fall asleep, and Marc sat across the coffee table from him, hands clenched around the arms of the chair nearest the front door. No one spoke. We looked like children lined up outside the principal's office, waiting to be called in. And essentially, that's what we were doing.

My father had locked himself in the dining room with the other Alphas to brief them on what we'd done. Try as I might to overhear their meeting, I could only catch the briefest of urgent whispers. They had Beethoven cranked on the stereo again, probably trying to make me sweat.

It was working.

It was nearly 8:00 a.m., and though I was on my second cup of coffee in under five minutes, no one had even started breakfast, because there was no one around to cook. My father and a couple of the other Alphas had called in extra backup to help with the search, but none of the flights would land until evening, so Jace and Michael were about to head into the woods. One of the other enforcer pairs had had to take a double shift because Marc and Lucas were in trouble along with me and Dr. Carver.

Everyone who'd searched until dawn was now sleeping.

So after another night without finding either the strays or the missing human hikers, we were understaffed again, and now walking on eggshells.

Still straining to hear something useful from the dining room, I nearly jumped out of my skin when a sudden pop

sounded from the kitchen, followed by a soft fizzing sound—
someone opening a can of soda. An instant later Jace stepped
into the doorway with a Coke in one hand. "Anyone else
thirsty?" He smiled at us hopefully.

My eyes met Jace's, and irritation fueled the fire of nerves
smoldering deep inside me.

"Don't look at me like that." Jace's eyes pleaded with me
as the can hovered in front of his mouth. "Your dad was
already up when I got to the cabin, and I couldn't very well
lie to him, could I?"

"Of course not." I sighed. It wasn't Jace's fault. We'd
known the Alphas would find out eventually. "I'm not mad.
I'm just…nervous." I'd told my dad I was ready to accept the
consequences of my actions. But that didn't mean I was
looking forward to it.

"Look, you were actually doing them a favor, and no one
got hurt." He gestured with the can as he spoke. "They'll
bluster for a while, then the whole thing will blow over.
Right?" Leaning against the door frame, Jace took a long
swallow of his soda, and when no one answered, a tight,
cautious smile stole over his face. "I mean, what are they
going to do? Execute you twice?"

"That's not fun—" I started. But then Marc's fist slammed
into the coffee table, and my last syllable was lost beneath the
splinter of wood as it broke in two.

"You think this is a joke?" He stood, kicking one-half of
the table out of his way. "Because I can *guarantee* you the
Alphas are taking it seriously." He turned from Jace to glare
at me, but I saw the truth in his eyes. He wasn't mad at either
of us. Not really. He was mad at himself. "I should *never* have
let you go in there." He pulled his foot back and kicked the
other half of the coffee table, and I flinched when it smashed
into the wall near the door.

Michael appeared from the bathroom, looking surprisingly

comfortable in jeans, hiking boots, and a thick flannel over-shirt rather than his usual lawyerly attire. He took one look at Marc, then pulled Jace behind him out the door, on the way to the forest.

When they were gone, Lucas stood calmly and picked up one half of the coffee table. Marc took the other piece and followed him out the front door. Their footsteps disappeared around the corner of the lodge, and I assumed they were taking the broken table out back to join the chair he'd broken the day before.

Marc was hard on furniture.

"He'll be okay," Dr. Carver said, and I glanced up to find him watching me. "The bottom line is that you got through to her when no one else could have, and they'll have to see that."

"I hope so." But I wasn't holding my breath. Marc was right. The Alphas obviously didn't think the ends justified my means.

A door creaked open at the back of the lodge, and the clas-sical music ended in midnote. "—bring them in," Uncle Rick said, and a moment later he appeared in the hall, his face a mask of anger and frustration. He stopped in the middle of the living-room floor, the tension in his expression giving way to momen-tary confusion. "Where are Marc and Lucas?" He paused, eyeing the newly open floor space. "And the coffee table?"

"Collateral damage." Marc stepped into the living room from the front porch and Lucas came in behind him.

"I see." But my uncle didn't look like he saw.

Marc shrugged and met his gaze unflinchingly. "So… what's going on?"

"I'm not entirely sure." Uncle Rick sighed, and rubbed his forehead, then met my eyes. "Your dad and I tried to get this handled on an individual-Pride basis, so we could each dis-cipline our own. But Malone didn't go for it. He made a con-ference call to the rest of the council and got a simple majority vote of six to four." With that, my uncle sank into the chair his son had just vacated. He looked angry, frustrated, and very, very tired.

I knew just how he felt.

"Vote to do what?" Lucas settled wearily onto the couch cushion on my right, closest to his father.

"To turn jurisdiction over to the Territorial Council."

"Jurisdiction for what?" I asked, my voice soft with dread.

Uncle Rick met my gaze with eyes the same crystalline blue as my mother's. "You're being charged with insubordination."

Beneath his reddish freckles, Lucas's face went pale with alarm, but all I could work up was mild irritation.

Insubordination was a relatively minor offense—what amounted to a misdemeanor. Under normal circumstances, a guilty verdict would call for the offending enforcer's immediate dismissal, but it was hard for me to work up much fear over that, considering I was already suspended. And that I was facing the fucking *death* penalty.

"Insubordination, huh? Is that it?" I asked, and my uncle nodded. "Okaaay, but doesn't that seem kind of pointless, in view of the other charges against me?"

He nodded again. "I don't understand what they're going for. Why bother to slap your wrist when they're planning to break your neck with the next blow?"

My heart dropped into my stomach. I knew what the death penalty meant, of course, but hearing it stated so bluntly wasn't exactly pleasant. I liked my neck *intact*.

Lucas took my hand in his, and I looked up to find everyone watching me.

"Wait." A brief wave of calm flowed over me as a nugget of werecat political trivia clicked into place in my head. "There aren't enough of you here for that. Three Alphas are enough for a tribunal, but you need at least four to officially convene the council." *Ha! Take that, Malone!*

But Uncle Rick didn't look anywhere near as pleased as

he should have been by my near-perfect recall of Territorial Council policy. Though Marc looked pretty damn impressed.

"The council ruled that your insubordination—"

"*Alleged* insubordination," I insisted, though I knew damn well I was guilty.

"Wrong." Lucas forced a smile. "Michael says that here, you're guilty until proven innocent."

"Whatever." I ignored him, exercising my right to scowl in protest.

"Anyway," Uncle Rick continued as all eyes refocused on him. "During the conference call, the council ruled that this is a separate issue from the hearing already in progress. They agreed that your father can avoid bias on such a minor indiscretion."

Shit. With Daddy, they had enough Alphas to officially call the Territorial Council into session. *Screw 'em!* What were they going to do? Revoke my suspension in favor of dismissal? So what? As much as I was starting to like my job, I liked my life better.

"So, is that it? One more charge leveled against me?" As if that were no big deal. Maybe if I acted like I didn't care, they'd believe me. Maybe I would, too.

Uncle Rick shook his head, eyeing me intently to underline the importance of what he was about to say. "It's not just you, Faythe. We're charging you *all*."

Eighteen

"What?" My hand went cold in Lucas's as his broke into an instant sweat. "No. They can't." I leaned forward on the old, dingy couch, staring at my uncle in search of some sign that I'd heard him wrong. I'd known *I* would get in trouble, and Marc and Dr. Carver would probably get yelled at, too, especially since I'd accidentally ratted the doc out. But I'd hoped they'd rant and rave, then let my father handle the situation privately. And I'd had no idea they'd drag Lucas into the fray, just because he was there. "You can*not* hold *them* responsible for what *I* did."

My uncle's normally warm blue eyes went as cold as glacial ice, and he stood, physically distancing himself from me. "Yes. We *can*. You all broke the rules, and you're all going to pay the price, whatever that turns out to be."

Then his gaze singled me out, his lips drawn into a tight, straight line. I'd seen that very expression on my mother's face hundreds of times, and now I knew where she got it. "Do *not* mistake my sympathy for an inclination to bend the law for you every time you step out of line. I believe you killed Andrew in self-defense, so I'm doing my best to keep the hearing fair. But you intentionally disobeyed a direct order this time. So you keep that in mind when you open your mouth in there."

Well, crap. He had me there.

Ten minutes later, I was officially charged with insubordination, once again seated at the end of the long dining-room table, as revoltingly cheerful morning sunlight poured through the windows along the east wall.

I'm starting to really hate this room.

Dr. Carver, Marc and Lucas sat in chairs against the wall, but this time no one sat in the chair on my right. They'd given Michael the option to act as my adviser again, but he'd joined the search efforts instead, refusing to stand by me on matters of principle. Or, as he put it, I was a damn fool to pull such a stunt, and he wasn't going to interfere with the heavy hand of justice. Or some such shit.

The point was that he thought I deserved whatever token punishment they gave me—and I sincerely hoped he was right about the "token" part—so he and Jace scoured the mountainside with the other enforcer teams while I spent most of the next hour trying to convince the council that I meant no insult to their authority by visiting the tabby against orders. I was simply trying to help meet her immediate needs without wasting time with a bunch of pointless formalities.

That line of reasoning might have worked well for me if not for the fact that the council—indeed, the very werecat political model—was founded on that same bunch of pointless formalities.

Since my father had already had his say, he seemed content to sit back and determine which way the council's collective wind was blowing before taking an official position. Unfortunately that wind was all blowing in one direction.

Though my uncle was more moderate in his censure than were Malone and Blackwell, he was disinclined to go easy on any of us in his official statement, for fear of being seen as soft on his own son and niece, and thus less than impartial. Also, he was truly and deeply pissed at having his authority disregarded, even if I *had* ultimately helped both Kaci and the council.

And the real bitch was that this time Malone didn't have to say a word. He just sat back and grinned smugly while my uncle gave me a public dressing-down. The bastard even spoke up in my *defense* at one point, interrupting Uncle Rick to insist I was "probably doing what I thought was right at the time." Which effectively implied that I had no idea what "right" really was.

Malone's little show of support was no doubt also intended to combat rumors that he was unnecessarily harsh in matters concerning me. The manipulative prick.

After each of the Alphas had his say, I got a chance to defend myself. My father warned me to be good with his eyes as I stood to address the panel. "Look," I started, but judging from his deep scowl, that wasn't the proper way to address the Territorial Council. So I started over.

"You guys are probably every bit as tired of seeing me here as I am of being here, so I'm just going to lay it all out for you. The truth." I gave them all a moment to object, and when no one did, I continued.

"Yes, I disobeyed a direct order in going in to see the tabby alone. So I guess technically, I am guilty of insubordination. But this whole thing?" I spread my arms to take in the entire room and the proceedings therein. "This is *why* I didn't ask first—because she wouldn't have calmed down enough to Shift in front of a roomful of enforcers, so we would have wound up right here, arguing about it for hours while that poor little girl sat up there stuck in cat form and scared to death. She's weak, confused and half-starved, and every single moment we leave her like that, we're guilty of neglect. She's a *child*. She doesn't know anything about your rules and forums. She doesn't know a thing about us, *period,* and I was trying to help her. To help *you,* by getting her to talk. Which none of you could have done, if I may point out."

But apparently I was *not* supposed to point that out. Who knew?

My father chose that moment to stand, and I couldn't help but think he'd timed his statement carefully, so I would have my say before he pronounced me guilty for the same reason Malone had come to my defense—to show that he could be fair too.

"Faythe, your motives and even your results are immaterial here. What matters is that you disobeyed a direct order." He paused to look at each of his fellow Alphas. "Now, I'm sure everyone here understands the value of the work you've done with Kaci Dillon. But surely *you* acknowledge that your action must have a consequence?"

Aw, crap. He was going to make me say it.

"Yes, of course." I sighed, and my shoulders sagged in defeat. *In for a penny, in for a pound, Faythe.* "I knew that when I went in, but I did it anyway because I believed then— and now—that the result would be worth whatever penalty you throw at me. *Not* going in would have been taking the coward's way out. Staying in the hall because I was scared— of you guys or of her, it makes no difference—would have been shirking what I consider my moral duty. Knowing the right thing to do is easy. Doing it when you know there will be consequences is not. *You* taught me that."

My father nodded, and I thought I detected a little flush in his cheeks, though that might have been wishful thinking on my part. Either way, my uncle looked a little less furious than he had moments earlier.

I met each council member's eyes for just a moment, silently acknowledging their authority even as I asked them to acknowledge my good intentions. "I did what I had to do. Now you have to do the same."

With that, I took my seat, my heart pounding in my throat,

my palms sweaty enough to leave damp streaks on the polished surface of the dining-room table.

"Personally," Paul Blackwell said, and I narrowed my gaze on him, surprised to hear the old fart speak up, "I see no reason to sentence her now, considering that her future is…*uncertain.*"

That didn't sound good.

"I agree." This from Malone, who'd looked less than pleased by one of my better attempts to talk my way out of trouble. *Tough room.* "I move that we hand down her sentences all at once, when the hearing is over."

"No." My father leaned back in his chair. "I have a right to my say in this procedure, but am not a part of the tribunal."

"Fine." Malone rested his elbows on the table. He watched me, though his remark was obviously directed at my father. "We'll decide this one separately, but announce them all three together."

A small-but-vocal part of me wanted to point out that I hadn't actually been found guilty of murder yet, so there *was* no sentence to be handed out on that one. But since my mouth had actually talked me *out* of trouble this time—at least for the time being—I saw no reason to press my luck.

Unfortunately, the tribunal's ire wasn't directed solely at me. When my part was done, I sat in a chair against the wall, at the end of the line of toms waiting to face the music.

Dr. Carver came under fire for asking me to disobey a direct order. In his defense, he told the Alphas that as a physician, his first duty was to the young tabby's well-being, and that he did what was in her best interest—provided her with immediate nourishment and counseling from the only person she would let near.

The council members seemed unmoved, and Malone insisted that if Dr. Carver had explained the urgency to them, they would have immediately provided the tabby with whatever she needed. But we all knew she wouldn't have cooperated with them and they would *not* have let me go in alone to earn her trust.

When they'd all had their say, the doc was strongly reprimanded and warned—by my father—that any future transgressions would result in him being exiled from the Pride.

Lucas got off with an angry warning and a month's suspended pay, since he was the lesser-ranking tom present. But as my father's second-in-command, Marc technically had the authority and the responsibility to stop us all from doing something so irresponsible and potentially dangerous. Yet he hadn't.

My stomach twisted in on itself as Marc walked solemnly into the center of the room. He stood with his hands clasped behind his back and his feet spread—at ease, though he was probably anything but. He elected not to sit. He was going to take it like a man.

Because of me.

I couldn't remember Marc ever even being reprimanded by the council before. He'd been reproached by my father for his quick temper on occasion, but that was nothing compared to this. That was a slap on the wrist from a loving father figure. Malone didn't love Marc, and would just as soon rip off his hand as slap his wrist.

Malone opened his mouth to begin, but my father cut him off. "Marc…" He trailed into a pained silence, and I fervently hoped I was the only one who could read the disappointment in his eyes. "What were you thinking?"

"Honestly?" Marc asked, and my father nodded, giving him permission to say something the others probably wouldn't want to hear. "I was thinking that it didn't matter what I did. If Faythe wanted to work with the tabby, she was going to do it no matter what any of us said or did."

Daddy didn't smile. Instead, he nodded wearily, as if to say he shared Marc's pain.

"So you let her disobey a direct order?" Malone demanded,

leaning so far forward, the table must have been digging into his waist. "You just stood there and watched your Pride's only tabby—the professed love of your life—walk alone and unarmed into the room with a strange, violent werecat? Why?"

I could only see Marc's face in profile, but that was enough to showcase jaws bulging in anger, and a single brow drawn into a fierce frown. "Because *someone* had to do it, and Faythe is best equipped for the job. She has previous experience counseling a traumatized young tabby." My cousin Abby, of course. "And a couple of days ago she took out a full-grown stray in the grip of scratch fever, and this was just a *child,* weakened by hunger and exhaustion. Also, Faythe wasn't completely unarmed. She had a tranquilizer."

But he wasn't saying it all. He wasn't saying that he'd tried to stop me, and that I'd refused to listen. He wouldn't lay the blame on me—even when I deserved it.

I leaned forward, my hands clenched around the arms of my chair. *Why isn't he defending himself?*

"What if the cat had attacked?" Malone gripped the edge of the table with tension-white fingers. "Faythe's barely recovered from several gashes in her stomach. What if she'd been injured again?"

"Like you care!" I mumbled. My father's head whipped around and his eyes settled on me with the weight of my own conscience. But I'd had enough. I stood, glaring at them all at once. "What? It's the truth! Aren't you guys after the truth? Because we all know Councilman Malone would order Marc to break my neck here and now if he thought he'd get away with it. Yet there he sits, browbeating him for something *I* did! Where's the justice in th—"

Lucas tugged hard on my arm, and when I fell into my chair, I bit my tongue, effectively cutting off my tirade. Blood flowed into my mouth and I swallowed it, wiping at my lips with the back of my sleeve even as I glared at my cousin. He ignored me, eyes glued to the Alphas seated at the front of the room.

"One more word and I'll have you escorted out of the lodge," Malone said, and somehow he made "escorted" sound much more menacing than it should have. Anger blazed up my spine. The bastard was threatening me!

I opened my mouth to say…*something*. I didn't have the details all worked out yet, but that turned out not to matter because Marc beat me to the punch, no doubt trying to save me from myself, as usual.

"I'm not protesting this." He glanced at his feet as if fighting for patience, and when he looked up again his eyes held a complacent strength the likes of which I'd never felt in my entire life. I would have given almost anything for a fraction of the self-control Marc wasted on the council. "I let her go in," he said. "I'm not arguing otherwise, so let's get this over with."

"Fine." Malone nodded, like that's exactly what he'd wanted to hear, when I knew for a fact it was not. He wanted to berate Marc some more, now that he'd finally found a legitimate forum for his irrational prejudice. But Marc had taken that opportunity away, and I would have applauded, if Lucas hadn't chosen that moment to clasp my hand, ostensibly to comfort me.

Malone's eyes gleamed with barely repressed joy, which I wanted to pound in one side of his head and out the other. "We're charging you with insubordination, and with neglect and endangerment of the tabby under your protection, which confounds me, frankly, considering you once wanted to *marry* this particular tabby."

That slimy son of a bitch!

Marc's hands fell into fists at his sides, and my uncle rushed to fill the silence. "Calvin, keep the editorializing to a minimum."

Malone ignored him, but wisely moved on. "I'm recommending a sentence consisting of a public apology, dismissal and *exile*."

Marc jerked as if he'd been slapped, and someone gasped out loud. I think it was me.

Blood dribbled down my chin when my mouth gaped open, and I wiped it away with that same sleeve, as the nails of my other hand sank into Lucas's skin. He hissed and tried to pull his hand from mine, but I barely noticed.

No. Marc had said he'd accept his sentence, but he couldn't have known Malone would pull a stunt like that.

"That's *completely* unreasonable." My father growled, now on the edge of his chair. His jaw bulged with obvious anger, which could only mean he was closer to losing his temper in public than I'd ever seen him. "No one was hurt, and Faythe actually helped both us and the tabby."

Every gaze in the room moved from my father to Calvin Malone, waiting to see how he'd respond. We were exploring new territory in the landscape of werecat political structure, at least as far as I knew, and no one seemed very sure of his footing at the moment.

Malone's eyes blazed with anticipation "He sent your daughter—in direct opposition to our orders—to be slaughtered by a half-wild werecat who'd already sliced open Dr. Carver's arm. If a full-grown tom couldn't handle her, Marc had no reason to believe Faythe could."

My father's voice went dangerously soft and deep. "He's a much better judge of her capabilities than *you* are, and he was right. She's fine."

"The happy ending doesn't matter—it could easily have gone another way. What matters is that he made a very poor decision that could have gotten your daughter killed." Malone and my father faced off against each other, the rest of us forgotten in a rarely seen Alpha battle of wills. "He has to pay for that, Greg, and letting him remain in your house and in your Pride is as good as saying you value *his* life over hers. You can't trust him to protect her now. You might as well hand him a knife and tell him to get it over with!"

Blood rushed to my face, scalding my cheeks, and I had to force air from my lungs in order to draw a fresh breath. He couldn't be serious. He was *not* accusing Marc of wanting me dead! If that wasn't the pot calling the kettle black, I'd… I'd…pound the shit out of the pot myself!

For several seconds I saw nothing but a thick film of angry red, as shocked silence settled around the room like a fog too thick to breathe through. When my vision cleared, my gaze settled on the first thing in the room to move.

To my utter horror, Blackwell was nodding, staring at Marc in disgust now. He was buying Malone's steaming pile of horseshit!

Uncle Rick looked as sick as I felt. But my father just looked pissed.

He stood slowly to face Malone, and his chair squealed on the floor. "You will *not* tell me how to run my Pride, nor will you dictate whom I include among its numbers. You've stepped over your boundaries, Calvin, and if you don't step back quickly, I *will* meet you toe-to-toe."

Yes!

Malone stood, and I couldn't stifle a petty surge of glee when his forehead only reached my father's nose. "My vote carries as much weight here as yours does, Greg, and my allies appear to equal yours."

Blackwell nodded, formally throwing his frail weight behind Malone's bullshit sentence. "Greg, Marc doesn't seem to have the best interest of your Pride at heart."

"That is for *me* to decide," my father thundered.

But two votes in favor of Malone's suggestion were enough to keep the jury hung until someone switched sides, or the world ended. Or they appealed to the rest of the council for a tiebreaker. However, that in itself was a risky move, because there were several other Alphas who shared Malone's prejudicial dislike of Marc. If the tiebreaker cast his vote with Malone, I would lose Marc for good. He'd be publicly humiliated, fired, and exiled as a traitor.

I could *not* let that happen.

"No!" I was out of my chair in an instant, and too far away for Lucas to grab without standing along with me, which he wasn't willing to do. He knew better than to draw attention to himself in a room filled with so much tension. He was a lot smarter than I was, because I planned to soak up *all* the attention, to keep it off Marc.

Unfortunately, that's as far as my plan went.

"Faythe…" My father turned furious eyes on me, but beneath the anger I saw true terror. He knew he was losing Marc, and he was afraid that if I didn't keep my mouth shut he'd lose me too. But that wasn't motivation enough for me to cooperate, considering he might lose me anyway.

"No." The end of my ponytail slapped my cheeks as I shook my head vehemently. "I won't let them do this. Marc didn't do anything wrong. He tried to stop me, but I wouldn't listen. If he'd held me back, I would have fought him. He would have had to hurt me to stop me, and he wasn't willing to do that. The only thing he's guilty of is trusting me enough to believe I knew what I was doing."

"That was not his call to make!" Malone yelled.

"It most certainly *was!*" I shouted, glowering in fierce loathing of every corrupt ideal he represented. "Marc was the highest-ranking tom there, which *made* it his call. And he made a *good* one, which you'd know if you'd listen to what Kaci told me."

"Faythe, *sit down!*" Marc hissed, turning to stare at me in horror. For once I knew exactly how deep a hole I was digging for myself, but my more immediate concern was that Malone not get away with such a selfish, blatant travesty of justice. Marc could not be exiled. I would *not* stay at the ranch without him.

"No!" My hands curled into fists at my sides, and I glared at him, almost as angry over his submissive silence as I was over Malone's despicably out-of-proportion sentence. "There's no way I'm letting them kick you out for something *I* did. I can't *believe* you're not fighting this!"

But I could, really. Marc's sense of honor was flawless. He'd said he would accept his sentence, and he was now honor-bound to do so, even if it was completely, outrageously unfair.

Malone crossed both arms over his chest. "The standard sentence for insubordination is dismissal. And for endangering a tabby's life? I'd say exile is getting off easy. A less tolerant Alpha might ask for something more...*permanent*." Beneath his disapproving scowl a grin was just dying to break free.

And to be pounded into a mutilated mass of split lips and shattered teeth. My fists ached for that honor.

On his end of the room, Blackwell was nodding, convinced that Malone was doing Marc a *favor*. And Marc just stood there, jaws bulging, hands clenched, lips sealed.

The last thread of hope unraveled around my heart, leaving frayed bits of despair in its place. I dismissed the rest of the Alphas and focused on my father; he was the only one who could stop this now. "Daddy, you can't let them do this." Rushing past Marc, I leaned over the table and placed my ice-cold palms flat on the smooth surface, staring down the length of the room at the patriarch of my bloodline. "Do *not* do this!"

My father frowned at me, seemingly at a loss for what to say in the face of such chaos, and that very concept sent me into a tailspin of panic. I didn't know how to function in a world where my father was speechless and Marc was absent. They'd always been the great constants in my life, and without their ironclad support in place, nothing made sense. Nothing I did or said mattered, because life would never be the same again.

My vision began to blur again, and when I blinked, tears slid down my face, oddly cool against the vicious heat in my cheeks. I wiped moisture with my fingers and could only stare at it in astonishment, as if those tears somehow held the explanation for what the hell was happening. How had I gone from trying to help a fellow tabby to watching my entire life's foundation stomped beneath the steel-toed boots of injustice?

"This doesn't make any sense, Marc. He wants to have me executed. He wants *you* to do it. And now he wants to throw you out for letting me put my own life in danger? That's bullshit! He can't have his fucking cake and eat it, too. I won't let him!"

I was no longer crying over only his sentence. I was crying over Andrew's death, and my part in it. Over my inability to help myself, because no matter what I said and did, I only managed to make things worse.

"Get her out of here," my Alpha—my *father*—ordered quietly.

"Hell no! I'm not going anywhere." I wiped more tears, then crossed my arms over my chest and spread my feet, prepared to make my stand—until my dad nodded at someone behind me.

I turned left to see who he was looking at, but Lucas took up my entire line of sight. I spun around, only to find Marc on my other side. He wrapped his arms around me and gently forced my head onto his shoulder, where I lost my already fragile control over the bulk of my anger and frustration.

Something pinched the back of my arm through my shirt-sleeve, and I flinched. I twisted to see Dr. Carver holding a now-half-empty syringe, his eyes brimmed with fright and regret.

"Traitor…" I whispered, my legs collapsing beneath me even as Marc scooped me into his arms.

Then, in the middle of a bright November morning, every-thing went dark.

Nineteen

Soft yellow light painted red streaks on the backs of my eyelids, and I moaned as I rolled onto my side. *Damn tranquilizers…* I opened one eye to take in a familiar pressboard dresser, on top of which lay the suitcase Marc had given me when I'd told him I wanted to go to college instead of rescheduling our wedding.

Shit. I was back in my own room at the cabin.

"Wake up, Sleeping Beauty," Jace said softly from my right.

"Call me that again, and I'll tell the whole Pride you sleep in Scooby-Doo underwear."

"I don't sleep in Scooby-Doo underwear. Hell, I don't sleep in *any* underwear."

Waaay too much information, Jace. And for once, no mental image popped into my head. I wasn't in the mood for recreational speculation at the moment. Not by a long shot.

"It'll be my word against yours." Still scowling, I sat up and put one hand to my forehead, when the room spun around me. The tranquilizer hadn't quite worn off yet. That, plus the daylight leaking through the cracks in the blinds told me I hadn't been unconscious very long. Though my rumbling stomach argued otherwise.

"How long was I out?" I asked as Jace sat on the end of my bed.

He angled his wristwatch into the muted glow of my bedside lamp. "Just over three hours."

It could have been worse; I hadn't even missed lunch. "How bad is it?"

His pained expression said he knew exactly what I was asking. "Well, I doubt you helped your own case."

"*Fuck* my case." I threw the covers back, and my bad mood instantly worsened when I realized I wore no pants. "Nothing I do or say is going to make a damn bit of difference in that regard. They already have their minds made up."

"They do *now*…"

"They have from the start, but that whole damn ambush made no sense at all." I squinted into the shadows and spotted my jeans draped over the arm of a chair in the corner. "Where the hell do they get off charging Marc for endangering me, when they're going to order me executed as soon as they can fill out the proper paperwork?"

"You sound like your uncle."

I shot Jace a quizzical look over my shoulder, on my way to the chair. "What did he say?"

"I heard him tell your dad that Calvin's been in his room on the phone all morning, and he was on for nearly two hours yesterday, with music playing the whole time. He's up to something. Rick doesn't know what, but he's trying to find out."

Sighing, I sank into the chair and shoved first one foot then the other into the jeans I'd been wearing for most of the last eighteen hours. They were my most comfortable pair, and sometimes a good pair of jeans goes even further than good chocolate toward making me feel better. The only thing more effective would be a strong drink, which was out of the question at the moment. I needed to keep my wits about me, especially after convincing every Alpha within three hundred miles that I was certifiably *insane*.

Tranquilized for my own good. The guys would never let me live that one down.

"How's Kaci?"

Jace swiveled on his rump to watch me slink across the room toward my suitcase in search of a clean shirt. I needed a shower, but didn't want to waste time on such trivialities just then. "She's been asking for you. She won't talk to anyone else. Malone went in to see her, and she wouldn't even look at him. You should have seen him when he came out. He was so mad he wouldn't say what happened, but Lucas overheard it from the hall."

I pulled off the T-shirt I'd slept in and tossed it onto the pile of dirty clothes in one corner. "Well?" I faced Jace when it became clear that he was waiting for my response. "What did he say?"

"She told him to get the hell out of her room before she started screaming."

"Screaming?" I rummaged through the pile of clothes in my suitcase, looking for something that wasn't too wrinkled. But my entire wardrobe looked as if it had been wadded into one big ball, probably by someone searching for clothes for Kaci.

"Yeah. And apparently he didn't move fast enough to please her, because she *did* start screaming, and we could hear her loud and clear from the living room."

Unimpressed, I shrugged as I pulled a black lace bra from the top pocket of the suitcase. "That's not hard to believe."

"The living room of *this* cabin, not the lodge."

Oh. *Attagirl.*

With my back to Jace, I unhooked my bra and tossed it onto the pile of clothes in the corner, then scooped myself into the clean one. "So she's okay?"

"Yeah. That was about an hour ago, and they haven't sent

anyone in since. They're waiting for you to wake up and go talk to her."

"Are they planning to ask nicely?" My words were muffled as I pulled a black ribbed T-shirt over my head. I'd chosen it to remind everyone that I was still an enforcer, even if I was suspended. At least for the moment.

Jace huffed behind me as I shoved the sleeves of my shirt halfway to my elbows. "I doubt they'll ask at all," he said, smiling gently. "After your last big speech, they know you'll do it because it's the 'right' thing to do."

I should have *known* being nice would come back to bite me on the ass.

Rooting through the bag again, I tugged my hairbrush from a tangle of sleeves and ran it through my hair. My ponytail was gone, and the rubber band was nowhere to be found.

I kept my back to Jace as I asked the next question, both because I didn't want him to see my face and because I didn't really want to know the answer. "What about Marc? What did Daddy do?"

Jace sighed, and my shoulders sagged, my brush pausing in midstroke. I knew the truth before he even said it. "They didn't give him any choice, Faythe. It was all over by the time Michael and I got back, so I didn't hear what happened, but we both know your father would never have agreed to Marc's sentence if he had any way out of it."

No! How the hell could he do it?

"That's bullshit, and you know it!" My fist slammed into the side of my soft-shell suitcase, which flew across the dresser and smashed into the dark wood-paneled wall. The knuckles of my right hand throbbed with my pulse; I'd skinned them on the rough carpet weave of the bag. "There are *always* choices. *Plenty* of choices. What there's never enough of is courage—willingness to push past the easy option and see what else is available."

Jace scowled, an edge of anger showing through the sympathy defining his expression. "You think it was *easy* for your dad to lose Marc?"

"No." I closed my eyes and let myself sag against the dresser. "Of course not." Hell, there were times I thought he liked Marc better than *me*. "I just can't believe he did it. He's always talking about how important it is to do what's right. To keep those in power from running over those in need. But I guess that's a tendency he learned from the rest of the council—too much talk and not enough action. Too much politics, and not enough *truth*. If he and Uncle Rick would stand up to the others one good time—really lay it out loud and clear—this whole thing would be over in an hour."

"Maybe, but 'over' doesn't necessarily mean a happy ending." A sad smile tugged at the corner of Jace's mouth as he watched me. "You think you have all the answers?"

"In life? No." I plucked a folded pair of socks from the suitcase on the floor. "But in this case…yes. If my dad wants to keep this Pride intact, it's time for him and his allies to shut their mouths and start talking with their fists."

"What if everyone else has the same idea?"

"I don't know." I shrugged, pulling one sock free of its mate as I sank onto the nearest bed. "They lose, we win, and everyone goes home? Good triumphs over evil? That's how it works in movies."

Jace shook his head in sympathy and sat next to me. "This isn't Hollywood. If you want to change the system, you're going to have to do it from the inside. Even if Marc isn't there to help."

My eyes watered, and I wiped them on the clean sock, hoping Jace hadn't noticed. But of course, he had.

"I'm so sorry, Faythe."

"It's not your fault." Though I knew how he felt, as if he

were somehow responsible, just because his bastard of a step-father was spearheading the attempt to knock my world off its axis. But this had nothing to do with Jace. It was all Malone, and his petty grudges and power intoxication.

Fine. Maybe I couldn't stop them from kicking Marc out, but *they* couldn't stop me from going with him. We'd go together. After all, they couldn't execute me if they couldn't find me. Right?

Finally dressed, I stomped toward the door on my way to find Marc, but Jace appeared in my path from out of nowhere. I hadn't even seen him get up. "Move," I ordered.

He shook his head, arms crossed firmly over his chest. "I know what you're thinking and I understand, but you can't go."

"I can't do this with you right now, Jace. You know how I—"

A pained look crossed his face, chased away almost instantly by ironclad resolution. "This has nothing to do with *us*. I want to see you happy, even if it isn't with me. But you can't go with him."

I tried to shove him out of my way, but Jace refused to budge. I shoved harder, and he took my upper arms in both hands. "Think about Kaci. You're the only one she'll talk to. She needs you. Don't do this to her."

As badly as I hated to leave her, Kaci would be fine. My mother would know how best to help her. So would Manx. I tried to jerk my arms from his grip, but he wouldn't let go.

Jace saw the determination in my eyes, and he frowned. "Hell, don't do this to *Marc*. What will his life be like if you go with him? He'd spend every day fighting for you, and even Marc can't fight forever."

Fear sank through me like an anchor to the seafloor, pinning me to the spot where I stood. But Jace wasn't done.

"That's assuming the council doesn't go after him for kidnapping you. And you *know* Calvin would do it."

He was right. Marc was as good as dead if I went with him. There were strays in the free zone who would kill him for a shot at me. If the council didn't get him first.

And my father would waste incalculable time and re-sources looking for me.

Damn it!

I exhaled slowly, and when my shoulders slumped in defeat, Jace let go of my arms. "This isn't over," I whispered as he pulled me into a hug that bruised my heart as much as it comforted me. My eyes watered, and I blinked away tears. I would *not* cry about this again. I was done crying. It was time to get mad.

Anger was *so* much more productive than tears.

I pulled away from Jace gently so he wouldn't take it per-sonally, and met his eyes with a fresh layer of determination reinforcing my resolve. I would do what the council wanted; I would help them with Kaci. But I'd do it *my* way, and if they couldn't handle that, they could go fuck themselves.

I had nothing left to lose. Except for my life, which had less and less value each time they cut something out of it. So while I was playing their game, I would also be playing *mine*. I would find a way to get Marc back into the Pride. A loophole or something.

If I couldn't talk him out of submitting, his exile would only be temporary. I would see to that.

Bending, I snatched my hiking boots from the floor and pulled them on one at a time, so angry I tugged the laces tight enough to cut off the circulation in my foot, then had to loosen them. "When is Marc leaving?"

"His plane takes off first thing in the morning."

"Where is he?"

"In his room," Jace said, and I glanced at the wall separat-ing me from Marc, now aware that he'd probably heard every word we'd said.

"What about everyone else?" The cabin was silent around us, but for the distant hum of the refrigerator in the kitchen.

"At the lodge. Your dad said to take you over when you woke up." He followed me out of the bedroom and across the living room.

"Fine." I pulled open the front door and kicked the screen with one foot. It crashed into the exterior wall of the cabin then bounced back, and I held it open for him. "Consider your duty done."

He stepped outside and I pulled the screen shut behind him, locking it with a quick flip of one finger. "What are you doing?" Jace demanded, rattling the handle.

Instead of answering, I closed the heavy oak door in his face and twisted the knob lock, then slid the security chain into place.

"Faythe! It isn't really bringing you *in* if you don't come *with* me!"

"I'll be there in a few minutes. Walk slowly. I'll catch up."

"No. Faythe! Open the damn door!" Jace's fist slammed into the screen door and Plexiglas splintered. He could tear the screen right off its hinges if he wanted to, but the solid oak panel would take him much longer to get through. Satisfied for the moment, I was headed toward the kitchen to secure the back entrance when footsteps clomped across the front porch and his knuckles rapped the window, rattling it in its frame. "Don't make me break the glass, Faythe. You know I'll do it."

I exhaled in frustration, then marched back to the front door and unlocked it.

"Half an hour, Jace." I pulled the door open and stared at him through the screen, begging wordlessly for a few minutes alone with Marc. "Is that too much for a dying woman to ask?"

He scowled, unamused. "You are *not* dying."

"Somehow I doubt your stepfather would agree."

Hinges creaked behind me and I turned to see Marc

standing in his bedroom doorway wearing a faded Poison concert T-shirt and jeans with a hole in one knee. "What the hell are you doing, Faythe?"

"Bargaining for a little privacy. I need to talk to you, and I'm tired of everyone overhearing every word we say."

Marc hesitated, watching my eyes for several seconds. Then his gaze shifted from me to Jace, and he nodded.

"Marc…" Jace complained, and I turned to find confliction drawn in the deep lines around his frown.

"Go," Marc ordered, and Jace glanced back and forth between us in uncertainty. Technically, Marc had no authority over him anymore. But *I* wasn't going to tell him that, and apparently Jace wasn't, either.

"I'll wait here—on the porch—for half an hour. But the deal's off if anyone comes out here. Or calls."

"Fine. Thank you." I forced a small smile of gratitude, but he turned away before it was fully formed. I closed the door again, trying not to think about the dejection in his eyes. I had enough of my own emotional shit to shovel at the moment. I'd deal with Jace later. Assuming I *had* a later.

"What was that all about?" Marc leaned against the bedroom door frame and crossed his arms, pulling his shirt snug across the well-defined planes and bulges of his chest. The concert tee was his idea of casual Friday, though it was only Thursday. We'd been on the mountain four days, and so far I'd killed a stray, been gored, counseled a feral tabby and gotten Marc exiled.

Overall, not my best week.

"Nothing." I leaned with the sole of one boot against the closed front door, trying to decide whether to yell at him for leaving or beg him to stay. "You don't have to go, you know. You can't just roll over and bare your throat for Malone."

He sighed and shook his head wearily. "Don't do this, Faythe. It's over, and you have to let it go. Let *me* go."

"No." I shoved away from the door with my foot, jogging after him into his room. He swung the bedroom door shut but I slapped it aside with one palm. "*Hell* no. I'm not going to let you walk away from this. From me."

Marc sat on the rumpled right-hand bed next to his packed suitcase, his elbows resting on his knees. "What do you want, Faythe? What the *hell* do you want from me?" When he looked up, I saw fire in his eyes—a familiar blaze of indignation that made my heart thump harder in the hope that he might get mad enough to save himself. To save *us,* if we were to ever be *us* again. And I'd always assumed we eventually *would* be.

"I want you to *do* something, instead of bending over while they *fuck* you. I want you to stand up for what you want!"

"That's *not* what you want." He rose, eyes glittering furiously in spite of little available light, and stepped into my personal space. "I stood up for what I wanted two months ago and you handed me my heart—not to mention my balls—all wrapped up in your fucking pride and independence. And now you stand here yelling at me for not being willing to sing that song all over again? That's bullshit, Faythe. What is this about? What do you *really* want from me?"

"I said I didn't want your damn *ring,*" I said, flashing back to the night we'd broken up "I never said I didn't want *you.*" My words came out in a gutless whisper, which was the most I could manage without either crying or shouting. "This was *not* in the plan."

He huffed and leaned with both palms flat on the dresser, his back to me. "Plans change."

"Not if you don't let them."

Marc shook his head in either disgust or frustration; I couldn't tell which. "When are you going to learn? When are you going to *grow* the *fuck up* and understand that you don't make all the rules. Hell, you don't make *any* of the rules, and neither do I." He straightened and faced me expectantly, like he really wanted an answer, but I had no idea what to say because he was right. But he wasn't done.

"You don't want me to stand against the council. You want a *magic wand,* so you can walk around smacking people with it until everything's just the way you like it. But guess what, Faythe? Life doesn't work like that. Life *bites,* and the harder you fight it, the more leverage it has to tear your heart right out of your chest. And if you really want to wake this particular sleeping dog, the truth is that if you'd just taken that 'damn ring' five years ago, *none* of this *shit* would ever have happened!"

Stunned, I stared at Marc, blinking in silence as pain ripped through my chest, an echo of what Radley had done to my stomach, only infinitely worse. More personal. More agonizing. My breath abandoned my body in one long, ragged exhale. I fell against the wall and slid to the floor, my arms wrapped around my knees.

"I'm sorry." Marc's arms fell limp at his sides and his head dropped in defeat. Or in regret. "I shouldn't have said that."

"Yes, you should have. It's the truth." If I'd married him the first time he'd asked me, we'd probably have a home of our own several miles from the ranch, and a backyard full of swings and sandboxes. No excitement and no danger—for me at least. No capital crimes, no dead ex and no possibility of an execution.

"I've messed everything up. I know." And in that moment, if I could have taken it all back, I would have.

Marc exhaled deeply, and the sound settled into a fragile, excruciating silence. In spite of everything I'd done, he still respected me too much to sugarcoat the truth. To absolve me of all blame. And as much as it hurt, I loved him for it.

"Tell me what you want, Faythe. Just tell me what you want me to do, and I'll do it."

I wanted a do over. A time machine. That magic wand. But real life didn't have any easy outs, and very few happily-everafters. The real world was more like a Choose Your Own Adventure book, with most of the choices ripped out before you even opened the cover.

"I…" I stared at the floor so I wouldn't have to meet his eyes while I impaled my heart on my sleeve, where it could be shredded by a single sharp word from him. "I want you to love me enough to stay."

There, I'd said it—I'd admitted aloud what I hadn't *once* said directly in the ten weeks since we'd broken up. And it was too late to take it back now, no matter how he reacted.

I looked up to find surprise in the slack line of Marc's mouth and the slight tilt of his head. Pain rippled across his features like a repressed shudder, and when he spoke, it echoed in his voice, hollow and hurt.

"I'm walking away *because* I love you. Because Calvin Malone is after me, not you, and if I go, he'll leave you alone."

Twenty

"What?" I blinked, trying to make sense of the new information, without much luck. "Why would he leave me alone once you're gone?"

Marc gave me one hand, and I let him pull me up. "Malone never approved of your dad taking me in, and Blackwell can't see anything beyond his damn *good old days*. They aren't the only ones, either. This has been coming for a long time, and now they've found a way to get rid of me. They'll make your dad choose between you and me."

I shook my head, still confused. "I don't understand. How is Daddy choosing between us?"

"Malone gave him a choice—off the record, of course. If Greg doesn't fight my exile, Malone—as the head of the tribunal—will suddenly decide the death penalty isn't warranted for you."

What? "You can't be serious." Yet suddenly Malone's phony fear for my safety—even as he pushed to have me executed—made sense. The trumped-up charge against Marc was intended to force my father's hand, to make him kick Marc out.

And it had worked.

Marc pushed his suitcase over and sat at the head of his

bed while I sank onto the one opposite his. "Unfortunately, I'm completely serious. Your uncle thinks once I'm gone, Malone will have a change of heart. He's guessing they'll give you a warning, probation, and probably a long-term suspension, to make it look real. And the worst part is that that corrupt son of a bitch is going to come off looking merciful on us both."

But he was wrong there. The worst part was that Marc would be gone.

I let my skull thump against the headboard as I stared at the ceiling. "That's so *wrong!* My hearing has nothing to do with you! He can't make Daddy choose."

Yet we both knew he *could*. If he got a majority vote, Calvin Malone could do whatever he wanted. I'd known all along that he hated Marc; I just hadn't realized how far he was willing to go to get rid of the token stray.

The rest of the Territorial Council had been tolerant of my father's eccentricity at first, amused by the tenderhearted lion taking in the orphaned kitten. But when that kitten grew up big and strong—and especially when he became the front-runner in the race for my heart, a position as Alpha of our Pride, and a seat on the Territorial Council—a handful of them had panicked. For the last five years, several of the Alphas, including Calvin Malone, had been pressuring my father to marry me off to someone else—one of their sons, naturally. But he'd steadily refused, insisting that I would make up my own mind when the time was right.

But, shrew that I was, I'd proved him wrong; I'd turned down every offer of marriage that came my way—including Marc's. Now that I'd come home and was trying to win him back, those Alphas were evidently panicking anew at the thought of a stray sitting on the council with them. Led by Malone, they were going to all new lows to get rid of him.

And I'd just given them the perfect opportunity.

"So it's all a game!" Fury fused with relief and I sat up, my hand clenching and unclenching around the bedspread. "It's just a fucking game, and they've made their move. All we have to do is outmaneuver them. Which should be easy now that we know they aren't really going to execute me."

Marc shook his head slowly, sadly, and twisted to look at me. "It's not a game, Faythe. It's a power play, and they've already won. The death sentence isn't a bluff." He inhaled deeply, preparing to say something I was obviously *not* going to like. "I think it *was* a bluff at first, to scare you into letting one of their sons knock you up. But now they think they've found a replacement for you—a tabby with no connection to either me or your father. With whom they could edge us right out of our own Pride."

Kaci. Shit. Fear rushed through my veins, throbbing viciously with each beat of my heart. They wanted the young, scared, impressionable, orphaned tabby instead of the stubborn, uncooperative hellcat they thought me to be. "Son of a bitch!" Once they had Kaci, they wouldn't need *me,* at which point my existence became of no importance whatsoever. And that's exactly what Marc had been trying to tell me.

They had trapped my father in a lose-lose situation, and they didn't really care which option he chose. If he picked Marc, they'd execute me. Daddy would have no daughter, thus no heirs. He would eventually lose control of our Pride, and the council would give it to whomever they'd married Kaci off to—some tom they could easily control.

But if my dad chose me, Marc would already be out of the way, thus ineligible for a spot at my side and on the council. If I settled down with one of their sons, my chosen tom would inherit the territory and my father's seat on the council. If I still refused to marry, they'd replace me with Kaci.

A chill raced through me, sprouting goose bumps in its wake. "They're trying to handpick Daddy's replacement. They think they can pair Kaci with the tom of their choosing and cut us right out of our own territory!" My head whirled, my thoughts flying too fast to examine. "They'll probably pick one of Malone's boys." Who would one day become an Alpha, as well as a member of the Territorial Council, in effect giving Calvin Malone control of *two* territories, which would make him the most powerful member of the council. "We can't let him do this! Marrying Kaci off to a tom of their choosing is no better than what Miguel had in mind for me and Abby."

"I know. It's revolting." Marc swallowed thickly.

"Damn, I hope I'm wrong about her being a stray." If she was a Pride tabby, even an *orphaned* Pride tabby, there would be a gaggle of brothers and enforcers out there somewhere looking for her. And surely whatever she'd run away from was no worse than what Malone had planned for her.

Or maybe it was. Why else would she leave the security of her own home to wander on her own for weeks at a time, sick, starving, and injured?

Shit. There was a very good chance that poor thirteen-year-old tabby was stuck between the ultimate rock and hard place—a location I was intimately familiar with. I had to help her.

"We have to find out where she comes from and who might be looking for her. We have to protect her, Marc."

He shook his head slowly, as if it felt too heavy to move. "*You* have to protect her, and to do that, you have to be *alive*. That's why I'm leaving. It's the best thing I can do for both of you." His gaze burned into me, branding my soul with the memory of everything we'd once been. Everything we would lose once he was gone.

And he made it sound so damn *permanent*.

"There has to be another way to fix this." I shifted on the spare bed, and the mattress creaked beneath me. "I can't protect Kaci on my own, and losing you will make it worse, not better." And I sure as *hell* couldn't stomach the thought of spending the rest of my life without him. Much less ever replacing him, which the council would make me do eventually. The hearing had taught me that, if nothing else.

I brushed a strand of hair from my face, trying desperately to force down the fear clawing up the inside of my throat. "You can't go. I won't let you. I can't." My voice cracked as I spoke, and finally broke on the last word.

Marc crossed the room to stare out the window, as if it hurt to look at me. "I can't stay here and watch them kill you. Please, Faythe. Just let me go."

Tears blurred my vision, and I tried to blink them away, but they fell instead, scalding twin paths down my cheeks. "No." I stood and crossed the room, wiping my face with my sleeve. *Not for good.*

"Don't make this any harder," he whispered as my hands found his chest. "Please."

I stood on my toes and brushed my lips against his. His scent surrounded me, triggering memories I hadn't thought of in years, and reactions I'd never once forgotten.

"Faythe…" He pulled away from me, but I followed him, my fingers playing against the wrenchingly familiar planes and hollows of his chest beneath the faded cotton concert T-shirt he'd had for more than a decade.

I kissed him again, harder this time, demanding a reaction from him. Demanding an acknowledgment that we still had something together. That I still meant something to him. If I could make him remember what he'd be leaving behind, he might be willing to fight for it. For *us*. He just needed a reminder…

My hands slid beneath his shirt, and my fingers brushed the sparse, coarse hair on the rigid surface of his stomach. I inhaled deeply and his scent filled me.

My heart beat harder and my breath came faster. My hands skimmed higher on his chest, his flesh warm beneath my fingers. A long, low moan shuddered in his throat in spite of lips pressed together in denial of the sounds we both knew he wanted to make.

"Faythe, please…" But he didn't step back and made no move to push me away.

I slid my hands over each rib, dragging his shirt higher inch by slow inch. On my toes again, I trailed my mouth over his chin. I loved the rough, thoroughly masculine feel of his beard stubble against my lips. My hands moved farther up, my fingers splayed, and my thumbs brushed the hard edges of his pecs. His breath came faster, his mouth open now.

"Arms up," I whispered, my lips brushing his chin. Marc obediently raised his arms, and I slid the shirt over his head, then let it drop onto the floor behind him. My hands roamed his arms and chest, and my pulse roared in my ears, almost blocking out his heartbeat completely.

"Faythe, you don't have to—"

"Shh." My lips opened and my teeth found his chin, nibbling their way down the line of his jaw to his ear, where the delicious, musky Marc-scent deepened. I purred, capturing his earlobe between my lips. I was careful not to bite, but when I tugged gently, his hands finally found my hips, squeezing as his head fell back and a soft, throaty growl rumbled against my cheek.

My mouth dipped lower, nibbling the sweet, hot flesh of his neck, and his hands slipped beneath my shirt, kneading my waist in time with his own pulse. I murmured wordless pleasure against his throat and nuzzled closer, pushing us a step nearer to the bed. His hands slid beneath my jeans, cupping my hips eagerly, possessively. His skin was exquisitely warm against mine, his fingers wonderfully rough and willing.

He smelled so good. So intimately familiar and safe, yet dangerous at the same time, and I couldn't get enough of him. My lips found his again, and when my mouth opened, his parted in welcome. My hands trailed his torso once more until my fingers brushed the waistband of his jeans.

I pushed his button through its hole as his hands inched up the outside of my shirt and over my shoulders. His fingers tangled in my hair, tilting my head back to give him better access to my mouth. The kiss deepened and I shoved his jeans down, fighting not to wrap my legs around him where he stood. Marc hadn't touched me intimately in two and a half months and we only had a matter of minutes before the inevitable interruption.

Patience did not come easily.

He must have felt the rush, too, because he let go of my hair to grab my shirt, only pulling from my mouth long enough to tug the black tee over my head. He turned us so the backs of my knees brushed the edge of the mattress, my fingers still playing along his back. His mouth claimed mine again as his hands worked at the waistband of my jeans. A second later, they hit the floor, my underwear pooled inside them.

His arms encircled me, hands fumbling with the latch of my bra as I shoved his boxers down, my hands trailing over the tight curves of his backside, the granite expanse of his thighs. He growled in frustration and his arms tensed against me. Threads popped and my bra slid down my arms, the hooks ripped free from the material.

Damn. That was a good bra too. But Marc was better. He was worth however many articles of clothing he wanted to ruin, and if he'd stay, I'd gladly let him shred my whole wardrobe.

I let the bra fall as he stepped out of his underwear, and when his eyes found mine again I circled him, splaying one hand across his chest, my fingers half covering the old, white scars a psychotic stray had carved into him fifteen years earlier. Though I knew he hated them, I loved those marks because that was the injury that had brought him into my life. A permanent reminder of the moment that had ripped away everything he'd ever known, and given us to each other.

And after all that time, all those moments stolen, those cravings indulged, he was leaving—to save *me*. We'd been apart before, most notably the five years I spent at college. But this was different. Until I could get him reinstated, he wouldn't just be stomping around in the guesthouse out back, or waiting for me to come home from school. He'd be truly gone—out of reach and officially persona non grata.

But not until tomorrow. For now, Marc was everywhere. His chest hair tickled my palms, his heart beat against my fingers. His scent filled the air. His voice rumbled through me with each moan of pleasure, each groan of impatience. Soon, the free zone would have him. But until then, Marc was mine, and I was gonna give him one hell of a send-off.

I smiled and shoved him backward. He let himself fall onto the bed, and a little thrill raced down my spine to settle low and throb steadily. I was on him in an instant, straddling his thighs as my hands sought every inch of his flesh.

His hands squeezed my hips, grinding me against him as he arched up from the bed over and over again. I gasped, and my knees clenched on either side of him, pinning us together as he throbbed against the most sensitive parts of my body.

I sat up straight and Marc's eyes met mine. I nodded. He lifted me with both hands, guiding me forward. I closed my eyes, knowing he would watch my face the whole time.

He lowered me onto him slowly, inch by exquisite inch, until my thighs met his hips. I didn't realize I was holding my breath until it slipped from my open mouth in a sigh of contentment. Satisfaction. An indisputable *right*ness I never, ever felt except when we were joined so thoroughly, so intimately that our pulses raced in twin rhythms, each breath pushing in and out in tandem.

I felt him exhale beneath me, and with the next heartbeat I rocked forward, my head thrown back, my lower lip pinched between my teeth in concentration. He moaned and arched into me as I came back down. We started out slowly, letting the rhythm loiter, the pleasure build gradually. But that didn't last. It had been too long, and we had too little time.

He pulled me down for another kiss, and when I rose again, he grabbed my hips, rocking me faster, pulling in and out frantically as I clenched around him. My knees chafed against the cheap sheets, but I barely noticed because of the other, delicious friction building where Marc's body met mine. His grip on my waist tightened and our motions grew faster, more frenzied.

Sweat formed on his chest, slick beneath my hands. My thighs tensed and relaxed ceaselessly, raising me higher with each withdrawal, slamming us together with each thrust. He went taut beneath me. Each time we touched he cried out. Every stroke made me gasp, intensifying the need building within me until one last, brutal grind made his body jerk, his grip bruising my hips. And with his last thrusts, I shuddered around him, gasping, unable to think beyond that one endless moment.

I opened my eyes to find Marc smiling at me for the first time in months, and relief coursed through me on the tail of my orgasm. I fell limp on top of him, my cheek on his shoulder. He gathered my hair, spreading it to trail onto the bed, where he stroked it over and over, breathing hard beneath me as our hearts raced in echo of the rhythm we'd created.

For five solid minutes, we lay together on the bed, as close as we could be without doing it all over again. In spite of my raging anger at the tribunal and my recent sedation, my eyes were drooping when Jace's cautious shout splintered the peaceful silence.

"Hey, you guys? I hate to interrupt, but I think I just heard a door slam. Sounded like it came from the lodge."

"Thanks!" I called across both rooms and two closed doors. I rose reluctantly and donned my underwear and pants while Marc watched me from the bed, making no move to get up. He had nowhere important to be, for the first time I could remember.

I already had my bra over both shoulders before I remembered the hooks were ruined. Scowling in mock anger, I tossed it at Marc and grinned, already heading for my own bedroom to grab another one. "Consider it a souvenir."

"I believe handkerchiefs are customary. Or even a photograph."

"Sorry, I don't carry either." And I knew he'd take the bra, even though I'd meant it as a joke, because it smelled like me. For cats, even more than for humans, memories are triggered by scent. Which was why I had every intention of taking one of his T-shirts, just as soon as he left his stuff unguarded.

Five minutes later my father and brother walked through the front door of the cabin as I was sitting down to a plate piled high with formerly frozen waffles—so what if it was twelve-thirty in the afternoon? Marc was on his second bowl of Count Chocula, but I'd wanted something hot and sweet to replace the energy we'd just burned.

Jace waited for me in the living room, and when my father came in, my keeper rushed to explain that he was going to take me to the lodge just as soon as I'd had something to eat. Daddy waved off his excuses. "I need to talk to her anyway," he mumbled. Then he got a whiff of my scent and his gloomy scowl bloomed into a reserved smile that said he knew exactly what we'd been doing.

I knew *I should have taken time for a shower.* I'd smell like Marc—and vice versa—until I did.

Though I nearly swallowed my waffles whole, Marc still finished eating first, and when he stood, I shoved my leftovers across the table toward Jace and made my way into the living room. Marc sank next to me on the couch and we faced my father as a united front.

We'd gotten back together just in time to be separated by politics. I couldn't have had worse luck if I'd Shifted and broken a mirror on the underside of a ladder.

"I take it they've filled you in." My father settled wearily into the armchair on my right, in spite of lumpy arms and a too-low seat. From his bearing alone I knew better than to expect an apology for being sedated. Hell, I was lucky they hadn't knocked me out the old-fashioned way—with a solid blow to the head.

"Yeah." I hesitated, forcing myself to swallow my anger at my father. He wouldn't have made such a decision lightly. "They also said you had no choice."

He nodded. "As much as it pains me to admit it…"

For nearly a minute, no one spoke, and the only sounds were the ticking of Michael's watch and Jace's chewing. And that was all I could take. "So, how's this going to work?" I glanced from my father to my brother, then back. "Marc moves into the free zone for a while, then we find some reason to bring him back. Right? So how long are we talking? A few months?"

Michael suddenly became very interested in his loafers, and my brunch began to pitch within my stomach.

"A year? Surely it won't take that long…"

"I don't think it's going to be that easy," my brother finally said. "Malone and Blackwell are dead serious about this, and there are others on the council who will back them. If Dad goes back on his word—especially within just a few months— he'll lose a lot of credibility with the council. And he really can't afford that right now."

My father frowned, as if he wanted to disagree but couldn't. *Not* a good sign. But they couldn't really mean to leave Marc alone in the free zone forever. Or even for a couple of years. That was too long.

"Come on, guys, there has to be a way out of this. The Territorial Council has more pointless rules and regulations than any governing body in history. I'm sure we can find a loophole. Michael, you get out all the old logs and records and search for a precedent, Marc and Jace can keep the wolves at bay, and I'll…make some coffee."

At least that would prove that I was good for something other than getting people killed, concussed, or exiled.

"Faythe…" My father reached out to lay one hand on my arm, but I jerked away from him.

"No." I shook my head vehemently and clenched my hands in my lap so hard my knuckles ached. "We can't let this happen, Daddy. What did you actually agree to? Give it to me word for word. There may be some wiggle room in the phrasing. Did you happen to give a time limit for this so-called expulsion?"

"Stop, Faythe." Marc's hand landed on mine, and I didn't have the heart to pull away from him because I wasn't sure how long I'd have to wait to touch him again. "It's done, and we have some important decisions to make."

"Like what?" How long to make Marc pretend to be exiled before bringing him back? What to get him for a welcome-back gift?

He sighed. "Who to bring in as my replacement." His focus shifted to my father. "It should be someone we trust, and someone with a few years' experience. I was thinking maybe Brian Taylor."

"What?" I whirled on him, and a sudden flash of fear left my nerve endings singed. "You won't be gone long enough for that," I insisted, clinging stubbornly to the resolve that I could get him reinstated. Somehow. "Some new flea will crawl into Malone's fur and he'll forget about you, and when he does, we'll find a way to bring you back."

"Faythe." Marc took my hands and squeezed them, and his eyes held mine. Wouldn't let them go. "It's done. With any luck, it won't be forever." He glanced at my dad again, and on the edge of my vision, I saw my Alpha nod. "But it will be for a long time."

"No." I heard the plea in my voice and hated the sound of my own weakness, but couldn't seem to squelch it. "Not now.

Not after all this." My voice broke, and when I paused to regain what little composure I had left, I saw that Jace was standing in the doorway, watching me in an agony all his own. "Maybe Marc could work from the free zone. You know, patrolling the boundary from the other side, or—" I choked back a sob "—chasing down rogues. Of course, he'd have to come home now and then to file a report…"

"Faythe, I tried that," my father said gently. "I don't want to lose him either, and I did everything I could to put limitations on this. But Malone's a stubborn bastard, and Paul Blackwell's firmly in his corner on this one. And we don't have any leverage. Marc can't come back onto Pride territory while he's in exile."

"Okay." I nodded slowly, not because I understood, but because he'd just given me a solid obstacle to work around. A place to start. But I'd have to give it some thought. Come up with some leverage…

"And while he's gone," my father continued, shifting his gaze from me to Marc, "we have to bring someone in to replace him. Not as the top enforcer, of course. I'll bring up either Vic or Ethan for that. But we'll need an extra set of claws…"

I didn't hear most of the discussion that followed; I wasn't interested in replacing Marc. But ten minutes later, my father went into his bedroom and closed the door, behind which I heard him talking on the phone to my mother, probably calling in backup. We were shorthanded already, because of all the injuries, and it would only get worse when Marc left.

In fifteen short hours.

On the front porch, Marc squeezed my hand and gave me a lingering kiss goodbye, then Jace herded me down the steps. Now pissed, I stomped toward the lodge like a woman with nothing to fear and everything to prove, Jace jogging at my heels.

When we were halfway there, Jace called out from behind me. "Faythe, would you wait? I need to talk to you."

"So talk. But make it fast. I have something to say to the tribunal, and I want to get it over with before I lose my nerve." And anyway, I'd forgotten my jacket, and it was freezing outside.

"Well, you need to hear this, so stop for just a minute." He grabbed my arm and turned me to face him, returning my glare with a very grave expression when I jerked my arm free. "I sat with Brett for a little while you were sleeping off that tranquilizer, and he told me something you need to know."

Jace was closer to Brett than to any of his other half siblings, but I couldn't remember them ever sharing important information before. Or even much more than a greeting.

I frowned, set on edge by the urgency in his voice. "What's wrong?"

Jace ducked his head for a moment, as if he was embarrassed to say whatever was coming. But then he huffed and met my eyes, new resolve shining in his. "I heard Marc tell you why your dad let him go—" which meant that wasn't *all* he overheard "—and I'm afraid that if he finds out what I'm about to tell you, he won't go, and Calvin will push for your execution. So I need you to promise me you won't tell him."

"Jace, if it's that important, Marc needs to know."

"I know." His brow wrinkled as conflict flickered across his face. "But I'm not going to gamble with your life, even for this. So you have to promise, or I won't tell you."

I couldn't help but smile. "You know I'll find out eventually."

He nodded. "But I also know you don't have time to play snoop right now. Not if you want to stay out of trouble, or be any real help to that poor tabby."

Okay, he had me there. "Fine, I won't tell him." *Directly, anyway.* "Spit it out."

Jace sighed. "When your trial's over, Calvin's going to make a motion to have your father unseated as the head of the Territorial Council."

Twenty-One

"**H**ave him *unseated?*" I searched Jace's face for some sign that he was making a massively unfunny joke. But he was completely serious, and evidently every bit as angry about it as I was.

"Yeah." A cloud of steam puffed from his mouth with his answer. "Calvin claims to have the support of several other Alphas, though he's not naming names yet. At least, not to Brett."

Yeah, well, I was pretty sure I could guess at least a couple of them.

I closed my eyes in dread, curling and uncurling my fists to keep my blood circulating in the near-freezing temperature. "On what grounds?"

"Withholding information from the Territorial Council. Because he went after Andrew, Manx, and Luiz—" the stray who'd slaughtered a series of human strippers in and around our territory "—without alerting the other Prides." Jace rubbed my upper arms to warm them, and when I opened my eyes, he continued. "Cal's saying Wes Gardner should have had the opportunity to participate. Rumor has it Wes is seriously pissed because we didn't avenge Jamey's death. I wouldn't be surprised to find out he's one of the Alphas backing Calvin."

Wes Gardner was Alpha of the Great Lakes Pride, and his brother Jamey, an adopted member of our Pride, had been killed by Manx a couple of months earlier. We'd had every intention of avenging Jamey's death, but when we found out he was killed by a pregnant, abused, and emotionally fragile tabby, things got…*complicated*.

And my father had acted without consulting the Territorial Council for the same reason I'd gone into Kaci's room without permission—using the official channels always takes forever, and while the Alphas are wasting time, people die. In large part because men like Calvin Malone are more interested in flexing their political muscles than actually helping those depending on them.

That raging bastard!

"We have to tell Daddy."

"Yeah, I'm going to tell him while you're talking to Kaci. But Brett wanted you to know first. He thinks he owes you for saving his life. And he said he'd keep his ears open, just in case."

I nodded, already walking again to get my blood flowing. "Thank him for me, please."

Jace smiled. "I already did."

Anger buzzed inside me so fiercely my skin tingled all the way to the lodge. I yanked open the front door and stomped past my uncle and Lucas in the living room, hell-bent on standing up to Calvin Malone for once. He'd threatened to have me executed, gotten Marc exiled, and was planning to usurp my father's position on the council. If someone didn't drag his corrupt ass back down to earth soon, the bastard would probably start to think he could fly…

Furniture springs groaned as my cousin stood and fell into place beside Jace, making a show of support at my back like a member of some badass entourage.

I marched down the hall and into the dining room, where Councilmen Malone and Blackwell sat at the table, scooping huge spoonfuls of homemade chicken and dumplings from thick, ceramic soup bowls with cows painted on them.

When I appeared in his peripheral vision, Malone froze with his spoon halfway to his mouth, then lowered it slowly. "Miss Sanders." He nodded, acknowledging me politely, which shot my anger to the next level. His civil tone meant he knew he'd gotten rid of Marc and could now afford to be magnanimous. Slimy little pricks like Calvin Malone were rarely friendly under other circumstances. "What can we do for you?"

Several colorful answers popped into my head, but I kept my reply to the point, because if Paul Blackwell hadn't yet officially gone over to the Dark Side, one more outburst from me might very well send him there. My stand would have to be calm, and mature, and reasonable. Otherwise it would be very short-lived

I took a long, deep breath. "Jace said you needed something from me."

Malone's jaw tightened at my word choice. I'd said "needed" instead of "wanted," to emphasize the fact that they *did* need me. And if Malone expected my help, he was going to have to ask for it. *Nicely.*

Jace's stepfather nodded stiffly. "The tabby—"

"Her name is Kaci Dillon," I interrupted, my pulse spiking in petty satisfaction when his hand clenched around his spoon. That was just one more piece of information he wouldn't have had, if not for me.

"Of course. *Kaci* seems to have bonded with you, and we want to know where she's from and who her Pride is. And how she got here."

What, no pretty please?

I sucked in a deep breath and glanced over my shoulder, glad to see Jace and Lucas still had my back, even if they'd stopped near the doorway. "Fine." My focus narrowed on Malone. "I'm going to do this for you. But you're going to do something for me in return."

Malone's face flushed in fury. "You're in no position to ask for anything."

"I'm not asking."

Behind me, Jace chuckled, and the corner of my mouth quirked.

"What do you want?" Blackwell asked before Malone could come up with an original threat to my life or freedom.

"I want permission for Marc to visit the Lazy S every other weekend. Conjugal visits, if you will." I couldn't stifle a smile that time. Malone's whole reasoning for getting rid of Marc was to try to force me into a relationship with someone he considered more suitable for fathering the next generation. Preferably one of his sons.

My request would derail his entire evil scheme.

Malone's face went from "maraschino" to "red dwarf" in less than a second. "No. Absolutely not. An exiled tom has no business on Pride land, and no business with *you*."

"Fine. Go question Kaci yourself." I spun on one heel and was halfway to the door before Blackwell called after me.

"Don't you *dare* walk away from us without being dismissed!"

"Why not?" I turned to find the council's senior member standing, one wrinkled hand on the table for balance. *Let's find out where the swing vote stands on the matter of my death sentence...* "Aren't you going to have me executed no matter what I do?"

Surprise registered on the old man's face, followed by a flicker of confusion as he glanced at Malone. Did that mean he'd *participated* in Malone's capital punishment bluff, or only that he knew about it?

I couldn't tell. "Knowing that leaves me with no motivation to do what you want. What are you going to do, kill me twice?" I spared a glance over my shoulder at Jace as I borrowed his phrase, then turned back to the Alphas. "Next time you want to manipulate someone, remember to leave the poor bastard a little hope to keep him cooperative. Simple, but effective."

And apparently completely beyond the ken of Calvin Malone, who looked ready to burst from the pressure building behind his fake-reasonable mask.

I shrugged and propped both hands on my hips, eyeing Malone. "So, do we have a deal, or are you ready to go up there and make nice with Kaci. I hear you two got along *famously.*"

For several moments, no one spoke, and I could read indecision on their faces as Malone and Blackwell stared at each other, trying in vain to make a decision without discussing their options in front of me. But the Alphas were screwed, and they knew it. Or at least, Malone did.

Before he could use Kaci in his little coup, he had to make sure she didn't have a troop of angry brothers and enforcers coming after her. And if she didn't, it wouldn't hurt to get on her good side, to ensure her cooperation. But he couldn't do either on his own. He needed me. Not that I really had any intention of helping *him.*

"Fine. You find out where she's from, how she got here, and what Pride she belongs to, and we'll let Marc pay you a visit."

"Every other week…" I insisted.

Malone shook his head stiffly. "Once a year."

I laughed in his face, and enjoyed every second of it. "Once a month, or I walk."

Jace's stepfather growled and glared at me, and started to shake his head again. But Blackwell elbowed his fellow Alpha into silence and watched me with shrewd, glinting black eyes. "Once every six months. You either take that and consider yourself lucky or I'll fly my granddaughter out to bond with this new tabby, and you can kiss your lover goodbye forever."

Shit. I knew when I'd been had, and judging by the way Blackwell's face screwed up in disgust when he called Marc my lover, that time had come. Still, I'd stood up to Malone *and* pissed him off. And I'd kept him from completely cutting Marc out of my life.

I beamed over my victory. "Deal."

At the end of the upstairs hall, I snatched a bundle of my own clothing from the tom posted at Kaci's bedroom door, one of Paul Blackwell's enforcers, whom I barely knew. I had no idea how he wound up with the outfit I'd sent Jace for earlier, but I was glad he had it, since I'd completely forgotten the poor girl was still naked.

The garments tucked under one arm, I knocked on Kaci's door. There was no answer, so I knocked again, then turned the knob and slipped inside. Kaci was curled up on the floor in that same corner, still huddled beneath only the thin blanket, in spite of the late-November chill. The steady rise and fall of her small chest told me she was asleep.

I set the clothes on the nearest bed and dropped to my knees several feet from the sleeping tabby. I was afraid that if I woke her suddenly, she'd be frightened and disoriented, and I'd have to restrain her. She'd been through enough without having to fight me. So I waited.

My gaze was drawn to her face. She looked so…*normal*. Other than the fact that she was sleeping on the floor. And that she was too thin. And that she had mud and twigs caught in her hair. But her face could have been the face of any thirteen-year-old on the planet. Those well-formed lips and long, thick lashes could have belonged to a junior-high softball pitcher. Those thin fingers, now clutching the blanket to her chin, could play the piano in another life. And perhaps they would again, someday soon.

But the pessimist in me seriously doubted it. There was something unusual about this girl. Something different from every tabby I'd ever known. Maybe it was that she was an orphan. Maybe that was enough to account for the fierce determination to survive I'd glimpsed in her eyes each time fear faded from them. But I couldn't help thinking it was something else. Something connected to the reason she was on her own, instead of surrounded by the usual cocoon of brothers and enforcers.

As I watched, her eyes twitched behind her eyelids and her fists clenched around the hem of the blanket. She grunted in her sleep, and I was troubled by the obvious fear in such an inarticulate sound. My hand reached out before I could stop it, and I brushed a strand of dirt-caked hair from her face. She looked so fragile, so defenseless, and my urge to protect her was so overwhelming I couldn't breathe without tasting it in the air.

I stroked her hair one more time and suddenly realized her chest was no longer rising. She wasn't breathing. I pulled my hand away as panic flooded me. She'd gone stiff, her legs straight beneath the thin blanket, knuckles white where they gripped the hem. *Oh, shit!* Was she having some kind of seizure?

Then a small, quick movement drew my attention back to her face. Her eyes were open. She wasn't seizing; she was waking up.

Fear crept into those huge hazel eyes, but still she didn't move. She'd frozen in place, like I couldn't see her if she didn't move.

"Kaci?" I tried to project calm concern, to keep from setting her off, but it didn't work. She jerked into motion at the sound of my voice, backing away from me until she sat with her spine pressed into the corner, growling deep in her throat and glaring at me as if the fierceness of her expression should have scared me away.

Maybe it would have, if she'd been in cat form.

Damn, she doesn't remember. The realization hit me with a jolt of amazement. She'd just woken up in a strange place, after weeks spent in cat form. She had no idea where she was, likely didn't remember who *I* was, and probably had yet to realize she wasn't furry.

"It's me. Faythe." I reached for the bed behind me without taking my eyes from hers. My hand found soft, fuzzy material, and I pulled the sweater slowly into view. "I brought you some clothes."

Her gaze shifted to take in the sweater, and she must have caught sight of her arm, or some other obviously human part of her body, which ushered in memories from earlier in the day.

Kaci's head whipped up, her eyes studying me with a bit of cautious recognition now. Then suddenly they narrowed, and her forehead wrinkled in a frown. "Where were you? You said you'd be right back, but you were gone for *hours!* You *lied.*"

"I didn't mean to. I'm sorry. I…got in trouble." *May as well tell her the truth.* Part of it, anyway.

"I know. I heard them yelling at you." Her face relaxed a little, and she tugged the sheet up to her neck. "What did you do?"

I shoved hair back from my forehead and leaned against the mattress, wondering how much she'd already overheard. "I wasn't supposed to come talk to you without asking first."

"Asking who?"

"My dad, or one of the other Alphas."

Her brows dipped low in confusion, reaffirming my theory that she hadn't the slightest idea what I was talking about. But while I was dying to find out what she *did* know, I tucked my questions away for the moment. I would ask them once she was dressed and warm, and comfortable with me again.

"Um, I brought you some clothes." I held the sweater out toward her. "Why don't you put them on and we'll talk."

Kaci looked curious in spite of the distance she'd put between us. She peered at the bed over my shoulder, and I smiled as I pulled the rest of the clothing into my lap. She dismissed the black cotton pj's at a glance, but her eyes lingered on the cream-colored angora.

Smiling, I carried the whole bundle closer, expecting with each step that she would tell me to stop, or warn me off with another growl, but her attention never left the sweater. When I was close enough, she reached out and ran her fingers slowly across the material, clearly savoring the feel. Fear faded from her face and was replaced by…eagerness?

She wanted that sweater, and I'd gladly give it to her. If my two-hundred-dollar angora sweater was the price for whatever secrets had turned her out in the world alone, I was willing to pay. My mother had bought the damn thing anyway.

"Go ahead. Try it on," I urged, turning to face the door to give her privacy.

A minute later, she cleared her throat. "Okay. You can look now."

I turned to see her and couldn't believe the difference. She was still too thin, collarbones showing clearly above the neck of the sweater, and her hair was still matted with dirt and cockleburs. But donning clothes had changed her every bit as dramatically as Shifting had earlier. Maybe more.

Where before she'd been shy and scared, except during brief moments of fierce self-defense, now she seemed… content.

"You look beautiful. That looks like it was made for you." And it did, even though it was several sizes too large. Unfortunately, the pants were also too big. "Here. Let me help you tighten the drawstring."

A frown creased her forehead, and Kaci glanced at her tiny waist. I knelt in front of her and she held the black top and sweater out of the way while I showed her how to adjust the waistband.

"There." The pants still pooled around her feet, but they'd stay in place now.

Pleased by the progress she'd already made, I sat on the nearest bed, tucking my feet beneath me yoga style. Leaning to my left, I grabbed a pillow from the head of the bed and pulled it into my lap, hoping that if I looked relaxed and comfortable, she'd follow my lead, and we could have a nice tabby-to-tabby chat.

It worked.

As she perched hesitantly at the head of the bed, leaning against the sun-warmed windowsill at her back, I pictured her doing the same thing at some point in the past. Only then she would have been surrounded by girls her own age, at a slumber party, dressed in pink-and-purple pajamas and sharing a big bowl of popcorn or ice cream.

I shook the image off, bothered more than I wanted to admit by the thought of the normal life she'd probably never have again.

"So…" *Who are you and how did you get here?* But that was too direct, even by my own standards. Maybe we should start with something simpler. "Are you hungry?" If no one had brought her the clothes, she probably hadn't gotten lunch either, though it was nearly two in the afternoon.

She nodded shyly.

"I think we're out of chicken, but I'm sure we can come up with something else. You like frozen pizza? Warmed up, of course."

Her eyes lit up like an old-fashioned flashbulb. "I *love* pizza. And I haven't had any in, like…*forever*." Agitation flashed across her face as an old memory surfaced, but it was gone in an instant, likely buried by whatever inner strength had kept her going during all that time on her own. "Domino's is my favorite, but I guess frozen will do."

Spoken like a true teenager. Which I considered a very good sign.

Unfortunately, the goob at the door was under the council's orders not to leave his post, so I had to run downstairs and coerce Jace into warming up the pizza. I made him put it in the oven instead of the microwave to give me more time to talk to Kaci before food occupied her mouth. And because it would taste better that way.

Back in the upstairs bedroom, I shut the door behind me, cutting off the guard's curious look before he got more than a glance at Kaci. She was not going to come out of her shell so long as everyone kept treating her like an oddity.

"Pizza's on the way." I leaned against the closed door. "Should be here in about twenty minutes."

Kaci still sat at the head of the bed with her arms crossed over her chest, almost hugging herself. As I watched, unsure how to start the conversation we needed to have, Kaci's right hand left her arm and slid into the hair at her scalp, combing it in what was obviously a habitual gesture. But she got stuck less than a quarter of the way through, mired in tangles and dirt.

Kaci frowned and tugged her fingers free from the knot, then let her hands fall into her lap as she turned to stare out the window at the tree line, and the mountain rising in the distance. "Where are we?"

"In a private cabin complex. This is the main lodge, and there are several smaller cabins on either side." I crossed the room and settled onto the other end of the mattress.

"But *where* is this cabin complex?"

"Montana."

"Montana?" She twisted to look at me, and her eyes seemed to double in size. "Are you sure?"

I couldn't hold back a grin at her surprise. "Pretty sure. Why? You're not local?"

She shook her head and picked up a strand of her hair to peer at, as if checking for split ends.

"Me, neither."

Kaci plucked a cocklebur from her hair and dropped it onto the nightstand at her side. "Where are you from?"

"Texas. How 'bout you?"

She hesitated, frowning at the cocklebur for a minute before finally answering. "I'm not from anywhere anymore. I just…go wherever I can find food."

The crack she'd put in my heart widened a little more, and I ached to tell her she could stay with us as long as she wanted. But I knew better than to assume the council would honor any promise I made her. "Hey," I said, when her hand strayed to her hair for the third time in as many minutes. "The pizza won't be done for a little while. Would you like to take a shower before it gets here?"

"A shower?" She frowned for a moment, as if trying to pair the concept with the word, and again I wondered how long she'd been living in the wilderness. Then her eyes lit up at the prospect of doing something so…normal. "Yeah. I'd *love* a shower. And I really have to pee."

Twenty-Two

When I tried to take Kaci down the hall to the nearest bathroom, the guard at the door stepped into my path, refusing to let her out of the room. Kaci's eyes widened in panic at his less-than-gentle announcement that he was under orders to keep her inside. I cursed myself silently for not anticipating that little complication, then I cursed him aloud for being such a stupid asshole.

"She's a guest, not a prisoner!" I snapped, and my anger only grew when he told me to take the issue up with an Alpha. What made it even worse was that I couldn't blame him. He was just following orders.

It took me five minutes to calm Kaci down and convince her that she was indeed free to go if she really wanted to, all the while knowing that if I let her run, I could kiss my own freedom—and maybe my *life*—goodbye.

Once Kaci was calm, I had to run back downstairs, this time in search of an Alpha who could grant the tabby clearance to take a shower.

My father was still at our cabin with Michael, who was doing an Internet search for information about Kaci Dillon. Calvin Malone was seated at the head of the dining-room table, ostensibly going over his notes from my trial, but I didn't even bother asking him. Malone wouldn't push me out of the path of a speeding train, and I knew better than to expect his help in a less-than-critical situation.

Fortunately, my uncle walked through the front door just as I settled into the armchair across from Paul Blackwell, preparing to swallow my pride and ask the sexist old coot for some help.

Though he was probably still mad at me from earlier, Uncle Rick told the toy soldier upstairs to let me take Kaci to the second-floor bathroom, where he was to wait outside without bothering us. Then, before he went downstairs, my uncle shot me a conspiratorial wink from the end of the hallway. Evidently we were friends again.

Kaci followed me across the hall into the bathroom. I'd expected her to hide behind her hair and clutch at my arm, but to my surprise, she walked with her spine straight and proud, her head held tall. The only sign of discomfort I saw was the way her eyes rolled from side to side, constantly watching for anyone who might be lying in wait to attack her.

That was survival instinct, well developed during her time alone, and I wasn't going to discourage such impulses. They'd kept her alive, and they would continue to do so, which put her one step ahead of my brother Ryan in the game of survival. Ryan's idea of self-preservation was to suck up to our mother in hopes of keeping her checkbook open. Not that she was financing him anymore. He'd been locked in a cage in our basement since June, and he wasn't getting out anytime soon.

The upstairs bathroom was done in mountain-rustic decor, complete with framed black-and-white pictures of log cabins and shower-curtain hooks adorned with little brown plastic pinecones and moose antlers. I offered to wait outside with the guard, but Kaci asked me to come in. I think she was eager for company—not to mention security—after having been on her own for so long. So I stared at the fish-shaped coat hook on the back of the door while she stripped, then stepped into a separate cubicle to use the restroom.

I folded her—my—clothes, then set them on one side of the counter. She'd have to put them back on after her shower, since we had nothing else for her to wear at the moment, but at least she'd be clean.

The toilet flushed, then plastic rattled against metal as she opened the wilderness-themed shower curtain. A moment later, water burst from the tap to patter against the plastic-walled enclosure. Kaci squealed, then laughed at herself, and I smiled at the simple pleasure in her voice. "Okay, you can turn around."

I shoved aside an array of disposable razors, shaving cream, toothbrushes, and trial-size bottles of mouthwash littering the countertop, then hopped up to sit with my legs dangling. *This is definitely a guy bathroom.*

The cadence of the spray changed as Kaci moved beneath it, and after a moment she spoke, as if reading my mind. "I smell several…*scents* in here." At first I thought she meant shampoo, soap, and toothpaste—and maybe urine from whoever had splashed the rim of the toilet—but her next words set me straight. "Who are they?"

Oh. Personal *scents.* She smelled the other toms. And just like that she'd opened the very conversation I'd been struggling to start.

"They're enforcers. Several of the guys have been sharing this bathroom." I held my breath in anticipation of her response, and I honestly had no idea what to expect.

Kaci stepped out from under the flow of water, probably reaching for something at the end of the tub. A moment later the splatter of water was muted against her flesh again, and the aroma of soap flooded my senses. Irish Spring.

"What's an enforcer?" she asked, her tone as light as I'd ever heard it, giving the question no more significance than when she'd asked where we were.

But to me, her question spoke volumes. She hadn't known how to Shift, or even what the word meant. And now she didn't know what an enforcer was. Those concepts weren't foreign to a Pride cat, and again my focus centered on the possibility, however slim, that she might be a stray. I could see no other explanation for her ignorance.

"Enforcers are…like policemen. Or maybe soldiers. They protect their Alphas and defend their Pride's territory. And they protect their Pride's tabby, too, at all costs."

Wet sliding sounds told me Kaci was lathering soap in her bare hands, since I hadn't thought to give her a rag.

"Tabby…" The word lingered on her tongue, as if she were tasting it, and by the sound of things, she didn't find it unpleasant. "I heard you talking in the hall earlier. That's what you called me, right?"

"Yes. You're a tabby, and so am I." I couldn't see her through the curtain, but I felt her go still with some part of my mind that was more cat than human.

"You're…*like me?*"

"Very much so." I slid off the countertop, moved by the breakthrough I could sense coming. "Can't you smell me? Can't you detect the similarity in our scents?"

Silence settled beneath the harsh patter of water, and I pictured her inhaling deeply. "Yes. I can." Amazement layered her voice the way steam coated the mirror. Then Kaci was quiet for at least a full minute, and I heard her feet slosh on the tub bottom as she washed herself. When she finally spoke, she'd gone still again, and the scent of soap faded as fresh water rinsed it down the drain. "What *are* we?"

My breath caught in my throat and silent vindication coursed through me. I was right. She was a stray. There was no other way she could not know what she was.

I found myself in front of the sink, leaning with my palms flat on the counter as I stared into the fogged-over mirror.

"Kaci…we're werecats." It sounded ludicrous coming from my lips, and *I'd* known what I was all my life. I could only imagine how it must sound to her, not having been born into our culture. Because I was sure now that she *hadn't* been.

But she took it better than I expected. "Werecats." She paused while she thought it over, and I glanced at the curtain, as if the opaque vinyl would show me what she was thinking. "Like were*wolves* in movies, only cats, right?" I opened my mouth to answer, but she wasn't finished. "That makes sense." And she lathered up again for a second scrub.

"It does?" Surprised, I turned to lean against the countertop, my arms crossed over my chest, ignoring the sharp edge of Formica that bit into my hip through my clothes.

"Yeah." Another pause as she moved out from under the water again. "Hey, can I use this shampoo?"

I shrugged, then remembered she couldn't see me. "Sure." Though I had no idea who it belonged to.

"The bottle smells kind of like us. And kind of like a man."

Yup, that sounds about right. "You're smelling tomcat— one of the enforcers. They're werecats like us, only male." And messy, sometimes smelly, and often immature, just like human men.

Plastic clicked as she uncapped the bottle. "Like the guy in the hall?"

"Yeah."

"And those…cats in the woods?"

My heart stopped as a painful jolt of surprise lanced my chest. *Cats in the woods?* Had she seen the strays? Or had she seen our guys out *looking* for the strays?

"What cats? You saw tomcats in the woods?" My pulse raced, and I hoped fervently that she hadn't yet learned to listen for things like that.

"A few times." A new scent permeated the room, clean like soap, but threaded with a much heavier, musky chemical signature. Definitely a man's shampoo. "But I mostly smelled them and heard them."

Hmmm. "Did they smell like the guy in the hall?" Who was a Pride cat. "Or did they smell a little…different?" I didn't know how to vocalize the difference between the scent of a Pride cat and that of a stray, especially considering she probably didn't know what either of those labels meant.

"I don't know. They smelled like a man and like a cat. I tried not to get too close."

Good girl.

"At first I thought it was all a dream, all that walking in the dark. All the running… And that you'd woken me up from some kind of nightmare. But it wasn't a dream, was it?" Her voice quivered, even over the steady noise of the shower, and she took a moment to collect herself. "It's all real, isn't it?"

My hand tightened on the rim of Formica behind me. "'Fraid so."

A second later, the water cut off, and the sudden silence felt heavy with her disappointment, though that seemed too mild a word to describe the despair she must have felt upon discovering that her nightmare was real.

"Can you hand me a towel?"

"Oh. Yeah." I glanced around the bathroom for a clean towel, but had to dismiss the one hanging on the rack with one sniff. *Not even* kind *of fresh.* Fortunately, the cabinet over the toilet yielded several clean, folded towels. I shook out the one on top, then shoved it behind the shower curtain with my face averted.

Kaci took the towel, and the cheap cotton whispered against her skin as she dried. Then her thin, pale fingers—now immaculate—curled around the edge of the curtain and pulled it aside to reveal a thin, wide-eyed, towel-wrapped tabby, more little girl than young woman. Her hair hung past her elbows in a thick blanket of loose brown waves, struggling to curl on the ends in spite of the weight of the water soaking them.

I handed her the pile of borrowed clothing as she stepped from the tub onto a worn green bath mat. "You'll have to put these back on until we can get you some new clothes. Sorry."

She shrugged, and a drop of water fell from the end of her nose. "Hey, it's better than fur, right?"

"Sometimes. Though fur has its advantages, too." I smiled, but her expression clouded with a brief flash of fear before fading into doubt and confusion. She didn't look eager to return to cat form anytime soon, which was perfectly understandable, considering. However, if she waited too long to Shift, she'd pay the price, first with her health, then with her sanity.

And that's where you come in, Faythe. I could demonstrate what life as a werecat was *supposed* to be like. I could show her that she had nothing to fear from her cat form, and plenty to gain from it. I could teach her what I'd failed to teach Andrew.

I could *save* her, where I'd lost him.

I turned away while Kaci dressed and wrapped the towel around her hair, then I walked her back to her room. And now that she knew what he was, instead of ignoring the guard in front of the door, she gazed at him curiously.

"Why is he here?" she asked, settling onto the bed in front of the window as I closed the door on the tom. "Why do I need someone to watch me?"

I smiled in sympathy. She'd have to get used to the Alphas monitoring her every move. That was a fact of life for a tabby, and with Kaci, the council would no doubt double its efforts, especially if she did turn out to be a stray. She'd be unique— even more of an oddity than a tabby who goes to college instead of getting married to raise a litter.

My hands twisted the bedsheet as I tried to decide how best to explain without frightening her. She deserved the truth, and I was probably the only one who would give it to her. *Most* of it, anyway. "The council is afraid you'll get scared and run away. It's not safe for a tabby alone in the woods." But there was more to it than that, and after a moment's hesitation, I decided to tell her the truth. "They don't want you to go at all, but they *especially* don't want you to go before you've answered all their questions," I admitted, blushing a bit in shame for my fellow werecats' selfish motives.

Kaci didn't look surprised. "When I first woke up, I would have run if I could have opened the door." She unwrapped the towel on her head and pulled the bulk of her hair over one shoulder, combing through it with her fingers because I hadn't thought to bring her a brush.

"That's only natural. Cats hate being confined, and I've certainly done my fair share of running in the past. Hell, I've probably done *your* share too." I grinned wryly, and could tell I'd piqued her interest when her brows arched high on her forehead.

"Why did you run? Did they lock you in a room, too?" Her eyes grew wide, rimmed with an oddly calm fear, as if such a prospect was distant and not of real concern so long as I was there to protect her.

I cringed inwardly. There were many, many things I couldn't protect her from, and the council topped what was surely a very long list. But I had to *try*. A girl who grew up in the human world was *not* going to appreciate—or be willing to submit to—the werecat idea of what a woman should be. And no one could understand that better than I.

"Yeah, they locked me in several times," I said when I realized she was still waiting for my answer.

"Why?"

I sighed and leaned back on the bed with my weight on both hands. She wasn't ready to hear all the details. Hell, *I* wasn't ready to *think* about all the details. "It's complicated." I stared out the window at another beautiful fall day I wouldn't be allowed to truly experience. "I didn't want to do what they wanted me to do, and I thought the only way to get out of it was to leave. So I ran, and they found me and locked me back up. To keep me safe, of course." The last phrase sounded forced, even to my own ears.

"You don't sound like you believe that."

Her tone drew my head up until my eyes met the piercing, older-than-it-should-have-been gaze in hers. "You're pretty perceptive for a thirteen-year-old."

"My English teacher says that, too." Her head dropped for a moment, and when she looked at me again her eyes were damp with tears she'd thus far refused to shed. "She *used* to, anyway. When I went to school. Can I stay with you and go to school in Texas? Where you live?"

My heart throbbed painfully, and my throat suddenly felt too thick to speak through. How was I supposed to answer that? I would do my best to make sure she was safe, wherever she wound up, but I couldn't swear that would be with me. Or that I'd even be alive to *see* where they put her, because until my sentence was officially announced, I wasn't in the clear on the whole execution thing.

But I could hardly tell her *that*.

Still, she deserved the truth… "I don't know."

Kaci accepted my nonanswer with the patience of someone long accustomed to going without vital information, as were most children. Silence settled into the room around us, showcasing the ambient sounds from the house at large. Snippets of conversation came from the kitchen, dining room, and living room, and from two different bedrooms came canned fight-noises. In one room, the guys were playing another bloody, pointless video game. From the other, I recognized Jack Nicholson's distinctive nasal cadence, delivering one of his lines from *Wolf*.

But above all that was…footsteps.

A confident knock on the door preceded the aromas of pepperoni and tomato sauce by about a millisecond, and I knew from the way Kaci's nose twitched that she'd caught them both. When I pulled the door open, Jace's cobalt eyes shined at me in the dim hall light, and I couldn't help noticing that he carried not one formerly frozen pizza, but two. "I thought you might be hungry, too," he said, in response to the question plain on my face.

"Thanks." I took the plates from him and set them on the dresser beside the door. In truth, Kaci could probably have eaten both pies on her own, but I appreciated the gesture. And the food. And the two chilled Cokes he pulled from the pockets of his baggy jeans.

I set the cans on the dresser alongside the pizza.

Jace grinned, like he had a secret. "Your dad talked the tribunal into letting you go into town with me and Marc. Because we have no idea what to buy for a thirteen-year-old girl. Be ready in an hour."

A field trip? That was too good to be true. My eyes narrowed in suspicion. "What's the catch?"

His smile faded and Jace crossed his arms over his chest in a closed-off posture I recognized from every argument we'd ever had. "Calvin's sending one of his men, too, to make sure you don't make a break for it."

"Wonderful." I rolled my eyes in exasperation, stopping only when they landed on the eavesdropping enforcer in the hall. Malone's man would no doubt report everything Marc and I said during the shopping trip.

Jace glanced over my shoulder. "How's she doing?" He didn't bother to whisper; she'd hear him anyway.

"Coming right along, actually." I followed his gaze to where Kaci sat watching us both, making no attempt to hide her curiosity. "But the weird thing is that she knows nothing about us. As a *species*."

Jace's eyebrows rose, and he looked at the tabby again.

Then those same brows furrowed in a deep frown. "How is that possible?"

I scowled at the guard still watching us, then met Jace's eyes again. "I don't know, but I'm about to find out."

Twenty-Three

"Who was that?" Kaci asked as I tucked a can under each arm then bent awkwardly to pick up both plates of pizza.

"That was Jace Hammond." Leaning over the bed, I set both plates down on the rumpled comforter and let the cans fall next to them. "He's one of my father's enforcers, and my brother Ethan's best friend. He's a really good guy."

Kaci bit into her first wedge of pizza, then spoke around the bite with one small hand hiding her mouth. "Where's your brother?"

"Ethan?" I asked, and she nodded, still chewing. "He's at home. In Texas."

"Do you miss him?"

I chewed and swallowed my own bite before answering. "Nah. We've only been here a few days, and we'll go back soon." Assuming I survived my trial. And could stand living on the ranch without Marc...

Kaci shoved the crust from her first piece into her mouth then leaned against the windowsill and popped open her Coke. "So, Jace works for your dad?"

"Yeah, and my father has several more enforcers, including me, though I'm not really on duty at the moment."

The tabby's eyebrows rose comically and she swallowed a huge gulp of soda, still staring at me. "Girls can be enforcers?"

I couldn't help the little tingle of pride that surfaced inside me, in spite of my anger at the establishment that employed me. I was proud of being the only female enforcer, even if I'd been suspended from duty almost as long as I'd actually served. "Not usually, but my father has...*different* ideas than most of the other Alphas."

"So, can I be an enforcer when I grow up?"

I grinned as she shoved half of the next slice into her mouth at once. "I guess that's up to your father."

Kaci froze, her cheeks hollow beneath darkly circled eyes. Then she finished her bite in a hurry and frowned at me. "What does my dad have to do with it?"

Oh, shit. I'd forgotten about her father. "I just meant...you know...your Alpha."

"Oh." She took another bite and chewed in thoughtful silence while I did the same. "Who is my Alpha?"

I choked on my first gulp of Coke, and had to force it down while my nose burned from the little bit that had nearly gotten away. Once I'd recovered, I stared at her in amazement. "You really don't know anything about us, do you?"

She shook her head solemnly, leaning over her plate.

In spite of what I'd told Jace, until that moment some part of me had been convinced that Kaci knew deep down what we were and how things worked. That she'd suffered some sort of memory loss that would clear up with enough reminders—and time. But one look at her face now, a smear of pizza sauce on her upper lip and incomprehension in the depths of her eyes, told me that she truly knew nothing beyond what she'd learned alone in the woods.

I dropped the uneaten portion of my third slice back onto the plate and sat up straight, meeting her gaze cautiously.

"Kaci, I have to ask you some questions, and some of them might sound pretty strange."

She cocked her head to one side, just as she'd done in cat form earlier. "Stranger than running around in the forest as a panther, then turning back into a human?"

I grinned wryly. "Okay, you've got me there. But you're not a panther. There isn't really any such species."

"There isn't?" she asked around another bite, and I shook my head, smiling in sympathy with her confusion. "Then what are those black cats at the zoo? And what are we, when we're not human?"

Damn. I was going to have to start at the very beginning. "If you saw a black cat at the zoo, it was either a jaguar or a leopard with darker-than-normal pigmentation. That's called melanism. But we're neither jaguars nor leopards. We're just…us. Our own species, both human *and* cat, according to Dr. Carver." I paused, wondering how much she remembered. "The guy you scratched last night? Do you remember him?"

"Yeah. Sorry 'bout that." She flushed with embarrassment.

"Don't worry. He's fine. Anyway, Dr. Carver knows this tom from the West Coast Territory who's a geneticist, and he has these theories about—" I stopped when I realized that if she didn't know what we were, she would never understand the technical specifics. Hell, *I* didn't understand the technical specifics. "Never mind."

Kaci smiled around the bite in her mouth, then washed it down with another swallow from her can. "So, what were you going to ask me?"

Oh, yeah. "I need to know about your parents. Your whole family, actually."

As I'd expected, her entire body went stiff, her smile freezing into a parody of joy that looked more like a grimace. "Why?"

"Because you inherited everything you have from them. Genetically speaking."

Sudden comprehension gleamed in the green-brown of her eyes and her face relaxed. "You mean like how I got my dad's hair and my mom's fingers, right?" I nodded, and one corner of her mouth turned up in a sad little grin. "But I didn't get this from them." Her arms spread to define "this" as everything around her, and I understood that she meant her catself. "They didn't have this."

Breath burst from my throat, and only then did I realize I'd been holding it. "Are you sure?" I leaned forward in anticipation, fully aware of how ridiculous it was of me to ask the poor girl if she was certain of her parents' species. "Your father wasn't an Alpha, and your mother wasn't a dam?"

"You asked me that before. What's a dam?"

"A tabby who's given birth. A mother cat." I shook my head, as if to clear it of what was to me an irrelevant question. "What about your brothers? You never saw them Shift, either? Any of them?"

Kaci frowned, her last slice of pizza forgotten on her plate for the moment. "I never had any brothers. Just one big sister."

My cheeks went cold as blood drained from my face. "You have a *sister?*" The concept was too foreign to wrap my brain around. Sure, my *brothers* had a sister—me, of course. And most other Pride-born toms had a single sister. But I'd never in my life met a *tabby* with a sister, because it typically took a dam so many tries to deliver a tabby that the precious baby girl was her last. Which is why we were all the youngest of several children.

Kaci nodded in answer to my question, her eyes as wide as mine no doubt were. She was plainly amazed by my reaction to what was, for her, a lifelong fact.

"Okay, let me make sure I understand." I took a deep breath, rubbing the goose bumps that had popped up on my arms at the knowledge that I was *this close* to proving the existence of a female stray. "Your parents were *not* werecats, and you have no brothers. Your mother actually gave birth to *no boys*. Right?"

She nodded again, clearly astonished by the depth of my incredulity.

"And you have an older sister."

Pain flashed across her face, deepening the lines around her eyes. "I used to." Kaci dropped her head, staring at her plate as she poked listlessly at her remaining slice of pizza. "Her name was Charity. She…died."

Along with their parents—her pain made that obvious. In fact, they'd probably died in the attack that infected the tabby now sitting in front of me. The tabby who had, by some miracle, survived not only that attack, but the intervening weeks on her own, stuck in cat form and untold miles away from home.

"I'm so sorry, Kaci."

"Me, too."

We were both quiet for a while after that, as she stared at the busy floral bedsheet, aimlessly tracing a cotton calla lily. Then she picked up her last piece of pizza and bit into it, which I took as a signal that she was ready to continue.

"Kaci, when your family was attacked…were you scratched? Or bitten?"

"Wha?" she asked, still chewing. She swallowed thickly then looked at me in question. "Scratched or bitten by what?"

I set my plate—still half-full of pizza—on top of hers and pushed them both closer to her, gesturing for her to take the rest. She nodded in thanks and picked up another slice. "By one of us. In cat form. Were you scratched or bitten by the cat that killed your family?"

Blatant shock wiped her face clear of any other expression, like wiping chalk from a blackboard, and in her eyes I saw the truth and knew my guess had been a good one. Her family had been killed by a werecat.

Yet still she shook her head in denial. "No. No scratches. No bites."

I frowned. It was not unusual for a stray to have no memory of the attack that infected him, because the scratch fever that followed typically left him very sick for quite a while. That Kaci had survived scratch fever with no one to care for her was a miracle. Remembering her attack—or her attacker— was too much to ask of the poor girl.

But before I'd covered her with the blanket I'd glimpsed most of her body. I'd seen neither scratch-mark scars, nor any healed bites.

That didn't necessarily mean anything, though. I, of all people, knew that for a fact. I'd infected Andrew with nothing more than a nibble of his ear. The wound hadn't been visible at all, and I'd had no idea he'd been infected until months later. Theoretically, the same was possible with Kaci. Except that to my knowledge, no one else had mastered the partial Shift necessary to infect someone while in human form.

And then there was the fact that she was far too young to have such intimate contact with anyone, much less a partially Shifted werecat she hadn't even known existed.

"Kaci, think very carefully." I rolled my empty Coke can between my palms, the aluminum now warm from my body heat. "Are you sure you weren't bitten or scratched? In the shower, did you see any scars or marks you don't remember getting? Anything you can't account for?"

"No." She didn't even hesitate. "My hips are kind of pointy now, and I could see my ribs. And I have this sore on my hand, which is super-gross." She held her injured palm out for my inspection. "But that's it. Everything else is the same, except that my fingernails and toenails are really long."

I nodded absently, half convinced she had a small set of claw marks on her back, somewhere she couldn't see or feel.

There was just no other explanation for how she could be one of us, if no one else in her family was.

From the hall came a knock on the door, and I nearly jumped off the bed, startled half out of my wits. I'd been so absorbed by my questions and Kaci's answers that I hadn't heard anyone approach.

"Faythe?"

Marc. My pulse spiked, and I flushed, trying to ignore the curious arc of Kaci's eyebrows as she watched me.

Marc knocked again. "You ready to go?" He sounded tense, and I glanced at the door in concern. *Of course, he's worried. He's just been kicked out by the only family he's known for the past fifteen years.*

"Yeah. Just a minute." I didn't bother to shout, because I knew he could hear me. Like the guard in the hall, he'd probably heard everything we'd said for the last several minutes. Hopefully. That way I wouldn't have to repeat it.

"Who's that?" Kaci asked, grinning at me around the last slice of pizza as she bit the point from it.

"Marc Ramos."

"Does he work for your dad, too?"

My eyes closed, denying the tears that threatened to come. "He did."

"You like him." Her statement held an odd innocence, like she pictured me and Marc exchanging notes in the hall between homeroom and gym, clearly the extent of her own experience with boys. Kaci's shy smile and the tone of her voice set me at ease regarding her refusal to deal with the tomcats. If she'd had a recent bad experience with a man, she wouldn't blush so sweetly as she teased me.

She'd shied away from Dr. Carver and Malone because she didn't know them. Not because of anything tragic. *Thank goodness.*

"Yeah. I like him a lot." I smiled, seeing no reason to ruin

the girl-to-girl moment with the bleak facts, even if she'd
overheard some of them earlier. "Marc and I are going into
town to get some stuff for you. Clothes, shoes and other es-
sentials. What size shoes do you wear?" I was sure I could
guess her other sizes.

"Five."

"Thanks. We'll be back soon. I'll tell everyone to leave you
alone, if you want. But if Dr. Carver comes back in, please
be nice to him. He's the one who treated your hand while you
were sleeping, and he may want to check on you, to make sure
you're feeling good. Okay?"

She nodded slowly, and I relaxed a little more. "He's nice,"
I said. "I promise he won't hurt you."

"Okay." Kaci hugged her knees to her chest as I stood and
piled the empty soda cans on the stacked plates.

"Thanks for talking to me. When I get back, if you're
feeling up to it, I'd love for you to come down and have dinner
with the rest of us."

"Maybe…" Her gaze followed me as I backed toward the
door. "But not that guy who yelled at you. The one who came
in while you were gone. I don't want to eat with him."

Malone. "I don't want to eat with him, either," I said, and
she grinned. I had my free hand on the doorknob by the time
I remembered the question I'd forgotten to ask her. "Kaci,
where are you from?"

"Cranbrook." I must have looked confused, because she
elaborated to oblige my geographical ignorance. "It's about an
hour from the U.S. border. In southeastern British Columbia."

Huh. That was two Canadian strays in as many days. *What
are the chances?*

But then I realized the chances were far greater in
Montana than they would have been back on the ranch. The
cabin complex was less than a hundred miles from the
Canadian border.

Kaci's nose wrinkled in concern. "I think I crossed the border illegally. Am I going to be in trouble for that?"

I smiled, amused that she was worried about being deported, with everything else she had on her plate at the moment. "I don't think that'll be a problem."

Marc's eyes burned into mine as I shut the bedroom door behind me. "They called in backup a couple of hours ago," he whispered, taking the plates from me as we headed down the hall. "Ethan and Parker, and two more of Malone's men. Plus, whoever Blackwell's bringing in to replace Colin."

"Peachy." We were running low on uninjured enforcers and had yet to find the band of strays, so we could certainly use some extra claws on hand. But I didn't relish having a bigger audience when my verdict was finally read.

Downstairs, I dropped the empty cans in the trash and set our plates in the sink, then followed Marc out the front door, ignoring Malone and Blackwell entirely. Jace and Malone's enforcer were waiting for us on the porch, and from Jace's index finger dangled a set of keys attached to a bauble reading Hertz.

I had one foot on the floorboard when Michael called my name. I looked up to see him jogging toward us from the direction of our cabin. "What's wrong?" I asked, watching him over the roof of the car.

"I've spent the last three hours on the Internet, looking for your tabby. There is *no* girl by her name, fitting her age and physical description, anywhere in the western half of the country. Is there any chance she lied about her name?"

"No." I slid in next to Marc and pulled the car door shut, then rolled down my window as Jace started the engine. There were many things about Kaci I found hard to believe, but her name wasn't one of them. "She's Canadian. From Cranbrook, British Columbia. And you're probably spelling her name wrong."

Michael shook his head insistently, rounding the front of the car as Jace began to back out of the gravel driveway. "I tried *K-A-S-E-Y* and *C-A-S-E-Y*."

"It's *K-A-C-I*. And I think Dillon is with two *L*'s. Try it again." With that, I rolled the window up and scooted closer to Marc, watching my brother in the rearview mirror until Jace turned out of the driveway.

In town, we found a small shopping center that held both a moderately priced department store and a general store. In less than an hour, we bought a week's worth of clothing, shoes and toiletries for Kaci. And though the outing was a short one, the normalcy of a trip to the store—even a *chaperoned* trip—did wonders for my morale, simply because there were no Alphas around to remind me that each breath I took might be my last.

In addition to that perk, it was absolutely blissful to be surrounded by so many humans, who didn't give a shit who I was or what I'd done. I hadn't felt such freedom or anonymity since my last day of school, and wasn't likely to feel it again anytime soon.

Back at the lodge, Marc helped me haul the bags up to Kaci's room, then backed out after giving her a friendly smile. She returned his smile, and I couldn't help a flash of frustration that she was apparently warming up to the one tom she might never see again.

When Marc left the room, Kaci dug into the shopping bags with enough enthusiasm to rival her appetite. She was laying the outfits out on the spare bed, mixing and rematching tops and bottoms, when a shout from outside drew me to the window over her bed.

"Grandpa! We found him!"

I peered down at the lawn, where Paul Blackwell's grandson Nate marched across the dead grass alongside another enforcer I didn't know, who carried an oddly stiff, furry black form in both arms.

That's a corpse, if I ever saw one.

Twenty-Four

Kaci sat on the bed next to me and twisted to peer out the window, but I blocked her view with my body. "Hey, why don't you try on some of these clothes, and I'll be right back to see how they look."

"Why? What's wrong?" She frowned, standing to look over my shoulder. Fortunately, Nate and his partner had already taken their discovery around back, out of sight from Kaci's room.

"I'm not sure. Hopefully nothing." I couldn't lie to her, not when she'd just started to trust me. But neither could I tell her the whole truth. Not that I actually *knew* the whole truth yet. "I'll be right back. Okay?"

She nodded reluctantly, and I slipped into the hall without a word to the guard on duty, in spite of his obvious curiosity.

When I got downstairs, the living room was deserted, so I jogged through the kitchen and out the back door, where a group of toms—including all four Alphas—was gathered in a heavily shaded corner formed by the back porch and the rear wall of the lodge. Chill bumps formed instantly beneath my clothes, and my breath puffed from my mouth in thin white clouds.

"Oh, shit!" someone whispered, and no one admonished the guilty tom for his language in front of the Alphas. That couldn't be good. I tried to elbow my way through the huddle, but was shoved back like a runt at its mother's teat.

"Do you smell that?" Jace asked, and Marc nodded.

"Move!" I ordered, and when that got no response, I pinched Jace through his shirt.

"Ow!" he snapped, but shoved the guy on his left, then moved to make room for me.

I stepped into the narrow gap before it could close, and my gaze fell instantly to the cat on the ground at my feet. Something was wrong with it—other than the fact that it was dead—and it took me a minute to figure it out. The stray was missing his left rear leg. Not just the paw, but everything south of his knee.

Son of a bitch! Nate and his partner had found the missing honeymoon hiker, and not only was he dead, he was a *werecat*. He hadn't just been attacked by the strays in the forest. He'd been *infected*.

"I assume he was dead when you found him?" my uncle asked, and all eyes turned to Nate and his partner, who stood opposite me in the huddle.

"Yeah." Nate wiped his palms on his jeans, in either nervousness or excitement. "Looked just like that, only he was half under a clump of brush, like he'd crawled in there to die."

"I see no obvious signs of trauma," my father said. "Danny, what do you think?"

Dr. Carver knelt between the body and several pairs of dusty hiking boots, and began a quick examination of poor Bob Tindale. "Well, he still has complete rigor stiffness, and as cold as it's been the last few days, I'm gonna say he's been dead no more than twenty-four hours. This seems to be the source of the infection." He parted a section of fur over the stray's belly to expose a set of long gashes so inflamed and festered I couldn't tell whether they numbered two or three. Or four. "And based on the state of the wounds and the lack of other obvious trauma, my best guess is that he died of scratch fever."

"So, natural causes?" Jace said, stuffing his hands in his pockets.

"In a manner of speaking." Carver frowned up at him, then at me, which made me nervous. "He wasn't technically murdered, but in instances like this, I find it hard not to blame the infector. In most cases, anyway." The doc raised both brows at me, then tossed his head toward the corpse, telling me silently to take a whiff of the transmitter's scent, which would be forever laced through the hiker's personal new-stray smell.

Uh-oh. *This can't be good.*

I squatted next to Carver and sniffed Mr. Tindale's wounds from about a foot away. But that was close enough for me to understand what he'd been getting at.

Kaci.

The truth thundered through me, and I fell onto my rear on the cold ground. My eyelids slammed shut and refused to open, sparing me from sensory overload as I tried to make sense of evidence I didn't want to believe. If I'd had fur, it would have been standing on end.

No. She couldn't have. But no matter how badly I wanted to deny the truth, I knew better. Kaci's scent was layered through the handicapped stray's smell, forever binding her existence with his. And there was no other way it could have gotten there.

I rubbed my arms through my shirt, trying to fight off a numbness that came from inside me, rather than from the November chill. My nose ran from the cold and I dug a tissue from my pocket to wipe it.

"Faythe…" my father began, but I stood and backed away from the body before he could finish.

"No." My head shook in denial. Marc reached out for me, but I dodged his hand. "No," I repeated more firmly, turning to shove my way through the small crowd as I stuffed the tissue back into my pocket. "It's a mistake. She wouldn't do this."

"Not on purpose," my father admitted, and I felt the group's focus shift from the dead hiker to me. "She's been through a lot and probably had no idea what she was doing."

"She didn't." I whirled to face them again and my eyes went wide as I stared at my Alpha. "Kaci didn't even know she could Shift back. She had no *idea* what was happening to her, and she wasn't in her right mind. You can't *possibly* hold her responsible for this."

Silence closed in on me, but for the trilling of what few birds hadn't yet flown south for the winter. The weight of my father's gaze was suffocating, and those few seconds seemed to last forever. When he finally spoke, his solemn words did nothing to set my mind at ease. "Go talk to her. Find out what happened, and we'll go from there."

Fair enough. I'd ask Kaci, and she'd tell me it was a horrible accident. I'd report back to the council and they'd bury the body, clean up the mess, and forgive Kaci, who no doubt knew not what she'd done. I felt *horrible* for the poor hiker and his still-missing wife, but he was dead, and she probably was, too. There was nothing I could do for them. But the tabby was alive and in need of my help. And my protection. What kind of enforcer would I be if I didn't help her?

"One hour." Uncle Rick glanced at his fellow Alphas to confirm, and they each nodded silently. "We have decisions to make and work to do."

"Fine." I blinked to clear the fog of shock and confusion cushioning my shiny optimism from the sharp edges of reality.

On the way upstairs, dread slowed my feet as if I were

wading through knee-deep water, rather than fear for the poor, lost kitten upstairs. And really, fear is just as hard to negotiate as water—and in this case, it was a damn sight colder and more numbing.

At the end of the hall, I ignored the guard and knocked on Kaci's door.

"Faythe?" she asked from the other side, and I smiled in spite of the purpose of my visit. Either she'd come to recognize my footsteps, or she'd discovered that a quick whiff of the air would tell her who was at the door.

"Yeah, it's me. Can I come in?"

Soft footsteps approached and the door swung open slowly to reveal a teenage girl I barely recognized. Kaci wore tan hiking boots, a pair of slim, faded jeans and a soft pink sweater I'd known at a glance she'd love. She'd found the brush and ponytail holders and had twisted her hair into a long, thick braid on one side of her head. It trailed nearly to her waist.

"What do you think?" she asked as I pulled the door shut behind me. "There's no mirror in here. Can I go look at the one in the bathroom?"

"Sure. In just a few minutes."

Her forehead furrowed in disappointment. Then her features smoothed and she took my hand—her first voluntary physical contact—and pulled me over to the bed, where she'd laid out all the clothes. "This one's my favorite." She ran one hand down the sleeve of the sweater she was wearing. "But I like this one too. And that purple top? I have one kind of like it at h…"

Her voice faded into strained silence, and her gaze found the floor. I was eager to hear more about her family, and what her homelife had been like with no enforcers and a *big sister,* but this was not the time for those questions. I had fifty-five minutes to find out how and why the girl who hadn't even known she was a werecat until that morning had already managed to break one of our most serious laws.

She was the only girl I'd ever met who could get into trouble faster and more thoroughly than I could. Kaci fascinated me. And worried me more than a little.

"Kaci?"

"Hmm?" Denim rustled and plastic popped as she tore the tag from another pair of jeans, still avoiding my eyes.

I sat on the end of the bed and pulled her new leather jacket onto my lap. "We need to talk about something very… serious."

She finally looked at me, holding the jeans up to her waist to test the fit. "Like, you-look-stupid-in-those-pants serious, or you-have-terminal-cancer serious?"

I smiled, impressed all over again with her fortitude. "More like, where-were-you-on-the-evening-of-November-eighth kind of serious…"

"What?" Kaci frowned in bewilderment, and the jeans slipped from her grip. Then her expression relaxed, and her arms fell to her sides. "Is this about that guy you killed?"

"What?" My hand clenched around the sleeve of her coat. "Where did you hear that?"

She shrugged, flushing lightly. "That's all anyone talked about while you were shopping. I could hear them through the walls and the floors. And the vents."

Curious in spite of myself, I arched my brows at her in question. "What did they say?"

"Just that you killed a guy." She hesitated, then met my eyes boldly, as if she'd suddenly decided she deserved answers. "Did you?"

Um, yeah. The problem was that I couldn't say for sure which "guy" she meant. Eric, whose throat I'd ripped out over the summer? Or Luiz, whose skull I'd crushed with a dumbbell ten weeks ago? Or maybe the stray I'd tenderized forty-eight short hours before.

While that last one was a decent possibility, the most likely suspect was Andrew, the reason for our little vacation in the mountains.

"Yes." My hand found my forehead, rubbing before I'd even realized I felt the beginning of a serious migraine. "But it was self-defense. I had no choice."

Kaci sat on the opposite bed, facing me. "They don't believe you."

It wasn't a question, so I nodded my acknowledgment. "They never believe a damn thing I say," I mumbled.

"So…who did you kill?" Kaci stood with her back to me and pulled the pink sweater over her head, as if my answer didn't matter enough to interrupt her private fashion show. But I knew better. Her thin back was tense, her motions too stiff to ever pass for relaxed. My answers meant as much to her as hers would mean to me. She needed to know she could trust me. That I wasn't a cold-blooded murderer.

I sighed, and my hands found each other in my lap. "I killed a man I knew in college. If I hadn't, he would have killed *me,* and I wouldn't be here talking to you now."

Kaci considered that as she slid her arms through the sleeves of a silky red blouse. Then she turned to face me. "Do you ever think about it?"

"About killing him?" I asked, and she nodded solemnly. "I try not to, but sometimes…" *Sometimes I see his face when I close my eyes. His cheeks pale, blood spurting from the hole in his neck. His eyes accusing me of betraying him. Again.* "Sometimes I can't *not* think about it."

Kaci nodded, just the slightest bob of her head, but it was enough to send a jolt of understanding tingling down my spine to settle in my toes like pins and needles. She wasn't trying to decide whether to trust me with her life. She was trying to decide whether to trust me with her secret.

The female hiker. If she'd infected the man, she'd probably at least *seen* the woman, and I knew from experience how quickly a confrontation with a human could go very, very wrong. I'd almost killed a hunter once, when I'd lost control of fear-induced bloodlust.

It was an accident, I told myself as she unbuttoned the blouse with her back to me. *Whatever happened with Kaci and the hikers was an accident.* They'd surprised her, or she'd surprised them, and all parties had acted on instinct. That was it. It had to be.

"What are they going to do to you?"

I shoved hair from my face, wondering how much of my answer she could possibly understand. Or should even hear. "They're holding a hearing right now. It works kind of like the trials you see on TV, but I don't get a lawyer, and there are three judges. And no jury."

"That doesn't sound fair." Kaci leaned forward to grab a long-sleeved T-shirt from the bed I sat on. The front read Hands Off. I'd been tempted to buy one for myself.

"It *isn't* fair." I rubbed both hands over my face, suddenly very, very tired. "The Territorial Council doesn't care much about fair. They have to put the good of the group above the good of the individual, and right now some of them think I'm a threat to the group."

She pulled the T-shirt over her head and tugged it into place. Then she shoved her trembling hands into her pockets and took a deep breath, meeting my eyes with fear in her own. "Are they going to kill you?"

Apparently a sense of decorum doesn't come into play until late *adolescence.* But even I recognized the incongruity in that thought; my mouth had gotten me in far more trouble than my fists ever had.

I met her eyes, doing my best to project honesty in my voice. "I don't know. Maybe. But it's not over yet. They haven't even decided on a verdict so far, much less a sentence."

Kaci nodded as if she understood, but her face had gone pale with fear, and suddenly I realized my mistake. If they were willing to execute me for my crimes, it stood to reason that they might execute *her,* too. I'd just given her cause to fear for her life among those I'd sworn would protect her.

But the rules of the game had changed with the discovery of Bob Tindale's body, and I couldn't reassure Kaci when she hadn't even told me what had happened yet. She had no idea I knew about the hikers.

Too on edge to sit now, I folded a pair of khakis, then put them in the bottom drawer of the closest dresser. "Kaci, how long have you been here?" She shook her head, obviously thrown off by the change of subject, so I tried again. "In these woods, on this mountain?"

"I…I don't know." Her eyes narrowed in thought, and her hand absently stroked the sleeve of the pink sweater on the bed next to her. "What day is it?"

"November thirteenth."

Her eyes closed, and her pulse spiked noticeably. *"November?"* When she looked at me again, her eyes were glazed with fear, highlighting the pale green in a sea of deep brown. "Are you sure?"

"Yeah." I forced a small smile and bent to pick up a package of athletic socks that had fallen on the floor. "What month did you think it was?"

"I don't know." She half turned toward the window, her gaze going unfocused as she stared at the trees in the distance. "I knew it had gotten colder out, obviously, but the last time… When I…" Her mouth closed firmly, and she sank onto the bed facing me, without bothering to shove the clothes over. "August. It was the end of August."

Whoa. She'd been on her own for two and a half months. Not weeks. *Months.*

Part of me was impressed. But the rest of me was furious

at whoever was responsible for this girl. If Kaci was a Pride cat, some team of enforcers was *seriously* neglecting its duty. If she was a stray, someone had infected her, and whoever the bastard was, he was going to *pay* for that when we found him.

Just like I would pay for what I did to Andrew.

A sob caught in my throat and I forced it down, startled by the sudden reminder that I was in as much trouble as whoever was responsible for Kaci. Yes, I'd infected my ex by accident, but that had made no difference to him. What had mattered to Andrew was that I bit him, then abandoned him. His blood was on my hands, and I would pay.

But not before someone paid for what had happened to Kaci. And to the hikers by extension.

"Kaci, when you were in cat form, did you see any humans?"

"Not very often." She fingered the collar of the leather coat, her gaze tracking her hand up and down the smooth surface. "I followed the river most of the time, but I stayed in the woods, and there weren't many people out there. Mostly just animals. Deer and rabbits. And raccoons."

"But you *did* see some humans?"

She nodded slowly. "A few. Why?" Her voice grew cold with suspicion, and I steeled myself in preparation to simply spit the question out. Surely that would be easier on us both. But before I could do more than open my mouth, a soft, rapid series of knocks sounded on the door.

My nose supplied me with Dr. Carver's name even as he eased the door open.

Kaci froze, and startled recognition flashed across her face. "It's okay." I moved quickly to put myself between the two of them, facing her. "You remember Dr. Carver?"

Her head bobbed stiffly.

"Doc?" I twisted and arched my brows at him in question, which he took as an invitation to enter.

"I'm sorry to interrupt." He smiled confidently, but his

left hand rubbed the bandage on his right arm, a painful reminder of their last meeting. "But I need to borrow Faythe for a few minutes."

"What's up?" I glanced at my watch. I still had forty minutes.

"Michael's asking for you downstairs."

I scowled, showing him silently how bad his timing was. "Can it wait?"

"Um…no." The urgency in Dr. Carver's eyes sent an adrenaline-spiked surge of dread through my bloodstream, and I frowned. *What's wrong* now?

Twenty-Five

"Kaci, I'll be right back." I hesitated, one hand on the doorknob. "Can I bring you a soda?"

She nodded, eyeing us both suspiciously, but voiced no protest when I followed the doctor into the hall.

"Sorry," Carver said as soon as the door latched shut behind us, heedless of the guard obviously listening in. "But Michael—"

I cut him off with a harsh look and a firm grip on his arm, hauling the doctor quickly toward the staircase at the end of the hall. "She can hear us, genius," I hissed, clomping onto the first step.

One corner of his mouth turned up in surprise. "Yeah, I guess she can. Why is it we forget children can hear us, and we talk about them like they aren't even there?"

"Children? Hell, that's how most of you treat *women*. And that's not always a bad thing." I got most of my privileged information when some stupid tom or arrogant Alpha forgot I was within hearing range.

"I suppose you're right." The doctor shrugged, but had the sense to look embarrassed.

Downstairs, I found Michael surrounded by Jace and all four Alphas, all staring at whatever he held. Lucas and the other enforcers were gone, presumably having joined the search for the still-missing female hiker.

Marc hovered on the edge of the room, fists clenched in irritation. Though his flight wouldn't leave until early the next morning, he'd been removed from the proceedings by virtue of his official banishment, and I'd *never* seen him look more frustrated.

All heads turned my way as I thumped to the hardwood floor from the last carpeted step. "Is this about Kaci?" I whispered.

"Yeah, I found—"

I cut Michael off with a curt toss of my head toward the door as I marched past him, snatching my jacket from the back of an armchair on the way. "Let's take it outside. She can hear bits of everything said down here." To my amusement, they all followed me through the kitchen and into the backyard without a word of protest.

We wound up beneath the high, broad branches of an old oak, and I gave myself mental kudos for picking the side of the building the tabby *couldn't* see from her window. Michael stopped in front of me and the Alphas re-formed that same semicircle around him, Jace and Dr. Carver hovering around the edges.

"I found her," Michael announced. "Kaci, with a *K* and an *I,* and Dillon with two *L*'s."

"Yeah?" I'd been expecting that, of course. "What'd you find?" My gaze strayed to the thin stack of papers in his right hand. On the front page, a black-and-white school photo of a young girl stared up at me. It was upside down from my perspective, and her face was much fuller, eyes glittering with innocence and unspoiled youth. But it was Kaci, without a doubt.

Michael handed me the top sheet—an online-newspaper printout—and I turned it around to stare into Kaci's eyes while he spoke. "The Dillons were big news in their little town a couple of months ago. They even made a few of the papers down here."

The headline read: Father Mourns Missing Daughter.

Kaci's dad was still *alive?* If so, what the hell was she doing here alone?

Michael took a deep breath, then launched into an explanation he'd obviously already given the others. "On August 28, Roger Dillon came home from work to find his wife and sixteen-year-old daughter dead in their backyard. Mauled by an animal. Kaci was missing."

Cold waves of shock washed over me, combining with the frigid air to numb me from head to toe. My fingers throbbed with each painful beat of my heart. "How could we not know about this?" My voice sounded hollow, fuzzy.

My father sighed, clearly frustrated, and rubbed one hand across his creased forehead. "I'm sure the Canadian council knew. Has anyone ever heard of a Canadian Alpha named Dillon?" Heads shook silently, and my father's frown deepened. "If there is one, this could very well be a strike from a rival Pride. A play for more territory."

"That would explain why they left Kaci alive," Blackwell said, already nodding as he tightened his grip on his cane. "Take the land *and* the daughter."

"What about the sister?" I asked, bothered by such an obvious hole in the theory.

Malone shrugged, arms crossed over his chest. "Accidents happen."

Yeah, right. But that wasn't what I meant. "What kind of dam has two daughters and *no* sons?"

"That is unusual, but not really *impossible*," my father insisted.

"It's un*heard of*." I propped one boot on an exposed root at the foot of the tree and stretched to reach the branch over my head, just to have something to do with my free hand. "A werecat family structure like that would be big news all over the world, from the moment that first daughter was born. We'd all have heard of them."

"Unless the council tried to keep it quiet, to avoid just such an attack from an enemy Pride." Uncle Rick pointed at the printout I still held, and I handed it back to Michael.

Okay, that made pretty good sense. A tabby was her Pride's greatest resource, and rivals would be jealous of any Pride with two tabbies. But…

"Even if it were possible for one Alpha to have two daughters, what about the father? Wouldn't he be the primary target of such an attack? Why strike before he gets home? And what about the enforcers? The attackers would have had to go through at least half a dozen to even *get* to the wife and daughters. Right? But no other bodies were found. Which reminds me, why in he—" *Oops*. "I mean, why on earth would the father call the human authorities into a werecat matter? That's just *asking* for trouble from all involved. There would be questions, and biological evidence, and—"

"I think you've made your point," my father interrupted, his expression an odd mix of pride and embarrassment. He knew I was working my way around to my stray-tabby theory.

"No, she hasn't. What are you trying to say?" Malone demanded, scowling at me.

"Daddy…" I faced my father, pointedly ignoring Malone. Jace shook his head at me from over my uncle's shoulder. But the truth had to be heard sometime, and I was obviously the only one willing to say it. "It wasn't a hit. I don't think the Dillons are werecats."

"That's not possible," Blackwell said, just as Malone snapped, "That's ridiculous."

I arched my brows at them both. "More ridiculous than a single dam giving birth to two tabbies and no toms?"

"Well, there's an easy way to find out." My father put a hand on my shoulder, warning me to keep quiet. "Paul, has Colin Dean left yet?"

"No." Blackwell glanced at his watch, his other hand clutching his cane. "Not for a couple of hours. He's sitting with Brett." No doubt Blackwell's idea of the punishment fitting the crime. And I had to admit I liked it—though not as well as I'd like to see Colin neutered.

Daddy's iron gaze landed on Jace. "Go get him."

Jace jogged obediently toward the lodge. I trailed him with my eyes, not the least bit surprised to see Marc watching from the porch. He followed Jace inside, and though I couldn't hear what they were saying, it was obvious they were both upset.

Michael cleared his throat to regain our attention, flipping through the papers in search of something in particular. "The human authorities assumed it was a wild-animal attack because it *looked* like a wild-animal attack. And because the Dillon home is very isolated, surrounded on three sides by thick forest populated with deer, wolves, and at least two species of wildcat. *Actual* wildcats." He paused, still glancing through the pages, then pulled one from the pile triumphantly.

"Here we go. In the two weeks following the Dillon massacre—" my brother held up the page to show me the dramatic headline "—forest rangers shot four cougars, two wolves, a bobcat, and a bear. The locals went a little overboard trying to make sure they got the animal responsible."

Which they obviously had *not* done. Proof that werecats exist would have made front-page news the world over.

I squinted, staring at another black-and-white photo on the paper Michael held, this one of two men in hunting gear, grinning like fools as they held the corpse of a cougar upside down between them, the poor cat's head dragging on the ground.

Gorge rose in my throat, and I swallowed it, keeping my lunch down with sheer will. "Well, that's just…lovely." I couldn't find a word graphic enough to describe such point-less slaughter. At least we *ate* the animals we hunted. "What about Kaci? What does it say about her?"

"Officially, she's missing and the investigation is still open. But an aunt told the local paper that they don't expect to find her alive. Last month her dad bought a burial plot next to her sister and put up a stone memorial."

Well, at least *that* was in our favor. Morbid, but definitely good from our perspective. No matter what happened next, Kaci couldn't go back to live with her father, if he was truly human. That wasn't safe for him, or for us.

The back door of the lodge slammed, and we turned as one to see Colin trudging across the grass toward us, Jace on his heels.

"You rang?" the blond tom said, not bothering to screen malice from his tone.

Paul Blackwell stood straight on his crooked old spine, both hands on the curve of his cane. "Until that plane leaves the ground, you are in *this* jurisdiction and under *my* authority. You will adopt an attitude of respect, or I will see you pay for your impertinence. Can you wrap your thick skull around that, Dean?"

Colin nodded curtly, his gaze focused several inches over his Alpha's head. The Canadian import was one big mother-fucker—Lucas was the only one of us who could look him in the eyes—and he towered over the old man. But size isn't everything, which Colin's own cowardice had proved.

"Good. If you want to make it home in one piece, listen up and answer Councilman Sanders's questions."

Still scowling, Colin turned expectantly to my father, re-luctant curiosity written in each frown line on his face.

"Your father is Alpha of one of the Ontario Prides. Curtis Dean, right?"

Colin's curiosity deepened, as did his put-out glower. "Yes. Why?"

"Give me his phone number."

Colin's eyes went wide in panic. "Why? What did I do now?"

Paul Blackwell growled viciously, glaring at his disgraced enforcer, and I nearly choked on surprise. I'd had no idea such an ancient set of vocal cords could produce a sound so fierce. "Give him the number."

The unfortunate tom glanced from his Alpha to my father, and prattled off a series of numbers. My dad dialed, then dismissed Colin with one careless wave of his hand. Colin stepped back, but lingered at the edge of the circle to listen in, obviously still convinced the call involved him.

"Curtis?" my father said into his phone. "This is Greg Sanders, from the U.S. council." He paused, and we all listened to the elder Dean's gregarious greeting. "Yes, it has been a while." Another pause, during which Colin's dad apologized for his son's abominable behavior. "Don't even mention it," my father said, somehow managing to sound generous. "That's between you and your boy now. I have a question for you on a separate matter."

Behind me, Colin sighed in relief, but his stance remained tense. He clearly wasn't looking forward to the afternoon's family reunion.

"Do you guys have an Alpha named Dillon?" my father continued, turning to Michael for confirmation. "Roger Dillon?"

Michael nodded, and all eyes went back to my dad's phone, waiting for the answer. But I knew what it would be before Mr. Dean ever made a sound, because Kaci's father was no Alpha. He wasn't even a werecat. I had no doubt about that.

"No, there's no Dillon," Councilman Dean said, curiosity pitching his voice a little higher. "Why do you ask?"

"Oh, we're just trying to straighten something out down here. I'll tell you all about it when I have more time."

But we all knew that when he did, he would *not* be mentioning Kaci. Since she was either born into or infected in Canadian territory, one of the local Alphas might decide he had a legitimate claim on the "extra" tabby. Such an assertion would make it very difficult—politically speaking—for us to hold on to Kaci, assuming she wanted to stay with us. Which I didn't doubt for an instant.

Unfortunately, I also had no doubt Colin would fill his father in the moment he stepped off the plane, and there was nothing we could do about that, other than cross our fingers that the Canadian council wouldn't decide to make trouble.

We were all full up on trouble at the moment, and had no provisions in place for the overflow.

My dad thanked Councilman Dean, then hung up. "Jace, get on the phone and tell all of our search teams to go back to where they found Tindale's body for a second look around. We have to find his wife before the humans do. Michael, fire up your computer again and see what else you can find out about Kaci's father. Where is he? Is he still looking for her?"

Michael nodded and took off toward our cabin at a fast jog.

Then my father turned to me, and my heart tried to beat its way out through my rib cage with one look at his face. I wasn't going to like whatever he had to say. "Kaci infected Bob Tindale—we know that for a fact—which means she probably knows what happened to his wife, too. We need to know what she knows. What she *did*. And we need *you* to find out. Fast."

I smiled, well aware that my father was emphasizing the necessity of my participation for the other Alphas, as well as for me. "I'll get your answers." I stepped back, to look at all four Alphas at once. "But I think you should all be prepared for the possibility that you won't like what you hear, and I'd rather you not shoot the messenger."

"What is that supposed to mean?" Malone demanded, eyes narrowing at me in suspicion.

My father shot me a warning look, but I ignored it. Ignorance is dangerous, and ignorance on the part of our governing body could prove catastrophic. No pun intended. "That means there's a good possibility Kaci Dillon is a stray."

I felt the collective scowl on most of the faces surrounding me, but I didn't give a damn what they thought. There was no scientific basis for the impossibility of a female stray. Rarity, perhaps. But not impossibility. "Her family was human, then her mother and sister were killed by a werecat. Two and a half months later she shows up here on her own. And *she's* definitely *not* human. The conclusion seems pretty obvious to me."

"We don't know for sure that her family was human," my uncle pointed out. "We only know that her father isn't a Canadian Alpha."

"Or a U.S. Alpha," I insisted, reaching up again for the branch overhead. "Yet she speaks perfect English and was obviously raised in a North American culture." Based on her fashion sense, love of pizza and vocabulary.

"If you're so sure she's a stray, why doesn't she smell like one?" Calvin Malone demanded.

I opened my mouth to reply, but apparently the tact I was considering didn't show in my expression, because Dr. Carver rushed to reply for me. "I don't have an answer for that, Calvin. But with a sample of her blood and twelve hours to analyze it, I can tell you for sure whether or not she's a stray."

Malone looked intrigued, and I couldn't stop the smile blooming on my face, in spite of the inappropriate circumstances. The council could argue with me until the day I died—which might be tragically soon. But they couldn't argue with genetic evidence.

"Can you do that?" I searched Dr. Carver's face for the truth before my hopes rose too far.

"Me? No." He gave me an embarrassed smile. "I'm completely unqualified for that kind of work. But John Eames does it every day."

Dr. Eames. Of course. He was the geneticist Dr. Carver had been working with for the past few years, analyzing werecat DNA after hours in the lab where Eames worked. They were trying to find a way to increase the number—or at least the percentage—of tabbies born. Instead, they'd discovered a recessive gene present in all strays' DNA—a verifiable difference between natural-born werecats and strays. With his lab already prepared for such testing, we'd have the results in very short order.

My father nodded decisively. "Do it," he said to Dr. Carver. "Faythe, go with him and make sure Kaci cooperates. And find out what she remembers about the day her mother and sister were attacked, and what she knows about the female hiker."

I frowned and met my father's eyes. "I'll find out what I can about her family, but Daddy, I don't think she's ready to talk about the hikers yet."

"Ready?" Malone glanced around for support from his fellow Alphas. "Being ready doesn't figure into this equation. If she doesn't tell us where the woman is, the humans might find her first, and then we're all *screwed*."

"We're screwed just as hard and fast if I ask her and she freaks out and stops talking," I pointed out, oddly pleased by Blackwell's shocked reaction to my phrasing. But I was just expanding the metaphor *Malone* had started.

"Do you honestly think that will happen?" Uncle Rick asked, shoving both hands into his pockets as he eyed me in skepticism.

"Yeah, I do. She's been listening through the walls all day and has figured out that you guys are lobbying to have my head detached from my body for defending myself." My glare settled on Malone for that one. "She's a kid, not a *moron*. She has no reason to think you'll go any easier on her, ergo she has no motivation to tell us what happened. And she sure as *hell* has no reason to lead you to the proof needed to put the noose around her neck. Frankly, I can't say I blame her on that one."

Malone huffed in disgust, and even my father scowled. "Fine. Find out what you can about her family and we'll keep looking for the other hiker. But if we haven't found her by nightfall, you'll have to ask her about it. And you're going to *have* to make her answer."

I nodded, far from placated by the temporary reprieve, and headed toward the lodge—and toward Marc—with Dr. Carver a step behind. Just before I drew out of earshot, I heard one last line of the discussion now going on without me. "Wow," Colin said, no doubt watching us walk away. "That kid's almost as dangerous to be near as Faythe is. People around her drop like flies."

A chill raced through me and I stumbled; I might have gone down if the doctor's hand hadn't steadied me. It wasn't so much Colin's words that had startled me, though. It was the truth resonating in them.

Kaci and I had a lot in common, in spite of the differences in our age and upbringing. And with any luck, that commonnality would help me get the whole story out of her without shattering her already fragile sanity. Because unfortunately, that seemed to be all she had left.

Her sanity, and me.

Poor kid.

Twenty-Six

Kaci smiled when I opened the door, whirling to show off the one skirt we'd picked out for her. But her joy wilted like a cut flower when Dr. Carver stepped into the room behind me. "What's wrong?"

"Nothing." Yet I regretted my answer immediately, because though I hadn't meant to lie to her, I certainly hadn't been truthful. So much was wrong at the moment that I hardly knew where to begin. "Dr. Carver would like to run some tests, and he needs to draw a little blood."

Cellophane crinkled as Carver pulled the prepackaged, sterile hypodermic from one front pocket. His other pocket contained two similarly packaged rubber-topped plastic vials.

Kaci's gaze shifted past me and her eyes grew huge. "What tests? What for?"

"We need a little blood to prove to the men downstairs— the Alphas—that you're a stray. That your parents weren't… like us. *Aren't* like us," I corrected myself when I remembered that her father was still alive. "Kaci, why did you tell me your father was dead?"

She frowned in obvious confusion. "I never said that.

Why?" Panic stole over her expression and her eyes flicked from me to the doctor, then back to me. "Did something happen to my dad?"

"No. He's fine as far as I know." I sat on the empty bed, patting a spot next to me, inviting her to sit. "I guess I just assumed your whole family was…gone." Though I should have known better than to assume anything. Some enforcer *I* was.

"Do you want to…call him, or something?" Though I probably shouldn't have made such an offer. If her father really *was* human, the council probably wouldn't let her have any further contact with him, to protect the secret of our species.

But I needn't have worried.

"No!" Kaci's eyes widened in fear and her hands shook at her sides until she curled them into fists. "Not yet," she amended, though her heart still raced audibly, and eyes shone with unshed tears. "I'm not ready. He's been through enough."

But so had she.

Dr. Carver cleared his throat conspicuously, and I glanced at him. Since Brett was stabilized and the doc's return trip had already been delayed for more than a day, he was planning to hop on the next flight to Washington State, to hand deliver the blood sample to Dr. Eames and his genetics lab. Which meant he needed to leave within the hour.

"Will you let Dr. Carver draw some blood?" I asked.

Kaci hesitated, so the doctor showed her his too-friendly-to-be-a-threat smile. "I'm sure we can scrounge up some cookies and soda to get your blood sugar back up afterward."

That did it.

Kaci sank onto the bed next to me and pushed up her left sleeve. Dr. Carver sat on her other side and ripped open an alcohol wipe from his left pocket. The tabby jumped in surprise when the cold cloth touched the crook of her elbow, then laughed nervously and looked at me instead.

"Why don't the Alphas believe my parents are human?"

"Because *you* aren't human. You should be whatever your parents are, yet you're not. You're one of us."

"You're going to feel a little pinch…" Dr. Carver said.

She closed her eyes, steeling herself for it, and flinched when the needle slid into her skin. Then Kaci relaxed visibly and her eyes opened to look into mine. "So, how come I'm like you if my parents aren't?"

I smiled at her refusal to watch her blood being drawn. I didn't know many squeamish werecats. "Well, that's where it gets interesting. The only way you could have become one of us is by being infected by another werecat, which would make you a stray. But we've never found another female stray, and the council wants proof before they're willing to believe you are one. So Dr. Carver's going to take your blood to Dr. Eames to have it analyzed for that proof."

"A stray, huh?" Kaci asked, and I nodded, watching blood bubble into the vial. "That makes it sound like no one wants me. Like a stray dog."

"I assure you, that's *not* the case." At least for her. Unfortunately, regarding most strays, she had it just about right.

"How does a stray get infected?"

Dr. Carver removed the first vial from the needle cap and set it in his lap, then inserted the second vial.

"By a scratch or a bite from another werecat," I said. "But that won't work on just anybody. In order to actually be infected, instead of just getting really sick, you have to be born with a certain recessive gene inherited from a werecat ancestor. Dr. Eames's research proved that just a few months ago." And in the process, he'd stirred up one of the biggest controversies the Territorial Council had ever survived. Even bigger than…well, *me*.

It had taken half a dozen easy-to-understand lectures on genetic testing and several hundred dollars' worth of full-color graphic displays to bring the older Alphas to a functional understanding of a science they'd considered a bunch of mumbo jumbo only weeks before. Change did not come easily to a culture as old and secretive as ours. But eventually understanding *did* seep through the age-old cracks in tradition. Regarding werecat genetics, at least.

They were still decades behind the times on gender equality.

"If you don't have the gene, you'll just…well, you won't catch it." You'd die of infection instead, but I couldn't say that to Kaci. Not knowing what I knew about her family. And not with her looking at me as if her whole world had shrunk to include nothing but me and the protection I could offer her. In theory.

"But I wasn't scratched." She glanced at the doc, then back at me. "Or bitten."

Dr. Carver's gaze rose to meet mine as he thumped the second vial to get the blood flowing again. I knew what he was thinking, but I wasn't bothered by Kaci's statement. Very few strays had any memory of their attack.

"You probably just don't remember." I brushed a strand of chestnut waves from her thin face. "A newly infected stray gets pretty sick for a while. High fever, rabid hunger, delirium. It's a miracle you came through it okay with no one to take care of you."

"But…Faythe, I wasn't sick," she insisted. I nodded, humoring her, but she continued, even more vehement in her protests. "*I* was the first werecat I ever saw. No one scratched or bit me, and I never got sick."

Dr. Carver pulled the second vial loose and reached for the cotton ball he had ready, watching me the whole time.

"Honey, you just don't remember it." Hell, she'd probably blocked the whole horrible attack from her memory, to save her own sanity. My hand found hers, and I squeezed it. "You had to become one of us *somehow,* Kaci, and that's the only possible way." Unless someone else managed to infect her in human form, as I'd infected Andrew. But even if that were possible, it wouldn't explain why she didn't remember being sick.

Her eyes narrowed in doubt, but she didn't argue further.

Dr. Carver left as soon as he had his samples. He was obviously eager to study Kaci's blood, and frankly, I was just as eager for the results. I was sure they would prove my theory and earn me a little respect.

Okay, maybe not actual respect. I'd settle for a "Good job, Faythe." Though in truth, I was even less likely to get *that*.

"So, my blood will tell him that my parents were human?" Kaci scooted across the empty bed to lean with her back against the window, though the glass must have been cold through her blouse.

"Sort of." I tucked my feet beneath me on the bed, yoga style. "It'll tell him for sure whether or not you were born a werecat. If you were, then your parents were werecats, too. If you weren't, then they weren't either, and you must have been infected at some point, even if you don't remember it."

For several minutes she picked at the edges of the square Band-Aid in the crook of her elbow, evidently trying to absorb what I'd said.

I stared out the window over her head until a glint from the late-afternoon sun reminded me of the passage of time, and my own approaching deadline. *You need to ask her the important questions*. But I *really* didn't want to, even if it *would* prove my worth to the tribunal.

My finger traced a pattern in the comforter beneath me, and I steeled myself to hear things I wouldn't like. "Kaci, what do you remember about the day your mom and sister died?"

Her head snapped up so quickly I thought I heard her neck pop. "How did you know about that?"

"My brother found several news stories online." Her frown morphed into a mask of fright, and I did my best to relax her. "Kaci, we *had* to know who you are. Thirteen-year-old tabby cats don't just wander out of the woods—or into a bruin's backyard—on a daily basis. We had to know who's looking for you. Not to mention where you came from, and where you belong."

"I don't belong anywhere." She stood with her back to me and began folding the clothes still covering the other bed. "I can't go back to Cranbrook. Not after what happened."

She'd get no argument from me there. We could no more send her back to a human father than we could purge the infection from her body. "Are you ready to talk about it? About what happened to your mom and sister? And to you?"

She shook her head slowly and picked up her new coat on her way to the closet. "No, I don't want to talk about it. I don't remember much of it anyway." Suddenly Kaci's arms were empty, and something thunked into the wall. I turned just in time to see her new coat slide down the dark wood paneling, and by the time my gaze returned to where she'd been standing, she was gone.

Damn, she moves *like she was born a werecat!* But that wasn't possible. She was just a fast learner, and her learning curve was no doubt sharpened by more than two months spent exclusively in cat form.

Kaci paced the length of the room in long, furious strides, glancing at the window every few steps, as if the world outside was calling to her. It probably was. She'd spent the past ten weeks sleeping on a mattress of earth, under a canopy of tree limbs and stars, and now she'd been cooped up in a single room for nearly twenty-four hours. I could see cabin fever raging in her eyes. I smelled impatience and desperation in the fresh sweat beaded above her upper lip and along her hairline.

If I couldn't calm her down, she'd make a break for it, and at least half a dozen toms would chase her, making a bad situation several times worse.

"Kaci…" I stood, unsure how to approach her, but she turned on me, a mixture of fear and fury battling for control of her expression.

"No! I can't change what happened, so what's the point in thinking about it? Huh? Why are you trying to make me crazy? Don't you think I'm close enough now?"

Surprise numbed my tongue and stole my voice. Or at least my ability to use it with anything resembling skill or finesse. "I'm not trying to make you do anything." *Lie.* "I know exactly how you feel." *Lie.* "I need to know what happened so we can find the bastard who did this to you. We just want to help you." *Lie.* That wasn't *all* we wanted. The council wanted her womb, and Malone evidently thought this new tabby was the key to ridding himself of my entire family.

Kaci sniffled, and wiped one arm across her eyes. "No one did this to me. No one scratched me, no one bit me, and no one ever asked me if I wanted to be like this. Like *you*." She'd stopped pacing now and stared at me in so much pain I could barely stand to look at her. "If you want to help me, tell me how to make it stop. All of it. I don't want to hear people talking through the walls. I don't want to be able to smell the guy in the hall through a closed door. I don't want to know that you spent some serious time with that Marc guy earlier today. But I *do* know, because you smelled like him when you came in this afternoon. You *still* smell like him."

Okaaaay, this is awkward. I couldn't remember ever before being told by a child that I smelled like sex, which was basically what she'd just said.

"I'm sorry, Kaci."

She slid down the wall to sit with her knees up and her head in her hands.

I squatted next to her and stroked her hair, because I wasn't sure what else to do. I'd never been very good at comforting people. "I'm sorry this happened to you—more sorry than you can possibly imagine. But I can't fix it. No one can. The best we can do is to show you how to be one of us. How to deal with what you're hearing and seeing now."

"What if I don't *want* to deal with it?"

"You're gonna *have* to eventually." I sighed. I had no idea how to help a stray through her transition. But I might just know how to help a teenager relax… "But in the meantime…how about a video game? And maybe some junk food?"

Her head rose slowly, her brows arched halfway up her forehead in surprise. "Are you serious?"

"Why not? The guys have two different PlayStations set up downstairs. You ever play?"

She grinned. An honest-to-goodness, carefree-teenager grin. With teeth and all. "Yeah. Only every day of my life… until recently."

I smiled back; I couldn't help it. "I'm sure all their games are violent and bloody…"

Her smile faltered for a minute, then it was back in full force, her expression fortified with a healthy dose of resolve, like she was determination to have fun, even if it killed her. "The bloodier the better."

I had to admire the kid's grit.

"Good." I eyed the loose skirt and fitted blouse, then glanced at the pile of more casual clothes on the nearest bed. "Pick out something appropriate for video-game carnage and junk food. We have a selection of chips and dip downstairs that puts a supermarket to shame."

Five minutes later I pulled the bedroom door open and held it for a jeans-and-T-shirt-clad tabby who smiled in spite of the tense way her arms hung at her sides. She was nervous about meeting everyone, and I couldn't really blame her. I liked only about half of the people I'd be introducing her to, mostly because the other half wanted me dead. Or whored out to one of their sons.

"Where are you going?" the new guard asked, glancing from her to me, then down the hall toward the staircase, as if hoping someone would come to his rescue before he had to use the biggest muscle found *above* his neck.

"Downstairs. Kaci's ready to make some new friends. Would you like to be the first, or are you going to be a pain in our collective ass?"

"I have to clear it with an Alpha," the guard said, glancing uncertainly from me to Kaci, then back to me.

I shrugged. "So, go. Clear."

The guard jogged off in search of an Alpha, but I saw no reason to wait, so I led the tabby down the hall after him.

Kaci hung behind me on the stairs, so that I stepped into the living room first, and when she peeked out from behind me, all conversation stopped. The lodge became so quiet I could hear the individual heartbeats of everyone in the room— only a few toms recently back from the search, thankfully.

Marc sat in the armchair closest to the sickroom, from which he could see the entire room at once, including the front door. Jace sat on the end of the couch nearest him.

Dr. Carver was gone, a fact I verified with a quick glance out the front window at the empty spot his rental car had occupied. Blackwell and Malone were in the dining room at the rear of the lodge, their presence betrayed by the indistinct buzz of quiet conversation.

Presumably everyone else was still out searching for the missing female hiker. Except for my father, who stepped into the living room from the kitchen at that moment, the guard on his heels, frozen in mid-question.

He raised one brow at me in question, and when I only smiled in response, he nodded, then ducked back into the kitchen, as if the tabby coming out of her shell for the first time was no big deal. A rush of gratitude brought heat to my cheeks, and I would have thanked him if Kaci hadn't been practically clinging to my arm.

"Kaci, you remember Marc and Jace, right?" I tugged her gently into sight.

"Hi." She stepped warily around me, into the fringe of the room.

"Hey, kiddo!" Leaning forward on the couch, Jace favored her with his typical grin, all straight white teeth and cherubic lips. "'Bout time you joined the party."

I snorted, mildly amused by his description of my murder trial as a party. "I told Kaci we might be able to scrounge up something to eat and a game of…whatever pointlessly bloody exercise in time-wasting you guys have in there."

"Grand Theft Auto IV! You wanna play?" He was off the couch and across the room in an instant, pulling open the door to the empty first-floor bedroom.

Kaci glanced at me hesitantly, as if asking for permission. Or maybe looking for the all clear. I nodded, more pleased than I wanted to admit by her willingness to trust Jace—and by his apparently effortless ability to put her at ease.

She followed him into the bedroom and a moment later the game unit whirred to life softly, beeping a moment after that.

"You hungry?" I asked Marc, backing toward the kitchen so I wouldn't have to take my eyes from him any sooner than necessary.

"Always. I think I saw a can of Ro*Tel in the cabinet, and there's a block of Velveeta in the fridge."

"That'll work." I rounded the corner into the kitchen to find my father waiting for me. "Hey, did Jace talk to you about…" *Malone preparing to pull a Julius Caesar?*

"Yes, but we'll talk about that later, after the current mess is settled."

"But that'll be too la—"

Dad frowned at me in warning, and put one finger over my lips. Then he nodded toward the living room, where Marc's steady steps approached us. His message was clear, even unspoken. I would have to say goodbye to Marc eventually, and this was just as good a time as any.

But he was wrong. There was no good time to say goodbye to Marc, so I wasn't even going to try. I wasn't going to think about it until I had to, and that moment hadn't come yet.

Marc came in through one doorway as my father went out the other, and he headed straight for the fridge while I searched out the can of Ro*Tel he'd mentioned. We stood together at the counter, cutting the processed-cheese mush into much smaller blocks than necessary, just to have an excuse to be near each other.

My arm brushed his, and after a few minutes, he hooked his foot around my ankle, standing half behind me, my left foot sandwiched by both of his. His chest pressed into my back, and his breath brushed my bare neck, exposed by my high ponytail.

We worked in silence, content for the moment simply to be together. But cheese dip was a no-brainer, and try though we might, we couldn't drag the process out more than twenty minutes, even with the crappy, dented double boiler he found in the pots-and-pans cabinet.

He carried two bowls of dip into the bedroom, and I grabbed two unopened bags of corn chips on my way out of the kitchen. Marc and I lounged together on one of the twin beds, munching contentedly while Jace and Kaci sat on the floor, beating the crap out of digital drivers and grabbing drippy bites between rounds.

Over the next hour, other toms came and went as the search-party shifts changed. Kaci barely greeted each one with an absent nod and a wave, one hand still deftly working her video-game controller. Though she never gave any of the new arrivals much of an acknowledgment, neither was she upset by their presence.

By the time the sun sank below the horizon, Kaci and Jace

had gone through several levels in their game and seemed to be the best of friends. Or even brother and sister.

Marc and I lay quietly, rarely speaking, but constantly touching. Our hands were intertwined and my leg thrown over his when the dining-room door squealed open and the voices from the back of the house rose in volume.

I tensed instantly, knowing damn well what they wanted. The sun was down and Amanda Tindale had not been found. Time was up. Kaci would have to start talking, whether she wanted to or not.

Twenty-Seven

Marc's hand clenched around mine, silently asking me what was wrong, even as he sat up next to me on the bed. I nodded in the direction of the as-yet-unseen parade of Alphas, then toward Kaci, though I had no idea whether or not he could understand my makeshift sign language.

A long shadow fell through the open doorway, and to my surprise, the person casting it was not Calvin Malone, but my father—who had obviously beaten him to the proverbial punch. Daddy's eyes flicked from me to Kaci, then back to me, and his brows rose in question. His meaning was clear: playtime was over.

I nodded, and he retreated into the living room, herding the other Alphas along with him.

"Kaci?" I crawled forward to perch on the end of the bed, more relieved than I would have admitted when the warm curve of Marc's body settled in behind mine, his arm winding around my waist.

"Yeah?" Kaci hit a button with an eerily nimble thumb and the game on-screen froze as she twisted to look up at me. If she'd noticed my father's arrival and quick retreat, she showed no sign. "What's wrong?"

I inhaled deeply, unsure how best to prevent her from clamming up or freaking out when I explained what we needed from her. "I've put this off as long as I can, and now the council needs some information from you. *We* need some information from you," I corrected myself, hoping that she'd be more willing to help me and the guys than a bunch of old men, most of whom she'd never met.

She stiffened, and plastic creaked as her hand clenched around the video-game controller. "I told you I don't want to talk about my family."

"I know. This isn't about them." I pressed myself close to Marc, indulging my need to touch him as much as possible before he left.

"What then?" Kaci's forehead wrinkled, her youth-pouty lips tensing. On her left, Jace put down his controller and watched, ready and willing to help in any way he could.

"You told me earlier that you remembered seeing some human hikers in the woods. Do you remember seeing a man and a woman a few days ago? Somewhere near here?"

Kaci nodded slowly, her gaze drifting toward her lap. "I don't know how long ago that was, though. I lost count of the days a long, long time ago."

"That's okay." Jace scooted to lean with his back against the bed behind him. "Just tell us what you remember."

"I don't…" The controller fell from Kaci's hands to land in the ring created by her crisscrossed legs.

I waited for her to continue, and when she didn't, I shot a warning glance at Jace, telling him silently to let me do the talking. If I was good at anything, it was talking. "Do you remember the man, Kaci? Can you tell us anything about him?" To make sure we were all on the same page. Her expression was completely blank, so I nudged a little harder. "Do you remember anything about his legs?"

Recognition sparked in her eyes and she nodded. "He

had a fake leg. It looked like a metal stick. A pros…something or other."

I smiled. "A prosthesis. Yes, he had a prosthetic leg."

"Right," Kaci said, and a chill numbed my insides at the sight of her detached expression, as if she were reciting something she'd read somewhere once upon a time, rather than what she'd personally seen the day she'd infected the man in question. "It made him walk funny. Kind of hobbly."

That was exactly the kind of detail a werecat would notice, because a "hobbly" walk would make it difficult for the prey to run. Yet we knew for a fact that Bob Tindale had survived his encounter with Kaci, because he'd shown up later in cat form, bearing her signature scent in his bloodstream. What we didn't know about was his wife.

"I'm sure it did." I glanced at Jace, wishing I could see Marc well enough to judge his expression, but I couldn't, with him pressed so close to my back. "What we really need to know about is the woman he was with. Do you remember her?"

Kaci nodded again, staring at the floor now, but offered no further explanation.

I kept my voice low and soothing, noting that her eyes were no longer merely distant, but actually *vacant* now. "What happened to her, Kaci?"

"I don't…" She shook her head in slow, anguished denial, eyes squeezing shut tightly. "I don't remember." But it was clear that what she really meant was *I don't* want *to remember*. She wouldn't have been so upset if she didn't know what had happened to the female hiker.

"I need you to try, honey." I lay one hand on her shoulder, hoping physical contact would comfort her, rather than scare her. "We found the man this afternoon, but the woman is still out there, and we have to find her before the humans do. Do you understand why?"

Kaci shook her head again, but her eyes opened, vague curiosity flowing in to dilute her fear and denial.

"The police are looking for those hikers, and if they find the woman before we do, they'll do an examination of her body, which might give them evidence of our existence."

Things like that did happen on occasion, and the labs inevitably attributed their odd findings to contaminated samples. But eventually someone would link multiple "contaminated" cases, and our private existence depended on them finding as little evidence of us as possible.

"The woman is dead, isn't she?" I asked gently, when I realized we'd all been laboring under that unspoken assumption.

For a moment, Kaci only stared at me. Then her gaze dropped and she nodded.

"We need to know what happened." She started to shake her head again, but I continued, because if I couldn't get her to talk, there was no telling what the council would try. "No one's going to get mad, Kaci. We already know you infected the man. Your scent is woven with his. We've known that for several hours now, and no one's even said a harsh word to you, right?"

She nodded mutely, spinning the game remote on the floor.

"I promise you it's safe to tell me what happened. I won't let anyone hurt you."

Kaci glanced at Jace, then at Marc over my shoulder. I was about to ask them for some privacy when her eyes settled on me again and her mouth opened. "I didn't mean to do it. I was asleep, but something woke me up. Footsteps. Then smoke. I knew it was people and I got up to leave, but before I could get away, the woman…she just *appeared* in front of me. She had an armful of big sticks, but when she saw me she dropped them and just stood there staring at me. I tried to back away from her and she freaked out. She grabbed one of the sticks and ran at me. I…I didn't know what to do."

She glanced from me to Jace, then to Marc and back to me,

begging each of us with her huge hazel eyes to tell her it was okay. That she'd done the right thing—whatever that was.

"She tried to hit me, and I got really scared, but sort of mad at the same time. I can't explain it. I don't feel like that now, but I wasn't human then, and I couldn't really think about it. She ran at me with that stick and I hissed, but she didn't stop. When she got close enough, I just swung at her with one… um…paw." She held her right hand up for emphasis, swiping it across the air with her fingers hooked like talons.

"Were your claws retracted?" Marc asked, his chest rumbling against my back.

"Tucked in, you mean?" she asked, and he nodded. "No. I didn't even think about doing that."

Of course she hadn't. She'd never been taught how to defend herself without hurting anyone. She'd never been taught anything about being a werecat, and had only her own instinct to go on. Unfortunately, a cat's instinct didn't include concern over its foe's well-being.

"It's okay, Kaci," I said, surprised to hear the calm, soothing quality of my own voice. I didn't have much practice setting others at ease. In fact, I tended to piss people off more often than not, but Kaci reminded me a lot of myself, and even more of my cousin Abby, who brought out every protective instinct I had. "We can't change what happened, but we can help you deal with it. And I think the best place to start would be giving that woman a proper burial." Or at least a secret, moonlight-in-the-forest burial. "Don't you think? Can you do that for her?"

Kaci nodded, and I thought I saw an edge of resolve leak into the tense lines of her face.

"Good. Can you tell us where she is?"

Her brows furrowed, and she shook her head, the first sign of tears glittering in her eyes. "I don't know where I am. Or how I got here."

Of course she didn't. Keller had knocked her out with a length of firewood, and she'd woken up in a strange room with no idea what had happened while she slept.

Marc squeezed me from behind, and his stubbly cheek scratched against mine when he spoke. "Do you think you could show us, if we can get you back to someplace familiar?"

"Yes." She didn't hesitate, and actually looked a little relieved. *Thank goodness*. I stood and pulled the rubber band from my hair, mentally composing an appeal to the council, but Jace was already halfway to the door. By the time I got to the kitchen, Kaci clinging to my hand and fastened to my side, Jace stood in front of the Alphas seated around the kitchen table, launching into a formal request for the werecat version of a search-and-seizure warrant.

"You want to take *both* tabbies into the woods?" Blackwell asked, deep-set eyes wide in disbelief. Malone looked ready to spew lava from his ears, and even my father looked doubtful.

"Absolutely not," Malone thundered, shoving his chair back to stand with both palms flat on the table. "Faythe is still on trial here, and that child wears trouble like a snowman wears white."

I felt Kaci stiffen at my side, and my temper flared on her behalf. "This *child* is the only one here who knows where to find the missing hiker's body, and she can't tell us how to get there because she doesn't know how she got *here*." My gaze centered on Malone, and I struggled not to let contempt leak into my voice. Or to squeeze the poor tabby's hand off. "If you want the woman found anytime soon, Kaci is your best bet."

Malone glanced at Blackwell for support, but the old man only shrugged, clutching his cane like a security blanket. Malone scowled, and I knew that if I survived the hearing, he'd find a way to make me pay for forcing his hand not once, but three times in the last few days. Alphas don't like having their actions dictated to them. They like having their balls handed to them even less. But once again, he had no choice.

My father held his tongue and dared a small smile, obviously having come to the same conclusion.

"Fine. Take her out and find the body, but you're *not* going alone."

Honestly, I wouldn't have dreamed of it, mostly because I had no intention of carrying the corpse back by myself, and something told me Kaci wouldn't be much help in that department. But Malone faltered, glancing around the room to see who was left to accompany us. Other than Michael, who was currently playing nursemaid for Brett, he found only Marc and Jace. Marc had been officially dismissed, and Malone wouldn't trust Jace to clean his toilet, much less keep an eye on the tabbies he hoped would someday bear his grandchildren—whether they wanted to or not.

Watching Calvin Malone, I suddenly understood why inlaws the world over were so often maligned.

Finally Malone's gaze settled on the tom who'd been guarding Kaci's door, and he frowned, then rolled his eyes. Obviously the tom in question was not high on his list, which made me like the poor guy just a little bit. But before his stepfather could make the assignment official, Jace turned toward the front window with an exaggerated sweeping gesture. "Looks like the cavalry has arrived."

I followed his gaze and saw only darkness, but then the distant rumble of a car engine set my ears on alert. Seconds later headlights bobbed in the driveway.

"Who's that?" Kaci asked, and I glanced at her in surprise. I'd almost forgotten she was there, in spite of her death grip on my arm.

In the driveway, the engine choked into silence and the driver's-side door opened. The interior light blinked into life, outlining four different heads, one of which I would have recognized anywhere, under any lighting conditions. *Ethan.*

"More of the good guys." I pulled Kaci forward as we

followed the small crowd into the living room. My brother Ethan and Parker Pierce—one of my father's long-time enforcers—came through the front door moments later. On their heels were two more of Malone's enforcers, including one more of Jace's half brothers, whom I'd only met once. I think his name was Alex.

"Wow." Ethan stopped cold in the middle of the floor, and Parker had to nudge him aside to get past. "You must be Kaci." My brother's bright green eyes settled on the young tabby an instant before a huge smile took over his face.

At my side, Kaci nodded silently, but made no move to duck behind me. She already seemed to liked Ethan as much as she liked Jace, which didn't surprise me in the least. Women of all ages were defenseless against the Wonder Twins' charm. Including my mother, who let them get away with more than I ever had.

Ethan let his bag slide to the floor, then dropped to his knees in front of Kaci, staring up into her face as if she were the only person in the room. "You *are* something special, aren't you?"

Kaci's cheeks flushed bright red, and she stared at her feet, but she kept sneaking glances at him after that, when she thought no one was looking. I couldn't help smiling. Ethan was *way* too old for her under any circumstances, but at that point I wasn't willing to rule out anything that could possibly pull the poor girl out of her shell.

Including a crush on my stupid-cupid youngest-older brother.

While Malone's men unpacked in the room they'd be sharing, and Ethan and Parker took their stuff to our cabin, Malone and my father argued from opposite sides of the kitchen table over who should accompany us in the woods. If asked, my dad would have said they were having a "heated discussion," but I knew an argument when I saw one, and they were *definitely* arguing.

Daddy wanted Marc included—even though he was technically no longer a Pride cat—because he would fight the hardest to protect me if that proved necessary. But Malone refused to relent on that one. In the end, my uncle brought them to a compromise. Since my father's first choice was out of the question—everyone else sided with Malone on the Marc issue—my father would get to send two of his men along with one of Malone's.

My dad chose Jace and Ethan, even though Parker was older and more experienced, because they'd been best friends since childhood and work partners for the last seven years. They worked very well as a team.

Malone chose a tom named Reid Something-or-other—or maybe Something-or-other Reid—probably to avoid shoving another of his own sons into the danger zone. Reid was a senior enforcer in his early thirties, whose typically muscular body and nondescript face were crowned by a completely bald head. *Shiny* bald. In fact, I was already calling him Cue Ball in my mind.

We headed out minutes after the escorts were chosen, with Jace in the lead because he was the only one who knew how to get to Elias Keller's cabin, which was where we'd decided to start, since Kaci remembered being there. Jace carried an LED flashlight, and my uncle's handheld GPS unit because none of the rest of us were confident enough in his human-form memory to risk wandering for hours in the woods.

Bundled against the cold in her new coat, Kaci walked several steps behind Jace, and Ethan and I followed her, chatting as we picked our way up the side of the dark mountain through fall foliage and sometimes thick undergrowth. The exercise kept us relatively warm in spite of the near-freezing temperature, and I was oddly at ease, considering our mission, because of the folding knife in my jeans pocket, already warm from my body heat. This one was Michael's, and I'd promised not to lose it.

Cue Ball brought up the rear, armed with a backpack full of bottled water and snack bars, and a second flashlight.

"Cute kid," Ethan whispered, ducking beneath a low-hanging branch. Kaci heard him; I could tell from her suddenly tense, self-conscious gait, but like most men, my brother was completely clueless. "A little thin, but definitely a looker." Yet he sounded worried, rather than pleased or surprised. "Have they decided what to do with her yet?"

"Not officially. Though Malone apparently has several ideas…" I left the thought hanging in the air between us, and Ethan's scowl said he knew exactly what I was getting at.

"How old is she?"

"Thirteen."

His scowl deepened. "Damn. How is that even possible?" I opened my mouth, but he cut me off. "Don't say it. We all know what *you* think."

Evidently my female-stray theory had traveled beyond the Rockies via the miracle of cell-phone technology. Or maybe e-mail. There was no telling what Michael had told everyone at the ranch.

"None of the other ideas makes sense," I said for at least the thousandth time, grabbing a thick branch overhead for balance as I followed Kaci around a sharp curve in the barely visible path ahead.

"Neither does this one," Ethan retorted, but before I could argue otherwise, Kaci slipped going up a steep incline and Ethan lunged to catch her. He lifted her easily and set her on level ground then scurried up after her.

I followed him, then shoved my brother playfully. "Thanks for the help, ass wipe."

"You didn't need any." He shoved me back and was already dancing away from my slightly-less-teasing blow when Reid hissed sharply behind us.

I turned to ask what was wrong, but he shook his head

curtly and made a show of sniffing the air to his right—north of our current position.

Adrenaline spiked through me and my body went on instant alert. I grabbed Ethan's arm and he froze, glancing at me with both brows raised in question. I nodded at Cue Ball, now standing on my right, between two huge, moss-covered tree roots.

Ethan jogged on to stop Jace and Kaci without making any obvious noise while I sniffed the air in the direction Reid was facing. At first I smelled nothing but the normal medley of woodland scents. But then the wind shifted and I caught something else. Something out of place and so close that I should have noticed it earlier and probably *would* have if I hadn't been playing around with Ethan.

Stray. And blood. Lots and lots of blood.

Anticipation made my heart race, and my hands curled into fists in my jacket pockets. Nervous sweat broke out on my forehead and I shoved loose strands of hair back from my face, my eyes scanning the surrounding trees for any sign of the cat we smelled.

Somewhere nearby was a stray, likely standing over a recent kill. I'd already faced two stray werecats while in human form, and I had no urge to do it again, even armed, and with three toms at my side.

On my left, Jace stood protectively in front of Kaci, and Ethan was working his way quietly back to my side. Reid lowered his backpack silently to the forest floor, his eyes alert for movement. He took the lead, drawing a pocket knife from a pouch on the side of his pants and flipping it open in one sharp, practiced motion.

The leaf-shaped serrated blade was barely two inches long and would only be good up close, but the same was true of werecat claws, not to mention canines. Of course, werecats came equipped with *eight* front claws and *four* canines, to Cue

Ball's one little blade. Still, his knife was badass compared to the one I'd borrowed from Michael, and I was kind of hoping to see it in action.

Ethan and I followed Reid, and Jace came behind us. I glanced back to find Kaci clinging to his arm, her eyes wide with terror, her hairline damp with sweat in spite of the cold. She'd survived on her own in cat form for more than ten weeks, but in human form, she looked small, scared, and defenseless, all of which were probably accurate.

Reid led us around a broad, tall clump of evergreen shrubs. He stopped in a small, pine-carpeted clearing, going still as he sniffed and glanced around. I did the same. We couldn't pinpoint a prey's location by scent, but we *could* tell whether the scent was growing or fading. And this particular scent was growing stronger with each step I took. So strong, in fact, that we should have been right on top of the stray, threatening his possession of his meal and setting off his every violent, protective instinct. Yet I saw no sign of him or his prey.

Where the hell *is that stray?*

Frustrated, I turned to look at Ethan, and a warm, wet drop hit my forehead. *Rain?* But there wasn't a cloud in the sky, as evidenced by generous pools of moonlight aiding the flashlights.

I wiped the drop from my face and my finger came away smeared with something dark and sticky. And fragrant.

Blood.

Dread tightening my stomach, I looked up slowly, and my fists clenched around air, my nails cutting into my palms. My breath caught in my throat and made a soft strangling sound. Ethan followed my gaze, and Reid followed his. I couldn't see Jace, but when Kaci gasped, I knew that they'd seen it too.

Our mystery stray was enjoying a leisurely, treetop dinner—but neither predator nor prey had fur.

Twenty-Eight

"Oh, *fuck*..." Jace whispered, and I could *not* have agreed more. In my entire twenty-three years, I'd never seen *anything* as gruesome or completely *fucked up* as the tom staring down at us from his elevated perch, possessive instinct clear in his posture, insanity shining in his eyes.

On a broad, bare branch about eight feet off the ground, a stray perched in the sturdy nook where the limb met the trunk. He was nude and in human form, his face and hands so *completely* coated in blood that at first glance I thought he wore a pair of skintight formal gloves—until I noticed them glistening dark and wet in the soft glow from above.

Wedged into a fork in the thick branch he sat on was another tomcat—based on his smell—also naked and covered in blood. But this tom stared at the moonlit trees with unblinking eyes, his arms hanging limply, his stomach ripped wide open. As I watched, frozen in shock and desperate denial, a thick, blood-slick loop of intestines slid from his gaping abdomen to dangle at least a foot below his body.

My hand slid slowly into my pocket and wrapped around Michael's knife.

Behind me Kaci gagged, then staggered into sight on my left to vomit at the base of another tree. Jace was at her side immediately, holding her hair up and rubbing her back. But his eyes never left the sight that had made her sick.

Overhead, the stray hissed, and my eyes found him again. His lips parted, blunt, human teeth gleamed wetly in the available moonlight, and a thin line of blood-tinted drool dripped from his stained chin, disappearing into the shadows long before it hit the ground. But I staggered back just in case, scrubbing the smear of blood from my forehead with the palm of my free hand. I had to forcibly swallow back bile as it rose to burn deep in my throat.

"Faythe, you okay?" Ethan whispered. He hadn't moved since discovering the grisly stray, and neither had Reid, though the fingers gripping his knife were now white with tension.

"Fine," I whispered back, though that was far from the truth.

Wood creaked overhead, and the startled stray leaned forward. The limb bobbed beneath his shifting weight. He thumped to the ground in front of us, knees bent, gory arms out for balance.

Reid jumped back and Ethan did the same, tugging me with him. I stood with my feet spread and pulled the knife from my pocket, pressing a button to release the blade. Ethan mirrored me in the ready-stance our father had taught us back in junior high. The stray was alone and unarmed, but he was also nude, covered in blood, and apparently full of his fellow tom's organ meat—a definite no-no in every werecat society I'd ever heard of.

"Mine." The stray sprayed bloody spittle across the dead leaves at our feet, and to my utter humiliation, I jerked in response. But no one was watching me. We were all watching Hannibal Lecter, whose eyes darted among us like a junkie fighting off paranoia. It took me a moment to realize what he meant, but his next words made it clear. "Go find your own."

On my left, Kaci stood from her crouch and swiped one

forearm slowly across her mouth. The stray's agitated gaze flicked past me to land on her. "You smell good," he purred, his expression taking on a new hunger without losing the eerie *wrongness* setting off every inner alarm I had.

Kaci whimpered, and both Reid and Jace moved forward to block her from view.

He's sick. Understanding settled into place in my mind. The stray was recently infected and likely still raging with scratch fever. In daylight, we'd see the flush on his skin, though in the dark, with him covered in blood, it was hard to tell at a glance.

"He's mad," Ethan said, confirming my own thoughts. I nodded, and Jace murmured his assent, but Reid only motioned us back with a subtle wave of his left hand.

"We don't want your kill," he said, drawing the stray's gaze from what little he could see of Kaci. "We're looking for something else entirely."

The stray's fever-glazed eyes brightened, seeming to glow with their own light in the darkness. "I can help! I know where everything is. This is my territory!"

Reid's shoulders tensed. "*You* own this property?"

"Yeah!" His gaze flicked back and forth between us, clearly searching for approval or acceptance. "Well, my Pride does. The Rocky Mountain Pride." Hannibal straightened as he spoke, squaring his shoulders in obvious satisfaction.

Ethan snorted. "There *is* no Rocky Mountain Pride."

Reid gestured angrily to silence my brother with the hand behind his back. "We're here on behalf of the Territorial Council…"

On a diplomatic mission to Alderan… I thought half hysterically.

"…to greet your Alpha formally. The council would like to meet him. Can you tell us who he is, and where we can find him?"

"Zeke?" The stray's eyes widened. "You want to talk to Zeke?"

I'll be damned! Zeke Radley. A little thrill of discovery tingled up my spine, raising tiny hairs all over my body, and suddenly I had a great deal of respect for Reid. Whom I silently vowed to stop calling Cue Ball.

"Where can we find your Alpha?" I asked, following Reid's lead.

"That's a secret," the stray said in a stage whisper, one hand cupped to the side of his mouth. "I can't tell you, because Zeke doesn't want any more men. Calls us toms. But we don't really have anyone named Tom."

Zeke obviously understood Pride social structure and politics to some degree, which surely indicated that he'd had contact with Pride cats before. But I was betting he had just enough knowledge to be dangerous.

But Hannibal wasn't finished. "You and her—" his gaze flicked from me to Kaci, as his index finger swirled a pattern in the blood on his chest "—can come with me. Whoever brings her in gets to be second in command."

What? "Wait, you *know* her?" I asked, unbothered when Reid shot me a shut-the-hell-up look.

The stray nodded, smearing the blood across his cheek now. "Mission impossible. Top priority."

Oh, that's just fucking fantastic. If I understood correctly— and that was a big if—Zeke Radley had caught a whiff of Kaci at some point and decided he needed her to complete his little farce of a Pride.

Reid shifted his weight from one foot to the other, subtly drawing attention his way. "How many toms do you have?"

The stray started to answer, then hesitated with his mouth already open. Suddenly unsure, he let his gaze travel over us all, as if he was considering his next words carefully. "Enough. Zeke says we have enough."

"Where does your Pride live?" Reid asked, repeating my earlier question.

The stray frowned and glanced up at his kill, then back at us in silence. He grinned broadly, again flashing bloody teeth, and licked his lips.

A shudder of revulsion slithered through me.

Reid turned to raise his eyebrows at Ethan in question, keeping the stray in one corner of his vision. Ethan nodded silently. They'd agreed on something, and though I hadn't caught the question, I knew better than to ask aloud.

Ethan blurred into motion at my side, and an instant later, he'd pinned the stray to the trunk of the tree he'd dropped out of. My brother had one forearm pressed into Hannibal's bloody throat, the rest of his body held carefully away from the blood-covered werecat. "Last chance. *Where…is…your…Alpha?*"

But obviously Radley had managed to impart loyalty to his troops, if not sanity. Instead of answering, the stray snarled and snapped his teeth at Ethan, in spite of the pressure on his neck. Ethan's fist flew, and a muted crack fractured the air. It was over in less than a second. Ethan stepped back and the stray slid to the ground, his head lolling limply to one side.

For a moment I thought Ethan had killed him with one shot, and while that would have been impressive, it also would have been disturbing.

But then Hannibal's chest rose. And it fell. Then it rose again. He was breathing.

Velcro ripped behind me, and I turned to find Reid pulling a roll of duct tape from his backpack. "Here." He tossed it to me and pointed at the stray slumped against the tree. "Get his mouth."

I ripped a section of tape from the roll, then knelt beside the unconscious tom and pulled his head back with a handful of sticky hair. Covering his mouth without actually touching his flesh was tricky, but it was worth the effort, because I didn't want any more blood on me than necessary. Not with the majority of our hike still ahead of us.

Reid knelt at my side and I held the tape out to him, but he shook his head. "Tear me off a long piece for his hands. Two feet, at least."

As I stood to keep the length of tape off the ground, something electronic beeped on my left. Jace was dialing on his cell phone. While I ripped off the tape and helped Reid bind the cat's wrists at his back, Jace called the lodge to have a cleanup team sent to dispose of the corpse and pick up the prisoner—immediately, since they were both in human form.

Then Ethan and Reid taped the unconscious stray to the tree. They actually wrapped the tape around both Hannibal and the tree trunk over and over again, heedless of the blood now smeared on their hands.

And for just a moment, I wished I could be there when they ripped all that duct tape off his bare chest. That'll *wake the fucker up…*

When they were finished, Reid dug in his bag once again, this time coming out with a packet of antibacterial hand wipes and a clear plastic sandwich bag. To my amusement, he handed a wipe to Ethan, then used another one to clean every single spot of blood from his hands, double-checking with his flashlight before finally tucking the used wipes into the Baggie, and the bag into the front pocket of his backpack.

I liked him more with each passing minute.

After that, we pressed on, Jace in the lead again, this time with Kaci at his side, rather than behind him. She didn't speak, nor did she look around at the beautiful moonlit night. She walked with her head down, her gaze on the ground at her feet.

Half an hour later, Elias Keller's cabin rose in front of us, smoke trailing toward the moonlit sky from a picturesque stone chimney he'd probably built himself. Light flickered in the front window—an honest-to-goodness oil lamp, if I had my guess—

and the scent of venison stew made my mouth water in anticipation of a meal I had no time to eat. Even if we were invited.

Keller's yard was nonexistent, trees towering over his cabin so close that the roots disappeared beneath the small building itself. The front steps were made of four huge log halves set into the earth flat-side up. They were unsanded, and a distinct, sunken wear pattern marred the center of each one, the obvious result of a certain pair of huge boots hitting them in the same place day after day for years. Many, many years, apparently.

As is considered courteous when approaching another territory unannounced—which hardly ever happens because most of us have telephones—we made plenty of conspicuous noise to announce our arrival and our intent to do no harm.

We were still a good fifty feet from the cabin when the door flew open and Keller appeared on the top step, his scraggly face screwed up in a snarl, his huge right fist curled around a five-foot-long club apparently made of an entire small tree, stripped of its branches. Moonlight gleamed on the smooth, broad knob at the top of the club, no doubt polished by several years' accumulation of oil from his own hands.

In front of me, Kaci froze, and I almost walked right into her.

"What—" Keller growled, his low voice rumbling through me physically even across such a distance. Then he squinted into the dark and sniffed the air. His body tensed and the club rose into the air. "Cats. You'd best state your business before I decide the whole lot of you need to be skinned to save the Pride cats the trouble."

Pride cats? He thought we were the strays? Apparently a bear's nose was less capable of identifying individual cats by scent than ours were. At least when we were in a group including two cats he'd never met.

But then, having never smelled another bruin, I couldn't swear I could tell the difference between Keller and his own father if I had to.

"Mr. Keller, it's us," I called.

"Faythe?" He clomped down two more steps to stand on the last inverted split log. "Who's that you got with you?"

I exhaled in relief when the tension left his voice and the end of his club settled onto the step by his boots. "This is Ethan, my youngest-older brother." I pulled Ethan forward by one arm and caught just a glimpse of the amazement he was trying to hide. He'd been told about Elias Keller, but because they were rare almost to the point of legend, seeing a bruin for the first time wasn't something you could ever really be prepared for. I knew that from experience.

"And this is Reid…" Damn, it would be nice to know his last name. Or his first name. Whichever I was missing.

Reid stepped forward, rubbing one large hand over the shiny expanse of his bald head. He was either much less impressed with the bruin than my brother was, or he was in much better control of his expression. I was guessing both.

"Brother, huh?" Keller laughed, a deep, rough sound like the rumble of a plane overhead. "How many of those do you have?"

"Four." I had a relatively small family for a werecat, but Keller was an only child. My father was virtually certain of it. Bruins were so uncommon that it was rare for two members of the species to ever meet, much less breed. Fortunately, they lived a very long time—about twice the human lifespan.

Keller seemed to think about my answer, then dismissed it with a shake of his head, thick, grizzly beard swinging. "Well, come on in and have some dinner. I've got stew on the fire…" He turned toward the cabin, already clomping up the steps.

"Thank you, Mr. Keller, but we don't have time right now. We have to find one of the missing hikers before the human searchers show up at dawn.

"What do you need from me?" Keller asked, and I couldn't help but admire his frank mannerisms. I'd love to be able to say whatever I meant without worrying about the political fallout of my uncensored mouth. Apparently that was one of the advantages of living by oneself. I hoped to have the chance to try it someday.

"Nothing," Jace said. "We just need a chance to sniff around your backyard so Kaci can find her bearings." He chuckled, and whispered beneath his breath, "No pun intended."

"Kaci?" The bruin squinted into the dark. "Is that the kitten's name? Come on up, child, and let me get a look at you."

But Kaci wouldn't go, and I couldn't really blame her. She clearly remembered Keller—at least to some degree—and *I* would certainly hesitate to approach the giant who'd hit me on the back of the skull with a piece of firewood.

"It's okay." Jace put one arm around her shoulders and urged her forward. Kaci shrugged out from under his arm and clung to me, her wide eyes staring at me in desperation. I couldn't help being pleased that she still thought of me as her protector, even though we were surrounded by large men.

"She's a little shy," I said, running one hand over the thick length of her hair.

Keller nodded. "I imagine she doesn't hold any fondness for me, either." His frank gaze shifted from me to Kaci as he thumped down from the steps and clomped across the yard toward us, staff in hand. "Sorry 'bout that bump on the head, Miss Kaci. I mistook you for some other girl cat rifling through my garbage."

To my surprise, Kaci smiled just a bit, though I doubt Keller could see it in the deep shadows.

"Come on up and take a look around, and we'll see if we can't get you headed off in the right direction." He stopped halfway across the wooded yard and motioned us forward with one heavy, flannel-clad arm. And this time when we went, Kaci came with us, albeit reluctantly.

"Does any of this look familiar?" He flung both arms wide,

the club hanging from his right fist like a broken branch dangling from a huge limb.

Kaci shook her head, staring at the tangle of forest shadows surrounding us. "I know I've been here, though. I've smelled…all this before."

"I found her out back." Keller took off toward the side of the cabin, moving so fast on his long, thick legs that we had to jog to keep up. He came to a stop in a surprisingly normal-looking backyard littered with thick tree stumps, the largest of which was three feet tall and nearly as wide. From its center ring protruded the blade of a single-sided ax with a three-foot handle. Keller's monster of an ax made the one Marc kept in the back of his car look like dollhouse furniture, yet I knew the bruin's hatchet would look small and delicate in his huge hands.

"Do you recognize any of this?" Jace asked, and Kaci nodded, moonlit hazel eyes wide as she scanned the yard. Her gaze settled on the woodpile between two twenty-foot oaks, then the large metal trash can by the farthest tree.

"I came in over there." She pointed toward the tree line to the southwest. "I followed the stream, and it ended…back there a little way. I stopped for a drink and I smelled food. Meat."

"Venison." Keller scratched at the tangled mass of his thick brown beard. "There's plenty more, if you're hungry."

I smiled in thanks, but shook my head regrettably. Kaci looked as if she hadn't even heard him.

"So do you think you can take us from here?" Ethan asked, and Kaci's gaze settled on him, her eyes seeming to clear. She nodded mutely. "Mr. Keller, do you know where this stream is?"

"Yup. S'where I get my water. I've stomped a pretty clear trail 'tween here and there, which is probably how the kitten found me."

Keller was true to his word. The path between his cabin and the stream was narrow—at least for a bruin—but clear.

We walked mostly in silence now, and Kaci seemed to grow quieter and more withdrawn with each step. Ten minutes after we left Keller's, a soft rippling sound met my eager ears. A quick sniff revealed the scent of mineral-rich water, and a couple of minutes later the stream itself came into view.

I knelt at the edge of the bank and cupped handfuls of the frigid, unpurified water into my mouth, mentally turning my nose up at the bottled springwater in Reid's backpack. And to my amusement, Kaci dropped to her knees and joined me.

When we stood, the guys stared expectantly at Kaci. Water dripped from her chin, reminding me how cold my own face was, and I swiped one sleeve across my mouth. Kaci let hers drip in spite of the temperature, and I had no doubt that though she still walked upright and clenched tiny human fists beside slim, denim-clad thighs, she was thinking very much like a cat at the moment. Perhaps because she was intentionally trying to retrace her steps. Or maybe she was lost in memories of the last time she'd drunk from that stream.

Either way, she turned away from us without a word and started down the stream bank, stopping every now and then to sniff the air and look around. Kaci made eye contact with no one and walked with her shoulders hunched, her arms wrapped around herself as if for comfort. She was clearly reluctant to revisit this portion of her past and was obviously trying to detach herself from both the emotional ordeal and from us. Or rather, any comfort we might offer. And I chose to let her, at least until something changed.

After about twenty minutes and countless pauses to sniff the air or stare into the dark, Kaci stopped. She wandered off to the right, obviously looking for something, then headed straight for a narrow, immature oak with a distinctive sharp curve in its trunk. Her hand trailed over the bark and she sniffed the steep crook, then plucked a tiny tuft of black fur from the surface. Her eyes went unfocused briefly and the clump of fur fell from her hand. Then her focus sharpened and she took off into the woods, breaking away from the stream without hesitation now that she'd found whatever she was looking for.

Jace hurried after her, and Reid followed him. I bent to pluck the tuft of fur from the nest of thorns it had snagged on and brought it to my nose. A single sniff told me it was Kaci's. She was following her own trail, and based on the rapid, almost desperate pace she'd set, we were getting close.

Suddenly I wasn't sure I wanted to get there after all.

Ethan and I jogged after the others, and in a few minutes Kaci adopted an all-out trot, stepping over exposed roots and trampling tangles of thorns and bunches of ivy. Her head whipped back and forth as she scanned the trees around her, and my blood raced in anticipation. Could we be that close already? We were only half an hour's hike from Elias Keller's backyard. Could the body have been so close to his cabin the whole time without us knowing?

Simply put, yes, it could. We hadn't searched very close to Keller's property, assuming that if she was there, he'd know it. But if Keller hadn't been looking—and really, why should he?—there was no reason for him to have found her.

Several minutes later Kaci came to another stop, this time in the center of a tight clump of four or five trees, each no more than a couple of feet apart. Most of them were young and relatively thin; they probably didn't get much sunlight in the shade of the other trees. However, two of the bur oaks were older and larger, their branches sprawling in every direction, crisscrossing each other in multiple places, creating a loosely woven canopy of limbs above, from which the thick bed of crunchy leaves beneath our feet no doubt fell.

I glanced around anxiously, carefully scanning a thick undergrowth of brush and several deep drifts of dead leaves. I saw no human body, nor any hole or pile of leaves big enough to conceal one.

"Kaci?" Twigs cracked beneath my boots as I crossed the three feet of ground between us, yet when I put one hand on her shoulder, she jumped, as if she hadn't heard me coming. "Kaci?" I repeated, lowering my voice to an intimate pitch I hoped she'd find comforting. "Where is she, hon?"

Instead of answering, Kaci let her head fall back until she was staring at the sky overhead. Or rather, at the branches between us and the heavens.

My gaze followed Kaci's, trailing over the broad, twisted oak trunk and scanning the branches as they dipped and curved, weaving in and out of the arms from the other trees. At first, I saw nothing but the usual bare branches intertwined with heavily laden red-cedar bows, all of which was virtually impenetrable by the moonlight we'd grown accustomed to. But then something clicked, and jarring artificial light sliced through the night.

And there she was—a single pale hand dangling from the spiky foliage of the red cedar.

Shit, no wonder we hadn't found her yet. She was very well concealed in her perch, and the human searchers would never have thought to look for her over their own heads until the body began to smell, which wouldn't be anytime soon, considering the ambient temperature.

Hell, most *werecats* wouldn't have thought to look up either, because murderers typically bury their kills to cover their own crimes. In fact, the only bodies I'd seen werecats drag into trees were those of their prey, which they intended to…

Eat.

Oh, shit. I glanced at Kaci and found tears sliding down her cheeks as she stared into the branches, and somehow I knew without asking that I was right. There was more to our little lost tabby than any of us had expected.

Kaci Dillon was a man-eater.

Twenty-Nine

"How the hell are we going to get her out of there?" Ethan demanded, and Kaci flinched at the edge of anger in his voice.

I rubbed her back as she crossed both arms over her chest and hunched into herself. There was one obvious solution, but somehow I didn't think anyone would be willing to simply shove poor Amanda Tindale out of the tree, no matter how much easier that would have made things for us.

Reid dropped his backpack on a thick clump of ivy. "Take her over there." He pointed to a fallen log several feet from the tree cluster we stood in. "Hopefully this won't take long."

As I ushered the frighteningly unresponsive tabby toward the makeshift bench, Reid pulled a roll of black sheet plastic from his bag, and Jace helped him spread it to cover most of the available ground space within the cluster of trees. They would wrap the dead woman in the plastic, tape up the human burrito, then carry it back to the lodge by hand, a prospect I couldn't even bear to contemplate at the moment.

By the time Jace and Reid finished with the plastic, a straight razor, and a half-used roll of duct tape, Ethan had scaled the red cedar and was completely hidden from view among its branches. "Oh, shit." A branch creaked and swayed, as if he'd sat down too hard on it, and several thin, oblong cones thunked onto the plastic.

"You okay?" Jace paused with one hand around the smooth, bare branch of a cottonwood grown several inches thick against all odds in its current environment.

"No. She's been…um…eaten."

Vomit rose in the back of my throat and I clenched my jaws to keep it down. Having my hunch confirmed was not a triumph this time. It was a tragedy.

At my side, Kaci showed no reaction at all. She merely stared across the clearing at nothing, tears dried—or frozen—on her cheeks, eyes glazed in what could only be the onset of shock. And suddenly I understood why she had reacted so violently to the state and placement of Hannibal and his victim. They were a terrifying, distorted reflection of the very sight she had to show us. She probably thought that once Reid saw that, he'd want to tape her up and knock her out, too.

But that wouldn't happen. What Kaci had done wasn't the same, and anyone with half a brain would have to see that.

Hannibal—in all his lunatic glory—had killed and eaten one of his own while in human form. He wasn't noticeably thin, which meant he had plenty to eat. He'd committed murder and cannibalism, and his only defense—insanity—was the very thing that would render him useless to the werecat community at large.

But Kaci had been attacked by the woman she'd killed. She'd been alone, terrified, exhausted, and literally starving. She'd killed the woman in self-defense, and probably had no idea that eating her human kill wasn't acceptable.

I'd never seen a more clear-cut case of temporary insanity. Kaci hadn't even known what she was. One day she was a human teenager, the next she was a big black cat, and she had no reason to even suspect that she might ever see two feet again. She was starving and suddenly confronted with what looked and smelled like food. She would have been crazy not to eat.

Right?

Reid didn't look anywhere near as sure as I was. He stood with one palm spread on the trunk of the red cedar, staring at Kaci as if she'd just grown an extra head. Murder was a capital offense, and cannibalism an abomination. A taboo with such strong associations with damnation that even speaking of such things gave most werecats the creeps. Man-eaters were not tolerated. And I'd never even *heard of* a man-eating tabby cat. Much less a man-eating teenage tabby stray.

The council would have no idea what to do with Kaci now. Hell, *I* had no idea what to do with her.

It took Jace, Ethan, and Reid nearly half an hour to get the dead woman out of the tree without dropping her or pulling her limbs from their sockets. Kaci had somehow managed to drag her kill onto a branch more than twelve feet off the ground, and I couldn't imagine the hunger and desperation that would drive such a small, weak cat to such lengths to protect her meal.

Hell, I was rarely motivated to put leftovers into the fridge for later, rather than scraping them into the garbage disposal.

Another wave of nausea crashed over me at that thought, and at the realization that I'd just compared a half-devoured human corpse to a tuna casserole.

Once Ms. Tindale was on the ground, the guys got her wrapped and taped with little trouble, thanks in part to the fact that she was past the point of rigor mortis, but had not yet started to rot because of the near-freezing temperature.

When they were done, I left the nearly catatonic tabby long enough to pass out bottles of water and protein bars to refuel everyone before we started back, though Kaci refused both.

Even though there was very little smell coming from the

body, I knew without a doubt that carrying the plastic-wrapped bundle back to the lodge would be one of the hardest, most profoundly disturbing things I would ever have to do.

And I *would* help. I couldn't refuse, especially after letting the guys do all the hard work. So after I stuffed our trash back into Reid's bag—intentionally ignoring the fact that I'd voluntarily taken up the food-and-cleanup role—I picked up one end of the wrapped bundle without being asked. Fortunately, I got the woman's feet. I couldn't have handled carrying her head. Even so, Jace tried to take it from me.

I cut him off with a curt shake of my head and a determined look. I would pull my own weight, even if it meant shouldering some of Amanda Tindale's.

Ethan took the other end and together we carried the poor woman through the woods, then back along the stream, following Jace, who led the way with one arm wrapped firmly around the young tabby's shoulders.

Kaci stumbled once near the stream and almost fell into the water, and when Jace first picked her up, then physically turned her around to face us, I realized she wasn't watching where she was going. At all. She stared off into space, even when he shone his flashlight into her eyes, as if she could see neither it nor us. She walked, but only when and where he led her. She wouldn't answer any of our questions, or even meet our eyes.

After that, Reid and I switched places so we could move faster. We wanted to get Kaci back to the lodge as soon as possible. Jace and I walked on either side of her, each with an arm wrapped around her, and I called my father as we walked, more than relieved by the strong cell phone signal even in the middle of the woods.

I explained what we'd found, and about Kaci's current nonresponsive state, and in return I got a worried "Hmm." I could tell by the heated comments in the background that everyone else in the room had heard me, and that as usual, no two Alphas could agree on how the situation ought to be handled. My father hushed them sharply. Then he told me to "Hurry back," and hung up.

We followed the stream back to Keller's place, marching through his yard, around the cabin, and weaving among the trees out front. He watched through the front window, the base of an old-fashioned oil lamp in one hand, and I waved as we passed, but didn't stop. He nodded in return, his face deeply shadowed from the flickering flame beneath his chin.

Less than an hour later we stepped from the tree line fifty feet from the lodge. Reid and Ethan carried the body around back while Jace and I ushered Kaci through the front door, where Marc and my father were waiting for us, though everyone else had gone out to inspect the dead woman.

We put Kaci on the couch and my father sat next to her. He took her hand and asked several questions, including whether or not she knew her own name, the date, or where she was. She made no response. She didn't look at him, or at any of the rest of us.

Daddy sighed, patting her hand. "Her skin is cold, and I don't think she's heard a word I've said."

"She's in catatonic shock," Jace said. I was pretty sure there was no such state—medically speaking—but I kept my mouth shut because I knew what he meant.

When Jace and my father went out to join the other Alphas, Marc and I took Kaci upstairs and got her ready for bed. She neither protested nor helped when we dressed her in a nightgown, and once we got her in the bed, she only stared at the ceiling. She wasn't even blinking often enough to suit me.

Kaci had checked out of her body for the time being, and I saw no sign that she'd be back anytime soon. And I couldn't really blame her.

For several minutes, I sat on the extra bed watching her in

the light of the bedside lamp. Marc sat with me, and I let my head fall onto his shoulder, treasuring the whisper of each breath he took, even under such unfortunate circumstances.

We stayed like that until the back door squealed open downstairs, admitting a procession of heavy footsteps into the house below. Then I rose, pulling Marc with me.

He stayed in the upstairs hallway because if they saw him, the Alphas would send him back to our cabin. But I took the steps two at a time, eager to hear what—if anything—the council had decided.

As one, the Alphas converged on the living-room furniture, as I sank onto the bottom step. I'm not sure what I expected—arguments, maybe, or I-told-you-so's. But I did *not* expect the parade of grim faces and hanging heads. The Alphas all looked…*tired*. Not like they'd given up, really, but like they'd *aged*. Drastically. And for Paul Blackwell, that hardly seemed possible; he was old as dirt *before* this whole mess started.

Daddy took the armchair against the wall, and Malone sat opposite him, but for once I had a feeling he wasn't actually in *opposition* to my father. He just wanted somewhere to sit without crowding onto the couch with the commoners, who would be played in tonight's production by my uncle Rick and Paul Blackwell. Jace retreated to sit with me on the steps, while Ethan, Reid, Parker, and Alex Malone lined up against the wall.

The best policy for enforcers in a council meeting was to try to blend into the background. Sometimes if you don't give the Alphas reason to notice you, they won't. It's one of the best ways to glean otherwise privileged information, and we were all experienced eavesdroppers.

My father ran both hands across his face, as if trying to wake himself up. He hadn't been sleeping well, and it was starting to show. "Call off the search for the strays." He leaned back in his chair, templing his hands beneath his chin, for once heedless of the wrinkles in his suit jacket. "Radley is forming a Pride out of homicidal, likely mentally unstable, strays, and we have to take him out with one strike. We need everybody rested to do that."

One by one, the other Alphas nodded in agreement. Uncle Rick's gaze settled on Parker. "There's a list of cell-phone numbers on the fridge. Start at the top and work your way down. They're out in pairs, so make sure you cross off the partners as you come to them to save time."

Parker nodded and headed into the kitchen, digging his own phone from his pocket as he went.

"We still need a location," Malone said, meeting my father's eyes over the coffee table.

"Yes, we do. Normally I'd send Marc, but since he no longer works for me, I'm open to suggestions."

Send Marc to do what? I glanced up at Ethan and he slammed one fist into his opposite palm, miming a punch. *Oh.* They were sending someone to pound some answers out of Hannibal. Wherever the hell he was.

"Reid?" Malone twisted in his seat to make eye contact with the fastidious, bald enforcer.

"Ethan will go, too," my father said, rubbing his jaw now. "He's taped up in the shed. Don't come back until you know where Radley's housing his men and how many there are."

Ethan and Reid nodded in unison, then headed for the back door.

My father sighed and glanced at the rest of us in turn. "Everyone else should get some rest." He twisted to face the stairs, and I expected his eyes to meet mine, but his focus settled over my head instead. "Marc!"

"Yes?" Marc thumped into sight without hesitation, and I couldn't help but smile. Our Alpha had known he was there the whole time.

"Escort Faythe back to the cabin." My father's gaze settled

on me with an emotional weight too heavy to quantify. "I'll call you if anything changes with Kaci. For now, get some sleep."

It was a truly wonderful gesture. He was trying to give us one final night together. For goodbye. I blinked back tears, both because of his gesture and because of its significance. According to the clock over the door, it was 11:00 p.m. In eight hours, Marc would be gone.

I stood, and Marc wrapped one arm around my waist. We walked back to the cabin slowly, trying to enjoy the evening stroll as if it were a routine event, rather than the last of such for six whole months. We were both grateful for my arrangement for semi-annual visits, but May seemed like a very long time away.

My feet dragged as I climbed the porch steps. As glad as I was to be spending the next few hours alone with Marc, I knew that a good portion of that would be spent sleeping—though not *all* of it, of course—and that when we woke, it would only be to say goodbye. I wanted to delay that moment as long as possible.

Michael sat on the couch in the living room, his laptop balanced on his knees, his head thrown back with his mouth hanging open. He was sound asleep, and I couldn't imagine how he'd kept from dropping his computer. When I lifted it from his lap, he woke up. "What time is it?"

"Just after eleven."

"Shit. What did I miss?" He removed his glasses to rub his eyes while I shut down his laptop.

"Kaci led us to the body." The screen went black and I closed the computer with a soft click. "It was in a tree. Half consumed."

"Nooooo." Michael sat up, suddenly alert. "Not Kaci?"

I nodded. "Yeah. She's fucked up, Michael. Completely nonresponsive. I think she was okay as long as she didn't have to think about it. But now she's just…checked out. Nobody's home."

"She'll come out of it." Marc leaned against my bedroom door frame. "Dr. Carver will know what to do."

"I hope so." I circled the coffee table, headed toward him. But then I turned back to Michael when I remembered what I'd forgotten. "Oh, yeah. Zeke Radley is forming his own Pride out of a bunch of psychotic strays."

Michael's forehead crinkled and he replaced his glasses, leaning forward on the edge of the couch. "Are you serious?"

"Unfortunately. And they've evidently been chasing Kaci, trying to add a hen to their collection of roosters."

"Huh." He shrugged. "That kind of makes sense. They're both from Canada. He could have been following her for quite a while."

I hadn't thought of that, but Michael was probably right. Which made Kaci's survival all the more miraculous, in spite of the atrocities she'd had to commit to stay alive.

"Yeah, I guess." I stepped backward into Marc's embrace, surprised to realize he'd taken off his shirt. "Also, we found one of Radley's toms. Ethan knocked him out and they're beating some answers out of him now." The last little bit came out as one long word, rushed in my eagerness to put a closed door between my brother and us.

Michael frowned in confusion, then smiled when my rushed statement sank in. "Okay, thanks. Go…get some sleep."

Smiling, I shut the door. A moment later the front door closed as Michael left for the lodge. He wasn't supposed to go alone, but I appreciated the gesture. Privacy was the most valuable gift one werecat could give another.

Besides, Michael was a big boy. He could take care of himself.

I turned to find Marc watching me, hands stuffed into the pockets of his jeans, T-shirt forgotten on the floor. He didn't smile; this wasn't a happy occasion. But he didn't look entirely unhappy, either. My gaze trailed over the dark stubble strengthening an already well-defined chin, down his neck, then his chest, where four parallel claw-mark scars marred an otherwise perfect display of granite masculinity. My hands ached to travel the same path. So I let them.

The lovemaking that followed was slower and more deliberate than before, but no less urgent. Afterward, I fell asleep with Marc curled against my back, his scent surrounding me.

I hadn't slept so well in months.

A sudden slice of light fell across my closed eyelids, rendering the darkness in a dull shade of red. I opened my eyes reluctantly, automatically searching out the alarm clock. Surely it wasn't time for Marc to go yet.

It wasn't. The glowing red numbers read 5:18. We'd slept less than four hours.

"Faythe!"

I sat up, shoving tangled hair away from my face. A man's silhouette stood framed by the doorway, backlit by light from the living room. The wire-thin corner of an eyeglasses frame would have told me who was there, even if the voice and scent hadn't. *Michael.*

"Is it Kaci?" My fingers found the warm expanse of Marc's chest on the bed next to me. The steady rise and fall of his ribs said he was still sleeping, by some miracle.

"Yes, but she's fine. Well, no worse, anyway." Michael shrugged, leaning on the door frame. "She's asleep. Jace stayed at the lodge to watch her."

"So what's wrong?"

"Nothing's wrong. Just…weird. Dr. Carver called, and Dad told him to hop on the next flight back up here because we'll probably need him after a raid on the strays."

Wow. He'd only been gone fourteen hours. Still… "You

woke me up to tell me Carver's coming back?" I grouched in a whisper. "Couldn't that have waited until morning?"

He shook off my complaint in barely restrained excitement. "That's not the good part. He and Dr. Eames worked all night on Kaci's blood, and they have the preliminary results."

"Already? How is that possible?" I climbed out of bed carefully to keep from jarring Marc, because I had a feeling I was done sleeping for the time being.

"Well, it wouldn't have been if they had to wait for a commercial lab to open and assign someone to it. But they did the work themselves, and they knew exactly what they were looking for."

My heart thumped as I followed him into the living room, my bare feet silent on the frigid hardwood. "So…she's a stray, right?" She had to be. He wouldn't be so excited if she were a Pride cat.

But Michael shook his head, his smile beaming at me *waaaaay* too brightly for five o'clock in the morning. "She's not a stray. But she isn't a Pride cat, either. You're not going to believe this. I'm not sure I believe it yet…"

"*Damn,* Michael, get to the point!" I stomped past him into the kitchen, heading straight for the coffeemaker. I was too tired and anxious for his speechless disbelief. "What is she?"

"Carver's calling her a 'miracle of recessive genes.'"

"Which means what?" I set the pot beneath the faucet and flipped the cold water on. "Is she stray or Pride?"

"Neither. Or both. I'm not sure. Dr. Carver says her blood is like nothing he's ever seen. He was so excited I could hardly understand a word he said."

And it must have been catching, because I didn't understand, either. Not a damn word coming from his mouth.

Thirty

"Double recessive... What does that even mean?" Malone shoved back the sleeves of his robe and crossed both arms on the long oak table. The dining room looked different with no sunlight shining through the wall of windows. It was oddly dim, in spite of the overhead light. But that sort of made sense. Most people didn't serve meals at five-thirty in the morning.

"Okay, I'm a lawyer, not a geneticist, so you'll have to bear with me on this." Michael mirrored Malone's posture from across the table. Somehow, he managed to look professional even in green plaid pajama bottoms.

Our father sat at the head of the table, taking up a position of authority since this discussion had nothing to do with my hearing. Uncle Rick sat on his left, followed by Paul Blackwell, then Malone. Michael and I sat opposite the Alphas.

I'd come to the emergency meeting because of my relationship with Kaci. No other enforcers had been included, ostensibly to make sure they got enough sleep. But we all knew the real reason. The Alphas didn't understand the new information, and they didn't want to look stupid in front of their subordinate Pride members.

I couldn't really blame them. I didn't understand, either.

"This is how Dr. Carver explained it to me, using mostly generalities and layman's terms," Michael said. "The reality is quite a bit more complicated, but for our purposes, I think the preschool version will suffice. Agreed?" He glanced around the table, receiving mostly nods.

Paul Blackwell harrumphed, gripping the curve of his cane between his knees. "So long as it's the truth and it makes sense. I won't listen to any of this theoretical nonsense." Blackwell trusted science about as well as he trusted strays, and he understood it even less. He was like the first caveman presented with fire, frightened and angered by things he couldn't comprehend.

Michael's excitement faltered, but he recovered quickly. "No problem. Okay, now we all know about the recessive werecat gene, right? How a human has to have been born with that in order to be infected by a scratch or bite. Are we all on the same page?"

Everyone looked at Blackwell, who was most likely to answer in the negative. "Right, right." The old man twisted his cane, and the rubber tip squeaked as it ground against the hardwood. "I remember the recessive gene. What I don't understand is how it got into humans in the first place. I never was satisfied on that point…"

As if the gene's existence was debatable. The old turd was even grouchier without his beauty sleep.

"It's not in *all* humans, Councilman Blackwell. Remember? The recessive gene is actually pretty rare. And we're not entirely sure how it got there. The working theory at the moment is that we've actually been putting it there ourselves, by…well, breeding with humans."

"Toms can't breed with humans, boy!" Blackwell shouted, face flushing in anger, and I rolled my eyes before I could stop myself. "That's the part of this whole thing that never made any sense."

"I know that's always been the assumption." Michael folded his hands on the table and stared back at the old man with more patience than I could ever have summoned. "But Dr. Carver and Dr. Eames think we've been wrong about that one."

Blackwell slapped his cane, and it fell over, smacking Malone's knees. "Oh, balderdash!"

"Paul…" Daddy's voice was stern, which no doubt irritated Blackwell even further, considering the two decades he had on my father. "We've been over all this before. Those genes got into the human DNA somehow, and who else could have put them there but us?"

Blackwell scowled, and I couldn't help grinning. The source of his irritation was obvious, and he wasn't the only one suffering from it. He was no doubt wondering how many bastards he'd sired from whatever human women he'd known before conquering Mrs. Blackwell's heart and bed.

Any one of us could have put his mind at ease about that one, but no one bothered, because he was being a royal pain in the ass. But the fact of the matter was that while human-werecat breeding was now considered possible, it was also considered very rare.

Over the past several hundred years, werecat toms who had no shot at marrying a dam and starting a family had consoled themselves with human women willing to share their company and their beds. Dr. Eames's theory held that a rare few of those unions resulted in the birth of a human baby carrying that mysterious recessive gene, which was then passed on to the next generation.

In fact, I knew of at least one tom several years back whose ex-girlfriend claimed rather loudly that he was the father of her child. He assumed she was lying, naturally, and dumped her for cheating on him. And rumor has it that since Dr.

Eames's discovery, he's been trying to get back in touch with that woman to find out the truth.

That poor tom was facing some serious problems, but Paul Blackwell likely had nothing to worry about. However, just in case, every tom in the country had recently been told in no uncertain terms to either buy stock in Trojans or get familiar with the concept of celibacy.

Considering that most of them couldn't even *spell* celibacy, the popular choice was pretty obvious.

Blackwell's scowl deepened, and he crossed thin, wrinkled hands over his chest. "It still sounds suspicious to me, but for the sake of expediency, I'm willing to move on."

"Thank you." Michael's gaze met mine, and a grin flickered across his professional expression. "Anyway, what they found in Kaci's blood sample was not one, but *two* of these recessive genes."

My uncle leaned forward, drawing all eyes his way. "Which means…?"

"Which means she got one from *each* of her parents."

"So she's not a stray?" Malone asked, smirking at me from across the table. I smiled sweetly back at him because I was starting to see where this little detour was going, and the destination was worth admitting I was wrong. *Way* worth it.

Because Malone was wrong, too.

Michael shook his head eagerly. "No, she's not. Her parents were human, but they both carried the recessive werecat gene, which means that somewhere in each of their family trees—perhaps generations back—is one of us." He glanced around, beaming at each of us individually, looking for some spark of understanding. My father smiled, but no one else seemed to get it. And to be fair, my father had probably gotten the news—and thus the explanation—straight from Dr. Carver himself.

"Don't you see?" Michael demanded, his voice rising in

excitement. "This was bound to happen eventually. It probably already *has* happened. The human authorities would never have gotten it straightened out, and we would probably have attributed it to an attack by a stray, just like we did in Kaci's case."

My uncle's eyebrows shot up, confusion and eagerness battling for space in his expression. "Attributed *what* to an attack by a stray?"

I sighed. "Michael, I don't think they understand about dominant and recessive alleles."

For a moment my brother looked stunned, as if surprised that the confusion could be attributed to something so simple. Then he smiled. "Of course." He closed his eyes, thinking for a moment. "Okay, this is a bit simplistic, but if a person inherits the gene for blue eyes from one parent and the gene for brown eyes from the other, he's going to get brown eyes, because the gene for brown eyes is dominant, and the gene for blue eyes is recessive. Brown eyes sort of trump blue."

"So how did Jace wind up with blue eyes?" Blackwell asked, and Malone frowned, displeased by the indirect reference to his wife's first husband.

Michael's smile broadened. "I'm glad you asked that. Jace inherited the recessive gene for blue eyes from both his mother and his father, so there was no dominant gene to override the blue. And bear with me, these terms are all wrong."

Blackwell waved off his apology; we were all fine with his terminology. "So what you're saying is that the little tabby got two recessive werecat genes just like Jace got two blue-eye genes?"

"Sort of. There are actually more than two genes responsible. And I don't think *genes* is even the right word here. But basically…yes."

Enthusiasm bubbled inside my chest, tightening it so that

I could barely breathe. I couldn't wait any longer. They were dragging it out, and I wanted everyone else to be as excited by this as Michael and I were. "But instead of getting blue eyes, she got to be a werecat!"

For a moment there was only silence as everyone stared at me. Except Michael, who glared at me beneath furrowed eyebrows. Apparently he'd wanted to make the big announcement himself.

Uncle Rick was the first to speak. "Wait, let me see if I understand this correctly. Kaci's parents were both human, but because they each gave her a recessive werecat gene…she's one of us? A werecat born to completely human parents?"

I opened my mouth to answer, but Michael beat me to it, beaming. "Yes."

"Other than being born to two humans, she's just like one of us," I said, glancing around the table in excitement, in spite of the early hour. "At puberty she experienced her first Shift, and since she had no idea what had happened to her, she didn't understand that she could Shift back, much less how to do it. She's evidently been in cat form ever since."

"If all this is true—" Paul Blackwell left that *if* hanging in the air like a cloud of poison gas "—why wasn't her sister one of us? The sister is older, right? So she should have gone through puberty before Kaci."

Everyone looked to Michael for an explanation, as if they'd been wondering that same thing.

My brother shrugged. "The sister didn't get both recessive genes. She might not have gotten either of them, in fact. Regardless, she clearly wasn't one of us."

"So what about the stray who attacked the sister and mother?" Uncle Rick sipped from an early-morning mug of coffee, which I was seriously starting to covet. "Was that just a coincidence?"

The stray who…?

Oh, shit. My eyes closed as comprehension settled through

me, pinning me to my chair with a devastating weight. "There *was* no stray."

Someone on my left moaned, and my head turned toward the sound even as my eyes opened. I was astounded to find myself looking at my father, whose face registered more shock and horror than I'd ever seen on it in my entire life. He'd clearly come to the same conclusion I had, but based on the confused expressions around us, no one else had arrived at that point yet.

"Kaci killed them." My father said it because I couldn't. I couldn't make myself voice such a statement, even though I had no doubt of its accuracy.

"Nooooo." Michael sat back in his chair, stunned.

"She didn't do it on purpose." Desperation to defend her made me break my horrified silence. "She couldn't have. Put yourself in her place. She's just turned into a huge cat—out of the clear blue sky—and has *no* idea what's happening to her. She's terrified and in horrible physical pain. Remember how badly it hurts those first few times?"

What was I thinking? No one else in the room was close enough to puberty to remember what a first Shift felt like!

"Anyway, it hurts like hel—like nothing you've ever felt, even though you know what to expect. Imagine if you have no *idea* what's coming!" No one spoke, so I continued. "So there she is, suddenly covered in fur, swishing a tail she shouldn't have, and before she's even recovered from the physical trauma she's smacked over the head with instincts she can't possibly understand. Especially considering how badly her mom and sister were probably freaking out."

My hands shook with the thought of what she'd been through, and with fear for her life as the consequence.

"Faythe…" Uncle Rick's hand covered my fist where it lay on the table. He was trying to calm me, but it didn't work. Nothing could.

"I'm just trying to make sure everyone understands. She

didn't do this on purpose. She couldn't have. She had no idea what she was doing."

"We know." My father leaned forward, intruding on Michael's personal space to get closer to me. "It's okay. We know she didn't mean to. I can't imagine what that must have been like for her."

"She's only thirteen…" I trailed off as tears formed in my eyes, then rolled down my cheeks. I pulled my fist away from my uncle to wipe at the moisture on my face, too horrified for Kaci—not to mention her mother and sister—to worry about how weak my tears probably made me look.

Calvin Malone cleared his throat, and I looked his way through blurry vision. "I'm sure you're right," he said, and I thought I'd die from the shock of him agreeing with me. "I can't imagine anyone here holding her responsible for her actions, considering what she was going through at the time."

And that's when the bitter truth sank in. If Malone tried to have Kaci executed, he wouldn't be able to use her in his plot to take over the council. He was *such* a selfish bastard, and that time I couldn't even argue with him, because by all appearances, he was giving me what I wanted. Sparing the tabby's life.

"I think there's something important to keep in mind here, Faythe," my father said, but when I looked up at him, I found him facing the room in general, clearly directing his comment to everyone, though he'd addressed it to me. "Kaci has been through something horrible. Something truly unfathomable. And she's had to do some terrible things to survive. But she *has* survived. She's made it on her own, traveling several hundred miles across multiple geographical boundaries, with no idea that she could Shift back and ask someone for help. She fed herself, sheltered herself and protected herself under circumstances many grown toms would have found daunting. Kaci is strong. She's a survivor. She's just the kind of tabby we need, and I think with Faythe's help we can get her through this."

Wow. The positive spin he'd put on that one would have made a ballerina dizzy. And he'd managed to work my usefulness into it to boot. *Damn, he's good.*

Heads nodded all around the table. The only Alpha who didn't look pleased was Malone, who'd probably been planning to handle Kaci's adjustment *personally*…

My father pushed his chair back and stood. "We can decide how to handle all this—and what to do with Kaci—later today. For now, I suggest everyone try to salvage what's left of the night." He turned to me. "That means go back to sleep."

I nodded and was already headed for the door with Jace when Malone called me back.

"Faythe…" I turned to face him, and the look on his face sent alarm tingling through me. "The tribunal will meet one last time while the enforcers clean out Radley's 'Pride.' We expect to have a verdict by the time they get back." Having dropped that bomb on me, Malone stared at me expectantly, like I was supposed to say something.

What, I had no idea.

"Um…thanks?"

Michael groaned, and Malone scowled. Apparently that wasn't the proper response. Maybe I should have licked his fucking boots. But we both knew *that* wasn't going to happen.

"This isn't a joke," Malone snapped. "It's your future." Or lack thereof. He was saying that last part in his head. I just knew it. "Go to bed. The least you can do is show up rested."

Yeah, like I was gonna get any sleep after *that*.

Ten minutes later I followed Jace into the cabin to find Marc sitting on the couch with a cup of coffee in one hand. He turned to look at me when I came in, but I got the distinct impression that he'd been staring at the wall before that.

"Hey."

"Hey," I returned. Jace went straight to his room as I sank

onto the couch facing Marc, crossing my legs beneath me. "Sorry to bail on you in the middle of the night. Dr. Carver called. Turns out Kaci's neither Pride nor stray. She's some kind of genetic-recessive something-or-other—"

"I know."

I met his eyes in surprise. "You know?"

He handed me his half-full mug of coffee and I drank, pleased to discover that it was still warm. And perfectly sweetened, even though he took it black. "I heard you and Michael talking, so I called the doc myself after you left. He was already at the airport waiting for a flight back. He explained it to me."

"You were awake? Why didn't you say something?"

"I was afraid you wouldn't go if you knew I was up, and I didn't want you to miss the discussion."

Sighing, I closed my eyes. Then I drained his mug. "Thank you."

"You'd have done the same for me." That wasn't true, but it was a nice sentiment. If he'd been invited to an Alpha-only discussion without me, I'd have snuck along behind him to eavesdrop. "Did I miss anything?"

"Unfortunately, yeah. We think Kaci killed her mom and her sister. Not on purpose, of course. Probably out of fear and pain."

Marc's lips parted in surprise, then he closed his mouth and nodded. "That makes sense, in a morbid kind of way. Anything else?"

"They're announcing my verdict tomorrow."

"Of course they are. Just as soon as I'm gone."

"I'm sorry." I set the mug on the coffee table, then took his hand in both of mine. "You're going to miss the big offensive tomorrow, too. Of course, so will I. They'll never let me go." The council wouldn't risk a tabby's life for something as ultimately insignificant as clearing out a den of strays. Even a tabby they'd claimed to be willing to execute only days earlier. Apparently consistency means nothing to some people…

"Well, at least it shouldn't take too long. Ethan came in while you were gone. They finally got some answers out of the stray you guys brought in."

"Just now?" I glanced through the kitchen doorway at the clock hanging over the fridge. It was nearly six o'clock in the morning.

"A couple of hours ago. He and Reid had a few drinks to celebrate."

Or to help deal with the fact that they'd beat the shit out of a perfect stranger for information. I knew Ethan better than any of my other brothers. He was good at his job and would do what he was told to do in the line of duty without fail. But he didn't enjoy that particular aspect of the job. For his sake, I hoped my father had someone else in mind to replace Marc. It wasn't fair to ask Ethan to take on such responsibility full-time. Vic, maybe? I could see Vic doing it. But not Ethan, and definitely not Owen.

Marc frowned at the thoughts no doubt flashing across my face. He seemed distinctly uncomfortable thinking about what would become of the Pride after he was gone. I wasn't comfortable with it, either.

"Let's go back to bed." So we did. By the time we finally fell asleep after another round of goodbye sex, the sun was coming up. But by then we were too exhausted to care.

Thirty-One

The next morning was hell.

Marc was gone when I woke up, and in his place was an envelope lying on his pillow. Inside was a folded sheet of lined yellow paper, probably torn from one of Michael's legal pads.

I leaned over to flip on the lamp on the bedside table. My eyes watered as I unfolded the note.

> *Dear Faythe,*
> *I'm sorry. I left without waking you up because I wasn't sure you'd let me go if you had the chance to stop me. I'll call you when I get settled in somewhere. Do not come looking for me. I'm going to Mississippi and will stay as close to the territorial border as possible.*
>
> *I love you. I always have, and I always will. There's more, but I can't write it down. Not here, and not now.*
> *Love always,*
> *Marc*
> *P.S. You don't have to wear this, but I wanted you to have the option, should you change your mind. My offer still stands.*

Wear what? I set the paper down and peered into the envelope, where I found a familiar silver ring peeking out at me. A delicate carving of an ivy vine wound around the band. It was the one he'd tried to give me two and a half months earlier. The one we'd broken up over. And there it was again.

A tear fell onto the envelope, and suddenly every emotion raging inside me blazed into anger. Unspeakable, unthinkable, uncontrollable anger. Marc was gone, and there was nothing I could do about it. I had nothing left of him but that damn ring and his scent on the pillowcase. I hadn't even remembered to steal one of his shirts.

I shrieked in pain and fury, and in the kitchen, everyday sounds I hadn't even realized I'd heard suddenly went silent. Enraged, I threw the envelope containing the ring across the room, where it smacked into the wall with a soft clink, then slid to the floor. I wadded the letter in both hands, then threw it to join the envelope. Then I collapsed onto my own pillow, using it to muffle more sob-wracked shrieking that was no one's business but my own.

When the tears finally stopped, though the anger had yet to recede, I sat up, suddenly horrified by what I'd done. I scrambled off the bed and across the floor, then snatched the envelope and dumped it into my palm.

Nothing fell out. The ring was gone. *Shit.*

I retrieved the letter and smoothed it out on the floor, then folded it and slid it into my back pocket. Then I knelt to search for the ring, the cheap carpet rough against my hands and bare knees. Not under the bedside table. Not in the corner. Not under the armchair in the opposite corner. But there it was, under the dresser, glinting at me in the light from the bedside lamp.

I had to lie flat on my stomach to reach the ring, and when I did, I slid it immediately onto the ring finger on my right hand. For a moment I stared at it in consideration. Then I took it off, not because I didn't want to wear it, but because I didn't want anyone else to see it. Marc and his ring were my business. Private.

Standing, I pulled my jeans from the arm of the chair in the corner and shoved the ring deep into the front right pocket. Then I stepped into them. I was zipping the fly beneath the hem of my pajama top when someone knocked at my door.

"Faythe, you okay?" It was Ethan.

"Go away," I snapped, digging through my suitcase for a fresh shirt.

Instead, he opened the door. "Take a shower and get dressed. They're bringing Kaci over in a few minutes, then everyone else is heading out into the woods."

"What the hell does it look like I'm doing?" I demanded, whirling to face him with clean clothes in one hand, my bathrobe in the other.

Ethan frowned, a slice of bacon halfway to his mouth. "Don't take this out on me. I had nothing to do with him leaving, and you know it."

He was right, but at the moment, that didn't help. Marc was gone, and in a matter of hours the tribunal would hand down a verdict sparing my life in exchange for his absence. Well, *fuck* them. Fuck them *all*.

"You want something to eat?" Ethan's frown was gone and he now looked sympathetic, which pissed me off even more, though I knew logically that this had nothing to do with him.

"No. Just coffee."

"It's already made," he said, as I brushed past him on my way to the bathroom.

Minutes later I emerged, clothes on, hair brushed, foul mood intact. I joined Ethan, Michael, Parker, and my father in the kitchen.

I walked straight past them to the coffeepot, where the mug I'd claimed as my own for the duration of my hearing was sitting on the counter waiting for me. The handle smelled like my father. It was a sweet gesture, but not enough to make up for letting Marc go.

Still, as I poured my coffee, ignoring the silent tension at my back, I had to admit I wasn't really mad at any of the men in my life. Not even my father. He'd acted in my best interest, as well as that of the Pride. But I wasn't ready to talk about any of it. Not yet. So I stood at the counter as I stirred sugar and creamer into my mug, listening to the chewing sounds behind me.

A chair scraped the cheap linoleum and footsteps came my way. I expected to smell Ethan behind me, but it was my father's arm that set a full plate of bacon, eggs, and toast on the counter in front of me. "I know you're upset. And mad. And probably several other things I can't possibly understand. But there will be time to indulge your emotions later. Today is a very important day. I want you to eat and get ahold of yourself. Then I want you to be there for Kaci, who's going through something much worse than what you're going through, whether you believe it or not."

I glared at my father, sharp words ready to fall from my tongue. But he cut me off with a few of his own. "Marc isn't dead, Faythe. No matter how bad things look right now, none of this is irreparable. But everyone Kaci loved *is* dead, or might as well be." Because we all knew she could never see her father again. "We're all she has left now, and *you're* the one she trusts. You're going to get yourself together and be there for her. Then, when the time comes, you're going to go before the tribunal and say whatever you have to say to make a good showing and to accept their mercy. Gracefully. For once, you're going to keep your mouth shut and your smile in place. If you need to throw a fit later, in private, that's fine. We all expect it. But for today, you're going to earn your place in this family and in this Pride. And you're going to take back your paycheck. I need you at my back now more than ever, and you will *not* disappoint me."

"Daddy…"

"No." His expression went granite hard, frozen somewhere between a scowl and a firm request. "Now eat. *That is an order.*"

He didn't retreat until I bit into my first slice of bacon, forcing myself to chew even though it tasted not like the hickory smoke advertised on the package but like my own bitter anguish.

I cleaned my plate, standing at the counter not out of rebellion now, but out of embarrassment. I'd known I wasn't the only one having a hard morning, but until my father's speech, I hadn't realized just how much everyone else was suffering along with me.

Parker cleared the table while I ate the last of my eggs, and through the kitchen window I saw Jace and Reid heading our way across the front yard, Kaci walking between them. She had her eyes on the ground, as if watching her every step, which was a relief considering she'd been staring into space the last time I'd seen her.

Something brushed my arm as I set my fork on my empty plate, and I looked up to find my father standing next to me, watching Kaci approach. My heart flooded with guilt, my eyes with fresh tears. "I'm sorry, Daddy."

He looked away from the window to meet my eyes. "Me, too." His arms opened and I stepped into them, resting my head on his shoulder as I blinked back tears surrounded by the scent I'd long ago come to associate with absolute security—and authority. And for once, those were both okay.

The front door opened, and Kaci, Reid and Jace stepped into the cabin. I pulled away from my father and put my plate in the sink, then joined them in the living room, where Parker sat in an armchair, stuffing bottled water into a backpack.

"Hi, Kaci." I paused in the threshold, leaning against the door frame. Kaci met my eyes and nodded in greeting, then lowered herself onto the couch next to Jace without saying a word. Still, silence notwithstanding, she seemed much better. "Have you had breakfast?"

She shook her head.

"I think we still have some bacon and eggs in here, if you're interested."

She nodded again and I headed back into the kitchen to warm up a plate of leftovers for her. My father followed me. "Michael and I are going to the lodge to wait for the tribunal's verdict and to sit with Brett. Jace and Parker are going out with the other enforcers. Since they were up too late to get much sleep, Reid and Ethan are staying with you and Kaci."

"Sure." I shrugged, spooning scrambled eggs onto a clean plate. What he really meant was that Reid and Ethan would be *watching* me and Kaci. And what *that* really meant was that we'd be missing out on all the action. As I'd expected.

"I'll call you when the tribunal's ready." With that, Michael and my father left for the lodge, and Jace and Parker headed for my uncle's cabin, where all the other enforcers were meeting to briefly discuss strategy before Shifting and setting off into the woods.

When they were gone, Kaci sat at the table slowly eating her breakfast, as if it was an effort to chew each bite. Though she seemed to be pushing the food around on the plate more than anything. Ethan, Reid, and I watched her from the living room, guzzling coffee. None of us had gotten much sleep.

I cradled my mug in both hands, enjoying the warmth. "So, did Hannibal Lecter say anything useful, other than where the strays are hiding out?"

Ethan looked confused until he realized I was asking about the cannibalistic stray. "His name is Jeff, and yeah, actually, he had lots of good information. But the real trick was interpreting it. He was *blazing* with scratch fever, and his brain was fried, so once he started talking, words just kind of leaked out, in no particular order."

"Did he say where the hell they came from? Surely Zeke Radley didn't make all those strays." I knew that for a fact, because he hadn't infected either Jeff/Hannibal or the stray I'd killed.

Reid ran one hand over his bald head and set his empty mug on the end table to his right. "According to Hannibal…" His brows rose in mild amusement over my pet name for the crazy stray. "He hooked up with Radley a few days ago, near the Canadian border. Radley was already traveling with several toms, and they were on their way to 'claim their territory.' Presumably this free zone." He raised both arms to indicate everything around us. "We're assuming that at some point Radley had a run-in with a Pride cat who taught him a little about Pride structure and told him this land was unclaimed. So Radley set out to claim it. And he was generous enough to let the other strays they ran into join their ranks. Including your Hannibal."

Ethan cleared his throat and brushed black hair from his forehead. "If we're understanding correctly, Radley infected a couple of the strays himself before he understood what he was doing. I guess he just kind of collected them, instead of abandoning them, because Jeff didn't seem to know that most strays are loners. He—and presumably all the rest of them—got everything they know about being a werecat from Radley. And Zeke Radley seems to have told them only what he wanted them to believe."

I nodded, catching on. "He told them that he was an Alpha, and that this is his territory."

"Yeah." Reid nodded grimly, and lowered his voice to a whisper. "And when they got here, they picked up that tabby's scent." He paused to make sure Kaci wasn't listening—if she was, I couldn't tell it—then continued. "Radley decided he needs her to complete his Pride, and offered rewards to the first tom who could bring her in alive. That's why they've been

stirring up trouble all over the mountain for the past few days.
Looking for *her*."

I *knew* it. They were hunting Kaci. Thank goodness cats
can't track by smell. And that Kaci had gotten good at hiding
over two and a half months on her own. "Damn, those are
some ambitious strays." But my heart broke for them, in spite
of all the damage they'd done.

If they'd been found and taught by someone other than
Zeke Radley—someone with just an *inkling* of moral fortitude—they might have become completely different people.
They might have lived peacefully. And much longer. But
today our enforcers were under orders to leave no survivors,
because we couldn't afford to play around with the what-ifs.
The reality was that no matter what *might* have happened, the
strays *had* committed multiple capital crimes, and had already
been convicted and sentenced by our council.

At least I got a hearing.

While Kaci ate in silence and Ethan and Reid played cards,
I stared out the kitchen window, my thoughts flitting from the
Alphas deciding my fate, to Kaci and her unsure future, to
Brett recovering from the injuries I *hadn't* been able to save
him from. Then my mind turned to the enforcers, even then
on their way to Radley's hideout in the mountains, and how
badly I wanted to join them. I could really have used some
therapeutic ass-kicking right about then.

But then my thoughts came back to Marc, as they always
did eventually. Was he on the plane yet? Was he thinking
about me? Had he meant it when he'd written not to come
looking for him? Would it matter if he had?

A flicker of movement from the window snagged my eye,
pulling me from my thoughts like a sailor from the sinking
wreck of his own ship. I froze, staring at the tree line, and something moved again—a flash of black, then nothing but the
stirring of evergreen shrubs and half-dead grass in the breeze.

I stood for a better look, setting my mug on the coffee table as my eyes narrowed. Someone was skulking around out back and he obviously didn't want to be seen. Which meant he wasn't one of ours.

A shiver of fear and excitement raced up my spine. I'd thought I would miss all the action, but once again, the action had come to me…

Thirty-Two

"What's wrong?" Ethan held his cards to his chest, glancing at the window in mild curiosity. But Reid set his hand down and stood, heading for the sink before I'd even rounded the coffee table.

"Did you see it?" I leaned over the double basin by his side, déjà vu sharpening my sudden dread.

"A second ago." We stared some more, then Reid stiffened. "There. He just passed behind that twisted tree. Be on the other side in a second."

My eyes found the twisted trunk, and sure enough, a patch of shiny black fur slunk out from behind it as I watched.

"Do you recognize him?" I whispered, though I knew Kaci would hear us.

"Recognize who?" she demanded. Her fork clinked on the edge of her plate, but I didn't turn. I didn't want to lose sight of the trespasser again.

"Not yet." Reid ignored her question, as did I. We didn't have answers yet anyway. "Doesn't matter, though. Our guys are long gone by now, or else holed up in the lodge."

I nodded. "He's heading that way." Toward the lodge, where the Alphas were gathered with an injured tom, and no one to protect them, other than Michael. Michael fought damn well for a lawyer, but he was only one man, and there was no telling how many strays were really in the brush.

The tabby's chair slid back from the table and Ethan squeezed in at the sink on my other side. Kaci hung back in silence.

"I'll go. Keep an eye on him while I Shift." With that, Reid disappeared into the living room, already pulling his shirt over his head.

"What's going on?" Kaci's voice was tight with tension and encroaching panic.

I smiled and put one arm around her shoulder, pulling her close. "It's fine. Reid's just going out to take care of an intruder."

"Who is it?"

I blinked at the raw fear in her voice, then searched out the cat again when Ethan turned to comfort her. Or maybe to pull her away from the window. "We don't know yet. Probably one of the strays. Ethan, get her out of here."

"Come on, Kaci." He guided her by one shoulder, glancing at me in question as he ushered her out of the kitchen. "We have some movies set up in the living room."

She went reluctantly, but I could feel her eyes on my back. She wasn't happy being left out, and I couldn't really blame her.

Several minutes later, Reid huffed and I turned from the window to find him standing on the linoleum clad in nothing but shiny black fur rippling over long feline muscles. He huffed again and tossed his head toward the front yard, probably asking me if our unscheduled visitor was still there.

"Yeah. He's moving slowly, scouting everything out," I said. Reid nodded and padded toward the back door, where I let him out. "Be careful." He nodded, then took the steps at a trot.

I closed the door behind him and returned to the window. A second later he raced across the yard. Reid slowed as he approached the tree line, coming up on the intruder from the rear, his paws no doubt silent even on crunchy dead grass.

The stray paused, and his ears arched forward on alert. Reid dropped to his belly, and when the stray moved on, he rose. Three steps later two large black blurs dropped from the trees on either side of him.

"No!" I screamed, and Ethan came running. Outside, claws slashed, fur flew, and howls of pain sliced through the peaceful calm like a machete through birthday cake. "No!" I shouted again, leaning over the sink in fury. My fist slammed into the glass and it shattered, slicing open my knuckles. I barely felt the pain, I was so numb with shock and outrage. "They set him up!" I whirled to face Ethan, holding my bleeding hand in front of me. "They're here for Kaci. They waited for the guys to clear out, then they set a trap, and we let Reid walk right into it."

"Shit!" Ethan yelled, his eyes still glued to the fight outside. I turned back in time to see a spray of blood arc across the dead grass, staining the ground bright red. The shape in the middle of the huddle went still and the two remaining cats stepped back to reveal Reid, limp and unmoving. He was dead, his throat ripped out by the stray whose muzzle still dripped blood.

Ethan twisted on the cold water and shoved my hand under the faucet. "Pick out the glass!" he ordered, then raced over the linoleum to lock the back door. I plucked two shards of glass from my fist as he ran across the kitchen behind me, brushing past a newly shocked Kaci on his way to lock the front door. Then he was back again, wrapping a towel from the dish drainer around my bloody fist.

"Call Dad." He pressed my good hand over the makeshift bandage to hold it in place. "Call him, then Shift. Do you understand?"

"Ethan, I'm cut, not stupid." I had to let go of the towel to dig my phone from my pocket. Fortunately auto-dial made it possible to call my father with the press of only one button.

While the electronic tone rang in my ear, my gaze settled on Kaci, whose eyes were wide with mounting horror.

"They're here for me? Why?" she demanded, her voice shrill with fright, her arms wrapped around her torso.

I frowned, surprised and dismayed all over again by how little she knew about us. "They're trying to form a Pride, and you can't have a real Pride without a tabby. But don't worry. We won't let them take you." Or me either, because the consensus was that two tabbies were better than one.

Naked now, Ethan dropped to his hands and knees on the hardwood behind her. And still the phone rang in my ear. "Shit! He's not answering."

"Call someone else!" Kaci's eyes were huge in fear, and she glared at the phone, as if it were the source of all the trouble. "Call one of those other guys. The enforcers."

"I can't. They all went out in cat form. No pockets," I added when she shot me a confused look. But Michael hadn't gone out at all… I pressed End Call, then auto-dialed my oldest brother. The phone buzzed in my ear.

Then it buzzed on my right. *What the hell…?*

The phone rang again in my ear—than again somewhere to my right. I whirled around to see Michael's cell phone vibrating on the counter by the fridge. "Damn it!"

"What?" Kaci backed slowly toward the far corner.

"Michael didn't take his phone." *Dumbass!*

I glanced out the window to find the strays slinking across the yard boldly. And as I watched, a fourth form stepped from the bushes, in human form.

Zeke Radley. Shit!

Ethan moaned behind me and I turned toward the living room. My brother now resembled a bald jaguar, other than the occasional odd bulge where things were still changing and coming together. He was almost through Shifting, but even in cat form he probably couldn't hold off three toms, and I didn't stand a chance without claws. I'd have to Shift. And so would Kaci.

Thinking quickly, I redialed my father's number, then crossed the linoleum toward the terrified young tabby as the phone rang in my ear. I sat in one of the kitchen chairs and pulled her toward me. "Kaci, you have to Shift. We both do."

"No." She shook her head vehemently, her hair slapping both of us in the face. "No! I can't! I don't ever want to be that again!"

"We have to, hon. We can't defend ourselves otherwise."

"We'll keep calling," she insisted. "The doors are locked. They can't get in and we'll keep calling for help."

But help wasn't answering.

"Kaci, locked doors won't stop them. Dead bolts will slow them down long enough for us to Shift, but they *will* get in, and we need to be able to defend ourselves. We need canines and claws."

She shook her head again, not quite as violently this time, but with no less determination. "I can't do it, Faythe." Tears stood in her eyes. "I do bad things when I'm a cat. I can't do it again."

"Yes you can. You have to. I won't let anything bad happen."

"No!" she shouted, spraying me with spittle, then backed toward the table while I wiped my face.

In full cat form now, Ethan growled at me in warning, telling me to hurry.

"Kaci…" I began again, but she was halfway across the living room now, backing away from us both with eyes wide in horror, tears trailing slowly down her flushed cheeks.

"No. I'll let them kill me before I'll do that again."

"You don't mean that." Not that it mattered. They weren't planning to kill her. What they wanted was even worse.

Her face went suddenly calm, and she spoke with an eerie softness. "I won't Shift, Faythe. You can't make me."

She was right about that.

In the backyard, Radley walked behind the three cats, halfway to the cabin now. "Fine." I ended my call again and held the phone out to her. "Go into my bedroom and lock the door behind you." I gestured to the room at her back. "Then get in my closet and keep trying to call my father. He's programmed in as 'Daddy.'"

"Really?" Her eyes brightened with hope, which nearly broke my heart in spite of the circumstances. "You're not mad?"

"Of course I'm not mad. Here." I tossed her the phone and she caught it. "Go!" I didn't have to say it again.

The bedroom door slammed shut behind her, then metal scraped metal softly as she engaged the lock.

Ethan whined, pacing back and forth in front of the front door now. I had my shirt and bra off in an instant, and my pants followed quickly. I dropped to all fours on the kitchen floor, the faded linoleum cold and smooth against my hands. But I barely had time to feel the November chill coming through the broken window before a familiar, bone-cracking pain chased it away.

My spine bowed and my knees cracked. My shoulders ached, the agony especially acute in my left shoulder, which had been wrenched by a psycho stray the previous summer. My elbows creaked, my ankles lengthened, and my knuckles popped like a series of firecrackers all going off at once.

Muscles slithered into and out of place under my skin, burning beneath my flesh. My fingers curved and shortened, the pressure in my hands almost unbearable. My nails lengthened and hardened into retractable claws, digging into the linoleum before they were even fully formed.

The surface of my tongue rippled with an influx of backward-pointing barbs as my newly sharp teeth pushed up from my gums, my jaw taking on a whole new shape in the midst of the pain. And finally my skin began to itch all over— fur announcing its arrival with the pomp and circumstance appropriate for such a majestic covering of thick, glossy black.

I sat on my haunches, stretching my front paws just in time to hear the first bang of a fist against the front door. "Little pig, little pig, let me in!" Radley shouted, then laughed hysterically. Like I'd never heard that one. Fortunately, the current shape of my jaw prevented me from responding with the line expected of me.

When he got no answer, Radley pounded again, this time with his foot, from the sound of it. Since his lungs evidently lacked the strength, he was going to kick the door in. And we were damn well going to be ready for him.

I padded into the living room next to Ethan, who was sweating adrenaline and excitement, laced with fear. All of which fed my own rage and eagerness—two of the best mental states to be in when forced to fight.

From the bedroom behind me came the faint electronic ringing from my own phone as Kaci tried in vain again to get in touch with my father. *Why isn't he answering his phone?*

Radley kicked the door again, and we could do nothing but watch. And wait.

The door rattled in its frame, and his determination grew. Radley kicked over and over again, until finally the door frame splintered, cracking visibly. His next blow sent a long shard of wood flying into the living room as the dead bolt tore free of its home. On the next whack, the door swung open to bang into the wall.

Radley stood in the doorway beaming, clearly not surprised to find us in cat form and ready to fight. "Kill the tom, but try to keep the bitch intact. I'll find the kitten."

The moment he stepped into the living room, Ethan was in his face, growling fiercely. But his threat was cut off a millisecond later as one of the cats behind Radley launched himself at my brother. Ethan jumped and they met in midair, jaws snapping, claws flying.

The other two cats approached me slowly, growling in

unison. I backed away from them, not quite sure what to do with two at once. I'd never faced a pair of foes, outside of training.

Angry and beyond pissed off, I hissed, and the cat on the left hissed back. Then a dark blur flew across the room and smashed into the cat on the right. Both forms went down in a heap of black fur. But they were up in an instant, and both turned their attention to Ethan, who'd evidently tossed the flying stray.

Now I only faced one. He pounced, and his teeth sank into the back of my neck. The pressure on my spine was tremendous, but his canines barely penetrated my thick fur. Probably because he'd been told not to kill me.

He shoved my head into the floor. One broad, heavy front paw landed on my face, a black toe pad holding my eye closed. I twisted, and my jaws closed over his ankle. I pulled, growling deep in my throat. He bit harder. Blood ran down my neck. *I* bit harder, and my teeth hit bone.

He howled, and when his mouth opened, I dropped my grip and backed away, facing off against him again.

A door slammed down the hall, and Radley swore, apparently having no luck in his search for Kaci. So far.

On my right, Ethan had one stray's foot between his jaws, the other cat pinned to the ground, beneath him. He was holding his own, even with four parallel gashes across his left flank. They weren't pouring blood, so the injury probably wasn't grave. But it couldn't have felt good.

My opponent charged again. I met him with a pawful of unsheathed claws, aiming for his chest. He anticipated my move and twisted away. My blow only glanced him.

Across the room, Radley had discovered the locked door. Abandoning my furred opponent, I pounced on Radley, knocking him to the floor in front of the couch. I growled, my muzzle inches from his nose. But before I could decide whether or not to kill him—it wouldn't be self-defense since he was no real threat to me in human form—something hit me from the side, throwing me into the coffee table.

I used my momentum to roll over, regaining my feet smoothly. But the stray was already there. He swiped at me, and fire ripped across my right front leg, just beneath my shoulder. My howl of pain almost covered the splinter of breaking wood. Almost, but not quite. Radley had gotten into my room.

He shoved the door open. The stray's teeth snapped shut an inch from my muzzle. Radley raced into the bedroom. I slapped the stray away with one paw. Two lines of bright red opened across his nose. He hissed and backed away.

Behind me, Radley bellowed in frustration and rage. I turned to see him standing in the middle of my bedroom, staring out the window. The *open* window.

Kaci had run.

Thirty-Three

"She took off!" Radley shouted. An instant later the stray pounced on me from behind, driving me to the floor as Radley's steps drew closer. "I'm going after her. Kill the tom, knock the bitch out, then Shift and bring her back with you. Now! We don't have all day!"

The stray pinning me to the hardwood whined in acknowledgment. I couldn't see Radley, but his footsteps stomped toward me, then into sight, heading for the porch. And beyond him, I saw something moving through the open front door: Kaci—speeding across the grass toward the trees.

"There she goes!" Radley ran after his prize, still shouting as he raced down the steps. "Get done here and catch up."

Right. Like it would be that easy. Like we'd *let* it be that easy.

On my right, Ethan snarled, and I twisted to see him pinned by one cat. But he had the other stray's ear in his mouth, and as I wriggled to wedge one paw between myself and the bastard on top of me, Ethan wrenched his head, ripping his opponent's ear from its skull.

The injured cat screeched and backpedaled. Blood poured from the hole in his head, and one paw slid out from under him, smearing it across the floor.

Disgusted, I shoved with the paw I'd forced into place. My foe flew back, but his claws sank into my flesh as he went. I howled as pain sliced across my back and blood ran down my fur.

I leapt to my feet, ignoring the sting in my back and my front leg. He hissed. I pounced, anger and fear for Kaci taking over where my training left off. My front paws slammed into his right shoulder. He hit the floor on his left side, and my weight drove the breath from his body.

My back claws sank into his right flank, slicing viciously before I could get squeamish. Muscle tore. The cat screeched. Blood poured from the wound, drenching my feet, and steaming in the frigid air let in by the open door.

I sucked in a deep breath, steeling myself to rip out his throat. But Ethan's almost-human scream of pain stopped me cold.

I froze, and my opponent tossed me off. I hissed and swiped at him, and he backed away, snarling ferociously. Behind him, Ethan lay on the ground.

The half-earless stray stood over him. Blood pooled beneath Ethan. His eyes blinked almost as slowly as his chest rose and fell. Three long gashes were open on the left side of his rib cage.

My heart beat hard enough to bruise my sternum. I roared in fear and in fury. The earless stray hissed and stepped closer. I snarled at him, but my eyes never left Ethan. I couldn't get to him. And even if I could, there was nothing I could do for him. Not without hands. And a medical degree.

Ethan blinked at me and whined.

All three strays blocked the door, watching *me,* now that my brother was no longer a threat. Radley's order replayed in my head. They would knock me out now—probably by clamping jaws over my throat—then Shift and drag me off. I couldn't let that happen.

I took another step back, and the strays followed. My claws

scratched grooves into the hardwood. My pulse raced fast enough to make my head swim.

Ethan whined again. My gaze flicked to him. His head was moving, his muzzle sliding across the floor slowly, aiming at the door.

What? But before I could figure out what he wanted, a fourth black blur shot through the open doorway, colliding full force with the stray in the center. The stray went down, the new cat's jaws clamped over the back of his skull. The downed cat snarled, but his anger was cut off with a whine, then the crunch of breaking bone. The new arrival had broken his neck with a single bite.

The victor stood over his victim's body and roared in triumph. He blinked, and his eyes met mine.

Marc.

My heart pounded, my head swimming with more questions than I could sort out. But Marc was already in action again, backing the remaining strays away from both Ethan and the door. I came forward to help him, limping from my injury, but he growled at me and shook his head.

I tilted mine in confusion, and he tossed his muzzle toward the door. *Go,* he'd said, and suddenly I understood. He wanted me to go after Kaci.

My muscles tensed, preparing to leap. Agony lanced my injured front leg, echoing in the slash marks across my back. I hunched on all fours—then launched myself over Marc.

I landed four feet from the door, legs in motion before I hit the ground. But my back paw slid in a warm, slick puddle, and I scrambled for traction. I dashed over the threshold and across the porch, then soared over the steps. My feet hit the brittle grass at a full-out run, in spite of the pain in my leg and the grisly ripping sensation in my back.

Behind me, Marc yelped, and paws pounded the ground. I slowed for a glance back, just long enough to realize it wasn't him following me. But I kept going because Marc could take care of himself *and* Ethan, and based on the snarls and growls coming from the cabin, he was doing just that.

So I ran. I broke through the foliage at the spot I'd last seen Kaci, sniffing the air regularly as I ran, searching for any sign of her. Or Radley.

Trees flew by. Thorns snagged in my fur. My paws sank in piles of pine needles and bruised against stones. Movement snagged my eye ahead—a green T-shirt, brilliant against the drab colors.

Radley was wearing green.

Adrenaline fueled a fresh burst of speed, and the huffing and chuffing behind me faded. The spot of green veered left. I followed, gaining on him steadily. I was hurt, but he was on two legs, and I was damn fast. He couldn't outrun me.

Unfortunately, he wouldn't *have* to.

Kaci screamed, and the green shirt stopped moving. I skidded to a halt in a small clearing flooded with morning sunlight. Leaves swung in the cold wind. A pinecone crunched beneath my left rear paw. Then Zeke Radley turned to face me at the edge of the clearing, Kaci clutched to his chest by her upper arms.

I growled. *Let her go.* But we all knew he wouldn't, even if he'd understood.

Behind me, four-legged footsteps thudded, then slid to a stop. Radley's backup had arrived.

"If you want to help her, come peacefully." Radley smiled as he spoke, as if I should have been grateful for the invitation.

I snarled. *Fuck you.* I think that one came through loud and clear, in spite of the language barrier.

He frowned, and glanced at the cat behind me. "Take her."

Something slammed into my left flank. I hit the ground beneath the stray. But we both froze as an unholy snarl ripped through the air from somewhere to the east. Somewhere *close.*

All heads swiveled as a huge wall of thorny shrubs shook to the left. The roar of fury came again, and my ears pinpointed it at least seven feet off the ground. No werecat was that tall. Not on four legs.

The shrubs shook harder. The roar deepened, ringing in my ears and pinging through my brain. Then the greenery parted. An entire eight-foot shrub uprooted itself from the ground, roots dangling a foot in the air.

The bush flew across the clearing, and all eyes followed it. My gaze flicked back to the gap in the vegetation to find it completely filled—by a seven-foot grizzly bear, nostrils wide in fury, dark brown fur tangled around twigs and briars.

Keller.

Fur stood on end all over my body, and I knew from the sudden stench of fear in the clearing that I wasn't the only one about to piss my…um…pelt.

More foliage rustled on my right, and a new cat leapt into the clearing—another of Radley's toms coming to his aid. But the cat froze with one look at the angry bear and began backing slowly in the direction he'd come from.

Radley scooped up a terrified Kaci under one arm and swung around, running for his life as her scream trailed into the air at his back.

Keller sprang into motion, much faster than I would have thought possible for a creature of his size. He dropped to all fours and thundered past me.

I twisted beneath the stray pinning me to see Keller swipe one powerful paw at the new arrival. The black blur flew across the clearing, rolling to an ungraceful halt in a thick tangle of briars.

Keller turned on us, and my heart stopped. I wasn't at all sure he could tell me from the others. Or that he was on my side, for that matter. I had no idea what a bruin's thought process was like in bear form—or even if he had one.

I thrashed beneath the tom crushing me, digging into the dirt in an attempt to get to my feet. But the dumbass bruising my flank seemed frozen in place. I clamped my jaws around his leg, grinding my teeth together through his flesh. He howled and jumped up, snapping at me instinctively.

I backed away and the stray tried to follow.

Instead, he flew across the clearing and crashed into a tree, four feet off the ground. I heard his spine snap from ten feet away, but didn't understand what had happened until my eyes focused on the tower of brown fur standing over me. Keller had *thrown* a full-grown werecat all the way across the clearing. Hard enough to break his back against a tree. With one blow.

I backed slowly away from the bear, lowering my muzzle in submission, hoping he spoke enough werecat to know I was *not* challenging him.

Keller huffed at me and blinked. Then he turned without lifting a paw against me. *He knows me. Thank goodness.*

I leapt to my feet and raced toward the edge of the clearing, where Radley had disappeared between two trees. But before I'd gone four steps, something heavy slammed into my shoulder. I landed in a pile of leaves on my right side. Teeth sank into my right rear ankle. Pain sheared through muscle and into bone. I howled, and my eyes closed as I thrashed, but the teeth didn't let go. Inhaling, I took in the scent of the stray Keller had thrown into the briars.

Didn't learn his lesson the first time...

I forced my eyes open and my body into motion. My paws swiped at the form over me, claws snagging in flesh. I pulled harder, and that flesh tore.

The stray hissed, and lost his grip on my leg. I thrashed harder, and he slid onto the ground. I stood and slashed him again, swinging blindly now. My claws ripped through the flesh over his shoulder.

Keller roared again, and my gaze sought him out, even as

I slashed once more. The bruin was on all fours now, facing two new strays whose tails swished along the ground frantically. Their ears were flattened to their skulls, bodies hunched close to the ground.

Fresh pain thudded through my skull as a paw made contact with my head.

I whirled on my attacker, hissing, claws flying again. The stray pounced, driving me onto my side. I wedged my back paws between us, and this time I didn't hesitate. I simply slashed.

My rear claws slid through soft stomach fur and into muscle. Blood poured over me. The stray screeched, his scream trailing into pitches too high for me to hear. Organs slid from ruined flesh. Paws flailed weakly at my face and sides. The scent of blood permeated the clearing, saturating the ground as surely as the air. And finally the stray stopped moving.

For a moment, I lay still, horrified by what I'd done. But that passed quickly. I'd defended myself. And now I would defend Kaci.

I got to my feet just as one of the remaining strays sprung, pouncing on a bear nearly twice his size. Keller swung one mighty paw, fur rippling in the breeze he created. He connected with the cat in midair. Something crunched, and the stray's neck bent at an odd angle. He fell into a motionless black heap on the forest floor.

A feline roar of fury sliced the air, and the last black blur launched itself at Keller's back. The cat landed firmly and clung, sinking his claws into the bear's flesh through thick, matted fur. The idiot had balls, if not brains; I had to give him that.

I paused on the edge of the clearing, glancing back over the strays Keller had broken and the one I'd disemboweled. The remaining stray still clung to the bruin, probably afraid to let go now, knowing he was dead if he did.

Then I took off after Kaci, confident Keller could handle himself against the last terrified werecat.

I ran as quietly as possible, pausing frequently to listen for footsteps. Fortunately, Kaci was doing her part to help—screaming almost nonstop. Apparently Radley couldn't hold on to her and cover her mouth at the same time.

The woods flew by as I ran, and less than two minutes after I left the clearing, I caught up with Radley. And he didn't even know it. He was too busy trying to drag the thrashing teenager up a hill to realize I'd found them, and I wasn't about to warn him.

Instead, I pounced.

I drove them both to the ground on the upward slant of the hill, Kaci pinned beneath Radley. It was the only way I could think of to keep him from using her as a hostage—I'd been in that position, and didn't want to put her in it.

My jaws closed over the back of Radley's neck. My teeth broke his skin. Blood trickled slowly into my mouth. I didn't want to kill him until she was free, so my bite was mostly a warning. Still, his blood sent adrenaline rushing through my veins, demanding I finish it. That I taste the blood of my enemy: a victor's right.

Instead, I planted my paws in the dirt on either side of them both and pulled Radley backward by his neck, lifting him several inches off of Kaci.

She didn't move—apparently too scared to realize what had happened. I whined, and felt her squirm beneath us. Then she scrambled into motion, crawling out from under him in a series of short, panicked movements. Finally free, she scooted up the hill on her rear, staring at us both in horror. There was no recognition in her eyes. She'd never seen me in cat form and clearly didn't realize her nose worked in human form, too. She had no idea who I was.

Eyes wide in terror, she turned away from us both. Then she ran—again, and I could do nothing but watch her go.

"Please…" Radley begged beneath me. And I hesitated,

because Kaci was free and I was in no danger. I could hold him until someone else arrived—and surely the cavalry would show up any minute. They would probably want to talk to him.

I shifted, tightening my grip on Radley's neck as I settled onto my stomach on his back. I would wait.

I inhaled through my open mouth, listening as Kaci's footsteps echoed off to the west. Radley squirmed beneath me, and I growled, warning him to hold still. Then I heard a metallic click, completely out of place in the woods.

What the hell?

Pain lanced my right side and shot through my hip. My heart tripped in panic. Then understanding bit me just as deeply as the pain. The son of a bitch had a knife. He'd fucking *stabbed me!*

I roared around his neck in pain and fury, and in response, someone shouted my name from the woods. "Faythe?"

It was Jace. Footsteps pounded the earth frantically, headed in my direction.

Radley pulled the knife free, and my teeth bit farther into his skin, my paws digging into the dirt on either side of him to hold him still. But then the bastard stabbed me *again.*

I moaned in fresh agony. Blood soaked through my fur, drenching the form beneath me. Pain ripped through my side with each heartbeat, echoing in the lacerations in my back and the vicious bite on my ankle. Panic edged up on me, burning beneath my fur like an electrical charge.

The bastard pulled the knife out again, and I screamed around his neck. If he hadn't nicked any vital organs yet, he would soon, and I'd be dead. And he'd be gone long before the guys found us. The motherfucker would get away free and clear.

The hell he will.

My jaws clenched around his neck. Blood flowed into my mouth. My teeth met bone. He thrashed beneath me. I bit as hard as I could, but breaking someone's spine was harder than I expected; Marc made it look easy.

I concentrated, clenching my jaws so hard they ached. Radley bucked, and shoved the knife in one more time. My body jerked on top of his. Footsteps raced toward me from the trees, but I couldn't hold on. My whole world was pain. Pain, and anger.

I seized the anger and forced my teeth together. Finally, bone snapped. Radley shuddered beneath me, then went still.

Fire licked at my side, burning deep within. I rolled off him onto my good side, and thought of nothing but breathing through the pain. Minutes later, Jace ran into sight, followed by Kaci and a handful of toms in cat form. He knelt at my side and pressed his shirt to my worst wounds, as Marc had done two days earlier.

I growled to tell him he was late, as usual, and to my surprise, he actually seemed to understand.

He smiled, even as his eyes watered. "Better late than never, right?"

Says the man who wasn't used as a pincushion.

"Faythe?" Kaci knelt at my side, and her hand stroked my muzzle. "Is that you?" I nodded, and she sobbed. "You came for me. You didn't let him take me." She wrapped her arms around my chest and laid her head on my shoulder. "Thank you."

Thirty-Four

"Hey," Marc said, and I looked up to find him leaning against the door frame, a mug of coffee in one hand. He wore his leather jacket, even though a fire raged in the next room, heating the tiny cabin much more effectively than I would have thought possible. "How do you feel?"

"Like someone used me for target practice."

He smiled and sat in the sturdy, knobby wooden chair by the bed. The chair was handmade by Elias Keller, as was the bed frame. The whole building, in fact. They'd carried me to Keller's cabin because it was closer than ours, and the bruin had insisted I stay to recuperate. I think he liked having company, after fifty-odd years alone.

Which was why he'd invited Marc, too.

Instead of catching his flight the morning before, Marc had headed for Keller's cabin. According to the bruin, he showed up on the doorstep with determination in his stride and desperation in his heart. He'd asked Keller's permission to stay in the territory until my verdict and lightened sentence were official, to make sure I was safe.

Rather than simply granting him permission to camp in the woods, the bruin had insisted Marc stay on his couch.

Later that day, he'd loaned me his bed. And earned our Pride's loyalty for life.

Marc set the mug on a small table made of a section of tree trunk polished to a smooth finish on top. "Doc says you should wait at least a week before Shifting again. Radley got you pretty good. It's a miracle he didn't hit anything vital."

Yeah, *that's* what it was. It was a miracle I'd "only" been stabbed in the hip and the side. It was a "blessing" the knife had nicked bone, rather than intestines, on the first plunge, then gone clean through muscle and skin and out the other side on the last two attempts to end my life. Really, I should have been grateful.

Marc smiled, as if he knew what I was thinking. Hell, he probably did.

Dr. Carver had also said my arm and ankle would probably scar, but I didn't give a shit about that; I was just grateful there was no muscle damage. Besides, I didn't know any enforcers without a couple of claw marks to show off. And now I had scars to match Marc's.

"How's Ethan?" I asked, reaching for the mug.

Marc handed it to me before I could stretch far enough to hurt myself. "Heavily bandaged, lightly sedated and recovering nicely. His ribs look awful, but Doc says he'll heal fine."

"What about Kaci?" I hadn't seen her since Carver shooed everyone out of the room so he could stitch me up.

Marc's mouth turned up in a triumphant smile. "They're going to send her home with you, when you go."

"Really?" I grinned through the pain. That was too good to be true. "How did my dad manage that?"

"You play a pretty convincing hero." He brushed a strand of hair back from my forehead and I treasured the touch, wishing it would linger. "You've made lots of progress with Kaci. And Malone saved face by pointing out that your mother will be there to bail you out if you screw up. She's still well respected among the Alphas. Even by most of those who don't like your dad."

I nodded. My mom was strong, and Alphas respected strength. Especially in my mother, because she presented her strength all dolled up behind a dainty, well-appointed and feminine facade. She'd been playing the game for a long time, and she almost always won.

I was trying to learn from her, but my facade was nowhere near as shiny, and I was pretty damn disinclined to polish. Especially after such an obvious dig from Malone.

"Where is Kaci?"

"She's asleep at the lodge. Jace is there, too. The only way we could get her to leave you was by promising Jace would stay with her."

When Kaci had run from me and Radley, she'd run right into Jace and the other enforcers, who were following the sound of her screams. "What was he doing in human form?" I asked, letting the mug warm my hands. "I thought they all went out furry."

"They did." Marc picked up the old-fashioned alarm clock on the nightstand and fiddled with the dials to keep his hands busy. He was nervous about something. "When they got there, Radley's hangout was empty. Jace Shifted and snagged some clothes one of the strays left behind, then headed for Keller's. They were hoping he had a phone Jace could use to call the lodge. He wasn't home, though."

I shook my head, smiling at the memory of the bruin smacking a werecat hard enough to snap his neck. "No, he was with us."

"I know. He went out to catch some fish for dinner, and caught the scent of several werecats near the stream instead. The trail led in this direction. So he Shifted and followed, just in case."

"Where is he now?"

"Out hunting with Parker and Michael."

The guys were hunting with a bruin? "No fair. I always miss the good stuff." I took another sip from my mug, watching him. "What about the strays? Did we get them all?"

A glimmer of true satisfaction shone momentarily through Marc's melancholy. "You got one in the woods—two including Zeke Radley—and I finished off two of the three you and Ethan took on in the cabin. Keller got several more, and the other guys ferreted out the last two—we hope—shortly after they found you. It was a big mess, and a horrible waste of life. Such a shame, what Radley turned them into. But Keller should have some peace on his mountain now."

"What about Hannibal?" After seeing him in midmeal, I still couldn't think of the blood-covered cannibal by so benign a name as *Jeff.*

"He was dead before the hunt began. Ethan and Reid put him out of his misery as soon as they were done with him."

A shadow crossed the door frame and I glanced up to find my father smiling at me, an old-fashioned oil lamp hanging from one fist. He wore a faded button-down shirt and the only pair of jeans he owned. "How do you feel, kitten?"

"I'm fine, Daddy." I wasn't in much pain at the moment, thanks to a strong local anesthetic at the site of my stitches. And there was another pile of little white pills on the table, for when the shots wore off. "So, what's up?" In consideration of my latest injuries, the tribunal had postponed the announcement of my verdict until Doc finished sewing me up. But my father had spent the past hour at the lodge, and I was pretty sure I knew why.

"The tribunal has reached a verdict."

Marc's hand closed around mine, and I nodded, holding my breath in anticipation. I was still pissed about missing the announcement, but Dr. Carver would not let me leave the bed yet. Not even to use the restroom. And I was *not* fond of the bedpan, though I have to admit it was better than a coffee can.

My father smiled. "Guilty of infection." Which we'd already known. "But innocent of murder, by reason of self-defense."

I exhaled, but wasn't sure whether to be relieved or angry. The real news was yet to come. "What's the sentence?"

My father's smile widened, his eyes sparkling in the firelight. "Public service."

"Meaning what?" Marc asked, before I could.

"Basically, they want Faythe reinstated as an enforcer, but working for nothing for the next year."

Okay, that wasn't too bad. I didn't know what to spend my meager salary on anyway...

"And...they want you to teach the rest of us to do the partial Shift. Which means you'll have to spend five days with each of the other Prides over the next few months."

"Really?" Surprise tingled through me, and my father nodded. *Now* that's *interesting*. Though there were certainly a few territories I did not look forward to visiting...

"The partial Shift saved your job," he continued, transferring the oil lamp to his other hand.

Yes, and Marc had saved my life, as well as Ethan's. But they wouldn't cut him the same break they'd cut me. He was officially exiled. In fact, other than my uncle, no one on the tribunal knew he was still around.

"Thanks, Daddy. That's great." But my victory was bittersweet. Now that my life was no longer in jeopardy, Marc had no reason to stay.

Fortunately, my father seemed to understand my lack of enthusiasm, and his own smile didn't reach his eyes. "I'm going back to the cabin to sit with Ethan. If you need me, call his cell."

I nodded. He had dropped—thus shattering—his own phone on the floor of the lodge the previous morning, which was why he hadn't answered it. He and Michael both seemed to feel pretty guilty for being incommunicado at the worst possible moment. In fact, Michael had gone out twice already to get me my favorite treats, to aid my recovery. I'd let him off the hook soon. Once he got back with fresh game…

My father's gaze shifted to Marc, and his expression sobered even more. "Ten minutes." Marc nodded, and his former Alpha retreated into the main room, then out the front door.

I watched him go, then frowned at Marc in dread. "You're leaving now?"

His eyes closed for a moment, then opened to meet mine in obvious pain. "I have to."

"No, you don't." I shook my head vehemently as panic set in beneath my anesthesia-fueled fog. "The verdict's official. Daddy can take you back, and there's nothing they can do about it."

Marc sighed, and scooted to sit on the bed with me. "Faythe, Calvin Malone formally challenged your father's leadership last night on a conference call with the entire council. He's called for a vote of nonconfidence, and requested to be named the new head of the council. The bastard timed it perfectly—twelve hours before he pronounced you innocent of murder, which makes him appear just and unbiased."

Nooooo. My heart sank into my stomach, and the room seemed to spin.

It was too soon. My dad had two seriously injured children, one incarcerated son and a new, traumatized young tabby to deal with. Not to mention Manx and her upcoming childbirth. And trial. And the loss of his top enforcer. How could he possibly deal with Malone's coup on top of all that?

My gaze strayed to the empty doorway where my father had stood. "Why didn't he tell me?"

Marc sighed. "He doesn't want this to set your recovery back. But I know you're stronger than that, right?"

I nodded, numb. I'd have to be. "When's the vote?"

"February. They each have three months to present their cases to the other eight Alphas. Your dad needs five votes, other than his own, to keep his spot." He stopped, and stroked the back of my hand with his forefinger. "That's why I have to go. If your dad goes back on his word by revoking my exile, he'll be loading Malone's smoking gun for him." He set my mug on the table and took my hand in both of his. "I can't do that to him. You can't ask me to."

No. Of course I couldn't.

How the hell had Malone forced us each to choose between the other two? And why did Marc always wind up the loser in our little game, no matter how we shuffled the cards?

I sighed and let my head fall back. The ceiling came into focus—plank after plank of wood hewn from trees Keller had probably felled himself.

"So wait for me," I insisted. "I'll go with you as soon as I can Shift." But I knew it wouldn't work. Jace had been right about that. "Or we could stay here! This is free territory, and after what Keller did to those strays, no one with half a brain will come within five miles of his territory again. Including the Territorial Council."

He shook his head, squeezing my hand. "I came up with all those same ideas, Faythe, but they're no good. We can't drag Keller into this. He'll be hibernating soon, and he'll need peace and quiet, not tomcats yowling all over the woods in search of you." Marc sighed and his shoulders slumped in defeat so gloomy my heart broke to see it. "Besides, you belong with your Pride."

"*Our* Pride," I insisted as my vision blurred with unshed tears. "And so do you."

"I have to do this, Faythe. It's for the good of the Pride," Marc said. And that's when I knew I'd lost the argument. He would do whatever it took to keep the rest of us safe. Even if that meant not being there to protect us personally.

Marc was the Alpha Calvin Malone would never be, and the irony was that Malone would never see that. But my father had seen it from the beginning.

Marc stood, and his hand slipped from mine. He leaned down to kiss me gently, and when he tried to pull away, I held his head in place, so I could kiss him longer. If he was going to go, he was damn well going to say goodbye the right way.

He sank into that kiss, and fed from me like a starving man holding off famine. I drank from his soul in preparation for the drought to come. And when he finally pulled away, my throat was thick with unspoken words, my heart heavy with every apology I'd ever denied him.

But it was too late for promises. The time had come for goodbye.

"First I was sleeping, and now I'm stuck in bed." I wiped away my tears as soon as they fell. "Why do you always leave when I can't stop you?"

He smiled sadly. "We both know that's the only way this will work." He backed slowly toward the main room, and by the time he reached the front door, tears blurred my sight so that I could barely focus on his face.

I blinked them away in time to see him wink at me. "This isn't forever, Faythe. I swear on my life."

Damn right, I thought as he pushed the door open. If Calvin Malone took over the council, the days of female enforcers and stray Pride members would be over for good, and no one stood to lose more than the south-central Pride. Than me and Marc.

My father would stand against Malone; there was no question about that. But he would need all his enforcers standing strong at his back. Including Marc.

We would be together again soon, and I would do whatever I had to do to make that happen.

He smiled one last time. Then he stepped into the night and the door closed behind him.

And just like that, Marc was gone.